PRAISE FOR JAMES LEE BURKE

"James Lee Burke is the reigning champ of nostalgia noir."
—*The New York Times Book Review*

"A gorgeous prose stylist."

—Stephen King

"James Lee Burke is the heavyweight champ, a great American novelist whose work, taken individually or as a whole, is unsurpassed."
—Michael Connelly

"Burke's evocative prose remains a thing of reliably fierce wonder."
—*Entertainment Weekly*

"America's best novelist."

—*The Denver Post*

"Burke can touch you in few ways writers can."
—*The Washington Post*

"For five decades, Burke has created memorable novels that weave exquisite language, unforgettable characters, and social commentary into written tapestries that mirror the contemporary scene. His work transcends genre classification."

—*The Philadelphia Inquirer*

"Burke's writing [is] Faulkner-esque in its beauty, its feel on the ear like a southern breeze blowing through magnolia blossoms and oil fields."

—*Missoulian*

Swan Peak

A Dave Robicheaux Novel

James Lee Burke

SIMON & SCHUSTER PAPERBACKS

New York London Toronto Sydney New Delhi

Simon & Schuster Paperbacks
An Imprint of Simon & Schuster, Inc.
1230 Avenue of the Americas
New York, NY 10020

This Simon & Schuster trade paperback edition January 2018

SIMON & SCHUSTER PAPERBACKS and colophon are registered trademarks of Simon & Schuster, Inc.

For information about special discounts for bulk purchases, please contact Simon & Schuster Special Sales at 1-866-506-1949 or business@simonandschuster.com.

The Simon & Schuster Speakers Bureau can bring authors to your live event. For more information or to book an event, contact the Simon & Schuster Speakers Bureau at 1-866-248-3049 or visit our website at www.simonspeakers.com.

Manufactured in the United States of America

1 3 5 7 9 10 8 6 4 2

Library of Congress Control Number: 2008004965

ISBN 978-1-5011-9812-0
ISBN 978-1-4165-7921-2 (ebook)

For our son, James L. Burke III, and his wife, Kara, and their son, James L. Burke IV

Swan Peak

CHAPTER
1

Clete Purcel had heard of people who sleep without dreaming, but either because of the era and neighborhood in which he had grown up, or the later experiences that had come to define his life, he could not think of sleep as anything other than an uncontrolled descent into a basement where the gargoyles turned somersaults like circus midgets.

Sometimes he dreamed of his father, the milkman who rose at three-fifteen A.M. and rumbled off to work in a truck that clinked with bottles and trailed a line of melting ice out the back doors. When his father reentered the house off Magazine at midday, he occasionally carried a sack of Popsicles for Clete and his two sisters. On other days, his face was already oily and distorted with early-morning booze, his victimhood and childlike cruelty searching for release on the most vulnerable members of his home.

Sometimes in his dreams Clete saw a straw hooch with a mamasan in the doorway suddenly engulfed in an arc of liquid flame sprayed from a Zippo-track. He saw a seventeen-year-old door gunner go apeshit on a wedding party in a free-fire zone, the brass cartridges jacking from an M60 suspended from a bungee cord. He saw a navy corpsman with rubber spiders on his steel pot try to stuff the entrails of a marine back inside his abdomen with his bare hand. He saw himself inside a battalion aid station, his neck beaded with dirt rings, his body dehydrated from blood expander, his flak jacket glued to the wound in his chest.

He saw the city of New Orleans sink beneath the waves, just as Atlantis had. Except in the dream, New Orleans and the China Sea and perhaps a place in the Mideast, where he had never been, melded together and created images that were nonsensical. Blood washed backward off a sandy cusp of beach into a turquoise ocean. Soldiers who looked like people Clete had once known struggled silently uphill into machine guns that made no sound.

When he woke, he felt that his own life had been spent in the service of enterprises that today contained no learning value for anyone and would be replicated over and over again, regardless of the cost. A psychiatrist once told him he suffered from agitated depression and psychoneurotic anxiety. Clete asked the psychiatrist where he had been for the last fifty years.

His dreams clung to his skin like cobweb and followed him into the day. If he drank, his dreams went to a place where dreams go and waited two or three nights before they bloomed again, like specters beckoning from the edge of a dark wood. But on this particular morning Clete was determined to leave his past in the past and live in the sunlight from dawn until nightfall and then sleep the sleep of the dead.

It was cold when he unzipped his sleeping bag and crawled out of his polyethylene tent by a creek in western Montana. His restored maroon Caddy convertible with the starched-white top was parked in the trees, speckled with frost. In the distance the sun was just striking the fresh snow that had fallen on the mountain peaks during the night. The spring runoff had ended, and the stream by which he had made his camp was wide and dark and devoid of whitewater and running smoothly over gray boulders that had begun to form shadows on the pebble bed. He could hear the easy sweep of wind in the pine and fir trees, the muted clattering of rocks in the stream's current. For a moment he thought he heard a motorized vehicle grinding down the dirt road, but he paid no attention to it.

He made a ring of rocks and placed twigs and pinecones inside it and started a fire that flared and twisted in the wind like a yellow handkerchief and blew sparks and smoke across a long riffle undulating down the middle of the streambed.

The place where he was cooking his breakfast in an iron skillet set on top of hot rocks was the perfect site for a camp and the perfect place to begin wading upstream through canyon country, false-casting a dry fly over his head, watching it float delicately toward him on the riffle. He had not chosen this place but had found it by accident, turning onto the dirt road after he had found a snow gate locked across the asphalt two-lane. The countryside was grand, the cliffs sheer, the tops of the buttes covered with ponderosa pine, the slopes already blooming with wildflowers. Along the edges of the stream, there were no prints in the soft gravel except those of deer and elk. The air smelled of the woods and wet fern and cold stone and humus that stayed in shade twenty-four hours and the iridescent spray drifting off the boulders in the stream. The air smelled as though it had never been stained by the chemical agencies of the industrial era. It smelled as the earth probably had on the first day of creation, Clete thought.

He pulled his hip waders out of the Caddy and put them on by the side of the stream, snapping the rubber straps tight on his belt, looping a net and a canvas creel around his neck. He waded deep into the water, down a ledge, his feet slipping on moss-covered surfaces, until the drop-off sent the water over the edge of his waders. He whipped a dry fly over his head twice, then three times, the line forming a figure eight, whistling with a dull wet sound past his ear. With the fourth cast, he stiffened his wrist and let the fly float gently down on the riffle.

That was when he heard the sound of the truck again, mounting the grade just beyond a cut between two pine-covered hills.

But he kept his eyes on the fly floating down the riffle toward him. He saw an elongated shape break from behind a boulder, rising quickly into the light, the dark green dorsal hump roiling the surface. There was a flick of water, like a tiny splash of quicksilver, then the rainbow took the fly and went straight down into the shadows with it.

Out of the corner of his eye, Clete saw a bright red pickup with an extended cab and a diesel-powered engine crunch down the slope onto a bed of white rocks. Once stopped, the driver did not cut his engine, nor did he get out of the vehicle. Inside the canyon walls, the engine clattered like a vibrating junkyard.

Clete tried to strip line when the rainbow began to run. But his foot slipped on the moss, the tip of his Fenwick bowed to the water, and his two-pound monofilament tippet snapped in half. Suddenly his Fenwick was as light and useless as air in his palm.

He looked up on the bank. The truck was parked in shadow, its headlights sparkling, and Clete could not see through the dark reflection that had pooled in the windshield. He waded up through the shallows until he was on solid ground, then he slipped off his fly vest and laid it on a rock. He set down his fly rod and net and creel and removed his porkpie hat and reset it at a slant on his forehead. He looked at his convertible, where his Smith & Wesson .38 rested inside the glove box.

Clete walked to his fire ring and squatted beside it, ignoring the truck and the hammering of the diesel engine. He lifted his coffeepot off a warm stone and poured his coffee into a tin cup, then added condensed milk to it from a can he had punctured with his Swiss army knife. Then he got to his feet again, wiping his hands on his clothes, his eyes shifting back onto the front windows of the truck. He stared for a long time at the truck, drinking his coffee, not moving, his expression benign, his green eyes clear and unblinking.

He wore a charcoal corduroy shirt and faded jeans that were buttoned under his navel. On first glance his massive arms and shoulders and the breadth of his chest gave him a simian appearance, but his top-heavy proportions were redeemed by his height and his erect posture. A pink scar that had the texture and color of a bicycle patch ran through one eyebrow. The scar and his over-the-hill good looks and his little-boy haircut and the physical power that seemed to emanate from his body created a study in contrasts that attracted women to him and gave his adversaries serious pause.

Both front doors of the truck opened, and two men stepped out on the rocks. They were smiling, glancing up at the hilltops, as though they were sharing in Clete's appreciation of the morning. "Get a little lost?" the driver said.

"Somebody locked the snow gate on the state road, so I turned in here for the night," Clete said.

"That road is not state-owned. It's private. But you probably didn't know that," the driver said. The accent was slightly adenoidal, perhaps Appalachian or simply Upper South.

"My map shows it as a state road," Clete said. "Would you mind cutting your engine? I'm starting to get a headache, here."

The driver's physique was nondescript, his face lean, his brown hair dry and uncombed, ruffling in the breeze, his smile stitched in place. A half-circle of tiny puncture scars was looped under his right eye, as though a cookie cutter had been pressed into his skin, recessing the eye and dulling the light inside it. His shirt hung outside his trousers. "Have you caught any fish?" he asked.

"Not yet," Clete replied. He looked at the passenger. "What are you doing?"

The passenger was a hard-bodied, unshaved man. His hair was black and shiny, his dark eyes lustrous, his flannel shirt buttoned at the wrists and throat. He wore canvas trousers with big brads on them and a wide leather belt hitched tightly into his hips. The combination of his unwashed look and the fastidious attention he gave his utilitarian clothes gave him a bucolic aura of authority, like that of a man who wears the smell of his sweat and testosterone as a challenge to others. "I'm writing down your license number, if you don't have an objection," he said.

"Yeah, I do object," Clete said. "Who are you guys?"

The unshaved man with black hair nodded and continued to write on his notepad. "You from Lou'sana? I'm from down south myself. Miss'sippi. You been to Miss'sippi, haven't you?" he said.

When Clete didn't reply, the passenger said, "New Orleans flat-ass got ripped off the map, didn't it?"

"Yeah, the F-word in Louisiana these days is FEMA," Clete said.

"You got a lot less Afro-Americans to worry about, though," the passenger said. He rolled the racial designation on his tongue.

"What is this?" Clete said.

"You're on posted land, is what this is," the driver said.

"I didn't see any sign to that effect," Clete said.

The passenger went to the truck and lifted a microphone off the dash and began speaking into it.

"You guys are running my tag?" Clete said.

"You don't remember me?" the driver said.

"No."

"It'll come to you. Think back about seventeen years or so."

"Tell you what, I'll pack up my gear and clear out, and we'll call it even," Clete said.

"We'll see," the driver said.

"We'll *see*?" Clete said.

The driver shrugged, still grinning.

The passenger finished his call on the radio. "His name is Clete Purcel. He's a PI out of New Orleans," he said. "There's a pair of binoculars on the seat of his convertible."

"You been spying on us, Mr. Purcel?" the driver said.

"I've got no idea who you are."

"You're not working for the bunny huggers?" the driver said.

"We're done here, bub."

"We need to look inside your vehicle, Mr. Purcel," the driver said.

"Are you serious?" Clete said.

"You're on the Wellstone Ranch," the driver said. "We can have you arrested for trespassing, or you can let us do our job and look in your car. You didn't have situations like this when you worked security at Tahoe?"

Clete blinked, then pointed his finger. "You were a driver for Sally Dio."

"I was a driver for the car service he used. Too bad he got splattered in that plane accident."

"Yeah, a great national tragedy. I heard they flew the flag at half-mast for two minutes in Palermo," Clete said. He glanced at the black-haired man, who had just retrieved a tool from the truck and was walking back toward Clete's Caddy with it. "Tell your man there if he sticks that Slim Jim in my door, I'm going to jam it up his cheeks."

"Whoa, Quince," the driver said. "We're going to accept Mr. Purcel's word. He'll clean up his camp and be gone—" He paused and looked thoughtfully at Clete. "What, five or ten minutes, Mr. Purcel?"

Clete cleared an obstruction in his windpipe. He poured his coffee on his fire. "Yeah, I can do that," he said.

"So, see you around," the driver said.

"I didn't get your name."

"I didn't give it. But it's Lyle Hobbs. That ring any bells for you?"

Clete kept his expression flat, his eyes empty. "My memory isn't what it used to be."

The man who had introduced himself as Lyle Hobbs stepped closer to Clete, his head tilting sideways. "You trying to pull on my crank?"

Clete set his tin coffee cup on the rock next to his Fenwick and slipped his hands into the back pockets of his jeans, as a third-base coach might. *Don't say anything,* he told himself.

"You don't hide your thoughts too good," the driver said. "You got one of those psychodrama faces. People can read everything that's in it. You ought to be an actor."

"You were up on a molestation charge. You did a county stint on it," Clete said. "The girl was thirteen. She recanted her statement eventually, and you went back to driving for Sally Dee."

"You got a good memory. It was a bum beef from the jump. I got in the sack with the wrong lady blackjack dealer. Hell hath no fury, know what I mean? But I didn't drive for Sally Dee. I drove for the service he contracted."

"Yeah, you bet," Clete replied, his eyes focused on neutral space.

"Have a good day," Lyle Hobbs said. His head was still tilted sideways, his grin still in place. His impaired eye seemed to have the opaqueness and density of a lead rifle ball.

"Same to you," Clete said. He began to take down his tent and fold it into a neat square while the two visitors to his camp backed their truck around. The back of his neck was hot, his mouth dry, his blood pounding in his ears and wrists. *Walk away, walk away, walk away,* a voice in his head said. He heard the oversize truck tires crunch on the rocks, then the steel bumper scrape across stone. He turned around in time to see one wheel roll over his Fenwick rod and grind the graphite shanks and the lightweight perforated reel and the aluminum guides and the double-tapered floating line into a pack rat's nest.

"You did that deliberately," Clete said, rising to his feet.

"Didn't see it, Scout's honor," the driver said. "I saw them comb Sally Dee and his crew out of the trees. The whole bunch looked like pulled pork somebody had dropped into a fire. You're a swinging dick, big man. Public campground is five miles south. Catch a fat one."

CHAPTER 2

CLETE AND MY wife, Molly, and I had come to western Montana at the invitation of a friend by the name of Albert Hollister. Albert was a novelist and retired English professor who lived up a valley off the state road that ascended over Lolo Pass into Idaho. He was an eccentric, a gadfly, and in most ways a gentle soul. Unbeknownst to his colleagues, he had served time on a road gang in Florida when he was eighteen. He had also been a drifter and a roustabout until age twenty, when he enrolled in the same open-door, poor-boy college I had attended.

I had always admired Albert for his courage and his talent as an artist. But I tried not to let my admiration for him involve me in his quixotic battles with windmills. His rusted armor always lay at the ready, even though his broken lances littered the landscape. Unfortunately, many of his causes were just ones. The tragedy was they were not winnable, and they were not winnable because the majority of people do not enjoy the prospect of being tacked up on crosses atop a biblical hill.

But Albert was Albert, a generous and brave man who protected the wild animals and turkeys on his property, fed stray dogs and cats, and hired bindle stiffs and broken-down waddies most people would shun.

He gave us a log cabin that was shaded by cottonwoods next to a creek on the far side of his barn. He gave Clete the bottom third

9

of his massive stone-and-log home. Our plans were to spend the summer fishing the Blackfoot and Bitterroot rivers, with an occasional excursion onto the Lochsa River in Idaho or over east of the Divide to the Jefferson and Madison. The riparian topography of those particular waterways is probably as good as the earth gets. The cottonwoods and aspens along the banks, the steep orange and pink cliffs that drop straight into eddying pools where the river bends, the pebbled shallows where the current flows as clear as green Jell-O across the tops of your tennis shoes, all seem to be the stuff of idyllic poems, except in this case it's real and, as John Steinbeck suggested, the introduction to a lifetime love affair rather than a geographical experience.

I had taken leave from the Iberia Parish Sheriff's Department, where I made a modest salary as a detective-grade sheriff's deputy. Hurricanes Rita and Katrina had spared our home on East Main in New Iberia. But Clete had watched the city of his birth drown. He had not recovered, and I was not sure he ever would, and I had hoped Montana would offer a cure that I could not. Clete was one of those who always tried to eat his pain and shine the world on. There was only one problem. His pain didn't go away, and the booze he drank and the weed he smoked and the pills he dropped didn't work anymore.

But we would soon learn that the state of Montana, with all its haunting beauty, would not provide a panacea for either of us. Both of us had been here in the late 1980s, and neither of us had dealt adequately with the ghosts we had created.

Clete had left the valley the previous day for two days of fishing in the Swan River country. But at one P.M. on the following day I saw his maroon Caddy coming hard up the dirt road. He passed Albert's stone-and-log house up on the bench, passed the barn and horse pasture, and turned in to the rutted lane that led to our cabin. It was a bluebird day, one that had started off beautifully. I had a feeling that was about to change, and in truth I did not feel like fitting on a Roman collar.

He told me what had happened that morning beside the creek on the ranch owned by a man named Ridley Wellstone.

"You think they're neo-Nazis or cultists of some kind?" I said.

"A guy at the courthouse said Wellstone is a rich guy from Texas who moved here about a year ago. What doesn't flush is this guy who ran over my fly rod. He said he remembered me from Lake Tahoe, that he was a driver for a car service there. Then he said he saw Sally Dio and his gumballs combed out of the trees after their plane crashed into a hillside in Montana."

Clete tried to hold my eyes, then looked away. His association with Sally Dio was not one he was fond of remembering. The circumstances of the plane accident that killed Dio were not details he cared to revisit, either.

"Go on," I said.

"The guy was trying to tell me he never worked for Dio, but at the same time he was telling me he drove Dio around in Nevada and was at the site where Dio's plane crashed. It's coincidence he was in Montana on the res when Dio smacked into a mountain?"

"In other words, he was one of Sally Dio's people?"

"Yeah, and a perv who molested a thirteen-year-old girl on top of it."

"Blow it off," I said.

We were sitting on wood chairs on the porch now. My fly and spinning rods were propped against a hitching rail, my waders hanging upside down from pegs on the front wall. The hillsides that bordered Albert's ranch were dotted with ponderosa and larch and Douglas fir trees, and when the wind blew, it made a sound like floodwater coursing hard through a dried-out streambed.

"The guy deliberately destroyed my tackle and lied in my face about it," Clete said.

"Sometimes you've got to walk away, Cletus."

"That's what I did. And I feel just like somebody put his spit in my ear."

But I knew what was eating him. After Sally Dee's plane had smacked into a hillside on the Flathead Indian Reservation, the National Transportation Safety Board determined that someone had poured sand into the fuel tanks. Clete blew Montana like the state was on fire. Now, unless he wanted someone asking questions about his relationship to Sally Dee and Sally's clogged fuel lines, he had to allow one of Sally's lowlifes to shove him around.

"Maybe the deal with your fly rod was an accident. Why's a guy like that want to pick a beef with you? Sally's dead. You said it yourself. The guy in the pickup is a short-eyes. You don't load the cannon for pervs."

"Good try."

"You can use my spinning rod. Let's go down on the Bitterroot."

He thought about it, then took off his hat and put it back on. "Yeah, why not?" he said.

I thought I'd carried the day. But that's the way you think when your attitudes are facile and you express them self-confidently at the expense of others.

IT WAS EVENING when the red pickup with the diesel-powered engine came up the dirt road, driving too fast, its headlights on high beam, even though the valley was only in part shadow, the oversize tires slamming hard across the potholes. The truck slowed at the entrance to Albert's driveway, as though the men inside the cab were examining the numbers on the archway at the entrance. Clete's Caddy was parked by the garage, up on the bench, against the hill, its starched top and waxed maroon paint job like an automobile advertisement snipped out of a 1950s magazine.

The pickup truck accelerated and kept coming up the road, spooking the horses in the pasture. Molly was inside the cabin, broiling a trout dinner that we had invited Albert and Clete to share with us. I watched the pickup truck turn in to the lane that led to our cabin, and I knew in the same way you know a registered-mail delivery contains bad news that I had sorely underestimated the significance of Clete's encounter with the security personnel on the ranch owned by a man named Wellstone.

"Can I help you?" I asked, rising from my chair on the porch.

The two men who had gotten out of the truck cab looked exactly as Clete had described them. The one with the recessed eye socket stared up at me, a faint grin on his face. He wore a short-sleeve print shirt outside his slacks. "My name is Lyle Hobbs," he said. "That yonder is Albert Hollister's place, is it?"

"What about it?" I said.

He glanced at the Louisiana tag on the back of my pickup truck. "Because the owner of that Cadillac parked up yonder told me he wasn't working for any bunny huggers. But that's not so. That means he lied to me."

"He doesn't work for *anyone*. At least not in this state."

"My instincts tell me otherwise. I hate a lie, mister. It bothers me something awful."

I let the implication pass. "Maybe you should go somewhere else, then."

The other man, who was unshaved and had thick, uncut black hair with a greasy shine in it, stepped in front of his friend. "What's your name, boy?" he said.

"What did you call me?"

"I didn't call you anything. I asked you your goddamn name."

I heard Molly come out on the porch. The eyes of the two men shifted off me. "What is it, Dave?" she said.

"Nothing," I replied.

"You tell Mr. Purcel he's sticking his nose in the wrong person's business," Lyle Hobbs said. "Mr. Wellstone is an honorable man. We're not gonna allow the likes of Mr. Purcel to besmirch his name. You tell him what I said."

"Tell him yourself," Molly said. She was holding a heavy cast-iron skillet, the kind used to cook large breakfasts for bunkhouse crews.

The man with black hair rubbed his thumb and forefinger up and down the whiskers on his throat, his eyes roving over Molly's figure, a matchstick elevating in his mouth. "Sounds like somebody is whipped to me," he said.

I stepped down off the porch, my old enemy ballooning in my chest, tingling in my hands. "I strongly recommend y'all drag your sorry asses out of here," I said.

Lyle Hobbs continued to stare directly into my face, his eyes jittering. "We're leaving. But don't make us come back," he said. "Those aren't idle words, sir."

He walked back toward his truck, then turned around, cleaning one ear with his little finger. He ticked a piece of matter off his fingernail. There was an indentation at the corner of his mouth, like a wrinkle in clay. "It's Robicheaux, isn't it?" he said.

"So?"

"Sally Dee purely hated you and Mr. Purcel. Used to talk about what he aimed to do to y'all. I saw him knock the glass eye out of a hooker because she mentioned your name. He was a mean little shit, wasn't he?"

The sunlight was red across the valley as he and his friend drove back toward the state highway.

"Who are they, Dave?" Molly asked after they were gone.

"Trouble," I said.

AFTER SUPPER, I talked with Albert about our visitors, the summer light still high in the sky, the valley blanketed with shadow, Albert's gaited horses blowing in the grass down by the creek.

"They do security for a man name of Ridley Wellstone? From Texas?" he said.

"They seemed to know you," I said.

Albert had fine cheekbones, intense eyes, and soft facial skin that belied the nature of his earlier life. His hair was white and grew over his collar, and he often wore an Australian digger's hat that hung from the back of his neck on a leather cord. His profile always suggested Byronic images to me, a poet wandering in the wastes, kicking at stone fragments along the edges of a collapsing empire.

"They sound like worthless fellows to me. What was that other name you mentioned?" he said.

"Clete had a bad period in his life and got mixed up with some gamblers in Vegas and Tahoe. One of them was Sally Dio."

"You talking about the Dio family out of Galveston?"

Oops.

"That's the bunch," I replied.

"They weren't gamblers, they were pimps. They ran all the whorehouses. Clete worked for them?"

"For a while. They held his hand in a car door and slammed the door on it," I said.

Albert set his boot on the bottom rail of the fence and gazed out at the pasture. His wife had died of Parkinson's three years past, and he had no children. His whole life now consisted of his ranch in the valley and another horse ranch he operated on the far side of the mountain. I wondered how a man of his extreme passions lived by himself. I wondered if sometimes his private thoughts almost drove him mad. "If those fellows come back around, send them up to the house," he said.

Not a good idea, I thought.

"Are you hearing me, Dave?" he said.

"You got it, Albert," I said.

"Look at the horses out there in the grass. You know a more beautiful place anywhere?" he said. "I don't know what I'd do if a man tried to take this from me."

I'M NOT SURE I believe in karma, but as one looks back over the aggregate of his experience, it seems hard to deny the patterns of intersection that seem to be at work in our lives, in the same way it would be foolish to say that the attraction of metal filings to a magnet's surface is a result of coincidence.

On Saturday morning Molly and Albert drove into Missoula to buy groceries at the Costco on the edge of town. They stopped on the way home to pick up a new Circle Y saddle Albert had ordered from the tack shop in the back of the Cenex. While Albert paid for his saddle, Molly drank a can of soda inside the store and watched the customers gassing up their vehicles at the pumps or lining up at the fast-food drive-by window next door. The day was lovely, the sky blue, the Rattlesnake Mountains to the north glistening with lines of snow that had fallen during the night. It was what a Saturday in America should be like, she thought, a day when family people stocked up on groceries and spoke with goodwill to one another inside the freshness of the morning.

On a newspaper rack directly behind her, the front page of the

Missoulian contained a headline story about the discovery of a coed's body in a canyon one mile from the University of Montana campus. The girl's high school yearbook picture stared placidly at the customers walking in and out of the store.

A white limousine with several people seated inside it pulled up beside a gas pump, and a man who must have been six feet four got out of the back and came inside the store with the help of aluminum forearm crutches. He wore a pearl-gray Stetson, shined needle-nosed boots, an open-collar plum-colored shirt, and a gray suit that had thin lavender stripes in it. But it was his gaunt face and the suppressed pain in it that caught Molly's eye. It was obvious that walking inside and struggling with the heavy glass door was a challenge to him, and Molly wondered why no one from his vehicle had accompanied him. In fact, Molly had to force herself to look straight ahead so the man on crutches would not think she was staring at him. When he got in line at the counter to pay for a newspaper and a package of filter-tipped cigars, she could see the set of his jaw and the rigidity of his posture out of the corner of her eye. There was a controlled tension in his expression, the kind you witness in people who are experiencing unrelieved back pain, the kind that dwells at the base of the spine like a thumb pressed against the sciatic nerve.

One of the clerks tried to scan the man's package of cigars, but her scanner came up empty. "Do you know how much these are?" she asked.

"No, I don't," the man replied.

"I'm sorry, I have to get a price check," the clerk said.

"That's all right," the man said.

But he was not all right. His hands were squeezed tightly on the grips of his crutches, his face gray and coarse-looking, his breath audible. When he tried to shift his weight, Molly saw the blood drain from around his mouth. The teenage stock boy who had been sent on the price check could not find the rack where the cigars were.

"Sir, maybe I could help," Molly said.

"I'm fine here," the man said.

"I was a nurse in—"

"I'm fine," he said, not looking at her, his expression empty.

She felt her face tighten with embarrassment. She placed her soda can in a trash barrel and went outside. Albert was loading his new saddle in the camper shell that was inserted in the bed of his paint-skinned pickup. He shut the door on the camper and peeled the wrapper on a Hershey bar. "You drive, will you?" he said.

The morning sun created a glare on the window as she backed out of their parking spot. Simultaneously, the white limo was backing up from the gas pump to make way for a motor home. Molly's trailer hitch gashed the taillight out of the limo's fender molding, sprinkling glass and chrome on the concrete.

Lyle Hobbs got out from behind the wheel of the limo to inspect the damage. He chewed his lip, his fists propped on his hips, his dry hair blowing in the wind. He let out his breath and took off his aviator glasses and looked at Molly. "I guess if I was sitting on top of an elephant, you might have seen me," he said.

"That's very clever. But people don't usually back up from gas pumps. That's why this store has an entrance and an exit. You drive into the entrance. You put the gas in your car and drive out of the exit. That's usually understood by most literate people. Maybe the problem is with your dirty windows. Can you see adequately out of them?"

"You're Ms. Robicheaux, right?" he said. "Don't even answer. Yes, indeed, here we are once again."

"This truck is mine. Address your remarks to me," Albert said, standing on the pavement.

But Lyle Hobbs continued to stare into Molly's face and did not acknowledge Albert. "Can you tell me why we keep having trouble with you people?" he asked. "Is this 'cause I broke Mr. Purcel's fishing rod?"

"I'm sure 'you people' refers to a specific group of some kind, but I'm afraid the term is lost on me," Molly said. "Can you explain what 'you people' means? I've always wanted to learn that."

The charcoal-tinted windows of the limo were half down. A gold-haired woman in back pressed the window motor and leaned forward, the sunlight striking her tan skin and blue contact lenses. "We're late, Lyle. Check her insurance card and make sure it's current," she said. "The attorney will handle the rest of it."

"Your attorney won't handle anything. Your vehicle backed into me, madam," Molly said.

But Molly had difficulty sustaining the firmness in her own words.

The man sitting on the far side of the gold-haired woman was grinning at her, if indeed his expression could be called a grin. The skin on his face and head and neck looked like a mixture of pink and white and red rubber someone had fitted on a mannequin, except it was puckered, the nose little more than a bump with two holes in it, the surgically rebuilt mouth a lopsided keyhole that exposed his teeth. He toasted Molly with his champagne glass and winked at her.

She felt a wave of both pity and shame rush through her. Behind her, she heard the metallic clatter of the man who walked with the aid of forearm crutches.

"I saw it all from inside," the man with crutches said. "It's our fault. We'll repair our own vehicle and take care of theirs."

"This man here is Albert Hollister, Mr. Wellstone," Lyle Hobbs said.

The man on crutches paused. "You're him, are you?" he said.

"What's that supposed to mean?" Albert said.

"It doesn't mean anything," Wellstone said. "What's the damage to your truck?"

"The bumper is scratched. It's nothing to worry about."

"Then we're done here. You agreeable with that?" Wellstone said.

"Your driver owes Mrs. Robicheaux an apology."

"He's sorry," Wellstone said. He got in the front seat of the limousine, propping his crutches next to him on the rolled leather seat. Then he flopped open his newspaper with one hand and slammed the door with the other.

"Why is it I have the feeling someone just spit on the tops of my shoes?" Molly said.

Albert sniffed at an odor he hadn't detected earlier. He bent down and looked under the bumper of his truck.

"What is it?" Molly said.

"The trailer hitch punched a hole in the gas tank. I'll need to get us a tow and have the tank welded or replaced."

"I should have seen the limo backing up. Dave and I will pay for it," Molly said.

"I just remembered where I heard that snooty fellow's name," Albert said.

THAT AFTERNOON THE lead story on the local television news involved the death of the University of Montana coed. At sunset the previous evening she and her boyfriend had gone for a hike up a zigzag trail behind the university. When last seen, they had left the main trail and were hiking up through fir trees, over the crest of the mountain. The girl was found two miles away, in a stony creek bed. Her body was marbled with bruises, her skull crushed. The boyfriend was still missing.

CHAPTER
3

THE MISSOULA COUNTY high sheriff was a western anachronism by the name of Joe Bim Higgins. He had inherited the office after his predecessor fell off a barn roof and broke his neck. Joe Bim rolled his own cigarettes when no one was looking and wore his trousers stuffed inside Mexican cowboy boots, the kind stenciled up the sides with red and green flower petals. He had been at Heartbreak Ridge, and one side of his face was wrinkled like old wallpaper from the heat of a phosphorous shell that had exploded ten feet from the edge of his foxhole. He wore an oversize felt western hat of the kind Tom Mix had worn and seemed to care little about either his image or his political future.

In the early A.M. we thought dry lightning had ignited a fire on the far side of the ridge behind Albert's house. But when I walked out on the porch, the sky was clear, the stars bright, and there was no trace of smoke in the air. Then we realized we were seeing the lights of emergency vehicles wending their way through the Douglas fir trees and ponderosa pines and that a helicopter was sweeping the canopy with a floodlight from the far side of the ridge.

At sunup Joe Bim Higgins's cruiser pulled into Albert's drive. Fifteen minutes later, the two of them drove to our cabin and tapped on the door. Molly was still in her bathrobe. I went out on the porch in the coldness of the morning and closed the door behind me. A helicopter swept by overhead, its searchlight off now, scattering the horses in the pasture.

Joe Bim was smoking a hand-roll, its tip wet with saliva. He asked if I had seen any activity on the hill behind Albert's house two nights previous.

"I didn't see anything. Maybe I heard a vehicle," I said.

"What time?"

"After midnight. I didn't pay it much mind," I said.

"Know what kind of vehicle?" he asked.

"A car."

He wrote on a notepad. "You didn't think that was unusual?" he said, not looking up.

"Some loggers from the Plum Creek Company have been working up there," I said.

"After midnight?" he said. He glanced at my face.

"I told you I didn't give it much thought. I had no reason to."

"I know you're a police officer, Mr. Robicheaux, but I don't like loading dead college kids into the back of an ambulance. This is the second one in two days. The coroner says this one has been dead at least thirty-six hours. Your wife hear anything?"

"No."

"Let's ask her," he said.

"She's not dressed," I replied.

"How about we eat some breakfast and work on this afterward?" Albert said.

Joe Bim Higgins studied the hillside, his chest rising and falling. He folded his notebook and put it in his pocket, then buttoned the flap on the pocket. His face was fatigued, his breath sour. "You worked a lot of homicides?" he said.

"A few."

"Thursday evening a girl by the name of Cindy Kershaw went hiking with her boyfriend up Mount Sentinel, behind the university. She ended up at the bottom of the canyon with a broken skull. We couldn't find her boyfriend and thought maybe he was involved. Late last night a man called in a tip from a pay phone and told us where to look. He told us the kid was alive and tied to a tree, but we'd better get our asses up there soon. You ever get tips like that?"

"Yeah, from people who were jerking us around."

"The boyfriend's name was Seymour Bell. He was twenty years old. He wasn't tied up. He was shot four times at close range, all in the face. According to the coroner, he was shot on the hill, not moved there from somewheres else. From the looks of his britches, he died on his knees. The shooter took his brass with him. You didn't hear any shots?"

"No sir."

"You were in Vietnam?"

"A few months, before it got real hot."

"Maybe this prick used a suppressor. Why you figure he'd kill the girl in one place and her boyfriend in another?"

"Was the girl raped?"

"She'd had recent intercourse. It could be called rough sex. But that doesn't go with what people knew about either her or her boyfriend." Then he told me what the perpetrator had done to her.

"My guess is the girl was the target. The perp separated them so he could take his time with the girl," I said. "Maybe he locked the boy in the car trunk. Can cars get up the mountain behind the university?"

"There's a fire road for pump trucks along the face of the mountain."

When I didn't reply, he looked up at the hill again. The morning was blue with shadow, the wind channeling through the wildflowers and bunch grass. Farther down the valley, wood smoke was drifting off a stone chimney that was still dusted with frost. "If I owned Albert's place, I'd hang up my badge and mess with my horses and trout-fish in the evening," he said. "I wouldn't do this kind of work anymore."

THAT AFTERNOON I helped Albert dig knapweed and leafy spurge out of his pasture. Knapweed is a nuisance in the American West. Leafy spurge is a plague. The root system can go twenty feet into the ground and form a network that, once established, cannot be eradicated with chemicals or even excavation by giant machines. A shopping center can be constructed on top of it, and its root system will continue to reproduce and grow laterally until its stems find sunlight. That's not a metaphor.

Albert was sweating heavily, chopping at the ground with a mattock, his gloves streaked with the thick milky-white substance that a broken spurge stem produces. He hadn't spoken for almost a half hour.

"Something bothering you besides noxious weeds?" I said.

"That fellow Wellstone owes me for a punctured gas tank."

But I doubted that his mood had its origins in a minor car accident. The light had died in his eyes, and I had a feeling that Albert had gone to a private place inside himself that he shared with few people.

"Molly said you remembered hearing this guy's name."

"When I was eighteen, I was in a parish can on the Texas-Louisiana line. The electric chair traveled from parish to parish in those days. I was there when it was brought in on a flatbed truck, the generators all tarped down so people wouldn't see their tax dollars at work. They electrocuted this poor devil thirty feet from the lockdown unit I was in. The next morning I got in the face of a hack who had been a gunbull at Angola."

I kept my eyes straight ahead and didn't speak.

"He cuffed and leg-chained me and frog-walked me down to an isolation cell. It was almost fifty years before I told anybody what he did to me. I saw him in a feed store in Beaumont once, when I was about twenty-one. He was a foreman on a cattle ranch. He had no idea who I was, the man who was to give me bad dreams for a half-century. He asked me why I was staring at him. When I didn't answer, he told me it was rude to stare at people and I had better stop.

"I was buying a weed sickle. It had an edge on it that could shave hair off your arm. I wouldn't let go of his eyes. He laughed because he couldn't stop what was happening. He said, 'Boy, whatever it is you're thinking, you'd best take it somewheres else.'

"I stepped close to him and touched his hip with the point of the sickle. I said, 'I was thinking about killing you. If I see you again, I expect I'll do it.' "

I looked at the side of Albert's face. It reminded me of a dead fire after all the heat has gone out of the ash and stone. "You ever see him again?" I asked.

"At the Wellstone ranch outside Beaumont, when I went there looking for work. They were oil-and-natural-gas people and ranched on the side. They were also mixed up with tent-religion groups that were just starting to expand into television."

"I'd let Wellstone and the past go," I said.

"I did, a long time ago. But Wellstone gashed a hole in my fuel tank. I called his house about it last night. A woman hung up on me. I think it was the gold-haired one who was sitting in the back of his limo."

Albert arched his back, squinting slightly. He stared up at the hill behind his house. "Did you know Chief Joseph and the whole Nez Perce tribe came right down that draw? They were trying to outrun the U.S. Army. They got slaughtered down on the Big Hole—women and children and the old people, too. The soldiers mutilated the dead and later robbed the graves."

"Yeah?" I said, not making the connection.

"This place looks peaceful. But it's not. The degenerate who murdered that college boy up there is the canker in the rose. It doesn't matter where you go. The same fellow is always there. Just like that jailhouse I was in when I was eighteen."

THAT AFTERNOON CLETE came down to our cabin and asked me to take a walk with him.

"Where we going?"

He lifted his eyes up to the hill behind Albert's house.

"What for?" I asked.

"The sheriff, what's-his-name, Higgins, thinks it's just coincidence that kid was killed behind Albert's place."

"You don't?"

"Higgins says Albert called the Shrubster a draft-dodging fraternity pissant in the local newspaper. The paper actually ran the letter. He helped run a PCB incinerator out of town. He got into it with some outlaw bikers over a barmaid. He has a general reputation for causing trouble wherever he goes."

"Why would somebody execute a kid on his knees because he's got it in for Albert?"

"Somebody called in a 911 on the location. The caller also said the kid was alive. He wanted as many people as possible to suffer as much as possible. I don't think Higgins knows what he's dealing with. I don't believe Albert does, either."

"You didn't answer my question."

"To use your own words, why do the shitbags do anything? Because they enjoy it, that's why. Trust me, Streak, the guy who did this has got a beef with Albert."

I followed him up a switchback trail to the top of the ridge, Clete wheezing and sweating all the way. Then we walked up a gradual slope through pine and fir trees to a level place where yellow crime-scene tape had been strung through the tree trunks. The tape had been broken in several places, probably by deer or elk, and the dirt road that led off the hillside was rutted by tire tracks. At the higher altitude, the air had become cold, flecked with rain, filled with the sound of wind sweeping across the enormous breadth of landscape below us.

I believed our climb up to the crime scene was a morbid waste of time. Even though the tape was broken, we had no right to go inside what was obviously a proscribed evidentiary area. Second, the ground was soft and already crisscrossed with the footprints of investigative personnel. In all probability, any forensic evidence there had already been removed, disturbed, tainted, or destroyed.

Except for one element that was still in plain view: blood splatter on a rock the size and shape of a blacksmith's anvil that protruded from the softness of the ground. The blood looked like it had been slung from the tip of an artist's brush.

Clete put an unlit cigarette in his mouth and peered down through the trees at the roof of Albert's house. He removed his porkpie hat and messed with it idly, then replaced it on his head, the brim slanted down. Then he removed it again and twirled it on his finger.

"What are you thinking?" I asked.

"The guy who drove the kid up here beat the shit out of his own car. Why would he want to risk busting an axle or tie rod when he could have driven into the national forest just as easily? The kid died on his knees. The shooter probably made him beg or do worse. The shooter did all this right above Albert's house. He could see Albert's house, but nobody in Albert's house could see him. He chose this spot deliberately, and he knew who lived down below. This fuckhead is a classic psychopath. He stays high on control and inflicting pain while he's within sight of people who have no idea what he's doing."

"That doesn't mean he knows Albert."

"Maybe," Clete said. But his attention had already shifted to something down the slope.

"What is it?" I said.

Clete worked his way about five feet down the incline, holding on to pine trunks for balance. He took his ballpoint pen from his shirt pocket and tried to pick up a leather cord and a small wood cross that lay at the base of a lichen-encrusted rock. The cord was broken, and it slipped off his pen.

"Don't taint the scene, Clete," I said.

"If we hadn't found this, no one would have ever known it was here," he said. But he didn't touch the cord with his hand; instead, he lifted up the end with his pen. "Look, the break is dry and there's no discoloration. The kid tore it off the shooter, or the shooter tore it off the vic."

"A logger might have dropped it, too."

"No, something weird happened out here. This isn't a random abduction and killing. I'll call the evidence in to Higgins," he said.

"Okay, partner, but I think you're overreading the information," I said.

Clete pulled himself up the incline and stepped back on level ground. His face was blotched from exertion and the high altitude. He looked at me a long time.

"Say it," I said.

"What'd the guy do to the girl before she died?"

"Everything he could without leaving his DNA," I replied.

"We're going to hear more from this guy. You know it, Dave. Don't pretend you don't."

The mist was white blowing through the trees. The rock that was stippled with the dead boy's blood glistened in the weak light. I picked up a pinecone and flung it into space.

DURING THE WEEK we heard a lot more about Ridley Wellstone and his family, in the same way you hear a word or name for the first time and then hear it every hour for the next month.

The Wellstones had arrived in Montana with checkbook in hand, not unlike the Hollywood celebrities and Silicon Valley millionaires who had come in the 1990s, believing that the beauty of the state was simply one more gift that a just and wise capitalistic deity had bestowed upon them for their personal use.

I must make a confession here. After telling Clete to ignore the destruction of his fishing gear by the Wellstone security personnel, and after telling Albert to forget the past and write off Ridley Wellstone's arrogance, I had made calls to friends in the oil business in both Lafayette and Dallas. The information I gathered about the Wellstones may seem from another era. It isn't. To a southerner, the story of the Wellstone family is a familiar one. The coarseness and privation of their background, the occasional ruthlessness of their methods, and the exploitation of their fellow man are rites of passage that are forgotten within a generation, if not sooner. The battle-fatigued knight returning to his castle, dragging his bloodied sword across stone, does not have to give an accounting for his deeds. Why dwell on the sight of burning huts in a peasant village when you can thrill to the horns blowing along the road to Roncevaux?

Ridley and his brother, Leslie, were the children of a Texas wildcatter by the name of Oliver Wellstone who, at age ten, had carried water by the bucket to drilling crews in the original Spindletop Field outside Beaumont. At age twenty-three, during the Depression, he borrowed one hundred dollars from a Bible salesman and talked a black farmer into accepting a promissory note for the lease on a two-acre cypress bog. The rig was constructed of salvaged railroad ties; the drill was powered by a twelve-cylinder motor removed from a junked Packard automobile. Three weeks after drilling commenced, the bit punched into a geological dome that sprayed salt water and a stench like rotten eggs high above the swamp. When the air cleared, Oliver Wellstone was convinced his dreams of wealth had come to naught. Then the ground under his feet rumbled and shook, and a geyser of sweet black crude exploded out of the wellhead and showered down on his head like a gift from a divine hand. He peered up at the heavens, his mouth open, his arms extended, his face running with oil. If there was such a thing as secular baptism, Oliver Wellstone had just experienced it.

Ten years later, he owned six producing fields in Louisiana and Texas, three ranches, a string of canneries, and an Austin radio station.

He bought a home in Houston's River Oaks, a metropolitan oasis of trees and high-banked green lawns and palatial estates where success was a given and the problems of the poor and the disenfranchised were the manufactured concerns of political leftists. Unfortunately for Oliver and his family, financial equality in River Oaks did not necessarily translate into social acceptance.

Wildcatters like H. L. Hunt and Glenn McCarthy and Bob Smith may have respected him, but his peckerwood accent and fifth-grade education trailed with him like cultural odium wherever he went. The fact that his wife's face could make a train turn onto a dirt road didn't help matters, either. At formal dinners Oliver stuffed his napkin inside his collar and sawed his steak like a man cutting up a rubber tire, then ate it with his fork in his left hand, dunking each bite in obscene amounts of ketchup. A columnist in the *Houston Post* said his head looked like a grinning alabaster bowling ball. He had a phobia about catching communicable diseases, washed his hands constantly, and on cold days wore two flannel shirts under his suit coat and refused to take off his hat indoors. Every day of his life he ate a Vienna-sausage-and-mayonnaise sandwich for lunch and walked eight blocks to his office rather than put money in a parking meter. At any café he frequented, he loaded up on free toothpicks at the cashier's counter. When Oliver and his wife applied for membership in one of Houston's most exclusive country clubs, their application was denied.

That was when Oliver returned to his holy-roller roots, in the same way a man returns to a homely girlfriend whose arms are open and whose heart makes no judgments. Pentecostals speaking in tongues and writhing in the spirit or dipping their arms in boxes of snakes might seem bizarre to some, but tent crowds all across Texas recognized Oliver as one of their own. When Oliver gave witness, there was rapture and sweetness in their faces. No one there was overly concerned about stories of Oliver's involvement with slant drilling or stolen seismograph reports or, in one instance, pouring lye in the eyes of a competitor. If he was challenged by a fellow believer about the contradiction between his philanthropy and the sources of his wealth, Oliver's response was simple: "There is nothing the devil hates worse than seeing his own money used against him. Let the church roll on!"

But Oliver's sons turned out to be nothing like him. What they were is much more difficult to describe than what they were not.

ONE WEEK HAD come and gone since Molly had backed Albert's pickup into the Wellstone limo. Then another week passed, and I heard nothing more about either the accident or the murder of the two university students. Perhaps in part that was because I avoided watching the news, hoping I could slip back into the loveliness of the season, the mist in the trees at sunrise, the smell of horses and wood smoke on the wind, the summer light hanging in the sky until ten P.M.

Fond and foolish thoughts.

Saturday night a downpour drenched the valley and knocked trees over on power lines and washed streams of gravel down the hillsides. During the storm, for reasons I can't explain, I dreamed of the Louisiana of my youth. I saw the slatted light that glowed at dawn through the shutters on my bedroom windows. I saw the pecan and oak trees in our yard, the fog off the bayou like cotton candy in the branches. I heard my mother gathering eggs for our breakfast in the barn, and I heard my father loading his crab traps and hoop nets in the back of his stake truck. I could smell the humus back in the swamp and the fecund odor of fish spawning and the night-blooming flowers my mother had planted in her garden. Not far from our home, vast expanses of green sugarcane were swirling in the wind, as though beaten by the downdraft of helicopter blades, backdropped by a sky that was piled with blue-black thunderheads.

It was V-J Day 1945, and my half brother, Jimmie, and I were safe in our home because our countrymen had driven both the Nazis and the Imperial Japanese from the earth. In the dream, I heard my father drive away in his stake truck, and I saw my mother look up the dirt road toward a parked Ford coupe. Sitting behind the steering wheel was a blade-faced man in a fedora who, like a scale-covered creature of long ago, patiently waited to enter our green-gold Eden on the bayou.

When I woke from the dream, I went into the kitchen and sat a long time in the darkness by myself. The sky was black, the rain thundering on the cabin's roof. The dream was one I had carried with me from Louisiana and the Philippines to Vietnam. It dealt with a sense of loss that I knew I would never get over. My parents had done the worst thing human beings are capable of doing to themselves: They had destroyed their own home and all those in it, including themselves. But the dream was about more than my own family. The world in which I had grown up was gone. The country I live in is not the one of my birth. It might seem so to others, but it is not, no matter what they say.

Molly sat down beside me in the darkness. Before she married a sheriff's detective with a history of alcoholism and violence, she had been a Catholic nun and nurse at Maryknoll missions in El Salvador and Guatemala, and had come to New Iberia to help organize the cane workers and build homes for the poor. She was wearing a white bathrobe, and when lightning flared above the mountains, she looked like an apparition. "Want to come back to bed?" she said.

"I think I'm up," I said.

"Want me to start breakfast?"

"How about steak and eggs up at the truck stop?"

"Give me a minute," she said, getting up from her chair, squeezing my shoulder.

I followed her into the bedroom. When she untied her robe and let it slip off her shoulders onto the bed, I could feel something drop inside me, like water draining through a hole in the bottom of a streambed, as if all the clocks in my life had suddenly accelerated and I couldn't stop them. I put my arms around her and held her against me. Her shoulders and back were powdered with freckles, and her skin felt cool and smooth and warm under my hands, all at the same time. She had red hair, and it was thick and cropped on her neck, and it smelled of the perfume behind her ears. I squeezed her tight and bit her on the shoulder.

"You okay, Dave?" she said.

"Always," I said.

LATER, WHILE MOLLY and Clete and Albert were in Missoula, I mucked out the stalls in Albert's barn and scrubbed out the horse tank and refilled it with fresh water from the secondary well he had drilled in his pasture. By noon the chill had gone out of the morning, and the sky was a hard blue, the valley bright with sunshine, the trees a deep green from the rain. I saw a waxed black convertible, the top down, coming up the road, the driver steering straight over the mud puddles rather than around them. Three people were inside. When they stopped by the rail fence at the foot of the pasture, I had no doubt who they were.

I pulled off my gloves and walked to the fence. The driver was a gold-haired woman who wore blue contact lenses and a halter that barely contained her breasts. A tiny bluebird, its wings spread, was tattooed above one breast. The man in back had a pair of aluminum forearm crutches propped next to him on the seat. But it was the man in the passenger seat whose face caused one to either look away or to stare into neutral space so as not to offend.

I tipped my hat to the woman and waited.

"Is either Albert Hollister or Clete Purcel at home?" she asked.

"No," I said. "Could I give them a message?"

"You can give Mr. Purcel this," the man in back said. He handed me a tubular fly-rod case, then gathered up a paper sack from the floor and handed that to me, too. "There's a creel and line and a reel and a box of flies in there, the best in Bob Ward's store. Tell him I'm sorry about his gear being accidentally busted up on my property. Tell him I hope all of us are shut of this, too."

"Maybe you should tell him, Mr. Wellstone," I said.

He ignored me and slapped the back of the driver's seat. The woman dropped the gearshift in reverse and backed down the road toward Albert's driveway, then turned the convertible around and headed for the state highway.

I went back to work in the barn, glad they were gone. But a moment later, the woman stopped the convertible and backed all the way down the dirt road until she reached the gate to the pasture. Ridley Wellstone got out on his aluminum crutches, unfastened the chain on the gate, and began working his way across the pasture toward me, the bottom of his crutches sinking into the soft detritus of manure and dirt and rotted hay. I picked up a wood chair out of the tack room and reached him just as he was about to topple sideways.

"Sit down, sir," I said.

"I didn't come all the way out here just to deliver fishing tackle. You tell Mr. Hollister I want to talk to him, man to man, face-to-face," he said.

"Why don't you leave Clete and Albert alone? They haven't done anything to harm you."

"Leave *them* alone? This man Purcel has been following my security personnel around. Albert Hollister and a group of tree huggers filed an injunction against me. I can't drill test wells on my own ranch." He looked at my expression. "You didn't know that?"

"What are you test-drilling for?"

"Oil and natural gas, if it's any of your business."

"You want to open up oil production on the Swan River?"

"You listen, Mr. Robicheaux: Once people know money is under the ground, they're going to extract it. The only question is how and by whom. Better some than others, that make sense to you?"

"Not really, but I'll tell Albert and Clete what you said."

"You might also tell them I'm not the Antichrist and to stop treating me like I am. This is a fine-looking place. What if I told Mr. Hollister he shouldn't string horseshit all over it, less'n he wants an injunction against him?"

I tried to think of a response, but this time he had me.

He began clanking on his crutches toward the gate. Then one crutch sank six inches in a soft spot, and he fell sideways into the mud, landing hard. He stared up at me, the blood draining from his cheeks. I tried to lift him, but he was deadweight in my hands and obviously in severe pain.

"Is it sciatica?" I said.

I heard the woman and the man with the disfigured face coming across the pasture.

"Get me up," he whispered.

"I think you need the paramedics," I said.

"Don't let me lie in the mud like this."

I got both arms under him and pulled him erect, then sat him down in the chair I had brought from the tack room. His chest was heaving, his suit spotted and smeared with mud. "Thank you," he said.

"We'll need to drive the car into the pasture. You mind if we open the gate?" the woman said.

"Of course I don't mind," I replied.

She went back for the car. The man with the ruined face lit a cigarette and put it in Ridley Wellstone's mouth. Then he fitted his right hand on Ridley's shoulder. Two fingers on his hand were missing, and the skin was shriveled so that the bones were pinched together and looked as small as those in a dried monkey's paw.

"I'm Leslie Wellstone, Ridley's brother."

I waited for him to offer his hand, but he didn't. "I'm glad to meet you," I said.

"The woman is Jamie Sue. She's my wife." There was a mirthful light in his eyes, one that was not pleasant to look at.

"I see."

"You do?" he said.

I had no idea what he meant, and I didn't want to find out.

"Get me up," Ridley Wellstone said.

"Give Ridley a saddle, and he'll be sitting on one of your horses," the brother said. "That's how he fixed up his back. Ridley goes from hell to breakfast and doesn't stop for small talk."

"I said get me up and leave Mr. Robicheaux to his work."

"How do you know my name?" I said.

Ridley Wellstone lifted his eyes to mine. "I know everything about you. You've killed over a half-dozen men."

I felt my ears pop in the wind, or perhaps I heard a sound like a flag snapping on a metal pole. "Repeat that, please?"

He was breathing through his mouth; there were tiny flecks of spittle on his lips. "You've got blood splatter all over you," he said. "Maybe you did it with a badge, but you're a violent and dangerous man all the same. I don't judge you for it. I just don't want you dragging your grief into our lives."

"*What?*" I said.

"I've known your kind all my life. Every one of you is a professional victim. If you had your way, we'd be studying Karl Marx instead of Thomas Jefferson. This whole country would be run by faggots and welfare recipients. A man of your experience and education knows this, but he's at war with his own instincts. It's nothing against you personal. I just want shut of you."

I decided a little of the Wellstone family could go a long way.

CHAPTER 4

ONE MONTH EARLIER, on a piece of baked hardpan out in West Texas, within sight of the shimmering outline of the Van Horn Mountains, a convict by the name of Jimmy Dale Greenwood was finishing his second year on a three-to-five bit, all of it served in a contract prison, courtesy of a judge who didn't like half-breeds in general and smart-ass hillbilly singers like Jimmy Dale in particular.

The contract prison was a squat blockhouse nightmare that, except for the parallel rows of electric fences topped with coils of razor wire surrounding the buildings, resembled a sewage plant more than a penal facility. Most of the work done by the inmates was meant to be punitive and not rehabilitative in nature. In fact, both inmates and prison personnel referred to the work as "the hard road." The hard road came complete with mounted gunbulls, leather-cuff ankle restraints, and orange jumpsuits that rubbed the skin like sandpaper in winter and became portable ovens in summer.

The majority of the personnel were not deliberately cruel. But drought and wildfires and the loss of family farms weren't of their making, and shepherding prison inmates on a tar-patch crew beat delivering Domino's pizzas or clerking at the adult-video store on the interstate. The line "It's your misfortune and none of my own," from the classic trail drover's lament, seemed an accurate summation of the Texas contract gunbull's attitude toward his charges.

Most of the inmates in the contract prison were recidivists and didn't question their fate or the power structure under which they lived. That meant they didn't grab-ass, eyeball, complain about the food, dog it on the job, wise off to Hispanic guys with Gothic-letter tats, or sass the hacks. If you committed the crime, you stacked the time. Then one day you popped out on the other end of your jolt and got a lot of gone between you and West Texas. It was that simple. Or should have been.

Jimmy Dale went down ostensibly for grand theft, the arrest being made after he crashed the stolen vehicle he was driving at ninety an hour through a police barricade. In reality, the judge dropped the jailhouse on Jimmy Dale's head because of an unprosecutable knife beef that had taken place outside a saloon off Interstate 10. Jimmy Dale never denied he drove the shank hilt-deep into the victim's chest. Nor did he deny boosting the car. What was he supposed to do? he explained to the highway patrol. Hang around and hope the victim's friends in the Sheriff's Department didn't use him for a piñata? The problem for the DA was the fact that the victim pulled the shank, not Jimmy Dale. Another problem was that the victim was a pimp who believed he had the right to beat up his whores in the parking lot. Also, his claim that Jimmy Dale had butted into his business would probably not flush with a jury made up of First Assembly and Church of Christ members. Last, the stabbing victim was the judge's nephew, and the judge had indicated to the DA that he didn't see any need for feeding the liberal media's appetite for scandal.

After two years on the hard road, with a shot at early parole because of overcrowding in the system, Jimmy Dale had the bad luck to fall under the supervision of one Troyce Nix, a six-feet-five-inch gunbull who once confessed to his peers, "Nothing gives me more pleasure than watching a full-grown man piss his pants."

Nix had another inclination, one that for years he had satisfied with rental videos or on the Internet or across the border in Mexico. His inclination had cost him two marriages and his career as an MP in the United States Army. He saw nothing unusual about his behavior, much less perverse. In a coupling of any kind, he was always the male, never the female; hence, he was not a homosexual. Anyone who doubted that fact, particularly his sexual partner, was given a lesson about the true nature of physical dominance.

You set your parameters, you drew your lines. When people crossed your lines, you slapped them into shape. What was wrong with that? Troyce had worked at the Abu Ghraib prison, thirty-two klicks west of Baghdad. When one of his current colleagues asked him what it was like, Troyce replied, "At least none of the graduates come back for seconds."

"No, after y'all got finished with them, they was probably busy blowing the shit out of American soldiers with IEDs," one of the other hacks said.

The hack who made the remark was fired three weeks later.

Troyce's body was covered with reddish-blond hair that seemed to glow like a nimbus in the sunlight. On the hard road, he wore a white straw hat coned up on the sides, shades, and needle-nosed cowboy boots that a trusty spit-shined every night. His olive-green trousers and shirt, with red piping on the pockets, were always starched and pressed, his black gunbelt polished. With his military posture, his shirt tucked tightly into his belt, he was a fine-looking man, his face serene, his voice neutral in tone. In some instances, he was almost fatherly toward the inmates under his supervision.

Jimmy Dale Greenwood was a different matter. Other than his conviction for grand auto, Jimmy Dale came into the prison population without a sheet. More simply stated, he wasn't a criminal by nature and didn't belong there. Also, it was impossible to read his expression or to know what he was thinking. He had a way of making enigmatic remarks that seemed to float on the edges of provocation and insult.

"I hear you left pecker tracks in a lot of white women's beds," one of the gunbulls said to him.

"I reckon it beats writing your name on the washroom wall, boss," Jimmy Dale replied.

The gunbull was going to put Jimmy Dale on the barrel that night. But Troyce Nix intervened and, at the close of the workday, told Jimmy Dale to climb up in the truck cab and ride back to the prison compound with him.

"I stink pretty bad, Cap'n," Jimmy Dale said.

Troyce grinned at him from behind his shades, the gearstick knob throbbing in his palm. "You'll stink a whole lot worse if you spend the night standing on the barrel and dribbling in your pants," he said.

Troyce was silent as they drove toward the compound, the dust from the alkali flats drifting through the windows. Up ahead, another truck towed the trailer that contained the gunbulls' horses. Jimmy Dale could see the horses' rumps swaying back and forth with the motion of the trailer, desiccated pieces of manure blowing into the wind. Troyce pulled a cigarette from his pack with his mouth and lit it with the lighter from the dashboard. The smoke leaked from his mouth like damp cotton.

"If you was wanting to buy a used horse trailer, what would you look for first?" Troyce asked.

"The floor," Jimmy Dale replied.

"Why's that?"

"'Cause if it's got dry rot in it, your horse's foot can punch through it on the highway."

"If you was to build a floor on a trailer, how would you go about it?"

"I'd use only treated two-by-four planks. I'd use only bolts and screws instead of nails so there wouldn't be cracks to soak up moisture. I'd put the planks in snug but with enough space between them so they could drain and aerate."

"How come you know so much about horses and tack?"

"I'm a rodeo bum, boss."

"Thought you was a country-and-western singer."

"I guess shitkicking can cover lots of categories."

Troyce laughed, appraising Jimmy Dale through his shades. "I want you to put a new floor in that trailer for me. Do a good job, and I'll write you up for half trusty and give you an indoor job. In three months you'll be up for full trusty."

"I'll be up for parole before then."

Troyce swerved the truck around a jackrabbit that had bolted across the road. Or at least appeared to swerve around it. When he glanced into the side mirror, his face seemed to contain more than idle curiosity. "I wouldn't necessarily count on that," he said.

"I'll build you a good floor, boss. I appreciate anything you can do for me," Jimmy Dale said.

"Yeah, you're gonna do just fine. Have a smoke." Troyce shook a cigarette loose from the pack, offering the firm white cylinder to Jimmy Dale, holding his eyes when Jimmy Dale took it.

Just before they entered the compound, the truck bounced over a series of potholes. Troyce's hand slipped off the gearshift, and the pads of his fingers brushed softly across Jimmy Dale's thigh. For Jimmy Dale, the sensation was like the tiny feet of a small animal tickling across his skin, and it caused his penis to shrivel in his skivvies.

THE CONTRACT PRISON was run military-style. At 7:58 P.M. sharp, the count man shouted, "In the house!" At eight P.M. he shouted, "Locking it down!" Then the steel doors slid collectively into place, clanging shut in unison with a sound that reverberated through the building. The count man and the screw behind him began their walk down the bullrun, the count man whanging his baton on the bars as he passed each cell, the screw ticking check marks on his clipboard.

Jimmy Dale hated this part of the day, trapped between daylight and darkness, between motion and inertia, between the illusion that he worked under the same sky and breathed the same air as other human beings and the knowledge that he was little more than a state-owned cipher entombed in a five-by-eight-foot steel box.

The echoes of the count man's baton on the bars trailed away in the distance, then the lights dimmed and he could hear the commode in his cell gurgling in the gloom. Jimmy Dale's nightmares waited for him just beyond the edge of sleep. In the worst of them, he was deep underground, pinned in a long tunnel, his arms crushed against his sides, the breath squeezed from his lungs. In his dream he cried out for his mother to free him, but his mother was not there. A psychiatrist had told him once that he had probably been wrapped in a rubber sheet when he was an infant and left to his fate. For some reason, to Jimmy Dale, those words were even worse than the dream.

His housemate was Beeville Hicks, a four-time loser whose enemy was freedom, not confinement. Long ago Beeville had flattened all the veins in his arms, destroyed his career as a steel-guitar player, and murdered his wife along the way. He was toothless, his skin like plastic wrap on his bones, his forehead tattooed with a red swastika, his hair as long and coarse as a horse's tail. Oddly, in spite of his violent history and his tattoo and his friendship with members of the AB, Beeville was basically a kind man who, had he not been a heroin addict, probably would not have hung washlines of paper all over the western United States. When Jimmy Dale asked Beeville why he had killed his old lady, he replied, "I'm not rightly sure. I knowed she was screwing the milkman, but she was a homely thing, and I couldn't hold that against her. Yes sir, that's a good question."

For his last birthday, Beeville's daughter had brought him his old scrapbook, which she had found in her attic. It was probably the finest gift Beeville had ever received, since few inmates or prison personnel believed his stories regarding the celebrities he had known or worked with. Beeville plastered his "house" wall with torn magazine pages and cracked black-and-white photographs showing him with Billy Joe Shaver, Texas Ruby, Moon Mullican, Stony Cooper and Wilma Lee, Floyd Tillman, Waylon Jennings, and Bob Wills.

He was eating a piece of gingerbread cake on the bottom bunk, what he called "scarf," the crumbs dripping off his hand, his naked back rounded, his vertebrae trying to poke through his skin. "I hear Cap'n Nix is going to have you working for him in the shop," he said to Jimmy Dale.

"That looks like the plan," Jimmy Dale said from the top bunk. In the silence that followed, he leaned over the bunk and looked down at Beeville. "What about it?"

"You got a lot of talent. Not just in your fingers, either. You got an old-style voice, like Jimmie Rodgers. Ain't many got that kind of voice anymore. Maybe Haggard or Dwight Yoakam has got it, but not nobody else I know of."

"Will you take the collard greens out of your mouth?"

"I got this swastika put on my head in Huntsville because I thought it'd protect me. I was right. Nobody would touch me with a toilet plunger. When I come out, nobody in the music business would touch me, either. How's that for smarts?"

Jimmy Dale lay back on his pillow and stared at the ceiling. It was steel, painted white, and the rivets that held it in place were orange around the rims. He could almost feel the ceiling's weight crushing down on his chest. "If I don't go along with Nix, he'll screw me at my hearing."

"He'll screw you in the shop and do it at your hearing, both. Go out max time, Jimmy Dale. You'll still have your voice, you'll still be a solid con. How about that girl you sang duet with? She's still out there somewhere, ain't she?"

Jimmy Dale heard somebody scream in the block, maybe a fish taking it from a couple of AB guys who had paid a screw to provide them a fresh experience. He laid his arm across his eyes and felt the moisture on his skin.

"What was that gal's name?" Beeville asked.

"Jamie Sue," Jimmy Dale replied. "Jamie Sue Stapleton."

"I saw her at a gig in Austin once. She looked like a movie star. Where's she at?"

"Will you shut up, old man? Just for once eat your rat food and shut up."

Jimmy Dale's ears were ringing as though he were in a plane dropping out of clouds, the face of a rock cliff rushing toward him. He leaned over the side of his bunk again, hoping the walls would stop spinning. "I'm sorry, Bee. I'm just off my feed."

Beeville dipped his head down, eating the crumbs from his palm, and showed no indication that he had heard either the insult or the apology. When he finished his gingerbread, he wiped his hands with a piece of toilet paper and threw the paper into the commode. "Life's a bitch, ain't it?" he said.

DURING THE NEXT two weeks, Jimmy Dale built a floor for Troyce Nix's horse trailer, then a desk for his office and a gun cabinet for his house. Nix seemed to pay little attention to Jimmy Dale except to check occasionally on the progress of the work.

Then one scorching afternoon, while Jimmy Dale was running an acetylene torch in the shop, Troyce dropped a fresh set of state blues on a bench and told him to take a shower in back and change clothes.

"What's going on, boss?" Jimmy Dale said.

"I just got you bumped up to full trusty. I need you to go in town with me and load some spool wire," Troyce Nix said.

"Hidalgo going, too, boss?" Jimmy Dale said, half smiling.

Troyce Nix did not acknowledge the question.

Jimmy Dale lathered himself under the showerhead inside the tin stall in the back of the shop, staring through the window at the clouds of yellow dust blowing across the hardpan. A skinny Mexican kid pushing a broom glanced back over his shoulder, then looked at Jimmy Dale. His shirt was wadded up and hanging from his back pocket, his skin peppered with sweat and welding soot from the shop, his back tattooed with an enormous picture of the Virgin Mary. "Watch your ass today," he said.

"We're going to town for wire. It ain't a big deal, Hidalgo," Jimmy Dale said.

"Make him use grease. I heard a guy say it was like a freight train."

"You close your mouth," Jimmy Dale said.

Hidalgo paused in his sweeping, his expression reflective, his eyes downcast. "I thought you was stand-up, Jimmy Dale. You can't go out max time, man?"

The trip to town was uneventful. Jimmy Dale loaded a dozen wire spools in the bed of the stake truck, chained up the tailgate, and got back in the cab with Troyce Nix. The only thing that bothered him was that the employees at the hardware store could have loaded the spools and Nix actually had no need of him. On the way back to the prison, Nix took note of the time and yawned. "It's been a hot one, ain't it?" he said.

"Yes sir, and to be followed by a warming spell, I expect," Jimmy Dale said.

But Nix was not interested in Jimmy Dale's attempt at humor. He turned off the state road onto a dirt track that led across a long stretch of cinnamon-colored earth and mesquite trees and scrub oak. The dirt track wound into a bank of hills and a canyon where a paintless frame house with a gallery was tucked against a bluff, one side of it shaded by a hackberry tree.

"That yonder is my camp, a place where I drink whiskey and shoot coyotes and cougars sometimes. That windmill puts out the sweetest, coldest water you ever drunk. Take that sack out from under your seat."

Jimmy Dale reached between his legs and felt the tip of a paper bag. When he pulled on it, the bottle inside clanked against the seat.

"Crack it open and hand it to me," Nix said.

"Boss, I don't want to get in no trouble," Jimmy Dale said.

"All of you are the same, ain't you?"

"Sir?"

"Under it all, you're three years old and fixing to shit your diapers."

Nix took the pint of vodka from Jimmy Dale and cracked off the cap. He drank from the neck like he was swallowing soda water, his throat working smoothly, his eyes fixed on the shadows spreading across the canyon floor. He braked the truck between the windmill and the frame house. A dust devil spun across the hardpan and broke apart against the gallery. "Get out," he said.

"Boss—"

"That wire ain't for the compound. It's for a mustang lot I'm putting in before the federal auction. I been off the clock and on my own time since noon. There ain't nothing wrong that's going on here. Now, you move your ass, boy. You're starting to piss me off."

"Where you want it, boss?"

Nix let the heat die in his voice. "Up yonder, on the slope. Watch you don't step in none of them armadillo holes. I don't want to have to haul you to the infirmary."

Jimmy Dale worked the spools of wire off the truck bed and carried them one at a time up an incline, the heat in the metal scorching his hands and forearms. He set the spools in a row by a stack of treated fence posts, his heart beating, Nix's silhouette like a scorched tin cutout against the sun. Why had he been so foolish? Why hadn't

he listened to Beeville and Hidalgo? He tried to pretend that acceptance of Nix's explanation about the side trip to the camp would get
him safely back in the truck, on the road back to the prison, back
to eight P.M. lockdown and the chance to undo his own naïveté in
thinking he could outwit a career gunbull who had worked at Abu
Ghraib. But even as he had these thoughts, he knew that of his own
volition, he had climbed into a concrete mixer.

Nix took off his shirt, released the chain on the windmill, and
washed his face and chest and under his arms in the sluice of water
that exploded from the pipe. His shoulders were ridged with fine
red hair, his stomach corrugated, his chest flat, like a boxer's. He
removed a pair of yellow leather gloves from his back pocket and
fitted them on. As an afterthought, he removed his shades and set
them on top of his folded shirt.

"How hard you ever been hit?" he said.

"I been beat up by the best there is, boss."

"We'll see." Nix grinned and looked at the dust gusting down
an arroyo. The windmill blades clattered against the sky, and water
sluiced out of the pipe onto the tip of his boot. He balled his right
hand and made a gesture with it, causing Jimmy Dale to flinch. Then
he hit Jimmy Dale unexpectedly with his left, the blow landing like
a bee sting on his ear, just before the right fist caught Jimmy Dale
square on the jaw and knocked him headlong in the dust.

Nix pulled a pair of handcuffs loose from the back of his belt and
dropped them on Jimmy's Dale stomach. "Put these on, and let's get
you into the house. I got some iodine for that cut. You can yell all
you want. It won't bother nobody."

During the next half hour, Jimmy Dale tried to go to a private
place in his mind, one where he was inviolate and apart from what
was happening to his body. He was even willing to journey to the
tunnel in his nightmares where his arms were pinioned at his sides
and the breath was crushed from his lungs. But this kind of fantasy
anodyne was not available for Jimmy Dale. Hidalgo had mentioned
a freight train when he warned him about Nix's potential. But a
freight train didn't smell of testosterone and hair oil, and it didn't
have unshaved jaws that felt like emery paper, and it didn't have a

wet mouth laboring by Jimmy Dale's ear; nor did it make sounds that were less than human and simultaneously plaintive with need.

When Nix was finished, he bent over with his handcuff key and released Jimmy Dale's wrists. Then he looked down at him with the most bizarre expression Jimmy Dale had ever seen on a human being's face. "Go outside and wash yourself at the windmill," he said. "You turn my stomach."

THE NEXT MORNING was Saturday. When the gate screw hit the seven A.M. buzzer and opened all the cell doors on the tier, Jimmy Dale climbed down from his bunk, vomited in the commode, and climbed up on his bunk again.

"You ain't gonna eat?" Beeville Hicks asked.

"Got a touch of virus, I think."

"You look like you was rope-drug down a staircase," Beeville Hicks said.

Jimmy Dale stared at the steel-plated ceiling, one hand pressed on his stomach, wondering if he had bled into his skivvies.

"What'd he do to you, boy?"

"Nothing."

Beeville was sitting on the edge of his bunk, his back humped. He popped a pimple on his shoulder and looked at his fingers. "I got turned out when I was seventeen. It goes away with time." When Jimmy Dale didn't reply, Beeville said, "What you aiming to do?"

"I don't rightly know."

Beeville stood up and began buttoning his shirt. His toothless mouth was ringed with deep creases where the flesh had collapsed. "I'll see if I can sneak you a banana back," he said.

"I told you, I ain't hungry, Bee."

"Better eat up. It ain't over with Nix. He takes it out on the guy he's got the yen for. I feel sorry for you."

Jimmy Dale closed his eyes and swallowed.

The full-court press started Monday after lunch.

"Cap'n Rankin says he come in for some center cutters on the ditching machine. He says you sassed him," Troyce Nix said.

Jimmy Dale set down his acetylene torch and pulled his goggles up on his forehead with his thumb. The motes of dust were as bright as grains of sand in the shafts of sunlight shining through the windows. "I don't think I done that, boss," he replied. "I just want to stack my time and not bother nobody. I don't want nobody bothering me, either, boss."

"You calling Cap'n Rankin a liar?"

"No sir."

"Then why'd you sass him?"

"I guess it's just been one of them kind of days, boss."

Nix pulled his gloves from his back pocket and flipped them idly on his palm. "You're either the dumbest breed I ever met or the slowest learner. Which is it?"

"Probably both, boss."

Nix shook his head as he walked out of the shop. Through the window, Jimmy Dale saw him talking to two other screws. While Nix talked, the other two men stared in Jimmy Dale's direction, their expressions opaque in the shadow of their cowboy hats.

That afternoon at quitting time, Jimmy Dale was told he wouldn't be showering or heading for the chow hall. Instead, he was escorted to what was called "the barrel," an empty upended fifty-gallon oil drum that sat on a stretch of green grass in an alcove between two lockdown units. A flood lamp shone down on the barrel, bathing the inmate who stood on the barrel in a white light from evening until sunrise. Throughout the night, while he tried to keep his balance, the inmate could see the gunbulls in the roofed towers on the fence corners, their cigars or cigarettes glowing in the dark. Before an inmate climbed onto the barrel, he was allowed to relieve himself and to drink one glass of water. If the inmate fell from the barrel during the night, he not only had to climb back on it, he had to spend another night on it. If he relieved himself in his pants, he spent another night on it. If he called out to the hacks, he spent another night on it. An inmate who was sent to the barrel learned that his relationship to the barrel was open-ended.

Early Tuesday morning Jimmy Dale was escorted back to his tier, his knees like rubber, the backs of his thighs still tingling, his body crawling with stink. He was allowed to shower and dress in clean state blues and eat breakfast in the chow hall. Then he reported for work on time, at eight A.M., in the shop.

"You gonna give me a good day, Jimmy Dale?" Nix said to him.

"Yes sir, boss."

"You already eat?"

"Yes sir."

"Think I was too hard on you?"

"Stuff happens. I don't study on it."

"Stick this Hershey bar in your pocket."

"I'm all right, boss."

"A workingman gets hungry by midmorning. I'm going out to my camp Friday afternoon and put them fence posts in. You reckon you can screw a posthole digger into hardpan? It ain't a skill every man's got."

Jimmy Dale tried to look Nix in the face but couldn't do it. He wet his lips and tried to keep his eyes focused. His legs seemed to be buckling under him, a fetid odor rising from his armpits, even though he had showered that morning. For just a moment he thought he was going to be sick again. A grin tugged at the corner of Nix's mouth.

"Whatever you say, boss. I don't want no more trouble," Jimmy Dale said.

"Let me ask you something. That woman you was singing with, wasn't her name Jamie Sue Something?"

"I don't even remember, boss."

Nix removed a folded newspaper from his back pocket. It was pressed and rounded by the tightness of his buttock against the fabric of his uniform. "Is this her?"

Jimmy Dale studied the three-column color photo of a gold-haired woman singing onstage at an evangelical rally in Albuquerque. She was dressed in an evening gown that rippled like blue ice water on her figure. The HD-28 Martin guitar Jimmy Dale had given her hung on a braided strap from her neck. "Never seen the bitch," he said.

"Her name is Jamie Sue Wellstone. It says here she sung for the president of the United States."

"She sure ain't sung for the likes of me. Most of the women I hung with had bad cases of hoof-and-mouth. That's a fact, boss. I'm lucky I ain't loaded with diseases."

Nix rolled the newspaper into a cone and tapped it on the edge of a trash barrel, taking Jimmy Dale's measure. The barrel was stuffed with empty motor-oil cans, shredded cardboard boxes, and a windshield that had been ripped out of a wrecked pickup truck. Nix dropped the newspaper into the barrel. "Friday," he said.

Friday it is, motherfucker, Jimmy Dale said to himself, inhaling a breath that was as sharp as a razor in his throat.

EVERY JAIL HAS its own economy. Almost every item and form of service sold on the outside can be purchased for smokes, "scarf," or cash on the inside. Booze, skag, weed, yard bitches, and premium food delivered to your house are all available. You just have to know the right inmate or sometimes the right screws.

Weapons and contract hits are another matter. Frying a man in his house with a Molotov made from gasoline and paraffin can be done fairly easily. It takes little skill to make the Molotov, and usually a meltdown with little control over his life is assigned to race past the cell and light up the victim.

But a good shank is a work of both ingenuity and craft because the materials are limited and the process is time-consuming and must be accomplished in clandestine and circuitous fashion. If possible, the shank should come from a source other than the person who plans to use it. A toothbrush handle can be heated and molded around a razor blade. Nails can be sharpened on concrete, shoved through a block of wood, and turned into dirks. A scrap of tin can be cut into a pie shape, honed on all the edges, and inserted neatly into a grooved and wire-wrapped piece of mop handle. The materials are primitive, the craftsmen imaginative, their skill as traditional as that of medieval guild members.

Before his last fall for breaking and entering, Hidalgo had been a glazier in Pasadena, California. On Tuesday night a punk by the name of Mackey Fitch who did errands for the AB and sometimes for his cousin Beeville Hicks dropped two and a half cartons of smokes on Hidalgo's bunk.

"You turning sweet on me?" Hidalgo said.

"Bee said he owed you these smokes. He said if you want to drop something off at his house, that would be okay. But make sure you do it by Thursday night."

"I'll check my calendar on that, Mackey. Tell Bee thanks for these free smokes."

"Anytime," Mackey said.

IT WAS HOT and bright, and there was a yellow cast in the clouds Friday morning when Jimmy Dale left the prison compound in the stake truck with Troyce Nix.

"See them cows bunching up in the arroyo?" Nix said. "Bet it'll rain by noon."

"Got to ask you something, boss. I heard you took away my good time."

"You shouldn't have got in Cap'n Rankin's face."

"I spent the night on the barrel for something I didn't do, but I didn't complain about it. You shouldn't have taken away my good time."

"Sounds like you got up with a hard-on this morning." Nix pulled a cigarette out of a package on the dash and stuck it in his mouth. "What are we gonna do about that?"

"I want my good time back."

"I bet you do, you little bitch."

Nix didn't speak the rest of the way into town. After they picked up fifty bags of crushed white rock for the trim along the walkway and gardens in front of the administration building, Nix drove to a diner and went inside and ate while Jimmy Dale sat in the truck. When Nix came out, he handed Jimmy Dale a paper bag and a cold can of soda and started the truck. "You didn't think about taking off on me?"

"I just want my good time back," Jimmy Dale said.

"Come Monday, I think you'll be going back on the hard road. But that don't change the relationship we got, you get my drift?"

They drove in silence to Nix's camp, the land spreading with shadow, the temperature dropping, electricity leaking from the thunderclouds overhead. Jimmy Dale saw a solitary bolt of lightning strike the top of a distant mesa. It seemed to quiver there, as though it had sought out an animal and impaled it to the earth.

"You think we're doing something illegal here, you working on my property?" Nix said.

"I thought about it."

"You thought wrong. I'm a founding officer and stockholder in the corporation that owns this prison. That means my living quarters come with the package. Inmate maintenance here is just like inmate maintenance at the compound. If you was thinking about getting an ACLU lawyer—"

"I just want my good time back, boss."

"You got a bad case of mono-brain," Nix said.

He parked the truck by the windmill and told Jimmy Dale to get the posthole digger out of the toolshed. Then he went inside to use the bathroom. Just as the first raindrops struck the ground, Jimmy Dale heard the toilet flush. He twisted the posthole digger into the ground, busting through gravel and clay that had baked as hard as ceramic. He spread the wood handles to widen the hole. Then he cleaned the blades of the posthole digger in a bucket of water and started in again. The wind puffed the hackberry tree that shaded Nix's house. The air was cool and rain-scented, and Jimmy Dale could hear the windmill's blades ginning behind him. A bolt of lightning exploded on top of the cliff and startled him.

"When people is scared of lightning, it's usually 'cause they grew up in a strict church," Nix said. He was standing on the back porch, stripped to the waist, his yellow leather gloves pulled snugly on his hands. He had tucked his trousers inside his half-topped boots, as though he didn't want to soil his trouser cuffs. He stepped off the porch onto the ground, the wind blowing his hair, his chest taut and dry-looking in the shadowy light, the limbs of the hackberry tree thrashing above his head. "You scared of lightning?"

"Not really. Fact is, I ain't scared of a whole lot, boss."

"Lay the posthole digger down."

Jimmy Dale let it drop to the side, the handles clattering against the hardpan.

"I thought I was gonna go easy on you this time. But there's something about you that really pisses me off. I just cain't put my finger on it," Nix said.

"People cain't change what they are," Jimmy Dale replied, unbuttoning his denim shirt with his left hand.

"It makes me want to lose all restraint and flat tear you apart. Can you relate to that?" Nix said.

"All I wanted was my good time back, boss."

"Take off your britches. Or I can do it for you."

"I don't give a shit what you do, boss."

Nix looked at him quizzically. Jimmy Dale was still facing the cliff, his face turned to the wind when he needed to speak. He slipped his hand down toward his belt buckle or perhaps his side pocket.

Nix stepped closer. He touched Jimmy Dale's shoulder and slowly turned him around. "Say that again?"

The shank Hidalgo had made for Jimmy Dale had been fashioned from a triangular piece of automotive windshield glass, the blade three inches long, as pointed as a stiletto, as sharp on the edges as a barber's razor, the butt end inserted in the sanded-down handle of a shoe-polish applicator, all of it wrapped in a scabbard made from newspaper and electrician's tape.

"Sorry to hurt you like this, kid, but that's just the way it is," Nix said.

"You got it all wrong, boss," Jimmy Dale replied.

He turned with the shank and slashed Nix backhanded across the jaw, opening the flesh to the bone. Then he hit him twice in the chest, each time going deep, aiming for the heart or the lungs. Nix reached out toward him, either trying to keep his balance or to ward off the next blow. But Jimmy Dale got under his arm and drove the blade into Nix's chest again, going even deeper this time and snapping it off at the hilt, as Hidalgo had instructed him. Nix struck the ground heavily, his mouth puckered, his breath coming in short gasps, as though, somehow, through an act of will, he could control the massive hemorrhage taking place inside his chest.

Jimmy Dale went through the back door of the house and pulled a shirt and pair of work pants out of Nix's bedroom closet, streaking the interior of the house with Nix's blood. As he changed into Nix's clothes, he looked through the back window and saw Nix rise from the ground and then collapse below the level of the window. A sound like kettle drums was thundering in Jimmy Dale's head.

Moments later, he was roaring down the dirt road in the stake truck, hailstones bouncing off the windshield, his hands trembling on the wheel. He skidded in a cloud of dust onto the state road and headed due west, the front end shaking when he hit ninety, the engine needle on the dash climbing into the red. Nix's stolen clothes felt like an obscene presence on his skin.

CHAPTER
5

From where she sat at the bar, Jamie Sue could see out the back window of the saloon onto Swan Lake. The lake was vast and steel-colored in the twilight, ringed with alpine mountains, the white cap of Swan Peak razored against the sky on the south end. Down the shore was a group of guest cottages among birch trees, and when the wind gusted off the water, the riffling leaves of the birches made Jamie Sue think of green lace.

A man and a woman Jamie Sue didn't like were drinking next to her. They said they were from Malibu and driving to Spokane to catch a flight back to California. The woman's hair hung to her shoulders and was dyed black, and she had a habit of touching it on the ends, as though it had just been clipped. She had an ascetic face and gray teeth and wore dark clothes and purple lipstick. She seemed to have no awareness of her surroundings or the fact that the subject of her conversation would be considered bizarre and distasteful by normal people.

"After about a year I got tired of working for Heidi," she said. "Most nights I'd sit and watch while an eye surgeon freebased himself into the fourth dimension. I'd rather make five hundred a night having dinner and intellectual conversation, and maybe messing around later, than fifteen hundred watching a married guy freebase and pretend he's head of FOX, know what I mean?"

Jamie Sue tried to focus on what the woman was saying, but she was on her third whiskey sour, and her attention kept wandering across the empty dance floor to a face she thought she had seen behind the bead curtain that gave onto the café attached to the saloon.

"So you're in the entertainment business, too?" the man from Malibu said. He was deeply tanned, soft around the edges, his blond hair chemically sprayed so it dangled in wavy strands on his forehead. He wore black leather pants and a maroon shirt unbuttoned to his midsternum. His face was warm with alcohol, his elbow poised on the bar while he waited for Jamie Sue to answer his question.

"I used to sing professionally, but I don't do that anymore," she said.

"Is that really Bugsy Siegel and Virginia Hill in the picture?" the woman in purple lipstick asked the bartender.

The bartender glanced at the glass-framed color photograph mounted on the wall behind the bar. In it a couple were building a snowman on the edge of the lake. The woman in the photo wore a fluffy pink sweater and knee-high brown suede boots stitched with Christmas designs. Her hair was the color of a flamingo's wing.

"My boss says they used to stay up in those cottages there," the bartender said. He appeared to be a practical man who made a marginal living mixing cocktails in a rural area, and he was not interested in the visitors from California or their questions about gangsters from another era. His concern was with Jamie Sue Wellstone. She was probably one of the richest women in Montana, and she was now living year-round less than fifteen miles from the saloon. Jamie Sue Wellstone was watching the bead curtain at the entrance to the café. It was obvious to the bartender that she had seen someone or something that had disturbed her.

"You want another whiskey sour, Ms. Wellstone?" he asked.

"Yes, if you please, Harold."

Harold bent to his task, lifting his eyes once toward the entrance to the café. He was a powerful man who wore crinkling white shirts and black trousers and combed the few strands of his black hair straight across his scalp. "Somebody out there get out of line, Ms. Wellstone?"

"I thought I recognized a man. But I was probably mistaken," she replied.

"A guy who's maybe part Indian?"

"Yes, how did you know?"

"I saw him looking at you. In fact, I saw him around here a couple of days ago. Want me to check him out?"

"No, don't bother him. He did no harm."

"You just tell me whatever you need, Ms. Wellstone," the bartender said, wrapping a paper napkin around the bottom of her drink.

The man in black leather pants with the chemically sprayed hair had come in the saloon wearing a western straw hat, and had placed it crown-down on the bar. Stamped inside the rayon liner was the image of George Strait. The man noticed a greasy smear on the brim. He frowned at the bartender. "Give me some paper napkins," he said.

Without looking up, the bartender put a stack of at least ten napkins on the bar.

"Give everybody a round, including yourself. You might get the fucking grease off the bar while you're at it," the man in leather pants said. He went into the restroom and shot the bolt behind him.

"You okay on your drinks?" Harold said to the women at the bar.

"I'm feeling just right, but thanks for asking," the woman in purple lipstick said.

"When your friend comes back, maybe tell him this is Montana," Harold said.

"What's that mean?" the woman said.

"That this is Montana," Harold replied.

"That's your limo out front?" the woman in purple lipstick asked Jamie Sue.

"No, it's my husband's," Jamie Sue said.

"Are you talking about Ridley Wellstone? He must own half of Texas."

Jamie Sue's chin rested on her palm. Through the window she could see a boy in a red canoe spin-casting along the bank, the water's surface shimmering like pewter whenever the wind gusted. She could feel the rush of the whiskey sour taking hold in her nervous system, warming every corner of her heart, deadening memory, preempting expectations she knew would never be fulfilled. "I used to live in Texas, but I don't anymore," she said.

"I wasn't probing, honey. I grew up in a shithole in the San Joaquin. The biggest event of the year was the Garlic Festival," the woman said. "I would have screwed the whole Russian army to get out."

She removed a piece of mucus from the corner of her eye, then opened her purse to get a cigarette. Three joints were tucked neatly in a silk side pocket. While she lit her cigarette with a tiny gold lighter, she watched an unshaved man in corduroy pants and a work shirt and lace-up boots enter the bar and try the handle on the men's room door. When he discovered the door was locked, he shook the handle. A moment later, he returned and shook the handle harder, rattling the door against the bolt.

The unshaved man went to the bar and ordered a beer, drinking it from the bottle, scowling at the restroom door. Then he hit on the door with the flat of his fist. "You paying rent in there?" he said.

The man inside unlocked the bolt and pushed open the door with one foot. He was still cleaning his hat with the napkins the bartender had given him, the water running from the faucet. "I'll be done in a minute," he said.

The woman in purple lipstick watched the scene idly; then her gaze seemed to shift sideways and sharpen slightly. She took a drag off her cigarette, held the smoke in her lungs a long time, and released it slowly, blowing it at an upward angle. "That one isn't badlooking, if you don't mind them a little gamey," she said.

"That's Quince, my driver," Jamie Sue said.

"I'm talking about the Native American cutie-pie who was peeking at you from the café. You must grow them shy out here."

The bead curtain was still rustling when Jamie Sue turned on the bar stool. She walked across the dance floor, her footsteps echoing inside the emptiness of the saloon, the row of video poker machines winking at her in the shadows. Inside the café, two workingmen were drinking coffee at the counter, and a family was eating at one of the booths. A log truck was pulling onto the state highway, a dark-skinned man in a soft gray hat riding in the passenger seat, his arm propped on the window.

"Who was that who just left?" Jamie Sue asked.

The waitress wiped the counter and looked out at the highway. "A guy hitching a ride," she replied. She picked up a coin from the counter and dropped it in her apron pocket. "Not many drifters leave a four-bit tip."

Jamie Sue returned to the bar and sat down. "What did the Indian man look like?" she asked the woman from Malibu.

"The kind who used to make my nipples pop," the woman said, her eyes crinkling at the corners. "I traded up, but I still think about the guy who was my first. Seventeen and a gyrene. I think he's the reason I see a sex therapist. You ever think back on those years? I'd like to go back and maybe do things different, stay married and that kind of crap, but Maury there in the can isn't such a bad guy, I mean, it could be worse, right? Like, I could be one of the women in his films. Jesus Christ, if you think they're bad on the screen, you ought to see what some of them do in their downtime."

The restroom door opened again, and the man in black leather pants walked past Quince, blotting drops of water off his hat. "Ready to get out of here?" he said.

"It's been nice, everybody. Oops, who just tilted the floor?" the woman in purple lipstick replied.

She and her companion started to leave just as a man in a Mercedes pulled into the parking lot and entered the saloon. The scar tissue that constituted his face, and the eyes that seemed to laugh inside the burned shell of his head, made the woman in purple lipstick involuntarily clench her companion's arm. In fact, she seemed suddenly drunk, unprepared to deal with unpleasant realities that her rhetoric had kept at bay.

"My husband was a legionnaire. He was in a tank. In the French Sudan," Jamie Sue said.

"What? What did you say?" the woman in purple lipstick said, unable to look away from the handicapped man.

"His tank burned. He was trapped inside it. That's why he looks that way. Don't stare at him. What's the matter with you?" Jamie Sue said.

Leslie Wellstone grinned broadly. "Don't run off. Would you like to have another drink? Or maybe a dance or two?"

The couple from Malibu were out the front door like a shot.

"Why do you have to act like that?" Jamie Sue said, her eyes wet.

"They probably got a kick out of it," her husband replied, fitting his arm around her shoulders. "Harold, what do you have that's good and cold?"

EARLY WEDNESDAY MORNING, one day later, the sheriff of Missoula County, Joe Bim Higgins, called me at the cabin. The caller ID indicated he was using a cell phone. "Can you and Mr. Purcel come down to my office?"

"What's up?" I replied without enthusiasm.

"It's in regard to the college kids who were killed and to the little wood cross Mr. Purcel found on the ridge behind Albert's house."

"I don't see how we can help you, Sheriff."

"It also has to do with another double homicide. This one happened two nights ago at a rest stop west of town."

"Same answer," I said.

"I'm about seven miles from you right now. I'll be there in fifteen minutes or so. Thanks in advance for your time."

I walked down the road to Albert's house and knocked on the downstairs door. Clete was still in his skivvies, cooking breakfast in the small kitchen that was part of the accommodations Albert had given him. I told him about the call from Joe Bim Higgins.

"You're pissed off at me because I found evidence at a crime scene and reported it to Higgins?" he said.

"No."

"Then get that look off your face."

"You go out of your way to get us into it, Clete."

"I do?"

"Yeah, you do. No matter what the situation is, you can't wait to put our tallywhackers in the hay baler."

His back was turned to me as he flipped a pork chop inside a skillet. I could see the color climbing up the back of his neck. But when he turned around, his face was empty, his green eyes on mine. "You want to eat?"

"No."

"Suit yourself," he said. He sat down at the table and ate out of the skillet, pumping ketchup all over his meat and eggs. He stared at a documentary on the History Channel, then got up and shut off the TV set with the heel of his hand. "A kid got smoked on his knees up on that hill. Two of the Wellstones' gumballs rousted me because I strayed onto a posted stream. The same two dudes came here and made threats. I found a cross at the crime scene that was probably torn from the victim's throat. Can you explain how I caused any of those things to happen?"

"I didn't say you did."

"Yeah, but that's the signal you send. Now, how about we give it a rest?"

He was right. I had wanted to believe that somehow our journey into the northern Rockies, what some people call "the last good place," would take us back into a simpler, more innocent time. But trying to re-create the America of my youth through a geographical change was at best foolish, if not self-destructive.

"You have any coffee?" I said.

"In the pot, big mon," Clete said.

Ten minutes later, Joe Bim Higgins's cruiser pulled into the driveway. While hawks floated over the pasture and the sun broke across the mountain crest on fir and pine trees limned with frost, Joe Bim told us of the double homicide in a rest stop on Interstate 90.

"A trucker saw the smoke coming out of the women's side of the building and thought somebody had set fire to a trash barrel. He said by the time he got his extinguisher out of the rig, he smelled the odor and knew what it was. He kicked open the stall door and sprayed her with the extinguisher, but she was already gone.

"We found the man out in the trees. A dead joint was lying in the grass. The entry wound was right behind the ear, muzzle burns all over the skin and the hair. From the blood pattern on the ground, the coroner thinks the vic was forced to lie on his face before he was shot.

"There was one bullet hole in the door to the stall where the female died. With luck, she got it before her killer soaked her in gasoline."

"Who were the victims?" I asked.

"The female had two arrests for solicitation in Los Angeles. The man was an independent film producer of some kind. LAPD says he may have been hooked up with some porn vendors. They were traveling on his credit card. From the charges, it looks like they were bar-hopping their way from the Swan Valley back to Spokane."

"I don't see how we figure in to this, Sheriff," I said.

"They were in a saloon in Swan Lake. According to the bartender, they were drinking with Jamie Sue Wellstone, the sister-in-law of Ridley Wellstone."

"I still don't get the tie-in," I said.

"Maybe there isn't one. But when Mr. Purcel called in about the little wood cross he found up on the hill, he mentioned two thugs who work for the Wellstone family, guys he had trouble with. Maybe that's all coincidence. What's your opinion?"

"We don't have one," I replied.

"Let me be honest here," Joe Bim said. "Sometimes I like to believe that the victims of violent crime invite their fate. Maybe this porn dealer and his hooker girlfriend were killed by their own kind. But the thought of what happened to those two college kids doesn't give me any rest. They were taking a stroll on a beautiful summer evening behind the school they attended, and a degenerate sodomized and raped the girl and snuffed out her life and made her boyfriend beg or commit oral sex on him before the perp blew his head off.

"We lifted Seymour Bell's thumbprint off the wood cross. There were no other prints on it, so the cross probably belonged to the boy. Why would somebody rip it from his throat? Why deny a kid about to be murdered a symbol of his religion? It's thoughts of that kind that make me want to blow somebody out of his socks. Did you guys ever feel like that? Did you ever want to blow the living shit out of certain people and drink a beer while you did it?"

Clete and I looked at each other and didn't reply.

JOE BIM HIGGINS was not an inept lawman or administrator and probably didn't need my help in his investigation. But an execution-style murder had been committed within sight of the cabin where Molly and I were living, and to pretend an act that evil had no relationship to our own lives, to wait for the authorities, with their limited resources, to assure us that our environment was safe, is the kind of behavior one associates with someone who relies on the weatherman to protect him from asteroids.

Clete and I drove to Missoula and went into the big stone court-house where the sheriff kept his office. We explained that we wanted to ask questions of some people who had known the two murdered college students, that we did not intend to impose ourselves on his investigation, that we would report any meaningful discoveries immediately to him, that, in effect, we would not become an unwelcome presence in his life.

He was sitting in a swivel chair with one booted foot on the wastebasket. He chewed on a hangnail and stared out the window at the trees on the courthouse lawn. "How would you describe your relationship with the FBI?" he said.

"We don't have one," I replied.

"That's what you think," he said.

"Sir?" I said.

"An FBI woman was in here an hour ago asking questions about Mr. Purcel. You worked for a greaseball up at Flathead Lake?" he said.

Clete was standing in front of the sheriff's desk, looking into dead space, his face impassive. "His name was Sally Dio. His private plane nose-dived into the side of a mountain."

"Really?" Joe Bim said.

"Yeah, I heard ole Sal looked like marmalade hanging in one of the trees. All the whores in Vegas and Tahoe were really broke up about it," Clete said.

"This FBI agent thinks maybe you had something to do with it," Higgins said.

"Funny none of them told me that," Clete said.

The room was quiet. Joe Bim let his eyes linger on Clete's face. "I got a shitload of open files in that metal cabinet. Don't make me regret what I do here today," he said.

"You won't, Sheriff," I said, trying to preempt any more of Clete's remarks.

Joe Bim removed his foot from the wastebasket. "I think the homicide of the two college kids is a random act. If that's true, we've probably got a serial killer operating on the game reserve. A connection with the double homicide at the rest stop is anybody's guess. The FBI says the male, the porn producer, was Mobbed up, so maybe it was a contract hit, an object lesson of some kind that has nothing to do with the college kids.

"The boy who was killed behind Albert's house was shot with a forty-five. The killer at the rest stop used a nine-millimeter. But there are a lot of similarities just the same. The shooter picked up his brass at both scenes, and he made both males show submission to him before he shot them. He also enjoys hurting women. You ever investigate a torch murder?"

"Both of us have," Clete replied.

"You saw the vic at the crime scene?" Higgins asked.

"I've never stopped seeing the vics," Clete said.

Joe Bim removed two manila folders from his file drawer and opened them on his desk. The faces of Cindy Kershaw and Seymour Bell stared up at us from their photos. Two of the photographs had been taken for school yearbooks. Two of them had been taken in the morgue. The disfigurement done to their features by their killer or killers was of a kind you hope no family member will ever be forced to look upon.

"Jesus Christ," Clete said.

"We have other open homicide cases here in Missoula County, cases that have been total dead ends," Joe Bim said. "One involves a guy we called the Mad Hatter. Some guy in a stovepipe hat went into a beauty parlor down in the Bitterroot Valley, made three women lie in a circle, then shot and killed all three of them. Then he cut off their heads. We don't have a clue who he was, where he went, or why he did it.

"Somebody out in Hellgate Canyon killed an eighty-year-old woman in a nursing home with a screwdriver. Maybe it was an inside job, maybe not, we just don't know. We've pulled ten- to twenty-year-old human bones out of campgrounds, but we have no idea who the vics are or how they died. This is supposed to be a place where tourists roast hot dogs on their summer vacations."

"We're going to start at Cindy Kershaw's dormitory, Sheriff. We appreciate what you've told us," I said.

"I pulled a week's worth of surveillance tape from the health club where the Kershaw girl worked. You want to check it out?"

"What's in it?" Clete said.

"A kid who could be my granddaughter," Joe Bim replied.

We went into a separate room where the sheriff plugged an edited and synthesized cassette of the health club's surveillance tapes into a VCR.

Most cops and newspeople tend to use categorical names for both the victims and the perpetrators of crimes, particularly violent ones that involve depravity and sadism. Why? The answer is simple: It's easier to believe the perpetrator is a genetic aberration or the product of a subculture that is unconnected to our lives. By the same token, the victim is someone unlike us, perhaps a person who, like a candle moth, chose of his own accord to swim through flame, perhaps someone actually seeking an executioner.

Then you look at a videotape of an eighteen-year-old girl wearing down-in-the-ass jeans, her baby fat exposed, vacuuming a rubber-matted floor with headphones on, the vacuum pack on her back swaying to music that only she heard.

In the background, people in workout dress clanked iron and sweated on the vinyl padding of the Life Fitness and Hammer Strength machines and pounded along on the treadmills as though they were traversing great spans of topography. On the opposite side of a glass window, a man lay on a table while a physical therapist pushed his knee up toward his chest; his mouth opened wide with a muscle spasm.

"Would you back it up a few frames?" Clete said.

"You see something?" Joe Bim asked.

"Yeah, the guy by the watercooler," Clete replied. He waited a moment. "Hold it right there." He studied the frozen image of a lean man with uncut hair who wore his shirt outside his slacks. The man was watching Cindy Kershaw, his arm propped on top of the watercooler. His face appeared only in profile on the screen. But there was something wrong with one of his eyes, as though a drinking glass had been cupped over it and pressed deeply into the skin, recessing the entire socket.

Clete tapped a fingernail on the television monitor. "I can't swear to it, but he looks like a dude by the name of Lyle Hobbs. He was a driver for Sally Dio. He also does security for Ridley Wellstone. He also has a sheet for child molestation in Reno."

"You're fairly certain about this?" Joe Bim said.

"I'm not real objective about this guy. Hobbs is a bucket of shit. That guy by the watercooler looks like him. That's all I can tell you," Clete said.

"It's Hobbs," I said.

Both the sheriff and Clete looked at me. "How do you know?" the sheriff asked.

"That's Ridley Wellstone on the therapist's table," I said.

CINDY KERSHAW'S ROOMMATE at the university had graduated with Cindy from a high school on the other side of the Sapphire Mountains. Cindy's father had died in a logging accident when she was five, and she had been raised by her mother, who cooked in a café and ran a small feed business with a man she sometimes lived with. The roommate's name was Heather Miles. On her shelf were a half-dozen stuffed animals and three trophies she had won as a barrel racer. Her eyes were ice blue, her features Nordic, the anger in her face like a cool burn.

"No, she didn't have other boyfriends. She didn't sleep around, either, because that's what you're talking about, right?" she said.

"No, not at all," I replied. "But when a woman is attacked in a ferocious manner, as Cindy was, the driving engine is almost always sexual rage. So if we exclude the people who knew her—old boyfriends, maybe somebody who felt rejected by her—we can start looking at what we call a random perpetrator. He's a hard guy to catch, because usually he has little or no connection to the victim."

"Seymour Bell was her only boyfriend. Everybody liked her. It was the same in high school," Heather Miles said.

"Were she and Seymour intimate?" I said.

"She didn't talk about it. Why do you keep asking those kinds of questions? What do they have to do with her death?" Her bed was neatly made, the blanket tucked tight on the corners. She was sitting on top of the blanket, her face turned up at mine, her hands opening and closing on her thighs like those of someone who was trapped. "You're making it sound like it was Cindy's fault she got killed."

"Did she know a guy named Lyle Hobbs?" Clete asked.

"I never heard of him. Who is he?" she said.

"A geek and a child molester. He showed up on the surveillance tape at the health club where Cindy worked," Clete said. "You know a guy by the name of Ridley Wellstone?"

"No, I never heard of him, either."

"Did Cindy wear a small wood cross, one attached to a leather thong?" I asked.

"No." Heather glanced sideways. "I saw Seymour with one. Maybe a week ago. His shirt was unbuttoned, and it fell out. Seymour was a Pentecostal. Or at least he used to be. What about it?"

"You know someone who might want to tear it off his throat?" I asked.

"What are you talking about? Cindy was raped and beaten. I heard Seymour was shot through the face," she said. I saw her eyes go out of focus; she looked like someone who has lost her footing and is not sure she will find it again. "I don't understand why you're here. Cindy and Seymour were taking a walk. They climbed up the mountain and never came back. Some sick fuck killed them. Why don't you assholes go out and do something about it? Why do you keep asking me these sick fucking questions? I identified Cindy at the morgue. Did you see her face? God, I hate you people."

She started to cry, then beat her fists on her knees.

WE DROVE UP the Clark Fork River to Bonner to interview the two roommates of Seymour Bell. They lived in a small rented house on a slope close to where the Clark Fork and the Blackfoot rivers formed a bay below a steel-girdered train bridge. The main residential street of the town was lined with willow and birch trees, shading the rows of neat sawmill houses on either side of the street. The yards of the houses were blue-green inside the shade, the flower beds bursting with tulips, the small porches dotted with cans of geraniums and begonias.

It was a fine day, cool and scented with flowers and sawdust from the mill, but Clete had remained morose and had spoken little since we had left the sheriff's office. At first I thought his mood was due to the nature of our errand. But Clete's involvement with Sally Dio and the Mob still held a strong claim on his life, and I suspected the furrow in his brow meant he had taken another journey to a bad place in his head and he was sorting through it with a garbage rake.

"I don't think the sheriff took the FBI too seriously, Clete," I said.

"No, somebody spit in the soup. They're going to try and hang a murder beef on me."

"You think Wellstone stirred up the feds?"

"Of course I do. That's how his kind operate. They call up Fart, Barf, and Itch or somebody in the attorney general's office or another bunch of bureaucratic asswipes just like them. They never hit you head-on."

"I'd shitcan this stuff. Sally Dee was a pus head. He got what he deserved."

"I got news for you. People who get in the way of Ridley Wellstone and his friends are going to be speed bumps."

"Yeah?" I said, glancing at Clete.

"Lose the Little Orphan Annie routine, will you?" he replied, his big head hanging down, his expression empty, like that of a stuffed animal.

We sat on the back porch in sun-spangled shade with a tall, lean, bare-chested kid by the name of Ben Hauser. He told us his dead friend Seymour Bell had grown up on a cattle ranch outside Alberton, west of Missoula. He also said Seymour was nothing like his girlfriend, Cindy, that Seymour had one foot in the next world, and no matter what Cindy said or did, Seymour would find a church where the congregants glowed with blue fire or neurosis, depending on how you wanted to define it.

"Seymour was a little eccentric about religion?" I said.

"No, he believed in it, full-tilt. The crazier, the better," Ben Hauser said. "He joined a Pentecostal group here, but he quit because they didn't give witness in tongues. Then he started going to revivals hereabouts. That's when him and Cindy got into it."

"Excuse me?" I said.

"Cindy went to church on occasion, but she thought these revival people were hucksters. Sometimes Seymour trusted folks when he shouldn't. Cindy would get mad as hell at him."

"Did he wear a small wood cross?" I asked.

Ben Hauser looked into space. "Yeah, come to think of it, he did. Or at least I think I saw him wearing one. Why?"

"Would someone want to tear it off him for any reason?" I said.

"No, people respected Seymour. He was a good guy. I don't understand how something like this happened."

Ben Hauser's hair was buzz-cut and already receding above the temples, giving him a look beyond his years. Down below us was the Blackfoot River, and a group of kids were diving off the railroad bridge into the water, shouting each time one went off the side. Ben Hauser seemed to stare at them, his face wan, his eyes unfocused.

"You okay?" I said.

"Sure," he replied.

"You don't know anybody who had it in for Seymour?" Clete asked.

"No," Ben answered. "I tell you one thing, though. Seymour was smart in school. He had a three-point-eight GPA. He was tough, too. The bastard who did him in had a fight on his hands."

"How's that?" I said.

"Seymour might have been churchgoing, but he rode bulls in 4-H. I told the cops the fuckhead who kidnapped him must have used handcuffs. You get Seymour mad, he'd take on three or four guys with fists and feet and anything else they wanted. He did it one night in front of the Oxford when some guys made a remark about Cindy. I bet there were handcuff burns on his wrists, weren't there?"

He stared up at me, waiting for my answer.

I LET CLETE drive and used my cell phone to call Joe Bim Higgins. "We just interviewed Ben Hauser," I said. "He told us Seymour Bell wouldn't have gone down without a fight. He says if Bell was kidnapped, the perp probably used handcuffs."

"That's a possibility," Joe Bim said.

"Say again?"

"There were abrasions on Bell's wrists. They didn't look like they came from rope or wire. I thought I mentioned that."

He had not, but what do you say under the circumstances? "I was just double-checking, Sheriff," I said.

"Anytime," he said.

I closed my cell and looked at the highway rushing at us.

"Where to?" Clete asked.

"Let's see what we can find out about the California couple who got killed at the rest stop. Let's start at the saloon where they were drinking with Jamie Sue Wellstone."

"You got it, big mon," Clete said, putting an unlit cigarette in his mouth.

We drove up through the Blackfoot Valley, through meadowland and across streams and sky-blue lakes that eventually feed into the Swan Drainage. The weather had just started to blow when we pulled into the saloon, and the lake was chained with rain rings, the mountains gray-green and misty on the far side, like images in an Oriental painting. Some fishermen were drinking in a booth, but otherwise, the saloon was empty. A heavyset bartender in black trousers and a white shirt was looking out the back window at the rain falling on the lake. He turned around when he heard us sit down at the bar. "What are you having, fellows?" he said.

I opened my badge holder. "I'm Detective Dave Robicheaux. My friend here is Clete Purcel. We're helping out in the investigation of the double homicide that happened in a rest stop west of Missoula Monday night. It's our understanding that the two victims were drinking here earlier the same day."

The bartender leaned on his arms. His cuffs were rolled, and his forearms looked thick and sun-browned in the gloom, wrapped with soft black hair. "You want to show me that shield again?"

"Not really," I said.

"Because it doesn't look local. I'm wrong on that?" he said.

"No, you're right. But you can call Joe Bim Higgins on my cell if you think we're pulling on your crank," Clete said.

"It was just a question. What do you guys want to know?"

I opened my notebook on the bar. The bartender told us his name was Harold Waxman and that he worked part-time at the saloon and sometimes drove 18-wheelers after Labor Day, when the tourist season shut down. "Lot of the mills have closed. There's not that much log hauling anymore," he said.

"Did the California people have trouble with anybody here? Exchange words, something like that?" I said.

"Not exactly," the bartender said.

"How do you mean, 'not exactly'?" I asked.

"The guy was a negative kind of person, that's all. He wasn't a likable guy."

"What did he do?" I asked.

"Said the place was dirty or something to that effect. Look, there was a half-breed or a Mexican-looking guy hanging around. He was watching Ms. Wellstone or the California woman from the doorway over there. Maybe he's a cherry picker. It's not the season yet, but they'll be showing up at Flathead Lake for the harvest pretty soon."

"You told this to the sheriff?" I said.

"Yeah, or to the detectives he sent out here. You want a drink? It's on the house."

I shook my head. "Give me three fingers of Jack straight up," Clete said. "Give me a beer back on that, too."

"The woman and the guy with her?" the bartender said, fixing Clete's drink. "The way they talked, I think maybe they were in the life, know what I mean?"

"What did they say?" Clete asked.

"She said she'd been a high-priced hooker. She was talking about it to Ms. Wellstone like it was nothing. It was embarrassing to listen to. If you ask me, California is a big commode overflowing on the rest of the country."

He set down a deep shot glass brimming with whiskey on a paper napkin, then drew a draft beer and set it on a separate napkin. The foam swelled up over the lip of the beer glass and pooled onto the napkin. Unconsciously, I touched at my mouth with my knuckle, then looked out at the rain dancing on the lake. The mist on the water's surface made me think of Lake Pontchartrain years ago, long before Katrina, long before I had blown out my doors with Jim Beam straight up and a beer back.

"Did Ms. Wellstone seem to know these people?" I asked.

"No, not at all. I don't think she liked them, either. Ms. Wellstone is highly thought of hereabouts. She could be a Nashville star if she wanted to. She gave up her career to sing gospel. That pair from California were low-rent. To be frank, anybody who thinks Ms. Wellstone would be mixed up with people like that has got his head up his ass."

Clete knocked back his Jack and sipped the foam from his beer. I could see the color bloom in his cheeks and his eyes take on a warm shine. "I hear Jamie Sue Wellstone married a guy who was fried in a tank," he said.

"Mr. Wellstone was wounded in a war. But I don't know how. Maybe you ought to ask him about it," the bartender said.

"You know what I can't figure, Harold?" Clete said. "You're knocking people in the life, but you've got a photograph of Bugsy Siegel and Virginia Hill on your wall there."

The bartender looked at him silently.

"What I also can't figure out is why young, beautiful women never marry mutilated poor guys or even old poor guys," Clete said. "It's a mystery."

"You guys want anything else?" the bartender asked.

Clete looked at me and back at the bartender. "Not a thing," he said, and slipped a folded five-dollar bill under his empty shot glass.

We talked to the waitress in the café about the man who had been looking through the bead curtain at the murder victims and Jamie Sue Wellstone. Then we walked out to my truck.

"What was that stuff with the bartender?" I said.

"I don't like blue-collar guys who suck up to rich people," Clete replied. "The Wellstone place isn't far from here. Let's check out the broad."

"I don't know if that's a good idea," I replied.

"What are they going to do? Dime me with the feds? Lighten up, big mon. Everything is copacetic."

CHAPTER
6

THE WELLSTONE RANCH was only a half hour from the Swan River, up on a plateau of emerald-green meadowland bordered by sheer mountains that were still capped with snow. The house was Tudor, huge, more a fortress than a home. The barns and sheds were red with white trim, the pastures separated by the same hand-stacked rock fences that you see in the Upper South. At least a hundred head of bison grazed on one slope; Texas longhorns grazed on another. The Wellstones, at least ostensibly, had created a bucolic paradise. The fact that they wanted to dig test wells on it, or anywhere else in the Swan Drainage, was beyond comprehension.

The security man at the gate called up to the main house, and we were waved in and told to meet Ms. Wellstone at the entrance to the garden. She wore a bloodred dress with a white ribbon that was threaded through the eyelets at the top of the bodice. She carried a martini glass with two olives in the bottom. I thought perhaps alcohol explained the casual access she had given us to her home. But I quickly began to feel that Jamie Sue Wellstone was one of those rare individuals who could use booze selectively, perhaps to deaden the senses if need be, and not become hostage to it.

The garden was dissected by gravel pathways and surrounded by a gray stone wall that was stippled with lichen in the shade. The flower beds were planted with pansies, English roses that were as big as grapefruit, forget-me-nots, violets, clematis vine, and bottlebrush trees. I wondered if the eclectic nature of the ornamentals in the garden said something about the undefined and perhaps deceptive nature of the Wellstones and their ability to acquire an entire culture as easily as writing a check.

"Would you like a drink?" Jamie Sue said, indicating a redwood table where a bottle of vodka sat in an ice bucket.

"*I* would," Clete said.

"Is your husband home, Ms. Wellstone?" I asked.

"He's taking a nap. This is about the people who were at the saloon on the lake before they were killed?" she said.

"Yeah, the bartender said a guy who was maybe a Latino or part Indian was paying undue attention to either you or the homicide victims," I said.

"I don't remember that, really. I didn't see anything unusual there that day," she said.

The sky was still sealed by rain clouds, and it was cold sitting at the table. The garden itself seemed like an intrinsically cold place, dotted with stone benches and tarnished bronze sundials, shut off from the vistas surrounding the ranch. Clete poured himself a full glass of vodka and dropped three olives in it. "Bombs away," he said, and tanked it down.

"Would you like a beer or a Scotch, Mr. Robicheaux?" Jamie Sue Wellstone asked.

"No," I said. "It's odd you have no memory of a Mexican or Indian watching you at the saloon, because the bartender made a point about his being there."

"Maybe an Indian or Mexican *was* there. It's just not the way I remember it. I'm not saying the bartender is wrong," she said.

Know what the false close is in the ethos of a door-to-door salesman? The salesman backs off, concedes that the customer's reluctance is understandable, and seemingly gives up. It's a hot day. The salesman is tired and asks for a glass of water. A moment later, he's the customer's friend, a victim himself, a family man with a wife and kids depending on him. The customer gets sandbagged without ever knowing what hit him.

"I see," I said, nodding, studying my notebook. "Did the California couple indicate they'd had trouble with anyone? You think maybe they were mixed up with criminals?"

"The woman sounded like she'd lived a checkered life," Jamie Sue said.

"As a prostitute?" I said.

"I can't say that with authority."

"On an unrelated subject, why would y'all hire a man like Lyle Hobbs to work security for you?" I said.

"I beg your pardon?"

"Hobbs has served time for child molestation. He also worked for a Mafia pimp by the name of Sally Dio," I said.

"My husband and brother-in-law try to help ex-felons. They also believe in forgiveness. You don't believe in forgiveness, Mr. Robicheaux?"

"I think the best place for child molesters is the graveyard. But I'm not a theologian," I said.

She took a drink from her vodka and let her eyes rest on mine. She was pretty; her voice and accent were lovely. It would have been easier to dismiss her as deceptive and cunning, even villainous. But I had the feeling she was much more complex than that and would not fit easily into a categorical envelope.

"I saw you once," Clete said to her out of nowhere.

"Oh?"

"In a joint in Uvalde, Texas. A big live-oak tree grew up through the floor. I was chasing down a bail skip over there. You sang 'I Forgot More Than You'll Ever Know.' You reminded me of Skeeter Davis."

"I knew Skeeter. She influenced me a lot."

His green eyes lingered on hers. The moment was one that made me think of a red light flashing at a train crossing. "You ought to stay clear of Lyle Hobbs. Also that racist from Mississippi who works with him," he said.

"I wish I could oblige, but I don't decide who works here," she said.

"Can you describe the man who was watching you at the saloon?" I said.

"I don't know what you're talking about. I don't remember anyone watching me. How many times do I have to say that to you, Mr. Robicheaux?"

"That's perplexing. The waitress in the café remembered him. She also remembered you coming in and asking about him," I said.

"Maybe I did. I'd had more to drink than I probably should have," she replied, then turned her attention back to Clete. "When were you in Uvalde?"

The French doors on the back of the house opened, and Leslie Wellstone walked out on the flagstone patio, dressed in gray slacks, a print sport shirt, and a blue blazer. *"Comment va la vie, Monsieur Robicheaux? Et votre ami aussi?"* he said.

"Ça roule," I replied.

"I heard your remarks about the quality of our personnel. You don't think Mr. Hobbs quite fulfills the requirements of the reborn?" he said.

"I'm sure he's a special kind of guy. Most ex-cons with a short-eyes jacket are," I said.

He let the reference pass and inserted a cigarette into a holder. "Did you know in 2004 we were responsible for getting the anti–gay marriage initiative on the ballot in your home state?"

"Yeah, you got the fundamentalists into the voting booth, and once there, they pulled the lever to put your boy back in the White House," I said.

"Smart man. You should come work for us," he said.

"Not at gunpoint, Mr. Wellstone," I said.

"Time to dee-dee," Clete said.

"You must be a veteran of our Indo-Chinese experience," Leslie Wellstone said.

"Thanks for your hospitality," Clete said. He turned toward Wellstone's wife. "By the way, you didn't just remind me of Skeeter Davis. You were better than her."

Maybe the disfigurement in Wellstone's face or the somber atmosphere surrounding the garden colored my perception. But when he looked at Clete, I would have sworn there was an iniquitous presence in his eyes, like the liquidity you associate with an infection.

Minutes later, as we drove off the Wellstone property, I waited for Clete to explain his behavior. Instead, he gazed at the snow clouds up on Swan Peak and the cottonwood trees flashing past the window. He reached down and adjusted himself. "Something wrong?" he asked.

"Yeah, stop having the thoughts you're having about that woman," I replied.

"What's to think about? She was lying about the guy watching her at the saloon. She's protecting him for some reason. That doesn't mean she's dirty."

"Who are you kidding?"

"Did you check out that pair of ta-tas? My flopper was flipping around in my slacks like a garden hose."

We didn't need this kind of trouble.

OVER THE MOUNTAIN from his residence, Albert Hollister owned two hundred acres up a drainage that was dry most of the summer and fall. Years ago, he had bought the acreage cheap as rough land from a timber company, then had immediately set about stacking and burning the snags and splintered logs that covered the property. He drilled two water wells and scarified the soil and reseeded it with a mixture of upland grasses, fenced the bottom land with smooth wire, and built a cabin with electricity and plumbing and an eight-stall barn strung with heat lamps so it could also serve as a brooder house for his poultry.

He kept sheep and Foxtrotters and saddlebreds and Morgans, and in a few years the grass that he watered constantly from his wells was a deep blue-green, not unlike the pastureland of central Kentucky and Tennessee.

The waddies and drifters who worked for him were the kind of men who were out of sync with both history and themselves, pushed further and further by technology and convention into remote corners where the nineteenth century was still visible in the glimmer of a high-ceilinged saloon or an elevated sidewalk that had tethering rings inset in the concrete or an all-night café that served steaks and spuds to railroad workers in the lee of a mountain bigger than the sky.

Most of them were honest men. When they got into trouble, it was usually minor and involved alcohol or women or both. They didn't file tax returns or waste money on dentists. Many of them didn't have last names, or at least last names they always spelled the same way. Some had only initials, and even friends who had known them on the drift for years never knew what the initials stood for. If they weren't paid to be wranglers and ranch workers, most of them would do the work for free. If they couldn't do it for free, most of them would pay to do it. When one of them called himself a rodeo bum, he wasn't being humble.

Their enemies were predictability, politics, geographical permanence, formal religion, and any conversation at all about the harmful effects of vice on one's health. The average waddie woke in the morning with a cigarette cough from hell and considered the Big C an occupational hazard, on the same level as clap and cirrhosis and getting bull-hooked or stirrup-drug or flung like a rag doll into the boards. It was just part of the ride. Anybody who could stay on a sunfishing bolt of lightning eight seconds to the buzzer had already dispensed with questions about mortality.

The man who walked up the dirt road had come in from the highway that traversed Lolo Pass into Idaho. He was dressed in khakis and a denim jacket and a shapeless gray felt hat that was sweat-stained at the base of the crown. His boots were pointed, cracked at the seams, the color leached from the leather; the chain on his wallet was clipped on his belt, the links clinking against his hip. When he spied Albert in the pasture, he set down his duffel bag and his guitar case and leaned one arm on a steel fence stake. He removed his hat and wiped his forehead on his jacket sleeve. A truck passed, driving too fast for the road, covering him with dust. The man chewed on a blade of grass and seemed to look at the truck a long time before he turned his attention back to Albert.

"Climb through the fence if you want to talk to me," Albert said.

"I understand you might need a wrangler or a guy to handle rough stock," the man said.

"Where'd you hear that?" Albert said.

"At the casino in Lolo."

"You a rodeo man?"

"Not no more. Got busted up in Reno about four years back. I can still green-break them. I ain't a bad trainer, either. I been a farrier, too."

"I'll meet you up at the cabin in a few minutes," Albert said. "The elk popped a few clips on my back fence."

"Got an extra pair of pliers?" the man asked.

A half hour later, Albert drank a glass of iced tea on the porch of the cabin with the man in the denim jacket, both of them seated in wood rocking chairs. It was shady and cool on the porch, and the man in the denim jacket looked tired, filmed with road dust, not quite able to concentrate on the conversation. He asked if he could wash inside. When he came back out on the porch, his hair was wet and combed out on his neck, his shirtsleeves rolled up high on his arms.

"What's your name again?" Albert asked.

"J. D. Gribble."

"You never got tattooed, J.D.?"

"I guess I never saw the advantage in it."

"Ever spend time in jail?"

"Some."

"Care to say what for?"

"Not using my head, mostly."

"There's a lot of that going around these days. Let's see your guitar," Albert said.

J. D. Gribble unsnapped the lid on his case and lifted the guitar from the felt liner and rested it across his lap. "It was my grandfather's. Gibson stopped making this model about sixty years ago," he said.

Albert put on his glasses and leaned forward to read the names that had been signed on the box. "Ramblin' Jack Elliott, Lucinda Williams, Jerry Jeff Walker," he said. "You know these people?"

"I've sat in with them."

"When that truck threw dust all over you, what were you thinking about?"

"Nothing."

"Not a thing?"

"Except some folks don't have no business driving on dirt roads, throwing dust and rocks all over people."

"How about a hundred and fifty a week and rent and utilities?"

J.D. shifted the guitar on his lap and smiled. "That's pert' near the exact figure I had in mind."

"On the subject of jail?"

"Yes sir?"

"I was on the hard road when I was eighteen. I was in several other cans, too. I wasn't a criminal, but I could have turned out to be one."

J.D. waited, unsure of what he was being told. "Yes sir, I'm listening."

"That's all. You have a voice and an accent that are reminiscent of Jimmie Rodgers. That's quite unusual," Albert replied. "I hope you like it here."

CLETE PURCEL WAS the bane of his enemies and feared in New Orleans by pimps, drug dealers, cops on a pad, jackrollers, scam artists who victimized old people, and sexual predators of all stripes. Paradoxically, his closest friends included whiskey priests, strippers, stand-up cons, hookers on the spike, badass biker girls, button men, Shylocks, and mind-blown street people who claimed they had seen UFOs emerging from the waters of Lake Pontchartrain.

His reputation for chaos and mayhem was legendary. In the men's room of the New Orleans bus depot, he forced a contract killer to swallow a full dispenser of liquid soap. In the casino at the bottom of Canal, he blew a degenerate into a urinal with a firehose, then escaped the building by creating a bomb scare on the casino floor. He dropped a Teamster steward off a hotel balcony into a dry swimming pool. He filled a gangster's hundred-thousand-dollar convertible with concrete. He hijacked an earth-grader from a construction site and drove it through the front of a palatial mansion owned by a member of the Giacano crime family. No, that is not an adequate description. He drove an earthmover through the entirety of the house, punching through the walls, grinding the furniture and tile and hardwood floors into rubble under the steel tracks. Not satisfied, he burst through the back of the house and destroyed the garages and parked cars and all the grounds, uprooting the hedges and trees, pushing the statuary and flagstone terrace into the swimming pool, finally exiting the property by exploding a brick wall onto the avenue.

I could go on, but what's the point? For Clete, life was a carnival, a theme park full of harlequins and unicorns, a reverse detox unit for people who took themselves seriously or thought too much about death. In an ambience of palm trees and pink sunrises on live-oak trees, of rainwater ticking onto the philodendron inside a lichen-stained courtyard, inside the smell of beignets and coffee and night-blooming flowers two blocks from the Café du Monde, he had lived the ethos of the libertine and the happy hedonist, pumping iron to control his weight, eating amounts of cholesterol-loaded food that would clog a sewer main, convincing himself that a vodka Collins had little more influence on his hypertension than lemonade.

During all of it, he had never showed his pain and had never complained. The Big Sleazy was God's gift to those who could not find peace in either the world or rejection of it. How could one refuse life inside a Petrarchan sonnet, particularly when it was offered to you without reservation or conditions by a divine hand?

But the chink in Clete's armor remained right below his heart, and the same knife went through it every time.

It's fair to say most of his girlfriends were nude dancers, grifters, drunks, or relatives of mobsters. Most of them wore tattoos, and some had tracks on their arms or thighs. But the similarity in Clete's lovers didn't lie in their occupations or addictions. Almost all of them were incurable neurotics who went through romantic relationships like boxes of Kleenex. The more outrageous their behavior, the more Clete believed he had found kindred spirits.

Ironically, it wasn't the hookers and strippers and addicts who did him the most damage. It was usually a woman with a degree of normalcy and education in her background who wrapped him in knots. I suspect a psychologist would say Clete didn't believe he was worthy of being loved. As a consequence, he would allow himself to be used and wounded by people whose own lack of self-knowledge didn't allow them to see the depth of injury they inflicted upon him. Regardless, it was the quasi-normal ones who hung him out to dry.

TWO DAYS AFTER our interview of Jamie Sue Wellstone, Clete began acting strange. "I'd better cancel out on our fishing trip today," he said on our front porch after knocking at seven A.M.

"What's the problem?" I said.

"Just some doodah I need to take care of in town," he replied. He looked up at the sunlight breaking on the mountain, his cheeks bright with aftershave. His hair was freshly combed and clipped, his shoes buffed. He wore a pair of pressed slacks and a crisp new sport shirt.

"How about some coffee?" I said.

"I'd better run. Check with you later."

"What are you up to, Clete?"

"Why do I always feel like you're trying to staple my umbilical cord to the corner of your desk?"

"When will you be back?" I asked.

"Does anyone at your meetings ever say you have a control problem?"

By three that afternoon, he had not returned. I tried his cell but got no answer. I drove three miles down the highway to the little service town of Lolo and saw his convertible parked outside the town's only saloon. He was at the far end of the bar, hunched over his drink, perhaps twenty feet away from a table full of bikers who were half in the bag. The bikers were talking loudly, obviously getting Clete's attention, although they were unaware of it.

I sat down next to him and ordered a glass of ice and carbonated water. "What are you drinking?" I said.

"A gin gimlet," he replied. "It's summertime, so I'm having a gin gimlet."

"You look like you're shitfaced."

"I had the top down. It's windburn. Dave, will you get off my back?"

"It's the Wellstone woman, isn't it?" I said.

"She called me on my cell. She wanted to retain me."

"For what?"

"To find an old boyfriend. It's not an unusual situation." My eyes were boring into the side of his face. He took a sip from his drink and balled up a napkin. He looked over his shoulder at the bikers. "Can you guys hold down the noise?" he said.

The bikers turned and stared at us. They were stone-faced and head-shaved, unsure which of us had spoken, their eyes taking our inventory.

"We're just having a drink here. How you guys doin'?" I said.

They went back to their conversation, the tenor of their voices unchanged.

"Has this got something to do with the man who was watching her in the saloon?" I said.

"Jamie Sue used to—"

"Jamie Sue?"

"That's what I said. Jamie Sue used to sing with a guy who went to prison. He tried to stop a pimp beating up a hooker outside a nightclub. He ended up putting a shiv in the guy," Clete said. "She thinks he's out now and maybe hanging around. She's afraid her husband's security people might bust him up."

"You believe that crap?"

"Come on, Dave."

"You stop jerking me around. You tell me what happened today."

"I met her for an early lunch at this joint on Flathead Lake. We had a couple of drinks and took a boat ride. The water was blue as far as you could see, you know, like you're out on the Pacific Ocean rather than a lake. Man, she looked fine, too, sitting on the bow of the boat with her gold hair blowing in the wind."

"Yeah, Jane Powell on a yacht. Get to it, Clete."

"We went back to the joint at the marina and had a couple more drinks. Then she put some money in the juke and asked me to dance. She felt so little inside my arms. Then I felt this wetness on my shirt. She was crying. She denied it, but she was crying."

I propped my elbow on the bar and pinched my temples. I hated to hear what was coming. In fact, I wished I had not gone looking for Clete and this time had let him take the fall on his own. "You got it on with her?" I said.

"It's like my libido was on autopilot. Five minutes away, there's this motel on the point. We had the room on the end, looking over the water. Man, it was like I was twenty-five again."

"Oh, Clete," I said, more to myself than to him.

"We agreed afterwards it was a mistake. She was serious when she called about this Indian guy she used to sing with. It's over between them, but she doesn't want to see him hurt. I think she's a good woman, Dave."

I wanted to punch him off the bar stool.

Just then the bikers began laughing uproariously at a remark one of them had made about the drink waitress.

"How about shutting the fuck up?" I said over my shoulder.

"What'd you say?" one of them asked.

"I said close your mouth. You're disturbing a conversation here," I replied, my face tight, my hand opening and closing on the bar.

The entire bar became silent. Out on the highway, I could hear a tractor-trailer rig shifting down for the long haul over Lolo Pass.

"Let it go, man," one of the bikers said to the others. "They're cops."

"The Bobbsey Twins from Homicide, bud, Clete Purcel and Dave Robicheaux, NOPD's answer for every whore's wet dream," Clete said, winking at them. "Something to tell your grandkids about."

But none of it was funny.

THAT NIGHT IN bed I told Molly what had happened.

"Has he lost his mind?" she said.

"He wants to be young again. He wants New Orleans to be like it was when we were beat cops. Scarlett O'Hara comes along and stokes him up and lets him think he's Rhett Butler. She hit him with the perfect combo—beautiful victim protecting her ex-boyfriend needs help from chivalric PI."

"Stop making excuses for him. Clete went to bed with another man's wife."

"That's the point. It's eating his lunch," I said.

I heard her sigh in the darkness. "I'm really sorry to hear this," she said.

"Maybe we should go back to New Iberia," I said.

"I think that's a bad idea. We didn't do anything wrong. We're not going to let other people's deeds or behavior make choices for us. Clete needs to get his goddamn act together."

"He'll come around," I said.

"Who are you kidding? Clete's at war with himself. It's the only way he knows how to live."

She was right. Clete had slept with the wife of a mutilated war veteran, a man who had been burned in a tank. In Vietnam he had witnessed the death by fire of marines who had been trapped inside a burning armored vehicle. In his dreams, almost every third or fourth night of his life, he heard the sounds of ammunition belts popping in the heat and the voices of the men who couldn't free the hatches on their vehicle. Now he had an extra set of knives turning inside his chest. Jamie Sue Wellstone may have been the succubus who provided the temptation and the opportunity, but the most pernicious agency in Clete's life always remained the same. He would give up his life before he would willingly harm an animal or a friend or an innocent person, but daily he went about deconstructing himself without ever understanding that the child his father had irreparably injured was still living inside him. Clete had demons not even an exorcist would take on.

Had Jamie Sue Wellstone deliberately played him? I wasn't sure. As though she had read my thoughts, Molly said, "I think you and Clete got too close to something. I think the Wellstones know exactly what they're doing. I think you're next, Dave."

"Not me. I've fought my last war."

She turned toward the wall and didn't reply.

• • •

THE NEXT MORNING, Friday, Clete's troubles took on a different shade, in the form of Special Agent Alicia Rosecrans from the FBI. When she found no one home at Albert's house, she drove her automobile up the dirt road to our front porch.

She looked Amerasian and was dressed in a blue suit, white blouse, and conservative shoes, her dark hair touching her shoulders, her face narrow. She wore small wire-framed glasses that gave her a studious look, like that of a research librarian or a university professor devoted to an arcane subject that no one cared about. She said she wanted to speak to Clete Purcel. When I told her I didn't know where he was, her eyes shifted off my face onto the interior of the cabin. She looked into my face again, not blinking, her expression impassive.

"You're a sheriff's detective in Louisiana?" she said.

"That's correct."

"You don't know where Mr. Purcel is?" she said, repeating her question.

"That's what I said."

"You were here in Montana when Sally Dio's plane crashed into a mountainside on the res? You were here with Mr. Purcel?"

"I wasn't 'with' him. But yes, I was here in Montana when Sally caught the bus. It was a heartrending moment for everyone."

"The Bureau considers his death a homicide. I understand Dio's men smashed your friend's hand in a car door."

"Tell you what—a guy who can give you firsthand information on this works at the Wellstone ranch up in the Swan. His name is Lyle Hobbs. He did scut jobs for Sally when he wasn't molesting children. You know the Wellstones, don't you?"

Her eyes took on a sharper intensity at the implication in my question. "I know who they are," she said. "You think my visit here has some connection to them?"

"I have no idea why you're here. But I don't believe it's about Sally Dio. The feds didn't care about him nineteen years ago. I don't think they care about him now."

Molly opened the front door. "Would you like to come in for coffee?" she asked.

Wrong time for southern protocol.

"That would be nice," Special Agent Alicia Rosecrans said.

Inside the kitchen area of the cabin, Molly began setting pastry and cups and saucers on our breakfast table, which was spread with a red-and-white-checkerboard cloth. Alicia Rosecrans sat down and opened a notebook on the table. "You and Clete Purcel are now helping Sheriff Higgins in the investigation of the homicide that took place behind Albert Hollister's house?"

"How'd you know that?"

"I reinterviewed some of the same people you and Purcel interviewed. You're walking on the edges of meddling in a federal investigation, Mr. Robicheaux."

Molly had been moving pots and pans around on the stove, but she stopped and turned off the propane on the burner. The only sound in the room was the wind blowing in the cottonwoods that shaded the cabin.

"I'm a police officer," I said. "Any interviews I conducted were done with the consent of the Missoula County Sheriff's Department. I think the question we're not dealing with here is your involvement in the investigation of a local homicide. Why are the feds interested in the deaths of two college kids?"

"One of them was kidnapped."

I wasn't buying her answer. Since 9/11, the FBI had shifted its emphasis not only to the vast and attendant connotations of the word "terrorism" but to following thousands of Mideastern college students all over the United States. I doubted they had time or resources to worry about what appeared to be the random murder of two college students in Missoula, Montana.

"Dave, I completely forgot. I promised we'd take Albert's cat to the vet's office this morning," Molly said.

Alicia Rosecrans closed her notebook and returned it to her purse. She folded her hands and stared out the window at the cottonwoods swelling with wind. Her features were as immobile as those in an oil painting, her eyes full of private thoughts.

"Ma'am?" I said, wondering if indeed she had accepted Molly's invitation to leave.

"I think your friend is with the Wellstone woman this morning," she said.

"Can you say that again?"

"I believe he's about to get himself in a lot of trouble," she said. "Thank you for your time. Thank you for preparing the coffee, too, Ms. Robicheaux."

Then Alicia Rosecrans went out to her car and drove away. But I had a feeling we would be seeing a lot more of her.

"What was that?" Molly said.

"The feds have Jamie Sue Wellstone under surveillance. The question is why."

CHAPTER 7

Troyce Nix's hospital window gave onto a terrace planted with mimosa and palm trees, bougainvillea, yellow bugle vine, crown of thorns, and Spanish daggers. In the early-morning hours and at sunset, the automatic sprinklers clicked on and misted the plants and created miniature rainbows above the terrace wall. But Troyce Nix was not interested in the beauty of a tropical garden or the baked hills across the river in Old Mexico or the millions of lights that seemed to come on at night along the dry floodplains of the Rio Grande. His favorite time of day was high noon, right after lunch, when the nurse turned on his morphine drip and the sky turned a blinding white and he found himself inside a vast desert somewhere west of the Pecos where neither God nor civilized man bothered to lay claim, where a solitary figure waited for him, both Troyce's and the figure's tracks finally braiding together amid sand dunes that were as tall as mountains.

In Troyce's dream, the figure wore state-issue blues that were stiff with dried sweat and caked with salt under the armpits. His hair was blown with grit, his lips cracked from dehydration, his work boots split on his feet. The desert was devoid of shadows, even those of carrion birds. The only remnants of modern civilization that Troyce could see were the bodies of automobiles, half buried in the sand, the paint scoured from the metal. As Troyce approached the figure, the water in his canteen sloshing on his hip, he could feel a thickness growing in his loins. He felt his palms starting to tingle and the same sense of expectation that he always experienced just this side of orgasm. He heard sand rilling down the face of a dune, wind whistling through the glassless window of a Model T Ford. He heard the sound of water as he drank it from his canteen, his throat working steadily. He smelled the astringent, reassuring odor of his own manhood as he wiped his face on his shirtsleeve.

He could do and experience all these things because he was alive and growing stronger by the minute, in control of another's fate, about to measure out justice and vengeance in any fashion he chose.

The figure dressed in state blues was terrified, his mouth opening silently with his fear.

Been thinking about me, Jimmy Dale?

A whole lot, boss. Real sorry about what happened back there. You got some water?

Look down at your pants.

Sir?

You just pissed your britches.

What you gonna do, boss?

Nothing.

Sir?

I'm gonna make you do it to yourself. I'm gonna make you do it to what you love. I'm just gonna watch.

I don't understand.

You know what Chinamen call the death of a thousand cuts?

No sir.

It'll be quite a ride.

That don't sound good, boss.

You don't know the half of it.

When Troyce Nix would wake from his dream, his throat would be parched, his phallus throbbing, his big, flat-plated chest damp with perspiration. When the male nurse came in to give him fresh ice water and to sponge-bathe him, Troyce would sometimes convince him to turn the drip back on. Then he would lie back in a sleepy pink haze, a sliver of ice on his tongue, mentally constructing his next encounter with Jimmy Dale Greenwood, the images for redress so stark he had to touch the male nurse on the back of the hand to keep his bearings.

But this afternoon was different. In the morning he would be leaving the hospital, perhaps unsteadily, his system laced with painkillers, but leaving nonetheless. The only problem now was the deputy sheriff sitting by his bed, a pencil pusher with soft hands and a pink egg-shaped face and carefully combed hair and breath that smelled of peppermint mouthwash. Unfortunately, the man's mind-set did not go with his demeanor or appearance. His name was Rawlings, and he was the fourth investigative deputy to visit Troyce Nix's bedside. He was also the most unrelenting.

"A few millimeters either way and any one of them body thrusts could have done you in," he said. "I'd buy me a bunch of lottery tickets or go to the dog track. You ever go to the dog track?"

"No," Troyce answered.

"So you figure it was a tramp hiding in your closet?" Rawlings said. "He was in your house and he hid in your closet when he heard your truck come up the road? That's what you're saying?"

"It's not what I'm saying. It's what happened," Troyce said. His chest was crisscrossed with tape and gauze; he shifted himself on the bed to relieve a place where the bandages were binding under his heart.

"And Jimmy Dale Greenwood was digging postholes behind your house or cabin or whatever? Wasn't no way it was him who hurt you? I mean, here on your statement it says you laid down to take a nap and this guy come out of the closet when you woke up. Wasn't no way you just got confused about who attacked you?"

"I was fixing to make Greenwood a full trusty. I greased the way for his parole. Why would he attack me?"

"Maybe he was chewing on peyote buttons. I've seen Indians stick their hand in a fire when they were souped up on mescal. He might have been down on grand auto, but he also put a knife in a guy."

"Jimmy Dale Greenwood stole my truck and took off on me when I was near bleeding to death. But it wasn't him who cut me up. It was a white man, not a breed."

"Trouble is, that shank your attacker busted off inside you was made from automotive window glass, the same kind that was in the shop where Greenwood worked. What would a tramp be doing with a prison-made shank?"

Troyce turned his head on the pillow and looked at Rawlings. The slash wound on his cheek had gone to the bone, and the connective tissue on one side of his face didn't work properly. "You wouldn't call me a liar, would you?"

Rawlings stared into space as though considering the question. He propped the heels of his hands on his thighs and returned Troyce's stare. "I understand you're checking out in the morning."

"That's right."

"Going to be doing some traveling, seeing the country, that sort of thing?"

"I got me a little woman in Las Cruces."

Rawlings nodded thoughtfully. He seemed to watch a fly crawling up the wall. Then he rose from his chair. He touched Troyce Nix on the thigh with his clipboard, through the sheet. "Take care of yourself, bub. Just one reminder, though."

Troyce waited.

"The worst fate can befall a lawman is to end up stacking time with the same sonsofbitches we been riding herd on," Rawlings said. "The thought of it makes something inside me shrivel up and die."

THREE HOURS AFTER Special Agent Alicia Rosecrans's visit to our cabin, Clete's Caddy pulled into our yard. The top was up, the maroon finish gleaming with a fresh wax job. Clete got out and shut the door firmly and stared back down the road. The sun was above the mountain crests now, and Albert's horses had moved into the shade of the cottonwoods along the creek. When the wind gusted through the trees on the hillsides, it made a sound exactly like rushing water. The sound made Clete look around him, as though he wasn't sure where he was standing. I wondered if he had been drinking.

I told him about my conversation with Alicia Rosecrans. I also told him she believed he had been with Jamie Sue Wellstone that morning. But he seemed distracted, his eyes closing and opening as he sorted through my words.

"Run all that by me again," he said.

"The feds probably have her under surveillance. They saw you with her at Flathead Lake. They probably saw you at the motel with her, too," I said.

He rubbed the back of his neck, staring down the road in the direction he had just come from, his consternation growing.

"Where have you been, Clete?" I said.

"To the Express Lube in Missoula."

"For three hours?"

"No, I picked up a tail. I think it was Lyle Hobbs. I tried to get him to follow me into the mall parking lot. He didn't take the bait, but I saw the same car again in Lolo. Why would Hobbs be tailing me? Why have I got a pervert like that bird-dogging me?"

"Because Jamie Sue Wellstone's husband is onto you. Because this is probably a way of life with them. Because she probably pumps everything in sight."

"Is Molly inside?"

"So what? Molly is your friend, too. You think she likes seeing you swallow a razor blade?"

"Who died and made you God? Lay off me, Streak. Maybe Jamie Sue played me, but maybe not."

"Don't even go near thoughts like that. You know what an old fool is? A guy who starts acting like an old fool."

I saw the injury in his face. My ears were ringing with my own words. I put my hand on his shoulder. It felt like boilerplate. "Take a walk with me," I said.

"What for?"

"Humor me."

"Humor *you*?"

"It's about the kid who was murdered up on the hill."

Clete was resistant and irritable, for which I couldn't blame him. But finally he took a deep breath, and the heat went out of his face, and we walked along the road together like the old friends we were, the wind blowing cool up the valley, the snow atop Lolo Peak wet and bright against a flawless blue porcelain sky.

"I got to thinking about something Seymour Bell's roommate told us. He said Seymour was both smart and tough. What if the little wood cross and the leather cord you found at the crime scene weren't torn off the shooter by Seymour or vice versa?"

"Go on."

"Joe Bim Higgins said there was only one print on the cross—Seymour's. Higgins assumed the killer had gloves on and tore the cross from Seymour's neck and flung it down the slope, probably in a rage. But what if Seymour broke the cord on the cross and threw it in the brush for us to find?"

"No, Higgins said there were cuff burns on Seymour's wrists. If he was forced to ride in a car, his wrists would have been cuffed behind him. He couldn't have gotten his hands on the cross."

"Let's go back up the mountain," I said.

We walked up the switchback trail through dense stands of fir trees until we reached the crime scene. It was windy and bright when we came out of the shade into sunlight, and both of us were sweating heavily. Far below, we could see the state two-lane that led over Lolo Pass into Idaho, and a long silvery creek meandering through cottonwood trees, the same creek Meriwether Lewis and William Clark and the Indian woman Sacagawea had followed on their way to Oregon.

"What are we looking for?" Clete said.

"Think of it this way: Maybe the killer brought Seymour up here in order to send Albert a message. But what if the motivation was more complicated? What if the killer was after information of some kind?"

"Too much of this is speculative, Dave."

"No, predators are always cowards. They don't take chances with guys like Seymour Bell. They kill them outright."

Clete bit on a hangnail and made a face. "You got a point."

The crime scene's forensic integrity had deteriorated dramatically since our first visit there. Deer and elk scat was everywhere. Tree branches were broken, and the soft layer of humus and pine needles was pocked with the hoofprints of large animals. A rotted larch trunk had snapped at ground level and crashed across the anvil-shaped rock that was stippled with Seymour Bell's blood.

"Figure it this way," I said. "The boy died within a few feet of that rock. The car tracks are about fifteen feet south of the rock. So everything that happened here probably took place within a circle that had a diameter of not more than twenty-five feet."

"Yeah?" Clete said.

I walked to the edge of the slope where Clete had found the small wood cross and broken leather cord. *What were you trying to tell us, kid?* I thought.

"Take a look," I said.

The rotted larch, shaggy with moss and decay, had cracked cleanly across its base and fallen in one piece, allowing sunlight to flood onto a fir tree next to it. At the bottom of the fir tree's trunk were gashes in the bark. They were lateral and thin and overlapping, as though a dull metal surface had been jerked repeatedly against the smoothness of the bark. I knelt on one knee and touched them with my fingers. "The killer locked that kid's wrists around the tree. Look at how the ground is churned up," I said. "I think maybe he was tortured here."

"But why would Bell throw away his cross?"

"Because he didn't want his executioner to take it with him," I said.

"Yeah, but why would a degenerate motherfucker like that want the kid's cross? Unless the guy is into fetishism."

I got to my feet, dusting grains of dirt off my hands. "I don't know," I said.

"Dave, if what Seymour's roommate told us is true—I mean about Seymour being a fighter—maybe there's another possibility we haven't looked at."

I waited for him to continue. In the distance, the wind was blowing the snowcap on Lolo Peak, powdering the sky with it, smudging the light.

"What if we're not dealing with just one guy?" Clete said.

• • •

TROYCE NIX HAD flown into Spokane on pain pills and adrenaline, then had gone directly to a Toyota dealership and purchased a re-possessed SUV. The vehicle had to be prepped before Troyce could drive it away, so he checked into a motel on I-90 east of the city and told the salesman to deliver his purchase when it was ready.

The motel was almost to the Idaho line, a leftover from an earlier time, constructed of pink stucco, set back in the deep shadows of cedar trees and fringed with purple neon. Next door was a steak house and saloon that featured live country music. Troyce ate a twenty-ounce porterhouse and sipped a Manhattan while he listened to the music from the bandstand. It wasn't long before a fellow trav-eler caught his eye and nodded politely to him.

The fellow traveler looked western enough, in tight stonewashed jeans and a hand-tooled belt and a short-brim cattleman's hat. But the clipped mustache hid a feminine mouth, and the wide shoulders inside the snap-button shirt couldn't disguise the flaccidity of his upper arms. Nor was the fellow traveler shy about glancing back at Troyce from the bar, flexing his buttocks against his jeans.

He wasn't quite Troyce's type, but it had been a long time between drinks.

The next afternoon Troyce's SUV was delivered to the motel. The only problem was that Troyce's interlude with the fellow traveler had proved both exhausting and complicated in ways he hadn't expected. As a result, his wounds ached, his pain pills and alcohol intake had collided in his nervous system, and he didn't trust himself to drive. Fortunately, he met another pilgrim, this one a honky-tonk in-your-face piece of work by the name of Candace Sweeney.

She said she would drive him all the way to Missoula for fifty bucks and drinks and the cost of a bus ticket to Livingston, where she claimed she had a job cooking at a dude ranch. "It's not a bad gig if you don't mind rich old guys scoping your jugs every time you lean over the table," she said.

It was twilight as they drove into the Idaho Panhandle and the mountains and lake country around Coeur d'Alene. In the glow of the dash, Troyce could see the tattoos of flowers on the tops of Candace Sweeney's breasts, and the tiny pits in her cheeks, and the black shine in her hair, which she wore in bangs, giving her a little-girl look that didn't fit anything she was saying.

"You're a cop, aren't you?" she said.

"What makes you say that?"

"I can always tell. Cops think behind their eyes. The ones on the make do, anyway."

"I look like I'm on the make?"

"No, you just think a lot. You see the ambulance take that guy out of the motel this morning?"

"No."

"Somebody knocked his teeth out with a blackjack. He wasn't saying who. He works the saloon sometimes, mostly married men who haven't figured out they're fudge packers."

"Too bad."

"Occupational hazard when you're selling your ass in a rawhide bar. He usually works hotels in Spokane or in Portland and Seattle. If you knew some of those sagebrush schmucks back there, you wouldn't mess with them. They've got no idea what goes on in their own heads. If they did, they'd stick a gun in their mouths."

"Never heard it put that way."

The sun had gone below the mountains, and the lakes on either side of the road were dark and glazed with the lights from boathouses and sailboats, the water sliding up onto rocky shoals.

"I used to have a little junk problem—tar, mostly. I got busted on a possession charge in Portland. The court sent me to a twelve-step program. I thought most of it sucked, then one night I heard these women start talking about certain sexual problems they developed with their own kids, like, they wanted to molest them. Puke-o, right?

"I didn't want to hear this shit, because I'd had a little boy myself that I gave up to Catholic Charities. Except the story these women told was a little bit too familiar, know what I mean, like yuck, they're talking about me. They all said they were molested themselves when they were little, and they knew if they did it to their own kids, their kids would have the same kind of miserable lives they'd had. This one woman said the only way she could spare her little boy was to drown him in the bathtub.

"Don't look at me like that. She didn't do it. But here's where it gets even worse. These women said that killing their kids was a way of looking out for them. Then they figured out that wasn't the reason at all. They wanted to kill their kids because they thought the little girl inside them was a whore and had to pay the price for what she did, I mean causing all the trouble for the grown-up. How sick does it get? Like gag me out, double puke-o again."

Troyce studied the side of Candace Sweeney's face for a long time. "Why are you telling me this?"

She glanced at him, disconcerted. They were headed up the Fourth of July Pass now, the forests on either side of them carving out of the darkness in the headlights. "I wasn't telling *you* anything. I was saying, you know, that—" Her words seized up in her throat. The muscles in one side of his face had been impaired by an incision of some kind, perhaps by a knife wound, and his expression looked disjointed, split in half, as though two different people shared his skin.

"You were saying what?" he asked.

"That whoever smacked around the bone-smoker back there probably hasn't figured out why he does stuff like that. Like he's a sick fuck. Like maybe I was, too. That's just the way the world is. People don't necessarily get to choose what or who they are." She turned her eyes boldly on Troyce's face.

"You're pretty smart," he said.

"Yeah, that's why I'm a cook for CEO titty babies who get their dorks mixed up with their deer guns."

Up ahead, the road was empty. Troyce twisted in the seat and looked through the back window. A car's taillights were disappearing in the opposite direction. "Pull in to that rest stop," he said.

"That's not a very good place."

"Why not?"

"They don't clean it. It smells like a bear took a dump in it six months ago and forgot to flush the toilet."

"That's all right. Pull in."

She parked the SUV by the public restroom, where an apron of electric light fell on the gravel and the roof of the vehicle and the giant log that separated the parking area from the sidewalk, all the things that should have looked normal and comforting but were now removed from the asphalt highway connecting Troyce Nix and Candace Sweeney to the rest of the world.

"You didn't cut the engine," he said.

"I was gonna listen to the radio," she said.

He turned off the ignition for her, then rolled down his window on the electric motor. The air was sweet with the smell of the woods, and water was ticking out of the trees. "Say that last part again. That part about the woman hating the little girl still living inside her," he said.

"I'm not into Jerry Springer. If you want to fuck me, I'll give it some thought. But I was talking about myself, nobody else."

"I want you to change my bandages. I'm leaking."

"What happened to you?"

"Who cares? Tell me about that woman again, the one who was going to drown her kid."

When she went into the back to retrieve the medical kit from under the seat, she saw a holstered, strapped-down nine-millimeter and a stitched leather-covered blackjack, the kind shaped like a large squash, the leaded end mounted on a spring and wood handle, one that could break bone and teeth and crush a person's face into pulp. The points of fir trees extended into the sky all around her. Directly overhead, the constellations were colder and brighter than she had ever seen them. She opened the passenger door and looked blankly into Troyce Nix's face.

"Do I end here?" she said.

"Little darlin', the Lord broke the mold when He made you. Ain't nothing gonna happen to you, at least not while I'm around."

"Take off your shirt," she said.

CHAPTER
8

On Monday morning Joe Bim Higgins asked me to come to his office at the Missoula County Courthouse. When I tapped on his partially opened door, he was standing at the window, gazing out on the lawn and the maple trees that shaded the benches by the sidewalk.

"Thanks for coming by, Mr. Robicheaux," he said, extending his hand. "Early yesterday morning somebody broke into the house in Bonner where Seymour Bell was living. Bell's roommates were gone for the weekend. Whoever broke in tore the place up pretty bad."

"You don't think it was just vandalism?"

"No, the drawers were all pulled out, mattresses peeled back, closets emptied. Somebody was looking for something."

"Was anything missing?"

"Bell's roommate says a cheap camera is gone, one of those little throwaway jobs. He said he was sure it was on top of Bell's bookcase when he left the house on Friday afternoon." Higgins paused, watching my expression. "What's your take on it?"

"If the camera was the object of interest and in full view, the intruder wouldn't have torn up the whole house. He was after something else as well, something more important."

"I talked with your boss in New Iberia this morning. She said you were a good cop."

I knew what was coming. "No," I said. "I came out here to fish.

I got involved in your investigation because the homicide took place behind Albert's house. Clete thought the killer might have been sending Albert a message."

"That's one reason I want you working for me. Albert is just like me. He's old and wants his own way. When he doesn't get it, he starts throwing horse turds in the punch bowl."

"Albert is going to have to take care of himself."

"You don't get it, Mr. Robicheaux. The West isn't the same place or culture I grew up in. People like Albert Hollister used to be the rule, not the exception. Albert believes in his country and his fellow man, and he'll let people kill him before he'll accept the fact that most of his fellow citizens care more about the price of gasoline than a volunteer soldier getting killed in Afghanistan. I want to deputize you right here, with a gentleman's understanding that this is a temporary situation confined to the investigation of these recent homicides. I've got good people working for me, there's just not enough of them. What do you say, partner?"

"What about Clete Purcel?"

"Forget it." He took a badge in a leather holder out of his desk drawer and dropped it on his blotter. "Tell me you don't want it and we're done."

ONE MILE AWAY, Clete had just parked his Caddy under a cluster of maple trees behind the university library when he saw a familiar green Honda pass on the street. He had seen the Honda twice that morning, in traffic, once outside the Express Lube Friday morning, and once later, at the mall.

Clete watched the Honda disappear around a curve at the base of the mountain behind the university. He walked across a knoll, through a grove of trees, and sat on the steps of a classroom building with a view of his Caddy. He sat there for ten minutes, sipping from a silver flask, each hit of Scotch and milk going down like the old friend it used to be, the wind blowing cool through the trees, the damp smell of the steps reminiscent of the Quarter in the early-morning hours. But the green Honda did not reappear, and Clete walked to the library, where he began to research both the life of the woman he had slept with and the life of the husband he had cuckolded.

As he did these things, he felt wrapped in a web of deceit and desire that he could not scrub off his skin.

The reference librarian helped him find articles about the young Jamie Sue Stapleton on the Internet and in music magazines and biographical books dealing with country-and-western personalities. Most of it was fluff, written by hacks who created caricatures of blue-collar people who rose from humble origins to a world stage where their brocaded and sequined western costumes told their audiences that fame and wealth could be theirs, too, if only they believed. The manufactured accents, the nativism and cynical use of religion, the meretricious nature of the enterprise, the cheapness of the disguise were all forgivable sins. It was the poor whites' answer to the minstrel show. Starshine allowed them to delight in the parody of themselves and to turn the poverty and rejection that characterized their lives into badges of honor.

Unfortunately for the hacks who wrote about her, Jamie Sue's life and career did not lend themselves to predictability.

She had been born to a blind woman and an oil-field roustabout in Yoakum, Texas, the inception point of the old Chisholm Trail. She left high school at age sixteen and worked as a waitress at a truck stop in San Antonio and as a dancer at a topless club in Houston. According to one interview, she earned an associate of arts degree from a community college when she was nineteen. She also married her English professor and divorced him one year later, after charging him with assault and battery and spousal rape.

With the money from her divorce settlement, she formed her first band.

At a time when Nashville music was transforming itself into a middle-class and popular medium, Jamie Sue used Kitty Wells and Skeeter Davis as her models, and a mandolin and a banjo as her lead instruments, and a Dobro instead of an electric bass. A song that always brought down the house was one written by Larry Redmond titled "Garth Ain't Playing Here Tonight."

She hooked up with Jimmy Dale Greenwood, a rodeo drifter some people said had the best voice to hit the Texas hill country since Jimmie Rodgers had lived there. Others said a hymnal duet by Jamie Sue and Jimmy Dale could make the devil join the Baptist Church. But two weeks before they were scheduled to cut their first album in an Austin recording studio, Jimmy Dale put a knife into the nephew of the meanest county judge in Southwest Texas.

Why had she married an older man, one terribly mutilated by fire? Was it simply money? Clete found only a few news articles on Leslie Wellstone: He had graduated from the University of California at Berkeley with a double major in anthropology and comparative literature, but he had disappeared into the post-psychedelic culture of Haight-Ashbury. He had made underground films and a documentary on migrant farmworkers. He had joined a New Age commune high up in the mountains above Santa Fe. He had also enlisted in the French Foreign Legion and gotten his Spam fried in the Sudan.

Clete had the feeling Leslie Wellstone was a man who had dealt himself almost all the cards in the box and had liked none of them.

Clete left the library and headed toward his Caddy. In a parking lot by the Student Union, he saw the green Honda again. A man was sitting behind the steering wheel, his face obscured by the sun visor. Out on the lawn, in the shade of maples not far from the Caddy, a college-age boy and girl were eating sandwiches on a blanket, the door of their parked vehicle yawning open behind them, their car radio playing softly. Clete looked again at the green Honda. *Showtime on the campus,* he thought.

He walked over to the college boy and his girl. The air in the shade was cool and smelled of clover. The two young people looked up at Clete uncertainly. He squatted down on his haunches, eye level with them, and opened his badge holder on his knee.

"My name is Clete Purcel. I'm a private investigator from New Orleans," he said. "See that guy parked in the green shitbox over there?"

They nodded but kept their eyes on his face and did not look directly at the parking lot.

"That dude has been following me, and I want to turn it around on him," Clete said. "The problem is, he's made my maroon Caddy over there. In the next couple of minutes, I'm going to flush him out of the parking lot. I've got about thirty-seven bucks in my wallet. It's yours if you'll follow him in your car and let me sit in the back-seat."

"He'll know who we are," the boy said.

"No, he can't see your car from where he is. He's not interested in y'all. He'll be looking for me and my Caddy."

"What's he done besides follow you?" the girl asked.

"He's a child molester," Clete replied.

"What do you plan to do to him?" the boy asked.

Take a chance, Clete thought. "Maybe nothing. Maybe break all his wheels," he said. "Anytime you want me out of the car, I'll get out."

The boy and girl looked at each other and shrugged.

Clete walked across the grass to Lyle Hobbs's vehicle and propped one arm on the roof above the driver's window. Hobbs had a box of Wheat Thins open on his lap and was feeding them one at a time into his mouth, chewing them on his back teeth. His recessed right eye, the one looped with stitch marks, glittered wetly, as though it had been irritated by the wind. Clete suppressed a yawn, his gaze wandering up the slope of the mountain behind the university. Then he watched a U.S. Forest Service plane, one filled with fire retardant, flying low across the sky, its engines laboring with its massive load. "Nice day, isn't it?" he said.

Lyle Hobbs turned on his radio and tuned the station to a baseball game in progress. "You gonna let it get personal, Mr. Purcel?"

A nest of small blue veins was pulsing in Clete's temple. "When I was with NOPD, I'd do just that, Lyle. Get personal, I mean. Know why that was? Because my pay was the same whether I was eating doughnuts or mopping up the sidewalk with a degenerate. Now I'm a PI. When it becomes personal, I get in trouble and lose my source of income."

"I noticed that about you when you were working for Sally Dee. A real pro. I was impressed. You always seemed to fit right in," Hobbs replied, his eyes fixed straight ahead.

"Does it ever get personal for you, Lyle? Ever know a guy with a short-eyes jacket who wasn't afraid—I mean, deep down inside, scared shitless? It's what makes them cruel, isn't it? That's why they always choose their victims carefully. You ever get a real bone-on and go apeshit on somebody, Lyle?"

"You're a real philosopher, Mr. Purcel," Hobbs said, suddenly looking up at Clete, just like the lead-weighted eyelids of a doll clicking open. He dropped his empty Wheat Thins box out the window. It bounced off the pavement, powdering Clete's shoes with crumbs.

Clete went into the alcove of the classroom building across from the library and waited. He unscrewed the cap on his flask and took a hit of Scotch and milk, then another one. After five minutes, he heard Lyle Hobbs start his car. He waited until he could see Hobbs's car heading toward the road that separated the campus from the mountain behind it. Then he walked quickly down the steps to the young couple sitting under the trees. "Let's rock," he said.

The three of them followed Hobbs across town to a park in the middle of the residential district. All of the adjoining streets were lined with maple trees, the park spangled with sunshine, children playing on a baseball diamond and in a wading pool with a fountain geysering out of the center. In the midst of it all, Lyle Hobbs stood under a tree, watching a group of young teenage girls practicing somersaults in the grass.

Clete took all the bills out of his wallet and handed them to the driver. "Thanks for the lift. You guys take care of yourself," he said.

"That guy's really a molester?" the boy said.

"From the jump," Clete said.

"Keep the money," the boy said. He was burr-headed and wore a T-shirt and a ball cap pulled down on his brow. "You might actually bust that guy up?"

"I exaggerate sometimes."

"You have booze on your breath," the girl said, trying to smile. "We don't want to see you get in trouble. You seem like a nice man." She patted Clete on the wrist.

After the college kids drove away, Clete walked into the park. Then his eyes focused on a picnic bench on the far side of the recreation building. Jamie Sue was sitting next to her brother-in-law, Ridley Wellstone. She was also sitting next to a stroller, watching a diapered little boy play in the grass. She set the boy on her lap and combed his hair with her fingernails.

Clete tried to assimilate what he was looking at. The Scotch he had drunk wasn't helping his thought processes. The light seemed to splinter into needles inside the trees; he opened his mouth to clear a popping sound in his ears. Then he realized both Wellstone and Jamie Sue were staring at him as though *he* were an aberration rather than the other way around.

"What are you doing here?" Wellstone said. His aluminum crutches were propped beside him.

"Following the asshole you put on my tail," Clete said. He looked at Jamie Sue and the little boy. "You have a kid?"

"Yes, I do. Why do you ask?"

"*Why do I ask?*"

"You don't look well," she said. "Do you want to sit down?"

"That's not a good idea," Ridley Wellstone said.

The popping sound in Clete's ears seemed to be gaining in intensity, like the thropping of helicopter blades. *How dumb can one guy be?* he asked himself.

"We made restitution for your fishing gear. Now get out of here," Wellstone said.

People at the other picnic tables were staring, and Clete's face felt tight and small in the wind. Again he thought he heard mechanical sounds from a distant war and smelled an odor like moldy clothes on his body and diesel fuel and mosquito repellent and mud that stank of stagnant water. For just a second he thought he felt the squish of trench foot inside his boot and saw the flicker of conical straw hats moving through elephant grass.

He walked away from Jamie Sue's picnic table, slightly off balance, his mouth dry, his forehead breaking a sweat. He passed Lyle Hobbs, who was still watching the teenage girls turning somersaults in the shade. Clete went into the restroom and washed his face for a long time. He dried his skin with a paper towel and looked in the metal reflector that served as a mirror. His face made him think of a pumpkin beaded with drops of water. Outside, he heard the music from an ice-cream truck. He thought of children playing in Audubon Park when he was a child in New Orleans. For a moment his heart was a kettle drum.

Lyle Hobbs walked into the restroom and relieved himself in a urinal. He was wearing shades, breathing through his mouth as he urinated, shaking himself off with one hand. He zipped his fly, then wet his comb under the lavatory faucet and began combing his hair. He never glanced at Clete.

"I catch you tailing me again, it's going to play out a whole lot different," Clete said.

Hobbs flicked the water off his comb and stuck it in his shirt pocket. "Mr. Wellstone came to town for his therapy. Nobody is tailing you, nobody is interested in you, Mr. Purcel. I cain't abide a self-righteous man, particularly one that didn't have a problem of conscience with putting his dick in another man's wife. You'd better count your blessings you're dealing with me and not Quince. Quince is mightily attached to the Wellstone family. Believe me when I say Quince is not a man you want mad at you."

"I saw you watching those young girls, you piece of shit."

Hobbs leaned toward the metal reflector, tilting up his nose, sucking in his lips. He plucked a hair from one nostril and dropped it in the basin. "Stay out of trouble," he said.

Hobbs walked out into the sunlight, his hair wet on his collar. Clete followed him, remaining in the shade, his heart still hammering. Hobbs was watching the teenage girls, who were now sitting on the grass under the maple trees, their knees pulled up in front of them. He bought a Popsicle from the ice-cream truck, opened his car door, and stood behind it, eating the Popsicle while he watched a girl not over fourteen climbing up on the jungle gym, her shirt sliding up on her hips.

Clete could see the outline of Hobbs's phallus against his trousers.

Walk away, Clete told himself. *You can't change what's happening here.*

Screw that, another voice said.

"You need to take your johnson somewhere else, Lyle," he said.

Hobbs turned, the Popsicle half in his mouth. He bit into it, clearly savoring the melt in the back of his jaws, his eyes lighting with a thought. "Sally Dee said you blew your career and marriage with booze and weed and ten-dollar street cooze. He said he felt sorry for you, Mr. Purcel. He said your wife was a muff diver, and that's why you were a gash hound and your colleagues at NOPD gave you a bad rap. That's why he gave you a job at his casino."

Hobbs's eyes remained fixed on the girl playing on the jungle gym, but Clete saw the indentation, the tug of a suppressed grin, at the corner of his mouth.

"I have a feeling there's paper on you somewhere," Clete said.

Hobbs dropped the empty Popsicle stick over the top of the car door into the gutter. He tilted his head inquisitively.

"Defective guys like you have outstanding warrants—a skipped bond, failed court appearances, a PV of a kind that only idiots commit," Clete said. "But what that means is I'm going to take you in and split the skip fee with whoever is looking for you. Lean against the vehicle and assume the position."

"Go blow yourself, Mr. Purcel," Hobbs said.

"I can't tell you how happy that makes me, Lyle."

Clete clenched one hand on the back of Hobbs's neck and slammed him against the side of the Honda. When Hobbs began to struggle, Clete swung him in a circle, flopping like a fish, and crashed him against the roof and against the hood. Hobbs's shades shattered on the asphalt, and blood leaked from his nose. Then he tried to run. He got as far as the grille of the Honda before Clete grabbed him again and threw him against the far side of the hood, kicking his ankles apart, shoving his face down on the hot metal.

The back of Hobbs's neck felt oily and warm in Clete's hand. The stench of deodorant layered over dry sweat rose from Hobbs's armpits. His head reared from the metal, his buttocks striking Clete in the loins.

Clete whirled him around and drove his fist into Hobbs's face. The force of the blow lifted Hobbs into the air and dropped him between his shoulder blades on the point of the hood ornament. It should have stopped there, but the red lights flashing and the bells ringing at a train guard deep inside Clete's head were of no value now. He realized what the popping sound in his ears had been. The stitches that held Clete Purcel together were coming loose one by one, and in the next thirty seconds he did things that were like pieces of liquid color breaking apart behind his eyes, dissolving and re-forming without sound or meaning. He thought he heard people screaming and a car horn blowing and the music from the megaphone on top of the ice-cream truck clotting with static. But none of these things deterred him. He felt his fists smashing into sinew and bone, the flat of his shoe coming down on the side of someone's head and face. He saw an old man pleading with him to stop, to grant mercy to the figure on the asphalt.

Then he was standing alone, as though under a glass bell, Hobbs at his feet, the children on the playground terrified by what they had just seen, the wind swelling the trees against a blue summer sky.

Think, he told himself.

He dropped to one knee, a handkerchief in his hand, and pulled a stiletto from a scabbard that was Velcro-strapped to his right ankle. He rubbed the surfaces of the handle clean, clicked open the blade, and wiped it clean, too. Then he pressed the handle into Hobbs's palm and folded his fingers on it.

In the background, he could hear sirens pealing down the street.

ONE HOUR LATER, Clete was sitting on a bench by himself in a holding cell that contained no plumbing and smelled of disinfectant and stone. Down the corridor, someone was yelling without stop in a voice that reflected neither coherence nor meaning, as though the person were yelling simply to deliver an auditory message to himself about his state of affairs. When Clete closed his eyes, he kept seeing the faces of the children in the park, their disbelief at the level of savagery taking place before their eyes. Clete wondered if it was he who was the ogre and not Lyle Hobbs.

The undersheriff who had cuffed Clete stood at the cell door, one hand behind his back. He was a pleasant-looking man, a bit overweight, more administrator than policeman, his face windburned, pale around the eyes where his sunglasses had been. "Hobbs is at St. Pat's. Did you use his head for a paddleball?"

"Sorry to hear that," Clete said.

"You told him you made him for a bail skip?"

"Yeah."

"And he came at you with a switchblade?"

"I guess that sums it up."

"Where was he carrying the switchblade?"

Clete glanced again at the undersheriff. The undersheriff's left hand was still concealed behind his hip. "It's my fault. I got sloppy on the shakedown," Clete said.

The undersheriff held up a Ziploc bag with a black polybraid scabbard inside. "My deputy found this under Hobbs's car. It's the kind of rig some plainclothes cops or PIs use."

"Wonder what Lyle would be doing with that," Clete said.

"You're lucky, Mr. Purcel. Hobbs has a couple of bench warrants on him. It's minor-league stuff, but as a bond agent, you probably have a degree of legality on your side. Anyway, there's a lady waiting for you by the front entrance."

"I'm sprung?"

"For now," the deputy said. "Be careful what you pray for."

Clete gave him a look.

A few minutes later, Clete emerged from the courthouse and saw an Asian-American woman on the sidewalk, a black purse hanging from a leather strap on her shoulder, her expression almost clinical, her wire-framed glasses perched neatly on her nose. "I'm Special Agent Alicia Rosecrans, Mr. Purcel," she said. "I'll drive you to your car."

"You're with Fart, Barf, and Itch?" he said.

"I think you're an intelligent man, regardless of what most people say about you. You can cooperate with us, or you can choose not to. You can also deal with the assault charge on your own. Do you want me to take you to your car?"

Clete saw a four-door silver Dodge Stratus with a government plate on it parked by the curb. Alicia Rosecrans waited for him to reply, then started toward her car. "I appreciate the offer," Clete said to her back. "I've always appreciated what you guys do."

But on his way to the university, he began to have second thoughts about accepting favors from Alicia Rosecrans. She made him think of a lab technician taking apart an insect with tweezers. She told him to open a manila folder on the seat. In it were a stack of photos, a copy of his discharge from the United States Marine Corps, and his medical records from the Veterans Administration.

"You guys followed me and Jamie Sue Wellstone to a motel?" Clete said. He tried to sound incensed, but he felt a knot of shame in his throat.

"No, we followed *her*. You inserted yourself into the situation on your own."

Inserted?

"Why are y'all interested in my medical history?" he said.

"Because we think you probably suffer from post-traumatic stress disorder. Because maybe there are people in the Bureau who don't want to believe you murdered Sally Dio and his men. Maybe some people believe there were complexities involved that others don't understand."

She kept her eyes straight ahead as she drove, her hands in the ten-two position on the steering wheel. Her face was free of blemishes, her profile both enigmatic and lovely to look at. Clete continued to stare at her, his frustration growing.

"I never had post-traumatic stress disorder," he said. "I drank too much sometimes and smoked a little weed. But any trouble I got into wasn't because of Vietnam. I dug it over there."

"Look at the photo taken at the homicide scene on I-90. There's a man walking toward a compact car. If you look closely, you can make out a rectangular shape in his left hand. We think he's the killer," she said.

"Where'd you get this?"

"There was a surveillance camera in the rest stop on the opposite side of the highway. Evidently it had been knocked off-center, and it caught the man in the white shirt in two or three frames. Unfortunately, it didn't catch the license number on the compact. Does this man look familiar?"

"No, it's too grainy. He's just a guy in a white shirt. Why are y'all investigating a local homicide?"

"Because during the last five years, there have been killings on several interstates that bear similarities to the one outside Missoula. The victims were made to kneel or lie on their faces. They were executed at point-blank range. They were sexually abused and sometimes burned or mutilated. Look at the next photo. Do you know that man?"

The eight-by-ten color blowup had been shot with a zoom lens in front of the saloon on Swan Lake. A tall ramrod-straight man wearing a short-brim Stetson hat and western-cut trousers and yellow-tinted aviator shades was looking directly at the lens. He had reddish-blond hair, and the sun on the lake seemed to create a nimbus around his body.

"I've never seen him. Who is he?" Clete said.

"We're not sure. That's why I asked you," she said.

"Why does the FBI have Jamie Sue under surveillance?" Clete said.

Alicia Rosecrans turned a corner carefully, her turn indicator on; she glanced in the rearview mirror. "Look at the last photo in the folder," she said. "Do you recognize that man?"

Clete lifted up the eight-by-ten and studied it. "He's a nice-looking guy. But I've never seen him before."

"Yes, you have, Mr. Purcel. That's Leslie Wellstone, Jamie Sue's husband, before he was burned in the Sudan."

Alicia Rosecrans didn't speak the rest of the way to the university.

CHAPTER 9

Clete had not called me from the jail, either out of shame or because he had thought he could elude a pending assault-and-battery beef by claiming he had feared for his life and acted in self-defense. Montana was still Montana, a culture where vegetarianism, gun control, and gay marriage would never flush. Nor would the belief ever die that a fight between two men was just that, a fight between two men.

That afternoon I went down to Albert's house to talk to Clete. He was already half in the bag, but not because of Lyle Hobbs.

"Why'd that agent show me the photo of Jamie Sue's husband before he was burned up?" he asked. "She wants to cluster-fuck my head?"

All of his windows were open. The weather had taken a dramatic turn, and the valley was covered with shadow, the air cold and dry-smelling, snow flurries already blowing off the top of the ridge.

"They're not interested in Jamie Sue Wellstone," I said. "They're after her husband or brother-in-law. But I don't know what for."

"These murders?"

"Whatever it is, they're not going to tell us. I don't think they're sharing information with Joe Bim Higgins, either." I told Clete I'd been deputized by Higgins.

"What about me?"

"You weren't here when he called," I said.

"Cut it out, Streak." He was spooning vanilla ice cream into a glass and pouring whiskey on top of it. "And stop giving me that look. Get yourself a Dr Pepper out of the refrigerator and don't give me that look."

"I don't want a Dr Pepper."

"Of course you don't. You want a—"

"Say it."

"Go to a meeting. I've got my own problems. I feel like I've got broken glass in my head. I porked the wife of a guy who had his face burned off. What kind of bastard would do something like that?"

"You're the best guy I ever knew, Cletus."

"Save the douche water for somebody else."

He drank the mixture of Beam and ice cream down to the bottom of the glass, his brow furrowed, his green eyes as hard as marbles.

TROYCE NIX HAD no trouble finding the location of Jamie Sue Wellstone's home in the Swan River country. The problem was access to it. An even greater problem was access to Jamie Sue.

He sat in the café that adjoined the saloon on Swan Lake and ate a steak and a load of french fries and drank a cup of coffee while he looked at the snow drifting over the trees and descending like ash on the lake.

"It always snows here in June?" he said to the waitress.

"Sometimes in July," she replied. "You the fellow who was asking about Ms. Wellstone?"

"I used to be a fan of her music. I heard she lived here'bouts. That's the only reason I was asking."

The waitress was a big, red-headed, pink-complected woman who wore oceanic amounts of perfume. "People around here like her. She's rich, but she don't act it. Harold said if you wanted information about her to ask him."

"Who's Harold?"

"The daytime bartender. He was gone when you were here before."

Troyce's eyes seemed to lose interest in the subject. He dropped coins in the jukebox, had another cup of coffee, and used the rest-room. When he sat back down on the stool, he felt the bandages on his chest bind against his wounds. He removed a black-and-white booking-room photo from his shirt pocket and laid it on the counter. He pushed it toward her with one finger. "You ever see this guy around here?"

She leaned over and looked at the photo without picking it up, idly touching the hair on the back of her head. "Not really."

"What's 'not really' mean?" Troyce asked.

The waitress took a barrette out of her pocket and worked it into the back of her hair. "You a Texas Ranger?"

"Why you think I'm from Texas?"

"You know, the accent and all. Besides, it's printed on the bottom of this guy's picture."

"You're pretty smart," Troyce said.

"I'd remember him if he'd been in here."

"Why's that?"

"Because he's almost as good-looking as you."

Troyce slipped the photo back in his shirt pocket and buttoned the flap. "What time you get off?"

"Late," she said. "I got night blindness, too. That's how come Harold drives me home. And if he don't, my husband does."

Troyce left her a three-dollar tip and took his coffee cup and saucer into the saloon and sat at the bar. Through the back windows, he could see the surface of the lake wrinkling in the wind and the steel-gray enormity of Swan Peak disappearing inside the snow. "Ms. Wellstone been in?" he said.

The bartender picked up a pencil and pad and set it in front of him. "You want to leave a message, I'll make sure she gets it."

"You're Harold?"

"What's your business here, pal?"

"This guy." Troyce put the mug shot of Jimmy Dale Greenwood in front of him.

"You have some ID?"

Troyce took out his wallet. It had been made by a convict, raw-hide-threaded along the edges, the initials T.N. cut deep inside a big star. Troyce removed a celluloid-encased photo ID and set it on the bar.

"This says you're a prison guard," the bartender said.

"I'm that, among other things."

"This doesn't give you jurisdiction in Montana. Maybe not a whole lot in Texas, either."

"You know that for a fact?"

"I used to be a cop."

"I think your waitress friend in there has seen this fellow. I'm wondering if you have, too."

The bartender picked up the photo and tapped its edge on the bar, taking Troyce's measure. The bartender's pate was shiny with the oil he used on his few remaining strands of black hair, his shoulders almost too big for the immaculate oversize dress shirt he wore. His physicality was of a kind that sends other men definite signals, a quiet reminder that manners can be illusory and the rules of the cave still hold great sway in our lives.

"A drifter was in here a couple of times. He was asking about Ms. Wellstone. He looked like this guy," the bartender said.

"You know where he is now?"

"No."

"Does your waitress?"

"She's not my waitress."

Troyce smiled before he spoke. "I do something to put you out of joint?"

"Yeah, you tried to let on you're a cop. We're done here."

ANYONE WHO HAS spent serious time in the gray-bar hotel chain is left with certain kinds of signatures on his person. Many hours of clanking iron on the yard produce flat-plated chests and swollen deltoids and rock-hard lats. Arms blanketed with one-color tats, called "sleeves," indicate an inmate has been in the system a long time and is not to be messed with. Blue teardrops at the corner of the eye mean he is a member of the AB and has performed serious deeds for his Aryan brothers, sometimes including murder.

Wolves, sissies, biker badasses, and punks on the stroll all have their own body language. So do the head-shaved psychopaths to whom everyone gives a wide berth. Like Orientals, each inmate creates his own space, avoids eye contact, and stacks his own time. Even an act as simple as traversing the yard can become iconic. What is sometimes called the "con walk" is a stylized way of walking across a crowded enclosure. The signals are contradictory, but they indicate a mind-set that probably goes back to Western civilization's earliest jails. The shoulders are rounded, the arms held almost straight down (to avoid touching another inmate's person), the eyes looking up from under the brow, an expression psychologists call "baboon hostility." The step is exaggerated, the knees splayed slightly and coming up higher than they should, the booted feet consuming territory in almost surreptitious fashion.

Every inmate in the institution is marked indelibly by it, and the mark is as instantly recognizable as were the numbers tattooed on the left forearms of the inmates in Nazi Germany's concentration camps. The difference is one of degree and intention. Time in the system prints itself on every aspect of an inmate's behavior and manner.

On Wednesday evening the weather was still cold, the air gray with rain, and at Albert's ranch we could hear thunder inside the snow clouds that were piled along the crests of the Bitterroot Mountains. Albert asked me to take a ride with him to check on the new man he had hired to care for his horses in the next valley. He said the man's name was J. D. Gribble.

Gribble's cabin was little more than one-room in size, heated by a woodstove that he also cooked on. He was unshaved and wore jeans without knees and only a T-shirt under his denim jacket. He smoked hand-rolled cigarettes and kept his cigarette papers and tobacco and a folder of matches in a pouch on the same table where he ate his food. In his ashtray were paper matches he had split with his thumbnail so he could get two lights out of one match.

Albert and I drank coffee and condensed milk with the new man, then Albert went out to the barn to check on his horses. Through the window I could see lightning tremble on the sides of the hills, burning away the shadows from the brush and trees. The cabin windows were dotted with water, the interior snug and warm, still smelling of the venison the new man had cooked for his supper. In the corner was a twenty-two Remington pump, the bluing worn away, the stock badly nicked. He followed my eyes to the rifle.

"I bought that off a guy in a hobo jungle for ten dollars," he said.

"Where you from, podna?" I asked.

"Anyplace between my mother's womb and where I'm at now," he replied.

"What were you down for?" I said.

"Who says I was down for anything?"

"I do," I replied, my eyes on his.

"It was a bad beef. But everybody in there has got the same complaint. So I don't talk about it."

"Albert is a friend of mine," I said.

He was sitting right across the plank table from me. He picked up his coffee cup and drank from it, his hand fitted around the entirety of the cup. "I already told Mr. Hollister I ain't necessarily proud of certain periods in my life. I had the impression he accepted my word and didn't hold a man's past against him."

"Is that your guitar?"

He rubbed the calluses on his palms together, his eyes empty. He stared out the window into the darkness as though he had found no good words to use. "There ain't nobody else living here. So I guess that makes it mine."

"It was just a question."

"I've had a lifetime supply of questions like that. They always come from the same people."

"Which people is that?" I asked.

"The ones who want authority and power over others. The kind that ain't got no lives of their own. The kind that cain't leave other folks alone."

"That's hard to argue with," I said. "But here's the problem, J.D. When a guy is still splitting matches, he hasn't been out long. When a guy is on the drift from another state, he either went out max time or he jumped his parole. If he went out max time, he's probably a hard case or a guy who was in for a violent crime. If he's wanted on a parole violation, that's another matter, one that's not too cool, either."

"I got news for you, mister. I ain't a criminal. And I ain't interested in nobody's jailhouse wisdom, either."

"Tell Albert I'm out in the truck. Thanks for the coffee," I said.

"You got a problem with me working here, tell Mr. Hollister. I was looking for a job when I found this one," he said.

There was a mean glint in his eye that probably did not serve his cause well. But I couldn't fault him for it. It's easy to come down on a man who doesn't have two nickels in his pocket. Actually, I had to give J. D. Gribble credit. He hadn't let me push him around. In truth, the crime of most men like him is that they were born in the wrong century. The Wellstones of the world are another matter. Maybe it was time to take a closer look at them and not scapegoat a drifter who was willing to risk his job in order to retain his dignity.

IT WAS STILL raining Friday evening when I drove to a revival on the Flathead Indian Reservation, up in the Jocko Valley, a few miles from Missoula. The light was yellow and oily under the big tent, the surrounding countryside a dark green from the rains, clouds of steam rising from the Jocko River and the unmowed fields, the Mission Mountains looming ancient and cold against a sky where the sun did not set but died inside the clouds.

I didn't know what I'd expected to find. The congregants were both Indian and white working people, most of them poor and uneducated. Their form of religion, at least as I saw it in practice there, was of a kind that probably goes back to the earliest log churches in prerevolutionary America. South Louisiana is filled with it. In the last twenty-five years, it has spread like a quiet fire seeping through the grass in a forest full of birdsong. It offers power and magic for the disenfranchised. It also assures true believers that they will survive an apocalyptical holocaust. It assures anti-Semites that Israel will be destroyed and that the Jews who aren't wiped off the planet will convert to Christianity. More simply, it offers succor and refuge to people who are both frightened by the world and angry at the unfair hand it has dealt them.

I sat on a folding chair at the back of the tent, a patina of wood chips under my shoes, ground fog now puffing out of the darkness. The minister wore a beard that was barbered into lines that ran to the corners of his mouth and around his chin. His navy blue suit looked tailored, snug on his hips and narrow shoulders; his silver vest glittered like a riverboat gambler's. His enunciation was booming, the accent faintly southern without properly being such, the words sometimes unctuous and empathetic, sometimes barbed and accusatory, like the flick of a small whip on a sensitive part of the soul. The congregants hung on every word as though he were speaking to each of them individually.

There was no overt political message, but the allusions to abortion and homosexual marriage threaded their way in and out of his narration. A woman with pitted cheeks and black hair cut in bangs was sitting on the edge of her chair next to me. She wore jeans with cactus flowers sewn on the flared bottoms and a black-and-red cowboy shirt with white piping below the shoulders and around the pockets. Her chin was lifted as though she were trying to see over the heads of the people in front of her. I offered to change chairs with her.

"That's all right, I was looking for my friend," she said. "*There* he is. I thought he had run off on me."

She smiled when she spoke, her eyes lingering on the opposite side of the tent, where a tall man wearing a nylon vest and a coned-up white straw hat and a pocket watch with a fob strung across his stomach was watching the crowd. I saw the tall man bend over and show what appeared to be a photograph to a couple of people sitting at the end of a row. A moment later, he showed the photograph to others. One of the ushers had taken notice of him and was staring intently at the tall man's back. The usher happened to be Jamie Sue Wellstone's driver, the man who seemed to have no other name than Quince.

Take a chance, I thought. "Is your friend a cop?" I asked the woman next to me.

"Why you want to know?" she said.

"He was showing a photograph to some people. That's what cops do sometimes, don't they?"

"Troyce looks like a cop. But he's not. How long do these things last?"

"Depends on how broke the preacher is."

She gave me a second look. Then she looked at me again. I could almost hear the wheels turning in her head. "You just happen to be passing by and decide to get out of the rain?"

"A guy has got to do something for kicks."

"That line is from a movie."

"Is that a fact?" I said.

"Yeah, *Rebel Without a Cause*. These kids who hate each other are about to drive stolen cars to the edge of a cliff to see who'll jump out first. But James Dean and this guy named Buzz become friends, and so it doesn't make any sense for them to try and kill each other anymore. So James Dean says something like 'Why are we doing this?' Buzz says, 'You got to do something for kicks, man.' "

While she told her story, her eyes were fixed steadily on mine. They were brown with a tinge of red in them, or maybe that was the distortion of the light under the tent. But she was pretty in an un-usual way, innocent in the way that people at the very bottom of our society can be innocent when they have nothing more to lose and hence are not driven by ambition and the guile that often attends it.

"But you are," she said.

"I'm what?"

"What you said."

"I'm a cop?"

"I can always tell. But you look like a nice guy just the same." She turned her attention back to the stage. "That's Jamie Sue Wellstone? If my boobs would stand up like that, I wouldn't be singing in a backwoods shithole under a piece of canvas in a rainstorm. I had mine tattooed, you know, chains of flowers, that kind of crap? They never recovered. They just flounce around now. What a drag."

The people in front of us turned and stared as though the crew from a spaceship had just entered the tent.

"What's your name?" I asked.

"Candace Sweeney. When I was a roller-derby skater, I got called Candy. But my name is Candace. What's yours?"

"Dave Robicheaux."

"A cop, right?"

"There're worse things."

"See, I can always tell," she said.

Jamie Sue Wellstone began to sing "Amazing Grace." Her rendition of it was probably the most beautiful I had ever heard. I believe its author, John Newton, would have wept along with the congregants in that unlikely setting of a rain-darkened tent in western Montana, far from an eighteenth-century slave ship midstream in the Atlantic Passage. I believe even the wretched souls in Newton's cargo hold would have forgiven Newton his sins against them if they had known how their suffering would translate into the song Jamie Sue was singing. Or at least that was the emotion that she seemed able to create in her listeners.

The crowd loved her. Their love was not necessarily spiritual, either. To deny her erotic appeal would be foolish. Her evening gown looked like pink sherbet running down her body. Her hands and pale arms seemed small in contrast to the big Martin guitar that hung from her neck; it somehow made her diminutive figure and the loveliness of her voice even more mysterious and admirable. In an act of collective faith, the congregants both elevated her and reclaimed her as one of their own. Her wealth was not only irrelevant; that she had turned her back on it to join with her own people in prayer made her even more deserving of their esteem. Her songs were of droughts, dust storms, mine blowouts, skies peppered with locusts, shut-down sawmills, and crowning forest fires whose heat could vacuum the oxygen from a person's lungs. How could she know these things unless she or her family had lived through them?

When the congregants saw Jesus' broken body on the cross, they saw their own suffering rather than his. When they said he died for them, they meant it literally. In choosing to die as he did, rejected and excoriated by the world, he deliberately left behind an emblematic story of *their* ordeal as well as his.

When the audience looked up at the sequins glittering on Jamie Sue's pink gown, when they saw the beauty of her face in the stage lights and heard the quiver in her voice, they experienced a rush of gratitude and affirmation and love that was akin to the love they felt for the founder of their faith. Idolatry was the word for it. But to them it was little different from the canonization of saints.

Their tragedy lay in the fact that most of them were good people who possessed far greater virtue and courage than those who manipulated and controlled their lives.

At intermission, the ushers poked broomsticks up into the canvas to dump the pooled rainwater over the sides of the tent. The air was damp and cold, the Mission Mountains strung with clouds. In the distance I could see a waterfall frozen inside a long crevasse that disappeared into timber atop a dark cliff. The people around us were eating sandwiches they had brought from home, and drinking coffee from thermos jugs. I told Candace Sweeney I was surprised no basket had been passed.

"They don't ask money from folks here. If you don't like it here, go somewhere else," said a man in strap overalls sitting behind us.

Candace turned in her chair. "Why don't you learn some manners, you old fart?" she said.

But I wasn't listening to the exchange between Candace and the belligerent farmer. Instead, a big Indian girl sitting next to him had captured my attention. She wore a purple-and-gold football jersey embossed with a silver grizzly bear. She realized I was staring at her.

"I was admiring your cross," I said.

"This?" she said, clutching the small cross with her fingers. It was made of dark wood and hung from her neck on a leather cord.

"Yes, do you know where I could get one?"

"I don't know which store they come from. I got mine at Campus Ministries."

"Pardon?"

"At the Campus Ministries summer training session. Everybody in Sister Jamie's campus outreach program gets one."

"Did you know Seymour Bell?"

"Who?" she said.

I repeated the name, my eyes on hers.

"I don't know who he is," she said.

"His girlfriend was Cindy Kershaw."

"Those kids who were killed? I read about them in the paper. But I didn't know them."

"I think Seymour wore a cross just like yours. I'm almost sure of it."

I could see the confusion and nervousness in her face. "I don't know what you're saying. Sister Jamie gave me this cross. I think you can buy them at that religious store in Missoula."

"Why are you bothering my granddaughter? Who the hell are you?" said the man in overalls.

"Nobody is talking to you," Candace Sweeney said to him.

It was not the way I wanted to conduct an interview. "Thanks for the information," I said to the Indian girl.

But it was about to get worse. Candace Sweeney's friend, who had been showing a photograph to congregants on the opposite side of the tent, reoccupied his chair, then leaned forward so he could see past Candace and look at me. A lateral indentation, a concave wound of some kind, ran from below his right eye to the corner of his mouth, and the muscles didn't work right when he tried to smile. He still seemed oblivious to the fact that his every movement was being watched by the man named Quince. "How you doing?" he asked.

"Pretty good," I said.

"You a fan of Ms. Wellstone, too?"

"I've heard a couple of her songs. I always thought she was pretty good."

I could see the edge of the photograph sticking out of his shirt pocket, and what appeared to be gauze and white tape at the top of his chest. He slipped a toothpick in his mouth and seemed to take my measure. His hands were broad, his fingers splayed on his knees, the backs of his forearms covered with fine, reddish-blond hair. Upon first glance, he seemed likable, his eyes crinkling at the corners, his trim physique and neat appearance suggestive of a confident man who had no agenda and didn't need to prove himself to others. "You from down south?" he asked.

"How'd you know?"

"I'm from West Texas, myself. I'm looking for a guy. Haven't had any luck, though."

"Who's the guy?"

He put his fingers on the edge of the photo in his pocket as though preparing to show it to me.

"You picked the right fellow, Troyce. Dave's a cop," Candace Sweeney said.

"You vacationing in Montana?" Troyce said, his eyes flat, the way people's eyes go when they have no intention of allowing you inside their thoughts.

"Fishing, mostly," I replied.

I waited for him to hand me the photo. But his fingers didn't move from his shirt pocket. Instead, he straightened the flap on the pocket and buttoned it. "I'm helping settle an estate down in Texas. I've got some money for this guy, but I don't think he's here'bouts. The money comes from a church trust the guy's family was involved with. That's why I was hanging around here. Big waste of time. I think the guy got drunk and fell off a freight-car spine outside Billings. Candace, I think we need to get us a chicken-fried steak and some Indian bread up at the café. What did you say your name was again?"

"It's Dave Robicheaux."

"It's good meeting you, Mr. Robicheaux."

We shook hands. His handshake was neither firm nor soft but neutral, just like his expression and his eyes.

Candace Sweeney was staring over her friend's shoulder at the aisle. "Troyce, there's a guy burning holes in your back."

"Unshaved dude, greasy black hair, blue shirt buttoned at the throat without a tie?" he said without turning around.

"You got it," she said. "He walked past me a while ago. He's got a serious gapo problem, like it's ironed into his clothes."

"What's gapo?" Troyce said.

"Gorilla armpit odor," she replied.

"Good night, Mr. Robicheaux," he said.

"Good night," I replied.

But they didn't get far. Just outside the apron of light that fringed the tent, I saw Jamie Sue Wellstone's driver buttonhole them. I walked up behind the three of them. Quince, the driver, was planted like a stump, his arms pumped, his hands opening and closing at his sides. "Don't lie to me, boy," he said. "I saw you pestering people as soon as you come in."

"Boy?" Troyce said, smiling easily.

"You answer my question."

"I didn't hear you ask one."

"You calling me a liar?"

"No sir, I wouldn't do that."

"Then state your goddamn business."

"I work for a faith-based foundation in El Paso. I was trying to find a man who's inherited a lot of money. But I ain't had no luck in that."

"The man on that photo you were showing around?"

"Could be."

"Let's see it."

"I don't know if that's a good idea."

"It is if you want your evening to go on in a reg'lar way."

Troyce looked into the darkness, his forehead undisturbed by wrinkles or thought. He removed the toothpick from his mouth and looked at Candace rather than Quince. "I guess it cain't hurt," he said. He unbuttoned his shirt pocket and slipped the photo from it. The image on it had been cropped with scissors, snipped clean of the jailhouse location and numbers under it. "Seen that fellow around?"

Quince studied the photograph for a long time. Even in the shadows, I could see his scalp flex. "No," he said.

Troyce smiled again, his eyes tolerant, faintly amused. "Sure about that?"

"I said it, didn't I?"

"Yes, you did. You've been a good little fellow. If I get the chance to talk to your mistress up yonder on the stage, I'll tell her that myself."

Candace Sweeney and Troyce walked into the mist and ground

fog, the vast silhouettes of the Mission Mountains stretched across the sky behind them.

Quince turned around, noticing me for the first time. "What are you looking at?" he asked.

"Not a whole lot," I replied.

I walked to the end of the tent area and up the dirt road that ran by the Indian powwow grounds. A moment later, an SUV with Candace Sweeney behind the wheel and her friend Troyce in the passenger seat went past me, the taillights braking where the dirt road intersected with the state highway. I wrote down the plate number, then drove home in an electric storm that lit the Bitterroot River and the cottonwoods like pistol flares floating down from a forgotten war.

CHAPTER
10

CANDACE SWEENEY HAD never understood abstract concepts connected with death, geographical permanence, or what people called "planning for the future." She associated those particular concerns with people who either lived in a different world from the one she knew about or who deluded themselves about the nature of reality. The kind of people who spent their time at garage sales, window-shopping at the mall, or watching the Business Channel. Like they were going to take any of that crap with them.

The future didn't exist, right? So what was the point of trying to control what hasn't happened? The same applied with relationships. People came and went in your life, just like people entered turnstiles and exited them on the other side. In and out, right? Why place your trust in anyone who was just passing through?

She didn't remember her mother. Her father was nicknamed Smilin' Jack. He claimed the mother had died of ovarian cancer up in British Columbia, where he had worked as a gypo logger and sometimes on commercial fishing boats. But others said Candace's mother was a morphine addict and a prostitute who ran a brothel in Valdez. When Candace was thirteen, Smilin' Jack left her with a cousin in Seattle and went into the Cascades to pan gold. He was never seen again. He didn't abandon her. He wasn't profligate or mean or selfish. He had simply walked off in the rain, just like he was entering a turnstile, and had been absorbed by the great green-gray mass of mountains east of Seattle.

Now it was early Thursday morning in a budget motel not far from the Blackfoot River, downwind from a sawmill that smelled like the Pacific Northwest where Candace had grown up. The lights were on in a truck stop across the road, and log trucks were parked outside the café area, their diesel engines hammering. The rain had quit, and Candace knew it was going to be a good day. Or did she just *want* it to be a good day? The latter thought was disturbing to Candace, because wanting or needing anything, particularly when it had to be granted by other human beings, was an invitation to dependency and trouble.

She had made a cup of instant coffee from the hot water in the bathroom tap, and she drank it in her pajamas by the window and watched Troyce sleep. She didn't understand Troyce. He was not like any man she had ever known. He opened doors for her, waited for her to order first in a restaurant, and didn't use profanity in her presence. He seemed to genuinely like being with her and gave her money for whatever she wanted to buy without her even asking. But their first night together in a motel, she had clicked off the television set with the remote and turned off the overhead bed lamp and pulled the blanket up to her chin, waiting in the darkness for his hand to touch her. When he fell fast asleep, his back to her, she attributed his behavior to the fatigue that the injuries in his chest caused him.

In the morning she had felt his hardness against her hip, his breath touching her cheek like a feather. Then he'd opened his eyes and smiled at her like a man who wasn't quite sure where he was. He'd gone into the bathroom and brushed his teeth and shaved and combed his hair. When he came out, drying his neck with a towel, his cheeks ruddy, he was completely dressed. He asked her what she wanted for breakfast.

She did not question him about his past, less out of fear of what he was than fear that he would lie to her. If he lied to her, she would know that in reality he was like other men, that he did not respect her and his attitude toward her had been dishonest and manipulative from the beginning. Her realization that she had stepped over a line and had made herself vulnerable to a man she hardly knew—except that he reminded Candace of her father—filled her with trepidation and anxiety and a growing sense of distrust about herself.

She had taken care of herself since she was thirteen. She didn't need any more lessons in the school of hard knocks.

But now she found herself residing in a canyon wet with dew, across from a truck stop whose neon signs smoked in the cold, wondering if all her experience on the ragged edges of America had adequately prepared her for the relationship she had entered with a six-feet-five man by the name of Troyce Nix.

He pushed himself up in bed, his face flinching with the pain his wounds caused him. He had never been specific about the origin of his injuries. He had said simply, "A fellow tried to do me in. He dadburned near pulled it off." He never denied he had been a cop of some kind. By the same token, he didn't indicate he *had* been one, either. From the way he talked, she believed he had been in the army, maybe even to Iraq, and had encountered some kind of trouble there, maybe even in an army stockade. He always read the articles about the war first when he opened the newspaper. But wherever he had been or whatever he had done, he was a man's man, and other men knew it. When she was with him, other men didn't let their eyes wander as they would have if she had been alone. He seemed to find no fault in her, never criticized, and always laughed at her jokes and her irreverence. He had become the man who had always lived on the edge of her dreams, one who had chased float gold in the Cascades, believing rocks washing down from snowmelt could make him and his daughter rich.

In short, she had fallen in love with a man who didn't touch her under the sheets in the darkness. Ironically, he had become the elusive figure who had been absorbed on the other side of the turnstile.

She sat down on the mattress and picked up Troyce's hand in hers. She made circles with her fingers on the round outlines of his knuckles and brushed back the hair on his forearm. "I feel like I'm not being the friend I should be," she said.

"You're real special. You just don't know it," he said.

"Somebody hurt you, Troyce. Last night you didn't want to tell that fellow Mr. Robicheaux why you were looking for the man in the photo. I didn't talk to him about you, but because you don't tell me what's going on, I could have opened my mouth and said the wrong thing."

"Well, you didn't, and that's all that matters."

"Don't you like me?"

"Sure, I do. Any man would. You're heck on wheels, little darlin'."

"Is it something about the way I look? My tattoos or the pits in my face?"

He lifted his hand from hers and touched his fingers on her cheek and around her mouth and eyes and behind her ears. The top of her pajamas was unbuttoned, and she saw his eyes drift to the tattoos of flowers on her breasts. His fingers grazed her nipples, his lips parting slightly. "I'm cut up too bad inside," he said. "That fellow broke the shank off in me. I like to bled to death."

But she'd seen the lie in his eyes before he even spoke it.

"It's all right. You've been good to me, Troyce. I'm not complaining," she said.

"A woman like you is the kind every man wants. You're loyal, and you're not afraid. Background or schooling don't have anything to do with what a man likes. You'll give a man your whole person and stick with him to the graveyard. I know men better than you do. Believe me when I say that."

She searched his eyes, her heart twisting inside her, a terrible truth suggesting itself right beyond the edge of his words.

"Don't cry. I wouldn't do anything to make you cry, little darlin'," he said.

THAT SAME THURSDAY morning Molly and I drove into Missoula and had breakfast, then went to the courthouse, where I told Joe Bim Higgins of my conversation with the Indian girl who had been wearing a cross similar to the one Seymour Bell had probably worn around his neck the night he was murdered.

"The Indian gal is some kind of campus minister with this revival group?" he said.

"That's what she says. But she didn't seem to know Seymour Bell or Cindy Kershaw."

"You think Bell was mixed up with Jamie Sue Wellstone somehow? Like a junior minister with her group?"

"Could be."

"I think we have a random killer on our hands. I don't particularly care for rich outside folks buying up the state, but I don't make the Wellstones for killers."

"You were at Heartbreak Ridge, Sheriff?"

"What about it?"

"Places like that have a way of altering our views on our fellow man."

"I saw things I don't talk about, if that's what you mean. But I don't believe in the notion that everybody is a potential killer," he said.

I didn't pursue it. I told him about my encounter with Candace Sweeney and her friend named Troyce who had gotten the attention of Jamie Sue's driver because he had been showing a photograph to members of the audience. "I got the guy's tag number. I'd like to run it," I said.

"Who do you think he is?"

"Not who he pretends to be," I replied.

"Come back in an hour." He paused. The glare through his office window silhouetted his face, and I could not read his expression. "Mr. Robicheaux?"

"Call me Dave."

"Your friend Purcel is on a short tether."

"Clete's a good man, Sheriff."

"So is my son-in-law. I just put him in jail for carrying a firearm into Stockman's bar."

Molly and I walked to a religious store two blocks from the courthouse. It was a fine morning, the sunshine bright on the mountains that ringed the town, the wind smelling of the river, the streetlamps hung with baskets of flowers, the main thoroughfare filled with bicyclists on a run to Flathead Lake. I kept thinking about the sheriff's words. He had said the deaths of the two college kids and the California tourists at the rest stop were probably random killings. I thought he was sincere, but I also believed his attitude was facile. In a sense, most killings are random. The causality of violence of any kind is more complex than we think, a homicidal act in particular. The latter is usually the conclusion of a long sequence of events and involves players who will never be brought to task for the actual crime. Rocky Graziano made a career out of bashing in his father's face in prizefight rings while the crowds cheered. I knew a Navy SEAL who cut the throat of a sleeping Vietcong political operative and painted the dead man's face yellow so his wife could find him that way in the morning. He told me it was his fervent wish that his own wife could wake by her lover in a similar fashion.

The term "serial killer" is equally specious. I've known racists who I suspected participated in lynchings years ago. After the civil rights era passed and a general amnesia regarding their crimes set in, they found ways to position themselves in other situations where they could injure and even kill defenseless people. The irony is, after they ensconced themselves inside the system, their deeds were often considered laudable.

My point is that when people use the term "random" or "serial" in referring to a type of homicide, they are leaving out the element that is central to pathological behavior. The motivation is not financial. It's not even about power. The attack on the victim is almost always characterized by a level of ferocity that is out of proportion to any apparent cause. Its origins reside in the id and are sexual and perverse in nature. The perpetrator's appetites are insatiable, and his desire to do more injury increases as he releases his self-loathing and fury on his victim. That's why family newspapers don't include details about the physical damage done to the victims of sociopathic predators, and that's why defense attorneys try to suppress morgue photos, and that's why a lot of cops drink too much.

Molly walked with her arm in mine. "I think you're on the right track. I think Sheriff Higgins is not."

"Why's that?" I asked.

"Let's see what we learn at the store," she said.

The bell rang on the door when we went inside the religious store. The owner was a very elderly woman, her back bent with bone loss, her eyes diffident over the top of her glasses. When I asked her about a wood cross attached to a leather cord, she removed a box filled with them from under the counter. "They're made in India," she said. "They're three dollars apiece." She waited, as though I were there to make a purchase.

I showed her the deputy sheriff's badge Joe Bim Higgins had issued me and told her I was conducting a homicide investigation. She tilted her head up when she comprehended the gravity of the subject; the angle caused her eyes to magnify behind the lenses.

"Do you receive any large orders for these crosses?" I asked.

"Once in a while. Not often. A young people's group has used them," she replied.

"Which one would that be?"

"Just a moment. I'll look." She went into the back of her store and returned carrying a shoe box packed with sales slips. It took her a long time to find the purchase order. "Here it is," she said. "It was a phone-in order."

"From the Swan Valley?" I said.

"No, in Spokane. A Baptist church there runs a summer Bible camp. The children are given these as rewards for learning their Bible lessons."

"Do you know the Wellstone family?" I asked.

"I know a Blackstone family. They used to live here in Missoula. Mr. Blackstone worked for the Forest Service. Is that who you mean? Since the timber industry has gone down, a lot of old customers have moved away. Mr. Blackstone was such a nice gentleman."

I tried to hide my exasperation. I showed her the class yearbook photographs of Cindy Kershaw and Seymour Bell that Joe Bim Higgins had given me. "You remember either one of these kids?"

"I remember that one." She pointed at the photo of Seymour Bell.

"How about the girl?" I asked.

She stared out the front window of the shop. There was a line of parking meters along the curb, and she seemed to be re-creating a scene that had taken place there. "The boy came inside. I'm not sure about the girl, though. A girl who looked like this one was with him. She was waiting for him by a big black car. She was mad about something. I remember thinking it was a shame a girl that pretty and young should have such a scowl on her face. I thought maybe it was the brightness of the day and the light hurt her eyes. But that wasn't it. She was angry about something."

"The boy came in by himself and bought the cross?" I said.

"No, a man was with him. I didn't care for him. He had an odor."

"An odor?"

"Like he'd been working outside and should have taken a shower. Or maybe he had been riding too long in a hot car, I don't know. His clothes were pressed and clean, but he hadn't showered. They had words outside."

"Who did?"

"The girl and the man. She walked off, and the boy went after her. I think the man followed them in the car and they all went off together. I'm not sure."

"Did the driver have a beard?"

"I don't remember. He wore a blue suit and a white shirt without a tie. It was too hot a day to wear a navy blue suit. I think he even had a vest on."

"What kind of car was he driving?"

"I didn't pay attention. I think it was a dark color."

I thanked her and left my business card on the counter, and Molly and I walked back toward the courthouse. I couldn't sort out the information the owner of the religious store had given me. In truth, I had wanted her to tell me Jamie Sue Wellstone or her husband or brother-in-law had either come into the store or phone-ordered the crosses. I had grown to dislike the Wellstones for many reasons, maybe because they were rich and powerful and arrogant, maybe in part because Jamie Sue had dragged my friend Clete Purcel into her life. Regardless, I didn't like them, and I wanted to bring them down. I doubted there was any tie between the Baptist Bible camp in Spokane and the cross Seymour Bell had worn. The big question was the identity of the driver who had accompanied Seymour into the store. Was it Quince? He didn't seem like the kind of man Cindy Kershaw and Seymour would be attracted to.

"Maybe Seymour Bell's purchase of the cross didn't have anything to do with the Wellstones and their religious crusade," I said.

"It did," Molly said.

"Why?"

"People don't buy a wood cross on a leather cord for ornamental reasons. The cross is important to the person who wears it because it was earned. It's not a piece of jewelry. It's a badge of merit."

I stopped in the middle of the sidewalk and stared at her. "Wait here a minute," I said.

The bell above the door rang again when I reentered the religious store. "Who paid for the cross, ma'am?" I asked.

She thought about it. "The man," she said. "His wallet was on a chain, the kind that loops around into the back pocket, even though he was wearing a suit. He counted out three one-dollar bills and made me give him a receipt."

"Do you keep copies of your receipts?"

"Not for walk-in purchases like that. I tore it off the cash register and handed it to him."

"You'll call me if he comes back, won't you?"

"I'm not sure I will. When something like this happens, I think the devil is involved in it. I think it's a mistake to believe otherwise. I think it's a mistake to put your hand in it."

This was the best source of information I had found so far regarding the origins of Seymour Bell's wood cross.

When Molly and I got back to the courthouse, the sheriff told me the SUV I had asked him to run was registered in the name of Troyce Nix, a supervisory employee at a contract penitentiary in West Texas. Joe Bim said I could call a deputy sheriff by the name of Jeff Rawlings if I wanted more information. "You think this fellow is worth all this trouble?" he asked.

"Probably not," I said.

He gave me the use of a spare office, and I called an extension at a sheriff's department in a rural county east of the Van Horn

Mountains. Jeff Rawlings explained that he had been one of four investigative sheriff's deputies who had interviewed Troyce Nix at his bedside in an El Paso hospital. At first Rawlings was taciturn and noncommittal, and I had the feeling he did not want to revisit his experience with Nix. "Has he got hisself in some kind of trouble up there?" he asked.

"I met him at a revival while I was investigating a double ho-micide. He seemed to be looking for somebody. I'd like to find out who."

"Why don't you ask him?"

"I had the sense he doesn't easily share information."

"Nix is on paid medical leave from a contract prison. He's also a major stockholder in the prison. So he might be on leave a long time. He has a hunting camp not far from the prison. He had a con-vict under his supervision at the camp when he said a tramp come out of the bedroom closet with a shank and cut him up. According to Nix, the convict was digging postholes when it happened. Nix says the tramp must have come in from the highway and was rob-bing the house when Nix and the convict drove up. The tramp hid in the closet, and when Nix opened the door, the tramp sliced him up. The convict took off with the truck, and Nix called 911 on his cell. That's the story."

"You're not convinced that's the way it went down?"

"There was blood all over the bedroom. He was lying in a ball on the floor when the paramedics got there. But there was also blood behind the house. He says he went outside and tried to get the con-vict to help him, but the convict had took off."

"What's Nix's background?"

"I was afraid you'd get to that."

I waited, but he didn't speak. "He's an ex-felon?" I said.

"Nix worked as an MP at Abu Ghraib. It got him kicked out of the army. So he got into jailing on a privatized basis. I hope he's up there enjoying y'all's alpine vistas. I hope he ain't up there for other purposes."

"Like what?"

"No comment."

"Was the convict under his supervision ever caught?"

"Not to my knowledge."

"You think he's the guy who cut up Nix?"

"There's no motivation. The boy was half-trusty and probably gonna make parole at his next hearing. Every write-up Nix put in his jacket was positive. For me, the convict as suspect don't add up. But nothing about Nix does. If you figure it out, give me another call."

"What's the background on the convict?"

"He was down for grand auto, but the way I understand it, his real crime was stopping a pimp from beating up a chippie in a parking lot. The pimp happened to be the nephew of the meanest bucket of goat piss to ever sit on the Texas bench. I wrote up my report on all this and shut the drawer on it. I don't think Nix belongs in law enforcement. I don't think the kid belonged in a contract jail. But I don't get to make the rules. Anything else?"

"What's the escaped convict's name?"

"Jimmy Dale Greenwood. Some of the other cons called him Jimmy Git-It-and-Go 'cause he was a guitar-picking man."

JAMIE SUE WELLSTONE and her husband kept separate bedrooms, not at her request but at his. Leslie Wellstone was an insomniac and wandered the corridors and downstairs rooms of his enormous house in slippers and robe for hours on end, sometimes reading under a lamp, sometimes fixing warm milk that he didn't drink. Perhaps his life of sleeplessness was due to his war injuries. Perhaps it had other causes. Whatever the cause, he never discussed it. Leslie Wellstone never complained and never discussed personal matters of any kind.

He was undemanding in his attitude toward Jamie Sue. She could buy anything she wanted and go anywhere she wanted. The best care possible was available for her child. Her driver, Quince, would probably lay down his life for her. A wave of her hand, the tinkle of a bell, a touch of her finger on the house speaker system could summon any type of domestic or security personnel she wanted. There were implicit understandings about her and her husband's sexual congress and the number of times a month they entered into it, but it was never he who initiated it. She left her bed and came to his of her own accord, usually in the dark, just before sunrise, when she woke hot and disturbed and filled with longing from a dream she would never tell him about. She didn't hold back when she made love with Leslie, but she did it with her eyes closed, thinking of the man in the dream, thinking perhaps just momentarily of the terrible trade-off that had made her despise herself and wonder if her soul was forfeit.

Then she would lie beside him, her naked body damp under the sheets, his hand in hers, and try to convince herself there was redemption in charity and that maybe even in committing sin, she had brought a degree of happiness into a blighted man's life.

It was in moments like these that she saw into another corner of Leslie's soul. She wondered if, inside his veneer of gentlemanly manners and self-deprecating humor, he had found ways to mock and injure her. Worse, she wondered if his cynical statements were made with forethought and in contempt of her poor education and background. In the predawn hours of the morning after the revival on the res, she had gone into Leslie's bedroom and undressed and gotten in bed beside him. After they had completed their particular form of lovemaking, he had disentangled himself from her and lay quietly in the gloom, staring at the ceiling, his breath as audible as wind whistling in a dry pipe.

"Is everything all right, Leslie?" she asked.

"I was curious about your rotund friend."

"Who?"

"Purcel is the name, isn't it? I bet he's a ton of fun to bounce around with."

She started to speak, but he turned on his side and touched his finger to her lips. "I have a question about the way you keep your eyes shut even though the room is dark."

"Leslie, don't."

"Tell me, when you're going at it, really outdoing yourself, do you secretly feel you're on top of a giant crustacean?" he said.

Then she knew that the man lying next to her believed in and respected absolutely nothing, and, if confronted with his nihilism, would probably ask her why it had taken her so long to figure that out.

AT NOON SHE had Quince drive her and her son to the café on Swan Lake. She carried her son on her shoulder and got a high chair from the waitress and set the little boy inside it, then ordered a grilled cheese sandwich for him and a buffalo burger for herself. After Quince ordered, Jamie Sue called the waitress back and asked her to bring a gin gimlet from the saloon next door. "Would you like something from the bar, sir?" the waitress said to Quince.

"Just the food I ordered. Water is good," he replied, tapping his nail on the water glass that was already full.

After the waitress was gone, Jamie Sue said, "You can have a beer if you like."

"Thank you just the same, Miss Jamie."

"I've never seen you drink."

"I'm hired to drive y'all. That means with a clear head. You know that alcohol stays in the bloodstream for three weeks?"

"No, I didn't know that. But you're a loyal employee, Quince."

"That's a fine compliment coming from you, Miss Jamie."

She let the personal nature of his remark pass and looked out onto the lake. She could see the wind cutting long V's in the surface, and Swan Peak rising into the clouds, blue-black against the sky, as sharply delineated as the edges of a broken razor blade. Her gimlet glass was frosted with cold when the waitress brought it, and she drank it empty in three swallows, the gin sliding down inside her like an icicle starting to melt. The food had not been placed in the serving window that separated the kitchen from the counter area, and she called the waitress back and ordered another gimlet.

"Miss Jamie, I heard about you in Miss'sippi, long before I went to work for the Wellstones. I listened to your music on a station up in Tennessee. The jukebox up at the café had a couple of your songs on it," Quince said. "People played them all the time. People said you were as good as Martina McBride."

"Yes?" she said.

"Liquor always messed me up. I'd have these blackouts and wake up with spiders crawling all over the room. I'd have memories that didn't make any sense. That's what I was trying to say. A lady like you don't need to—"

"You shouldn't worry about me, Quince. We're all doing fine here. Has Mr. Leslie said something about me? Are you troubled in some way?"

His face blanched. "No ma'am, I mean he didn't say anything to *me*. I ain't a bedpost, though. I hear things. I'm supposed to look out for you."

Quince kept talking, trying to undo his ineptitude, but she heard nothing else of what he said, as though his lips were moving beyond a piece of soundproof glass. The waitress brought her the gimlet, then came back with their plates. Jamie Sue cut the little boy's grilled cheese sandwich into small strips that he began eating with his fingers, smiling with a mouthful of toasted bread and yellow cheese. She let her own food grow cold on the plate and drank from her gimlet and looked out on the lake and thought about a scene many years ago in a little town in Texas at the bottom of the old Chisholm Trail.

It was a historical place in ways that nobody cared about. The most dangerous gunman in the West, John Wesley Hardin, had grown up in Cuero, right down the road. Bill Dalton's gang used to hide out there after robbing trains and banks. The biggest herds of cattle ever assembled were put together there and trailed across the Red River, through Indian territory, all the way to the railhead at Wichita. The Sutton-Taylor feud, probably the worst outbreak of violence in the postbellum South, began with the rope-dragging and murder of a cowboy on her grandfather's ranch.

In reality, she did not care about these things. When she thought about the town where she had grown up, she thought in terms of images and faces rather than events, of kind words spoken to her, of a time when she believed the world was an orderly and safe place where she was loved and one day would be rewarded because she was born pretty in a way that very few little girls were pretty.

Her father, an oil-field roustabout who was barely five feet five, had left one lung at Bougainville and had fixed the other one up with two packs of Camels a day. But he and his wife, a woman born without sight, had opened up a hamburger joint and for five years had made a living out of it and a truck patch they irrigated with water they hand-carried in buckets from a dammed-up creek. Each noon during the summer months, except Sunday, when they attended an Assembly of God church, Jamie Sue's mother fixed her grilled cheese sandwiches in the café kitchen and let her eat them with the customers at the counter. Every day she drank a Triple X or a Hires root beer with her sandwich, and was the darling of the cowboys and pipeliners and long-haul drivers who frequented the café. Then her father took his last trip to the cancer ward at the U.S. Navy hospital in Houston and died while smoking a cigarette in the bathroom.

The hamburger joint became a video store, and Jamie Sue and her mother lived on welfare and the charity of her grandfather, who owned the remnants of a dust-blown ranch that was blanketed by grasshoppers and filled with tumbleweed and dead mesquite trees. The grandfather cooked on a woodstove and had no plumbing. If a person wanted to bathe, he did it in the horse tank. If he wanted to relieve himself, he did not go to the outhouse, or at least one that would be recognized as such. The "outhouse" consisted of a plank stretched across two pine stumps. The disposal system was a shovel propped against a scrub oak.

In revisiting her childhood, Jamie Sue did not dwell on the years she had lived at her grandfather's. Instead, she tried to remember the grilled cheese sandwiches that she ate in her parents' café, and the attention and love she saw daily in the faces of their customers.

The only problem with traveling down memory lane was that you didn't always get to chart your course or destination. In her sleep, she sometimes heard grasshoppers crawling drily over one another on a rusted window screen, matting their bodies into the wire mesh, blotting out the stars and shutting down the airflow. She saw herself pulling wood ticks off her skin and sometimes out of her scalp, where they had embedded their heads and grown fat on her blood. The admiring patrons of the café were gone, and the only men who took a personal interest in her were the occasional caseworkers from the welfare agency who, while checking off items on a clipboard, asked her if she bathed regularly and whether she had seen worms in her stool.

"I'm going to the restroom. Would you watch Dale for me, please?" she said to Quince.

"Yes ma'am, I'll make sure he chomps it all down. He needs to drink all his milk to be strong, too. Don't you, little fella? You all right, Miss Jamie?"

"Of course I am, Quince. What a silly question," she replied.

When she went into the restroom, she felt the floor tilt sideways. Was it the gin on an empty stomach, or was she coming down with something? No, the gin was not the problem. She felt worse when she didn't drink it. So how could the problem be connected to her alcohol intake or the time of day when she drank it? If Leslie had not spoken so cynically to her, she wouldn't have needed the drink. She didn't crave alcohol, she was not addicted to it. It served to anesthetize her temporarily, but what else was she supposed to do? Excoriate herself because her husband talked to her like she was white trash and stupid on top of it?

Years ago another dancer at the topless club where she used to work started attending A.A. meetings for reasons Jamie Sue didn't understand. As far as she knew, her friend did a few lines now and then and, on her day off, might drink a few daiquiris on a rich man's boat, but she wasn't a lush or a junkie. When Jamie Sue told the friend that, seeking to reassure her, the friend replied that the chief symptoms of alcoholism were guilt about the past and anxiety about the future, that the booze and the coke and the weed were only symptoms.

Those words never quite went away.

After Jamie Sue washed and dried her face and put on fresh makeup, she went to the bar and sat on a stool, waiting for her head to stop spinning. The daytime bartender walked over to her and leaned on his arms. "Want another gimlet, Ms. Wellstone?"

"Can you make an Irish coffee?"

"We don't get a lot of calls for that one. But let's see what I can come up with," Harold replied.

He poured coffee into a tall glass from a carafe on the back bar, then added a brimming shot of Jack Daniel's and covered the top with whipped cream he sprayed from a can. He inserted a spoon in the glass and wrapped the glass with a napkin and set it on the bar. Then he placed another napkin and a sugar cube beside the glass.

"How much is that, Harold?"

"It's on me. It's not very professionally done."

"That's very kind. I don't want you to get in trouble with your employer, though." She took a ten-dollar bill from her purse and placed it on the bar.

He gathered up the bill in his palm. "Mr. Wellstone with you today?" he asked.

"No, he's not," she replied.

He brushed at his nose with the back of his wrist and looked out at the lake. "I wonder if I can ask you a favor."

"What is it?"

"Just say no and I'll understand."

She felt her impatience growing, as though an annoying person were pulling on her sweater to get her attention. She let her eyes go flat and drank from her glass without speaking.

"I got a camera here. If I ask Betty in there to take our picture, would you mind?" he said.

"No, of course I wouldn't mind. You asked about Leslie. Did you want to talk to him about something?"

"No, not really. He seems like a nice gentleman, is all I was saying. I bet he was a brave soldier."

"You'd have to ask him."

"Ma'am?"

She felt the mixture of caffeine and bourbon and gin take hold in her nervous system, and not in a good way. Her stomach was sour, and pinpoints of moisture broke on her temples. The bartender called the waitress, then posed stiffly by Jamie Sue's side, not touching her, while the waitress took their picture. "Thank you, Ms. Wellstone," he said.

"You're welcome," she said, sitting back down. "Take this away, will you, and give me another gimlet, one as cold as those others were."

"If that's what you want."

Of course that's what I want, you idiot, or I wouldn't have ordered it, she caught herself thinking.

"Sorry?" he said.

"You seem like a man of the world. Would you ever indicate to a woman she was your hired slut?"

The bartender's mouth opened.

"The question isn't meant to startle or to offend. Would you say something like that to a woman, *any* woman? Do you know any man who would?"

"No, Ms. Wellstone, I wouldn't do that. I don't associate with men who talk like that, either."

"I didn't think so. That's why I asked. The gangster in the photograph with his girlfriend? Why would they come to Swan Lake? Didn't they live in Beverly Hills? Why would anyone come here in the winter and build a snowman on the edge of a frozen lake? Didn't she commit suicide? Didn't she take an overdose of sleeping pills in Austria and lie down in a snowbank and go to sleep and wake up dead?"

"Ms. Wellstone, you're really worrying me," the bartender said.

"There's nothing wrong with me, Harold. I wish you would not indicate there is. I wish that lake was full of gin. It looks like gin when the sun goes behind the mountains and the light fades, doesn't it?"

"I guess you could say that."

"Would you like to call up my husband and talk with him? Were you in a war, Harold? My father was. A Japanese soldier stuck a bayonet in his chest and destroyed his lung. My father pulled out the bayonet and killed the Japanese soldier with it. My husband wasn't interested in the story."

Harold finished making the gimlet but didn't place it on the bar. He picked up a bar rag and wiped his hands with it, clearly caught between his desire to please and his fear that he was about to pour gasoline on a flame.

She propped her elbows on the bar and pressed her fingertips against her temples. "I'm sorry, I'm not feeling well," she said. "Please excuse my behavior."

"Everybody has those kinds of days. This morning a guy was tail-gating me. When we got to the red light, I walked back to his truck and—" Harold stopped, his attention riveted on the doorway that led into the café.

"What is it?" Jamie Sue said. Then she heard her little boy, Dale, screaming his head off.

Quince had just walked through the bead curtain, carrying Dale in his arms, the beads trailing off Dale's head. "I'm sorry, Miss Jamie. I got up from the table to get him some ice cream and he fell out of the high chair."

She got off the bar stool, the blood draining from her head into her stomach. She lifted Dale from Quince's arms and held him against her breast. He had stopped crying, but he was hiccuping un-controllably, and his cheeks were slick with tears. Quince got a chair for her, and they sat down at one of the tables by the small dance floor. "Miss Jamie, I don't talk out of school, but I know what's going on. It's that guy from New Orleans, Clete Purcel, isn't it? He's been nothing but trouble since we caught him trespassing on the ranch. He put Lyle in the hospital and went out of his way to cause disruption in y'all's home life. I'm not a blind man. I got my feelings. Excuse me for being direct."

She had her hands full with Dale, and she couldn't concentrate on what Quince was saying. The saloon was empty except for her and her little boy and Quince and the bartender, and every sound seemed to resonate off the polished wood surfaces and echo against the ceiling.

"Lyle just got out of the hospital last night. The cops aren't gonna do anything about it, either. I heard your brother-in-law talking to the sheriff. The sheriff must have said something about 'fair fight,' because Mr. Wellstone really got mad and said, 'Why don't you people grow up? This isn't a Wild West movie.' "

"Did he hit his head?" Jamie Sue asked.

"Who? You mean Dale? No ma'am. I mean I don't know. He did a flip right over the eating board and crashed on the floor. His little face just bashed right into it. I bet it damn near rattled his brains loose. The waitress come running around the counter and spilled a tray all over a guy's suit."

Jamie Sue thought she was going to be sick. "Bring the car around," she said.

"I was fixing to do that."

"Then go do it."

"Ma'am?"

"Shut up and go do it. But just shut up."

When Quince got to his feet, his belt buckle and flat-plated stomach and starched work shirt were so close to her face, she could smell his odor. For just a moment she saw a look in his eyes that went way back into her early life in the South—the kind of feral anger you normally associate with abused animals that have been pushed into a corner with a stick. Except the form of resentment she saw in Quince's face was far more dangerous than its manifestation in animals. It was hardwired into an entire class of poor-white southern males, like genetic clap they passed down from one generation to the next. They had perhaps the lowest self-esteem of any group of human beings in the Western Hemisphere and blamed Jews, Yankees, women, and black people for their problems, anyone besides themselves. They stoked their anger incrementally every morning of their lives; they fed on violence and exuded it through their pores. The mean-spirited glint in their eyes always seemed to be in search of a trigger—a word, a gesture, an allusion—that would allow them to vent their rage on an innocent individual. Blacks feared them. Their fellow whites avoided them. But no reasonable person deliberately incited them.

"Did you hear me, Quince? I've got more than I can handle right now," Jamie Sue said. "Where's my cell phone?"

"On the table."

"Don't just stand there. Go get it and bring it to me. Then get the car. You can bring the cell phone and bring the car around without my saying anything else, can't you?"

"I'll do just that. Yes ma'am, I'll get cracking on that son of a bitch right now," Quince said.

Moments later, Jamie Sue emerged from the saloon with Dale in her arms. His diaper was wet. Blinded by the brilliance of the sunshine, he looked about him as though seeing the world he lived in for the first time. Quince had backed up the Mercedes and was coming hard toward the entrance of the saloon, gravel pinging under the fenders. Jamie Sue held Dale tightly against her chest and turned her back, shielding her son from the dust Quince had scoured out of the parking lot. She could feel Dale's little heart beating against her own, his frightened mouth wet on her cheek.

As the dust drifted in an acrid-smelling cloud over both of them, she knew why the gangster's girlfriend in the photograph had come to Swan Lake in the wintertime. It was because of the cold. The cold numbed all feeling. It drove other people from the cottages and the saloon and the café and the highways. It sculpted the birch trees into bone and flanged the lake with ice and made the countryside white and sterile and pure. It left the girl in the photo free, because now she had nothing else to lose, and there were no comparisons in her ken to remind her of how much she had lost.

CHAPTER 11

I WENT EARLY FRIDAY morning with Clete to the health club on the Bitterroot highway, south of Missoula, and watched him work out on the heavy bag. He wore a purple-and-gold Mike the Tiger sweatshirt, the sleeves sawed off at the armpits, and a pair of shiny red rayon boxing trunks that hung to his knees. He was smacking the gloves hard into the bag, up on the balls of his feet, his weight forward, throwing his shoulders into it, vibrating the bag on its chain, *whap, whap, whap*. I could smell beer in his sweat.

I stood up from the chair I was sitting on and steadied the bag. I could feel the power of his blows thudding through the bag's thickness into my hands. He reminded me in his style of Two-Ton Tony Galento. He swung his left and his right with equal murderous effect, full-out, in sweeping roundhouse hooks, his face deadpan, his brow furrowed. And like Galento in either the ring or a broken-glass back-alley brawl, Clete was as indifferent to his own pain as a bull is when it advances toward a matador.

He had been in a funk for days, and I didn't know what it would take to get him out of it. He said his liver ached, and his blood pressure was probably through the roof. I thought if I stayed with him, got him into the steam room and a shower and a change of clothes, he could start the day fresh and clean and free of the boilermakers that daily fouled his blood. We could drive downtown to a working-man's café and enjoy a breakfast of steak and eggs and spuds, like we used to do when the two of us walked a beat in the French Quarter. It would be a modest start, but at least it would be a start. As the writer Jim Harrison once said, we love the earth but we don't get to stay. So why not have a decent sunrise or two while we're hanging around?

But I knew my chances were remote. I also knew the thoughts that were going on behind that furrowed brow. "That Wellstone woman isn't worth it, Cletus."

"Who said she was? What does it take to get you off my case, Streak?"

How do you tell your best friend that his problem is not the women in his life but himself? Maybe it had not been Jamie Sue Wellstone's intention, but she had driven the barb deep, twisted it, and broken it off inside Clete's elephantine hulk. In fact, she had done what is perhaps the worst thing one human being can do to another. She had made Clete feel that he had been used and used badly, led into a tryst and discarded like yesterday's bubble gum. Even worse, she had left him with uncertainty about her motivation. She had fixed it so he couldn't simply close the door on what had happened and mark off the whole episode as bad judgment, the kind of mistake that men over forty line up to commit again and again. Instead, he would repeatedly sort through each sordid detail with tweezers, wondering if he was being too severe in his judgment of her or if he wasn't simply an over-the-hill fool.

"Stop looking at me like that," he said.

"Like what?"

He smacked the bag hard, flinging sweat out of his hair. "Like it's me who's always got that problem. Like it's me who doesn't see the world as it is."

"I never said that."

He threw a left into the bag, then hit it with a right hook that was so hard the blow pushed me back, even though my feet were set and I was holding the bag with both hands.

"You didn't make Heckle and Jeckle over there?" he said.

At the other end of the building, two men in their thirties were shooting baskets, concentrating on their game, their backs to us.

"No, I didn't make them for anything except two guys playing with a basketball," I replied.

"How many guys have haircuts like that and look like jocks on crystal meth?"

"The FBI has other things to do besides follow guys like us around."

"Watch this," Clete said, cupping his hands by his mouth. "Hey, ladies, I got to grab a shower, then Dave and I are going to motor downtown for some eats. Join us if you like."

The two men stopped their game and looked at us blankly. I felt my face shrink with embarrassment.

"We'll see you at Stockman's," Clete shouted. "They make pork-and-beef sandwiches that'll rev up your dorks for a week."

"I'll see you out front," I said.

"Nobody believed Hemingway when he said the feds were bird-dogging him. After he blew his head off, somebody got hold of his FBI file and found over two hundred pages of surveillance on him. You're always quoting Hemingway. You think Hemingway was just blowing gas?"

"Why should the feds have this huge interest in you? Why don't you try a little humility for a change?"

"Maybe they're looking at me for Sally Dee's death. Maybe they're humps for the Wellstone family. How do I know what they're after? I camped on the Wellstone ranch by mistake and got in the Wellstones' crosshairs. Why should they care about a PI with a jacket like mine? I don't think it's about oil and methane, either. What's crazy is I think we're probably looking right at it, but we don't see it."

"See what?"

"I don't know. It's not just money. These cocksuckers moved past that a long time ago. They can punch wells all over the planet and send the bill to the taxpayers. Look at those two guys bouncing the ball off the rim. You don't think they have Quantico written all over them?"

I didn't want to hear any more of his obsession. I drank coffee in the lobby, then went outside and sat in his Caddy and waited some more. The two men who had been shooting baskets emerged from the health club, still wearing their sweats, looking back over their shoulders. They walked to the far end of the parking lot and got in a four-door black car with a fresh wax job and drove off. They got as far as a half-block from the club when one of them picked up a handheld and put it to his ear.

Clete and I drove to Stockman's and ate at the counter. Outside, the street was still cool and covered with shadow. The black four-door sedan was parked halfway down the block. The crew-cut, unshowered jocks from the health club were sitting in the front seat. I had a hard time concentrating on my food.

Clete followed my line of vision to the sedan. "Feel like voyeurs are looking through your bathroom window?"

"Order me a glass of milk," I said.

"Where you going?" he said.

I went out the door and down the street. I tapped on the passenger window of the sedan. The man rolled down the window. Neither he nor the driver spoke.

"Mind if I get in and have a word with you?" I said.

The driver hit the lock release on the back doors. Both men remained silent. I sat down inside and closed the door behind me. The car's interior smelled new and clean. I pulled out the badge holder Joe Bim Higgins had given me and opened it. "We're on the same side, right?" I said.

The driver peeled off the foil on a yogurt cup and began eating it with a tiny plastic spoon. The scalps of both men were shiny inside their crew cuts, the backs of their necks and heads somehow reminiscent of shoe spoons. "Why don't you guys share information, maybe cooperate a little bit with the locals?" I said.

No response.

"It sends a bad signal," I said. "We always get the sense we're the dildos and you guys are the serious dicks. Not cool, right?"

"Know what he's talking about?" the passenger asked the driver.

"Search me," the driver said.

"That's clever, coming from two guys who got made five minutes into their surveillance," I said.

"I'm a rep for a feminine hygiene spray. He's with Orkin Pest Control," the driver said, spooning yogurt into his mouth, glancing at me in the rearview mirror. "Who'd you say you worked for?"

"Here's what it is," I said. "The death of those two college kids is somehow hooked in to the Wellstones. Your guys are firing into the well when you spend time chasing Purcel around. The Wellstones are the target, not Purcel and not me. The murder of the two kids and perhaps the tourists on the interstate is the issue. Those aren't hard concepts to work with. If you want to follow us around, be our guests. Just try not to be so obvious. It's embarrassing to watch."

I got out of the car and closed the door behind me. The passenger rolled down his window again. "Your friend has a dirty jacket, and so do you, Mr. Robicheaux. Neither one of you has the right to lecture anybody. Your fat friend may have deliberately caused a plane crash that resulted in a mass murder. You think the two of you can come up here and fish and simply say 'fuck you' to the United States government?"

I leaned down to the window, right in his face. "Clete and I were fighting for this country about the same time your mother's diaphragm slipped. Stay away from us, you arrogant pissant."

I went back into Stockman's and started eating, my face hot and bright in the bar mirror, my food now as tasteless as cardboard.

"You lose your Kool-Aid out there?" Clete said.

"I wouldn't necessarily call it that."

He clasped his big hand on the back of my neck, his face suffused with a grin. "You're an awful liar, Streak."

"We need to do something about this crap."

"We take it to them with tongs, big mon."

"You're my kind of situational philosopher, Cletus," I replied.

"Give us fresh coffee and another plate of spuds and a bowl of gravy on the side, will you?" Clete said to the bartender.

REVEREND SONNY CLICK wasn't hard to find. He was listed in the Missoula phone directory in the Yellow Pages under the heading "Church" and the subheading "Charismatic Churches." His particular church was called the Wings of the Dove. Where was its location? Nowhere. He operated out of a farmhouse east of Rock Creek, and his church consisted of a sleek red twin-engine plane that he kept in a tin shed in a meadow bordered by the Clark Fork River on one side and a rock-sheer mountain on the other.

"You're sure this is the same guy who was at the revival on the res?" Clete said, getting out of the Caddy.

"Wait till you see him."

"What's different about this guy?"

"It's not what's different, it's what's the same. Every one of these guys looks like an actor playing a charlatan. I've never understood how anyone can look at their faces on a television screen and send them money."

"Check out the audience on the wrestling channel," Clete said, not really listening. "Is that the guy?"

A man had emerged from the front door of the farmhouse, his features dark with shadow under the porch roof. As soon as he reached the sunlight, he was wearing a smile that had not been there seconds earlier. His stylized beard made me think of lines of black ants running from under his earlobes, down his lower jawbone, and up to the corners of his mouth. He wore no coat but had on a white dress shirt and a silver tie tucked inside a sequined vest. There were rings on his fingers and two fine chains, one gold and one silver, looped around his neck.

When we introduced ourselves, his handshake was square and firm, his eyes direct and respectful, as though he was eager to help out with a criminal investigation. Everything about him reeked of disingenuousness and manipulation.

"You've been with Wellstone Ministries for quite a while, have you?" I said.

"Actually, I don't work for them. I work *with* them on occasion. There are several ministries I help out with. This afternoon I'll be in East Oregon and tomorrow up in the high country in Nevada. Tuesday I'm back here, and Wednesday I'll be in Winnemucca again. That little plane has carried the Word to many a remote community." He pulled back his shirt cuff to check the time on his watch.

"I need to be in the air pretty soon. What's this case you're working on again?"

Reverend Sonny Click wasn't very good at dealing with cops. Like all people who are afraid or who have something to hide, he continued to provide extraneous information we didn't ask of him, filling the air with words, controlling the conversation so others couldn't talk. In the meantime, Clete said nothing, his eyes roving over the farmhouse and the yard and the unwatered plants in the window boxes and flower beds.

"Can you take a look at the pictures of these two kids?" I said.

Click cupped the photographs of Cindy Kershaw and Seymour Bell in his palm and studied them. Studied, not glanced at or simply looked at. He studied them long enough to give himself time to think about his next statement and time enough to make me believe he was doing everything in his power to help us.

"No sir, I can't say that I've seen them," he replied. "They could have sat in my congregation at one time or another, but I don't remember them."

He tried to return the photos to me, but I didn't take them. Instead, I continued to look into his face without speaking.

"Wish I had more information for you, but it doesn't look like I do," he said.

"You're sure about that?" I said.

"Nobody can be absolutely sure about anything, except faith in the Lord. But in this case, I'm pretty sure I haven't seen these people."

I removed the photos from his hand and placed them in my shirt pocket. The wind was blowing through the canyon, stiffening an air sock at the end of the mowed runway. Clete had not spoken. He stuck a cigarette in his mouth but did not light it. His gaze was fixed on the front doorway of the farmhouse. "That your daughter?" he said.

"No, she's an assistant. In our campus ministry program," Click said.

"We'd like to talk with her," I said.

"She's a mite shy. She's had an unfortunate life. Her father was a drug addict and died in prison, and her mother became a street person in San Francisco. I created a little job for her helping out with my paperwork and such. She takes care of the yard and the plants while I'm gone, too. She's a good kid, and I hate to see her drug into something like this."

"Where'd she get that little wood cross around her neck?" Clete asked.

There was a beat like wheels stopping for an instant behind Sonny Click's eyes. "A number of youth ministers wear them on the UM campus," he said.

"Ask her to come over here, sir," I said.

"Fay, these gentlemen are here about that tragedy at the university. I've told them everything we know, but they thought maybe you—"

"At this point you need to be quiet, Mr. Click," I said.

"You don't need to take that tone. It's 'Reverend,' too, if you don't mind," he said. "Look, this other man here didn't show me his identification."

Clete took out his gold PI badge, which, like most of them, was bigger, more baroque, and more visually impressive than any state or county or federal law enforcement ID. "Have you ever visited Louisiana?" Clete said. "We've got the most famous faith healer in the country right there in Baton Rouge. Know what I can't ever figure? Instead of curing people onstage, why doesn't this guy go to emergency wards and hospitals and sanitariums where people are really in need of help? You know, rip the oxygen masks off their faces and tell them to get up and boogie? Walk over to my car with me, will you? My cigarette lighter must have fallen out on the seat."

In the meantime, I walked to the porch, into the shade, where the girl was watching us. She wore cutoff blue jeans and a plain T-shirt and Indian moccasins with soles, the kind sold to tourists in reservation stores. She was heavyset and plain and big-breasted, with no expression at all, wearing a cross and leather cord that was exactly like the one Seymour Bell had probably worn the night of his death. She said her name was Fay Travis, and she lived in a dormitory on the university campus.

I showed her the photos of Bell and Cindy Kershaw. Then one

of those strange and unexpected moments occurred, the kind that makes you feel every human being carries a secret well of sorrow whose existence he or she daily denies in order to remain functional. When she lifted her eyes to mine, I felt, rightly or wrongly, that I could see right into her soul. "You knew them?" I said.

Her eyes looked in Click's direction. "I saw them around the campus. Maybe in the Student Union sometimes."

"Did you see them other places?" I asked.

"You mean on campus?"

"No, I don't mean that at all. I think you know what I mean."

"What are you saying to me?" she asked.

"Don't be afraid of this man."

"I'm not. He's good to me."

"Don't look at him, look at me. Reverend Sonny Click is a fraud and a bum. I think you're a good person, Miss Travis. Don't let this man use you. Were Cindy Kershaw and Seymour Bell here at the reverend's house?"

I saw her swallow. I stepped into her line of vision so that she was facing me and not Sonny Click.

"At the end of the spring semester, the campus ministers met a few times for coffee at the Student Union. Brother Click was there as a guest. But I don't remember Seymour or Cindy coming out to the house."

"But he knew them?"

"Yes sir. He talked with them. He's real good with young people."

"Where did you get the wood cross?" I asked.

"From Brother Click."

"Did he tell you not to talk about Seymour and Cindy?"

"He just said we should pray for them."

I bet he did, I thought.

I removed one of my Iberia Parish Sheriff's Department business cards from my wallet and made an X through the printed information on it, then wrote my cell number and Albert Hollister's home number on the back.

"You call me if you have any other information about Seymour and Cindy," I said. "My wife and I will do whatever we can to help you. Do you understand what I'm saying? You get away from this guy, Miss Travis. He's a predator, pure and simple. He'll continue to hurt you as long as you allow him to."

"Why are you saying that? He hasn't hurt me."

In her eyes I could see the lights of shame and denial and self-resentment, and I tried to remember Saint Augustine's admonition that we should never use the truth to injure. "What I've told you is in confidence. Reverend Click didn't hear us. You don't have to be afraid—not of me, not of him, not of anyone."

She turned her face to the wind, pretending to brush at something that had caught in her eye.

"What are you majoring in?" I asked.

"Pre-veterinary, but I might have to drop out. My student loan didn't come through."

I wanted to wish her well and pat her on the arm, but I didn't want to send a signal to Click that one of his youth ministers had cooperated with the investigation at his expense. I put away my notebook and said goodbye to Fay Travis and walked back toward Click, trying to keep my emotions at bay. But how do you do that when you encounter a grown man who is probably sexually exploiting a young woman who can barely scrape together enough money to pay her college tuition?

"Before we go, Reverend, did you ever visit that religious store downtown?" I asked.

"I may have, but not recently."

"You didn't buy one of those little crosses for Seymour Bell?"

"No, I didn't."

"What kind of car do you drive?"

"A Mercury."

"What color is it?"

"Midnight blue. Why?"

"No reason. Have a good day. We'll be checking back with you later."

"I think you're wasting your time. I don't think I need to have any more conversations with you, either."

The wind changed and seemed to become colder, smelling of

animal dung and dead fish in the cottonwoods down on the river-bank. I stepped closer to Sonny Click, as though we were intimates, as though I feared my words would be smudged by the wind, their meaning lost on a man who long ago had abandoned moral nuances.

"I don't want to offend you, Reverend, but I despise men like you. You hijack Christianity and use it to manipulate trusting souls who have no other place of refuge. If I find out you're sexually abusing that young woman over there, I'm going to come back here and shove you into your own airplane propeller. It's not personal. It's just one of those situations when the shit really needs to hit the fan."

Clete lit his cigarette with his Zippo and snapped the lid shut. A bloom of white smoke rose from his mouth and broke apart in the wind. "Dave is probably exaggerating. But on the other hand, Streak gets out of control and goes apeshit sometimes. I'd err on the side of safety, Preacher. Keep your stiff one-eye on a short leash. We know you can do it."

THAT AFTERNOON, AT a shady roadside filling station and convenience store just south of Swan Peak, Candace Sweeney was gassing up the SUV while Troyce was inside buying a quart of chocolate milk and a bagful of Hershey bars, which he claimed thickened his blood and contributed to the healing of the wounds in his chest and face. Earlier that morning he had bought her a new pair of Acme cowboy boots, a snap-button western shirt that shimmered like pink champagne, and jeans stitched with roses on the pockets. It was a lovely afternoon, and she wanted to lie on the beach at one of the chain lakes that fed into the Swan Drainage, like other couples did on the cusp of summer in western Montana. Then she and Troyce could have dinner in a steak house built of logs and, later, dessert and drinks on the terrace, under a sky bursting with the constellations. It wasn't a lot to ask, was it? To have a normal relationship?

Or maybe it was. Troyce treated her with respect; his words were always tender. She seemed incapable of doing wrong in his eyes. But were his tolerance and patience and understanding a disguise for indifference? This morning she had gotten up early, brushed her teeth and gargled with mouthwash and combed her hair, then gotten back in bed with him, caressing his cheek, rubbing her hand down the length of his hip, feeling her internal organs melt when his sex hardened under her touch.

"Hi, little darlin'," he said sleepily.

"You sleep okay, baby?" she said.

"You never called me that before."

"You mind?"

"I've answered to a lot worse."

She propped herself on her elbow and looked straight into his face. "You want me to rub your back?"

"I think the world of you, Candace. I just got problems sometimes."

"Did you get hurt in the war?"

"I worked at a jail outside Baghdad. The army sent me back home 'cause of some things I did there. It wasn't a dishonorable discharge but right close to it."

"What things?"

"Giving some prisoners the worst day I possibly could."

"That doesn't sound like you."

He picked up a pack of cigarettes from the nightstand, then replaced it. "I was raised by an uncle who ran a truck-repair shop on the highway outside Del Rio. When I was about eleven years old, him and a couple of his friends come back from drinking all night in Coahuila. One of the friends took me in the bedroom and entertained me proper while my uncle and the other guy was playing cards. Then my uncle and the other guy had their turn. I can still smell them in my sleep sometimes. It's like a fog in the darkness, like stale sweat and mechanic's grease. I run away the next day, but my uncle brought me back, and the next week two different guys did it to me."

She laid her head on his shoulder and picked up his right hand in hers. "You like me?" she said.

"Sure I do."

"You trust me?"

"Ain't many like you, Candace."

"You didn't answer me."

"I trust you 'cause you don't want anything. 'Cause you accept folks for what they are."

"I want you." She took off her top and placed his hand on her breast. "You feel my heart? You feel how it beats when your hand touches my skin? It's going too fast to count the beats, isn't it?"

She could see the surprise, the puzzlement, in his face as he held his hand to her breast.

"You know what that means? It means I can never lie to you," she said.

"No, I don't believe you ever will."

"People like us are different, Troyce. It's in our hardwiring. It doesn't mean we're bad. We didn't get to vote about the kind of homes we grew up in. But here's the big joke. People taught us the homes we grew up in were normal. It's like somebody doing a double mind-fuck on you."

"What's that got to do with you and me?"

"It means I'm here whenever you want me."

He brushed a strand of hair out of her eyes. "I ever tell you you're always pretty when you wake up in the morning?"

"I got to ask you something, Troyce."

"About Baghdad?"

"Did you come out here to kill a man?"

"There's things I keep hid around a corner in my mind. When I get to them, I can make my choices and do what I need to do. It beats fretting your mind about events that ain't real yet. Would you not like me if I told you I got a long memory for people who do me harm?"

"Who hurt you so bad, Troyce?"

"A fellow who's right around the corner, just waiting for me to get to the end of the street."

Now she was in a breezy gas station shaded by pine trees, filling up the SUV, gazing at mountain peaks that looked like they belonged on a postcard. Twenty feet away was an unshaved man filling a five-gallon plastic fuel container. He was wearing a flannel shirt and laced boots and canvas work pants, obviously overdressed for the mild weather in the way that men deliberately overdress to indicate their indifference to their own discomfort. "Can I help you with something?" he said, catching her stare.

She didn't reply. She glanced through the window of the convenience store, where she could see Troyce counting out coins next to the cash register.

"Did you hear me?" the unshaved man asked.

She could feel the gas humming through the hose and handle into the SUV's tank. She heard the unshaved man drop his five-gallon fuel container onto the floor of his vehicle and slam the door. But he was still standing on the concrete slab, his eyes probing the side of her face, his hand squeezing his scrotum. Troyce came out of the store eating a candy bar. "Something wrong?" he asked.

"Check it out," she said, her eyes on Troyce's.

"What?"

"The guy from the revival."

"What about him?"

"Nothing. He's here, that's all."

"He crack wise or something?"

"I wouldn't call it that."

"What'd he say?"

"He's a jerk. Who cares?"

Troyce dropped the paper bag containing his candy bars and chocolate milk through the open window of the SUV and walked over to where the man named Quince stood by the pump. "You make some kind of remark to Miss Candace?" he said.

"She was eyeballing me, so I asked if I could help her."

"You been in the pen?"

"*What?*"

"You said she was eyeballing you. That's an expression that convicts on the hard road use."

"I got no idea what you're talking about."

"At the revival I showed you a photograph of a man I'm looking for. You said you'd never seen him. But that's not the truth, is it?"

Quince brushed at his nose and huffed air out of one nostril. Then he surprised Troyce Nix. "Maybe it's the truth, maybe not."

"How am I supposed to read that?" Troyce asked.

"What's in it for me?" Quince asked.

Troyce looked around and seemed to think about it. The breeze was blowing through the pine trees. His face looked cool and untroubled inside the shade. "I don't like talking out here. Go in the restroom and wait for me."

"You hold your negotiations in the shitter?" When Troyce didn't reply, Quince said, "I'll move my car."

Quince went inside the convenience store, looking once over his shoulder.

"Troyce, don't get in trouble. Not because of me," Candace said.

"Ain't gonna be no trouble, darlin'," he replied.

"Troyce, I don't want to lose you." She said this without emotion, as a fact, in the way women know facts that men do not, and he knew he had entered a new stage in his life. "You're a good man. You just don't know how good you are."

He looked at her for a moment, as though seeing her more clearly than he had ever seen her before. Then he winked and went inside the restroom. Quince was relieving himself in a urinal.

"You seen the man in the photograph?" Troyce asked.

"What kind of finder's fee we talking about?"

"Finder's fee?"

"Yes sir," Quince said, zipping his pants. He began touching at his face in the mirror, feeling the stubble, without washing his hands.

"How about you don't get charged with aiding and abetting a fugitive?" Troyce said.

"You aren't a cop."

"No, I'm not. But can I tell you a secret?"

Someone tried to open the door. "I got a sick man in here. You'll have to wait," Troyce said, squeezing the door shut again, shooting the bolt.

Quince stopped touching at his face and looked at the locked door.

"You know why you don't get a finder's fee?" Troyce said. "It's 'cause you're for sale. A man who's for sale suffers the sin of arrogance. What he don't understand is that nothing he's got is worth the spit on the sidewalk. You remind me of the tramps down at the blood bank. The blood you sell has disease in it, but you pass it on to other people to put wine in your stomach. You ain't no different from a whore, except your skinny ass ain't worth the time it'd take to kick it around the block . . . Where you think you're going?"

"I'm finished talking with you," Quince said.

"What'd you say to my lady friend out yonder?"

"You don't listen, do you, boy? That woman was staring at me like her shit don't stink. Your size don't bother me, either. Mess with me, I'll get you down the road. Take that to the bank, mother-fucker."

Quince tried to brush past Troyce and unbolt the door. Troyce ripped his elbow into the side of Quince's face, knocking him into the condom machine. Then Troyce hit Quince with his elbow again, this time in the temple, splaying him cross-eyed to the floor. He grabbed the back of Quince's neck and drove his face down on the toilet bowl, smashing it again and again on the rim. Blood and pieces of a dental bridge slid in rivulets down the porcelain into the water.

When Troyce straightened up, the pain that went through his chest felt like tendons were pulling loose from the bone. For a moment he was sure he was going to pass out. He forced himself to breathe slowly, his face draining in the mirror, his eyes out of focus.

Quince was on his knees, bent over the toilet, his hands cupped to his mouth, strings of blood and saliva hanging from his fingers.

Troyce pulled a half-dozen paper towels from the dispenser and wadded them up and stuck them in Quince's hand. "You dealt it, bubba. Don't come around for seconds," he said.

He slid the bolt and went outside, the racks of snack food bright and colorful under the fluorescent lighting, the glass doors on the cold boxes smoky with refrigeration, the cashier ringing up a purchase for a sunburned woman in a swimming suit, the world of normality back in place.

"Is that sick man still in there?" the cashier asked.

"He's cleaning up. He's gonna be fine," Troyce said. "Thanks for the use of your facilities."

"Anytime," the cashier said.

Troyce got in the SUV and let Candace drive. As they headed up the highway, she glanced sideways at him. "There's blood coming through your bandages," she said.

He touched her cheek with the backs of his fingers. "Want to rent a cabin at one of those lakes? Maybe have dinner at the steak house up the road this evening and dance under the stars? Like reg'lar folks, just me and you. What do you say, you little honey bunny?"

She was sure there were words that would adequately express what she felt, but she didn't know what they were.

CHAPTER
12

AFTER CLETE AND I interviewed Reverend Sonny Click, we stopped by the courthouse to see Joe Bim Higgins. I could tell Joe Bim was not happy to see Clete, but I didn't care. Clete had found the wood cross that belonged to Seymour Bell, and the wood cross had linked Bell to Wellstone Ministries. If Joe Bim didn't want to give Clete credit, that was his problem, not ours.

"You think this preacher might be involved with Bell's death?" he asked.

"Who knows? On one level or another, I suspect he's a predator," I replied.

"What do you base that on?"

"He had a coed at his house. She's poor and uneducated, and I don't think she's there to water his plants."

"Did she indicate she was being molested?"

"How many people willingly admit they're being sexually exploited, Sheriff?"

"Sounds like you didn't have the best morning."

"Click's dirty, Sheriff. He's hunting on the game reserve. In Louisiana we'd take him off at the neck," Clete said.

"I thought Click was from down south. Wonder why nobody got around to punching his ticket," Joe Bim said.

I tried to speak, but Clete had gone off cruise control, and I couldn't shut him up. "Somebody creeped Seymour Bell's house.

I think it was somebody working for the Wellstones," he said. "I think Bell had something in his possession that the Wellstones don't want anyone to see. Why not get a warrant on their ranch?"

"What you say might be true, Mr. Purcel, but there's no evidence the Wellstones are connected to a crime of any kind."

Clete stuck an unlit cigarette in his mouth. He wore a long-sleeve tropical-print shirt and cream-colored slacks, and he had not removed his porkpie hat when he entered the building. With his driving-range tan and sun-bleached hair and behemoth proportions, he looked like a misplaced Miami Beach tourist inside the spartan confines of Joe Bim's office. "Dave and I are just trying to help out," Clete said. "I think the person who killed those kids should be chain-dragged down the highway. But it's your backyard, not ours."

I wanted to punch him. I could see a thought growing behind Joe Bim's eyes, as though he were on the brink of making a decision he had postponed too long. Then he blinked and touched at the side of his mouth, and the moment passed. "I got a call from the Highway Patrol this morning," he said. "A man who works for the Wellstones got beat up in a convenience-store restroom near Swan Lake. His name is Quince Whitley. He claims he doesn't know who beat him up or why, but the witnesses say he was talking to the assailant out by the pumps before they got into it. The witnesses say the assailant was about six-four and had a Texas accent. Sound like anybody you know?"

"He sounds like Troyce Nix, the guy who was showing a photo around at Jamie Sue Wellstone's revival meeting on the res," I replied. "I saw Nix and this guy Quince get into an argument outside the tent."

Joe Bim was sitting behind his desk. He looked at a spot on the far wall. "I don't see how any of this has any bearing on those kids getting killed," he said. "To be honest, I think there's too much information in this case. Furthermore, I think people's personalities are getting too involved in some of the issues. There's times when less is more and more is less, get my meaning?" He let his gaze drift back to Clete. "You can't smoke in here."

"Sheriff, there are only one or two probable conclusions we can come to regarding the deaths of Bell and Kershaw," I said. "They were either killed at random by a psychopath who's operating in the area, or the Wellstones are involved. All the information we develop somehow leads back to the Wellstones. I don't think that's coincidental."

"You seem like a reasonable man, Mr. Robicheaux. How in God's name could a couple of kids from rural Montana be a threat to Ridley and Leslie Wellstone?"

"A heavy-hitter greaseball by the name of Didoni Giacano used to run all the vice in New Orleans," Clete said. "Frank Costello gave him the whole state as a personal gift. On his deathbed, a priest asked Didi Gee if he had forgiven all his enemies. Didi told the priest, 'I don't have any enemies, Father. I killed them all.' "

"This isn't Louisiana," Joe Bim said, the expression going out of his eyes. "I'd like to talk with Mr. Robicheaux a minute."

"Yes sir," Clete said. He had already put away his unlit cigarette and had nothing to do with his hands. So he took off his porkpie hat and fiddled with it, as though wondering how he could revise all the mistakes he had just made. He started to speak, then gave it up and left the room.

"The bad judgment is on me, not on you or Mr. Purcel," Joe Bim said. "I deputized you because I thought that was the best way to keep my old friend Albert Hollister from getting hurt. To be straight out, it hasn't worked worth a damn. I'll need your shield back. Some paperwork will be coming your way, and you'll receive some reimbursement for your expenses. It's been good knowing you."

He rose from his desk to shake hands. The scarred side of his face looked lined and creased, like old paper that had faded in the sun.

"It's the Wellstones, Sheriff. They're up to their bottom lips in pig shit, or they wouldn't have killed those kids. Don't let them blindside you," I said.

"Have a good one," he replied.

CLETE DID NOT try to apologize, nor did I want him to. Clete was Clete. You don't invite bulls into clock shops and act surprised at the results. Besides, crimes committed in the state of Montana were not our business. Perhaps it was time to accept that fact and leave other people to their own destiny.

At least that was what I told myself.

The next afternoon Clete borrowed Albert's pickup truck, in case the two FBI agents he called Heckle and Jeckle were still surveilling him. He showered and put on his sports clothes and told me he was going to listen to some music at a club down in the Bitterroots. I'm sure that was his intention. I'm sure that, like me, he was willing to go with the season and to let others do whatever it was they wished to do. But that was not the way it would work out.

IN THE NEXT drainage, J. D. Gribble was walking along the dirt road in the dusk, his twenty-two Remington pump gripped in one hand. He shielded his eyes from the late sun as Albert Hollister's truck approached him, stepping to the side of the road, pointing the rifle away from the vehicle. Then he realized Albert was not behind the wheel.

"Sorry to blow dust all over you," Clete said. "Are you the new fellow who works for Albert?"

"Yes sir."

"Have you seen him around? His wallet fell out on the seat."

"Not since this morning," Gribble said. He saw Clete taking note of the rifle in his hand. "A fox was in Mr. Hollister's brooder house. I think I hit him, but he went on up the hill."

"If you see Albert, tell him I left his wallet at the house." Clete had propped a long-neck beer between his thighs. Ten more long-necks were stuck down in a bucket of crushed ice on the passenger seat. He lifted the open bottle and drank from it. The bottle was still beaded with cold, and the late sunlight sparkled inside it. "Want one of these brews?"

"I wouldn't mind."

Clete pulled a bottle out of the ice and twisted off the cap. When he handed the bottle to Gribble, he noticed that Gribble was shaved and had on fresh clothes and that his hair had been wet-combed and had not had time to dry. He also remembered Albert saying that his new man didn't own a vehicle and walked everywhere and did not hitchhike under any circumstances, for whatever reason.

"I'm going down the road to listen to some music. Care to join me?" Clete said.

The club was thirty miles south in the Bitterroot Valley. The sun had gone behind the mountains on the west side of the valley, and the air was cool and smelled of the river and irrigated alfalfa in the fields. The sunset was one of the most extraordinary Clete had ever seen. A long stream of clouds, like curds of lavender smoke, flowed for miles and miles over the Sapphire Mountains in the east, pink-tinted on the edges, right next to an expanse of sky that was robin's-egg blue. Clete stood in front of the nightclub, his beer bottle in his hand, gazing at the vastness of the valley around him as though he had personally discovered and laid claim on it for the rest of mankind. "Do you believe this place?" he said to Gribble. "Good Lord in heaven, do you believe this place?"

Inside at the bar, Clete remained effusive, ordering double shots of Jack with a beer back, calling requests up to the bandleader, his voice louder than it should have been. He drank without sitting down, knocking back Jack and sipping from his beer, touching the foam off his lip with a folded paper napkin. His maroon shirt and beige slacks and shined oxblood loafers gave him a fresh and relaxed appearance that did not match the transformation Gribble saw taking place in him. The back of Clete's neck was oily and red. His green eyes were lit with a dangerous shine. His pumped forearms and the great breadth of his shoulders seemed to grow in size with his increased intake, like the boiler plate on a furnace expanding with its own heat.

"You can flat tank it down," Gribble said.

But Clete didn't hear him. He was talking to a blond woman who had serpentine tats on her arms and looked like she was about to burst out of her Clorox-white jeans and black Harley T-shirt. The woman seemed fascinated by Clete and the libidinal energies he radiated. But her friends at a far table were not impressed.

"Mr. Purcel, those bikers over yonder look pretty proprietary," Gribble said.

Clete responded by buying the woman a drink and raising his own in a toast to the bikers.

"I avoid trouble, sir. I hope you're the same kind of man," Gribble said.

"Drink up," Clete said, hitting him on the back. "It's Friday night. You ever hear of Sam Butera and Louie Prima? Every Friday night back in the seventies, I'd watch them blow out the walls in a joint on Bourbon Street." Clete turned toward the bikers at the far table. "Hey, you guys ever hear of Louie Prima?"

"Mr. Purcel, I'm getting a real bad feeling here," Gribble said.

"Lighten up. If those guys had anything going, they wouldn't dress in clothes somebody scrubbed out a grease trap with," Clete said. He signaled the bartender. "Give my friend here a draft with a depth charge. Give a round to the waxheads at the table while you're at it."

"You sure about that?" the bartender said.

"I look like I don't know what I'm doing, here?" Clete said.

"Three or four beers is about it for me, Mr. Purcel," Gribble said.

"Screw that," Clete replied.

The band was country-and-western. A cook was serving Mexican dinners from a pass-through window in the kitchen, and the crowd was happy and growing louder, and the dancers on the floor had reached that stage of cautionary abandon where they were bumping into tables and one another, with no sense of either ill will or danger. Clete asked the band's vocalist if she could sing "I Forgot More Than You'll Ever Know."

"That's Skeeter Davis's song," Gribble said.

"I knew a woman who could sing it just like Skeeter Davis."

"No kidding?" Gribble said, lowering his beer bottle, his expression mildly curious.

"Anyone ever tell you that you got a voice like Lefty Frizzell?"

"Not really. Where'd you know this lady at?"

"I heard her sing in a beer joint in Texas once."

Gribble looked straight ahead, his face empty, his beer bottle tilted forward in both hands, the heels of his boots hooked on the rungs of the bar stool. "There's not many can sing like Skeeter could. What was this lady's name?"

"Jamie Sue Wellstone."

Gribble wiped his mouth with a napkin, hiding his expression.

The woman in the Harley T-shirt grew tired of being ignored by Clete and rejoined her friends at the table. Clete stared at the woman's back, trying to remember why he had talked to her in the first place. He thought he could hear kettle drums beating in his head or tropical birds lifting from a jungle canopy, their wings flapping loudly against the sky.

"You ought not to keep looking at them men," Gribble said.

"You ever sleep with another man's wife?" Clete asked.

"Sir?"

"I hadn't ever done that, at least not knowingly. Ever sleep with the wife of a man who was burned up in a tank?"

"Mr. Purcel, I ain't up to this."

"Were you in the service?"

"No sir."

"See, when you watch other guys pay really hard dues, you accord them a certain kind of respect. That means you don't screw their wives or even their girlfriends, particularly when it's not an even field any longer. The guy who does that doesn't deserve to wear the uniform. He doesn't deserve to tell people he ever wore it, either."

"You slept with this woman you was talking about?"

"What difference does it make? It's yesterday's box score, right?" Clete said. "What are those guys over there looking at?"

"Her name is Jamie Sue Stapleton. Her husband might call her Wellstone, but for a lot of us she'll always be Jamie Sue Stapleton from Yoakum, Texas, 'cause that's where she comes from. Don't be talking about box scores, either, not when it comes to Jamie Sue."

Clete refocused his eyes on Gribble, as though looking at a different man from the one he had picked up on the dirt road.

"Where you going?" Clete said.

"I feel sick. I took some cold medicine today. I'm gonna lie down in the back of the truck," Gribble said. "I think I'm fixing to pass out."

Gribble went out the door, his hand pressed to his stomach. Clete ordered another round, wondering if he was the only sane person on the planet.

In the next hour, Clete lost count of the amount of booze he pumped into his system. The noise inside the club had become deafening, and the band had compensated by turning up its loudspeakers. The hands on the clock above the bar either had no motion at all or in seconds indicated that twenty minutes had passed. Clete was sweating inside his clothes, his ears filling with sounds like wind blowing across moonscape. For just a moment all sound stopped, as though the shapes and movements of people around him were one-dimensional and no more real than those of a silent cartoon on a screen.

A second later, the sound track returned with the power of someone clapping his hands on Clete's ears.

"Hey, Mac?" the bartender said.

"What?"

"You were in the Crotch?"

"Who told you I was in the Corps?"

"You asked me if I'd been at Parris Island." The bartender leaned closer. "Keep your eyes on me. Don't turn around. You hearing me, gunny?"

"Yeah," Clete said.

"Those guys at the back table must know you from some other gig."

"Yeah, they come into that joint on Highway 12 and 93."

"I heard them talking. Don't get yourself hurt."

"You telling me they want some shit?"

"No, I didn't say that at all."

"Give me another shot and a beer back."

"I tried."

"Semper Fi," Clete said, finishing the whiskey in his shot glass, sweat glistening on the tips of his hair.

He went into the restroom and came back out, looking directly at the bikers and the woman in the Harley T-shirt. They appeared to have lost interest in him. When he returned to the bar, a college boy and his girlfriend were standing on either side of his stool, trying to catch the bartender's attention. "Sorry, we didn't know you were sitting here," the boy said.

"Forget it. You guys have one on me. I think I fried my mush," Clete said, and put a five-dollar bill on the bar.

He walked outside, slightly off balance, the wind suddenly cool and fresh in his face, the stars arching across a black sky. He didn't bother to see if Gribble was still in the camper's shell; he didn't care if Gribble was there or not. He opened the driver's door to Albert's truck, pulling the keys out of his pocket, and bent over to get in. That was when he saw a shadow break across the corner of his vision.

The blow was as hard as a blow can be before a person loses consciousness. The weapon itself seemed to come out of the sky, whistling as it whipped across the back of Clete's skull. Inside a secluded place where Clete often lived, he knew he had been hit with a blackjack, one that had been manufactured in the classic design of a lead weight sewn inside an elongated sheath, mounted on a spring, balanced perfectly on a leather-woven grip that allowed the assailant to deliver a crushing, even fatal, blow with little effort.

Clete crashed across the seat and fell into a heap on the opposite side of the cab. With his blood running from his scalp into his collar, he felt himself being driven to a place and a final act that he had avoided for years—in Irish Channel street rumbles and on night trails strung with toe-poppers and booby-trapped 105 duds and in firefights with the death squads in El Salvador and up against the Mob in Reno and during Katrina when the levees collapsed and he had watched his first and only love, the Great Whore of Babylon, drown under the waves.

CHAPTER
13

For an indeterminate period Clete lay in the bottom of a dark well that was filled with memories and sensations that he thought he'd forgotten long ago. He saw himself stripping away a brick wall in an old house on Tchoupitoulas, where a corpse dancing with maggots had been entombed. He saw himself prying open the trunk of a car inside which a mobster had been locked before it was driven into Lake Pontchartrain. He felt his weight bounce tight inside a parachute harness when he was in Force Recon, the breath whooshing from his chest, his steel pot razoring down on his nose.

He wanted to get out of the dark well, away from memories that somehow were associated with confinement and suffocation and bondage. Where was he? Why wouldn't light enter his eyes when he opened them? All he could remember was the blow against the back of his head and tumbling into a great blackness that seemed to have no bottom.

When Clete actually awoke, to the degree that he knew he was still alive, he realized his eyes were wrapped with tape, his wrists locked behind a tree trunk with ligatures. He could smell pine needles on the forest floor and hear the wind blowing through the canopy. Above him, perhaps up a slope, he heard a heavy machine clanking and grinding over rocks and rough ground, then a sound like a steel bucket thudding into the earth, scraping up dirt and small boulders, unloading it all in a rasping downpour from a steel bucket.

The ground was hard under Clete's buttocks, the bark of the tree cutting into his back. He pulled against the ligatures, then tried to get to his feet, but the circumference of the trunk was such that he couldn't negotiate enough space to push himself into an upright position. His immobility was like that of a man prematurely sealed inside a coffin.

He scraped the tape back and forth against the tree bark, hoping to pull it loose from his eyes. But his abductor had wrapped it several times around Clete's head, winding it tightly into the scalp and hair and the bloody wound where Clete had been hit with the blackjack. Then it had been wound around the eye sockets and eyebrows, molding the layers so that they probably could not be removed except with scissors or a knife. Clete pushed his heels into the dirt and tried to bend the tree backward against its root system, but to no avail. Up above, the earth-grader or bulldozer or whatever it was continued to grind and clank and dump large loads of dirt in a pile, the stench of burnt diesel drifting off its smokestack.

Why was somebody excavating on the hillside? What was he digging?

A grave, Clete thought. *Or a place to bury someone alive.* He could feel sweat breaking on his forehead. "Who the hell are you?" he said.

But his words were lost in the engine's roar and the scrape of steel against dirt and rock. He tried to think. Was it the bikers from the club? Were they twisted on meth? Would they take a barroom beef this far?

It was possible. They nailed women's hands to trees. If he could work one wrist loose. If he only had a weapon. His twenty-five auto, his switchblade, even a can of Mace. Why had he messed with those guys?

But he knew the answer. Clete had spent a lifetime wading across the wrong Rubicon, provoking the skells and meltdowns, defying authority, ridiculing convention and normalcy. Women loved him for his vulnerability, and each one of them thought she was the cure for the great hole inside him that he tried to fill with food and booze and the adrenaline high that he got from dismantling his own life.

But one by one they had all abandoned him, just as his father had, and Clete had immediately gone back on the dirty boogie, once more postponing the day he would round a corner and enter a street where all the windows were painted over and there was no sign of a living person.

The operator of the heavy machine cut the engine. In the silence, Clete heard someone drop to the ground and walk toward him. The footsteps stopped, and Clete realized his abductor was standing above him, perhaps savoring the moment, perhaps positioning himself to inflict injury that Clete could not anticipate or protect himself from.

"Whatever you're going to do, just do it," Clete said. "But you'd better punch my whole ticket, because I'm going to hunt you down and—"

Before Clete could complete his sentence, the abductor crouched next to him and made a shushing noise, as though speaking to a troubled child. Clete turned toward the abductor, his scalp drawing tight, waiting for the blow or the instrument of torment to violate his body. He jerked at the ligatures on his wrists. "You motherfucker," he said.

He heard the abductor click open the top of a cigarette lighter and rotate the emery wheel with his thumb. The abductor lit a cigarette and drew in on it, the paper crisping audibly as the ash grew hotter. Clete felt the exhaled smoke separate across his nose and mouth.

"Fuck you," Clete said, his big heart thumping in his chest.

The abductor made no response and continued to blow his cigarette smoke on Clete's cheek and neck.

"Dave Robicheaux leaves hair on the walls, bub. Ole Streak is a mean motor scooter. You don't put the glide on the Bobbsey Twins from Homicide," Clete said, the words starting to break nonsensically from his mouth. "Streak dumped a guy's whole brainpan in a toilet once. That's no jive, Jack. Think of me when you eat a forty-five hollow-point."

The abductor got to his feet, dropped his cigarette into the pine needles, and ground it under the sole of his shoe.

"Who are you? Tell me who you are and why you're doing this," Clete said.

Instead of a reply, Clete heard liquid sloshing inside a container and the *pop* of a plug being pulled from an airtight spout on the container. A second later, gasoline rained down on his head, soaking his hair, burning the wound inside the tape around his eyes, drenching his shirt and skin, pooling in his lap. The abductor even pulled off Clete's shoes and soaked his feet and socks and drew the line of delivery up and down his legs.

"You sonofabitch, you cowardly piece of shit," Clete said, his voice cracking for the first time.

The abductor began to pile twigs and decayed tree branches and pinecones and handfuls of pine needles on Clete's head and torso and legs, whistling a tune, journeying back into the underbrush to gather more fuel for his enterprise. Clete struggled again against the ligatures, then tried to stretch his body forward so he could work one foot under a haunch and raise himself erect. All his efforts were futile, and he felt a sense of remorse and irrevocable loss he had not experienced since his fifteenth birthday, when he had torn the hands off a windup clock his father had given him.

He couldn't stop the tapes that kept playing themselves over and over in his head. The Big Exit should have come from a Bouncing Betty or at the hands of diminutive figures in black pajamas and conical straw hats threading their way through elephant grass that reminded him of Kansas wheat. But blood expander and a heroic navy corpsman who had dragged Clete down a hillside on a poncho liner had cheated Sir Charles out of another kill, and Clete had returned to the Big Sleazy and a battlefield of another kind.

The Mob had tried to kill him, and so had members of the NOPD. Whores had rolled him, and a sniper had put two twenty-two rounds in his back while he carried his patrol partner down a fire escape. He had skipped the country on a homicide beef and joined the leftists in El Sal, where he got to see up close and personal the handiwork of M16 rifles and death squads in Stone Age villages. But the real enemy always lived in his own chest, and like the gambler who hangs at the end of the craps table, bouncing the dice down the felt again and again, watching everything he owns raked away by the croupier's stick, Clete had finally wended his way to a dark hillside

in western Montana where he now lay powerless and defeated, waiting for a degenerate to roll the emery wheel on a cigarette lighter
and turn his body into a funeral pyre.

How do you shut down a tape like that? How do you explain to
yourself the casual manner in which you threw your life away?

LESS THAN FIFTY feet away, Albert Hollister's pickup truck was
parked in a grove of pine trees, the camper bladed with moonlight.
Inside the camper, J. D. Gribble was sleeping in a fetal position, a
blanket wrapped around his head, his dreams peopled with images
that he could not dispel or extract himself from. He heard the night
sounds of a jail—the count man clicking his baton against the bars,
somebody yelling in the max unit, a kid being wrestled down on a
bunk, a rolled towel jerked back against his mouth. But the dream
and the images in his head, brought on by the mixture of alcohol
and cold medicine, were not just about stacking time.

He saw a dark corridor with bars set in the middle, and on the
other side of the bars, a lighted world where a gold-haired woman in
a sequined blue evening dress was playing an HD-28 Martin guitar.
Her mouth was red, her expression plaintive, her dress as tight on
her body as the skin on a seal. Behind her was a backdrop of alkali
wasteland and low purple mountains that rimmed the entire horizon. She curved her palm around the guitar's neck to chord the frets
and seemed to purse her lips at Gribble as she sang.

In the dream, he walked down the corridor toward her until he
reached the bars and had to stop and rest with his hands clinging to
them. From out of the glare, a man in a linen suit approached the
woman and opened a parasol, lifting it above her head, shading her
from the sun. For the first time, Gribble noticed the woman's belly
was swollen with child. The man's face was disfigured and did not
look quite human, even though he was grinning at the corner of his
mouth. The woman wore blue contact lenses, and both she and the
disfigured man were staring oddly at Gribble, as though wondering
why he did not recognize the inevitability of his rejection.

Was it so hard for him to understand that a woman carrying

an unborn child must find ways to survive? Did he want the child aborted? Was she supposed to live on welfare while the father of her child spent his most productive years in a contract prison?

Actually, he understood those questions and would not argue with the answers they implied. The real question was one nobody had asked. Was her choice of a disfigured rich man driven by her need to survive or the need to sustain her celebrity? No one who has ever been sprinkled with stardust walks away from it easily. In fact, no one of his own volition *ever* walks away from it. Like youth, fame and adulation are not surrendered, they're taken away from you.

It was cold inside the camper shell when the man who called himself Gribble woke from his dream. He pulled the blanket from his head and sat up in the darkness. He could feel the wind blowing against the camper, and through the tinted glass in the side panel, he thought he could see pine needles sifting through the air and the shadows of the trees changing shape on the ground. Then he realized the shadows were not just those of trees.

He rubbed his hand on the glass and saw a humped figure at the base of a ponderosa with his wrists fastened behind the trunk. He saw a second figure walk out of the darkness, carrying an armload of organic debris from the undergrowth. The figure stood above the man fastened to the base of the tree trunk and poured the load of twigs and dead branches and leaves on the man's head and shoulders.

The man wore work boots and a dark suit and dark shirt. His hands and wrists were covered by rawhide gloves with cuffs that extended back over the wrists. He wore a full mask, one that was molded from thick plastic, bone-colored, hard-edged, and incised with slits to cool the skin. He seemed encased in his own darkness, his movements simian, his ritual one that he had learned and refined and fed in a private world that only his victims were allowed to witness.

Gribble could not understand how he had gotten where he was or what was going on by the pine tree. Through the back window of the camper, he could see a long wooded slope and part of a log road that zigzagged through the trees. He could see stars over the Bitterroot Valley and a creek full of white water notched deeply in earth that was soft with lichen and layers of damp pine needles. Had Mr. Purcel gotten into it with the bikers at the saloon? Had they followed the truck and forced it off the road? But there were no motorcycles here, nor any other vehicle that he could see.

The man in the mask was examining the ground as though he had lost something. He picked up a cigarette butt and put it in his pocket, then brushed his foot across the spot where the cigarette had been.

A pinecone fell from overhead and pinged on the pickup's hood. Suddenly the man in the mask was staring at the truck, his body motionless, a red gas container in his hand. Gribble froze, staring back at the man in the mask, afraid to move, afraid not to. His hand touched the barrel of the Remington pump.

What should he do? This wasn't his business. The worst trouble in his life had always come from messing in other people's business. He hadn't made the world. Why was it his job to change it? Why didn't people deal with their own damn grief? A good deed had sent him to the pen, on the hard road, spreading tar under a white sun that gave even black men heatstroke. It wasn't fair. He had just wanted to listen to music, to drink one or two beers and not think about the catastrophe he had made of his life.

Another pinecone toppled from the tree, hitting the camper's roof. The man in the mask looked upward and seemed to relax and lose curiosity about the truck, turning his attention to the figure sitting on the ground.

CLETE PURCEL TILTED up his head, listening, trying to sense the movements of the man who had covered him with debris from the woods. "Tell my why you're doing this? I know I'm not walking out of here. What's to lose?" he said.

A long time seemed to pass. Then the man got down on one knee, his breath echoing inside a hard surface of some kind. When he spoke, his voice was thick and ropy, hardly more than a whisper, like that of someone in the throes of sexual passion: "It's fun. Particularly when I do it to somebody like you."

Had Clete heard the voice before? There was no inflection or accent in it that he could detect. But all whispers sound alike, and the tonality of one has almost the same tonality as another.

The only life preserver available was time. *Make him keep talking,* Clete thought. *Keep him occupied with his own sick head. The sicker they are, the more they want to talk. Inside every sadist is a self-pitying titty baby.* "But I know you, right? Somehow I got in your space, jammed you up, maybe, not even knowing I was doing it?" Clete said.

No answer.

"I remind you of somebody," Clete said. "Maybe somebody who knocked you around when you were a kid. Ever do any reformatory time? It's a bitch in those places. You know what the Midnight Express is, right? A skinhead with Gothic-letter tats all over him holds a knife at your throat while he drives a locomotive up your ass. Is that what we're talking about here? The whole country is turning into *The Jerry Springer Show,* and the jails are worse. Someone make you pull a train when you were a kid?"

He heard the man chuckle and get to his feet. For a moment there was no sound at all, then the man kicked Clete in the ribs, waited a second, and kicked him again, harder.

"I was in 'Nam," Clete said, eating his pain. "I saw psychopaths do stuff that made me ashamed I was a human being. I always wanted to believe some of them got help when they came back. But the truth is, they probably didn't. Know why? Because nobody cares what they did. They did it to Zips, and we were in the business of killing Zips. 'How do you shoot women and children? Easy, you just don't lead them as much.' Ever hear that one? What I'm saying is, you're not as different as you think you are. You ever see a ville full of straw hooches naped? Nobody gave a shit then, they don't give a shit now. Somebody screwed you over when you were a kid. You got a legitimate beef. When I say 'screwed over,' you dig exactly what I'm talking about, right? I smoked a federal informant. That was in Louisiana. I could have ridden the bolt on that one. Instead, I've got a PI license and a permit to carry a piece."

"No cigar, fat man," the voice whispered.

The man standing above Clete was breathing deep in his chest, as though oxygenating his blood. Then he poured the rest of the gasoline on Clete's body and on the dried wood and leaves and pine needles, saving out a little to trail off of Clete's shoes so he could use it as a liquid fuse without exposing himself to the whoosh of flame that was about to burst from the base of the tree.

GRIBBLE WATCHED THE man in the mask set down his gas can and take his cigarette lighter out of his pocket again. Gribble's pulse was pounding in his ears. The man in the mask removed a piece of paper from his coat pocket, twisted it into a tight wrap, then flipped open the top of his cigarette lighter. He lit the tip of the paper and watched the flame curl along the edges toward his fingers.

Gribble grasped the stock of his Remington pump and pulled the lever on the door of the camper. He rolled onto the ground, momentarily losing sight of the man in the mask. Then he was on his feet, erect, throwing the stock to his shoulder, jacking a round into the chamber.

"Back away and put out the fire!" he shouted. "I'm holding a rifle. I'll pop you between the eyes."

The man in the mask stood stock-still. Then he seemed to make a decision, extending his arm away from his body, the twist of burning paper lighting the surfaces of his mask. He released the paper, letting it float to the ground, igniting the trail of gasoline he had poured on the leaves and pine needles.

CHAPTER
14

THE CRIME-SCENE TAPE enclosed an area not unlike a trapezoid on the hillside, the emergency vehicles from the Ravalli County Sheriff's Office lighting the trees with their flashers, firemen spraying the area outside the tape where sparks had blown into the underbrush.

J. D. Gribble sat in the back of a silver Stratus with a government tag on it while an Amerasian government agent stood outside the door, in jeans and a gunbelt and a windbreaker with the yellow letters FBI on the back, asking him one question after another.

"You didn't see where the guy in the mask went?" she said.

"No, I told you, he bagged ass while I was stomping out the fire," Gribble said.

"But you heard a vehicle of some kind?" she said.

"Yeah, but later, like it was way off down the road. It didn't have no lights. I just heard the engine, then maybe a door slamming."

"Like somebody was already in the car?"

"I don't know. I couldn't see anything, I done told you. I had to put the fire out before it got to Mr. Purcel. Then I had to get them ties off his wrists and drag him out of there before sparks set off the gasoline again. You could smell it everywhere. It was soaked into his clothes and on everything around him."

"Then you walked down the log road to the farmhouse?"

"An old man was up watching television with his grandson. He called 911. Then I come back up here to help Mr. Purcel."

"And you never saw a vehicle headed for the highway?"

"Maybe. I ain't sure. Long as that guy wasn't coming back up here, I didn't care what he did."

She put her hand on his shoulder. Because she was bent forward, her long hair hung on his cheeks and made her face look narrower, more intense. "You did a good job, Mr. Gribble. But we want to catch this guy. Every detail we learn from you can put us one step closer to this guy. Did you hear him say anything at all?"

"If he did, I didn't hear it. He had that mask on, and the wind was blowing in the trees. I pointed my rifle at him, and he dropped a piece of burning paper on the gasoline and took off. He looked back once over his shoulder. The moonlight on that mask was maybe the scariest thing I ever seen. Is that the guy killing people around here? Is that why the FBI is here? I read about the murders in the paper, those kids and that couple in the rest stop."

"Tell me again what you actually saw the man do. Don't leave anything out. Small things can turn out to be real important to us."

"I saw him throw an armload of sticks and leaves on Mr. Purcel. I saw him pour gas from that can yonder on Mr. Purcel. I saw him searching around on the ground. He picked up a cigarette butt and put it in his pocket. Then he kind of kicked at the ground with his foot."

She scratched at a place on her cheek and seemed to think about his last statement. It was cold in the trees, and a mist had started to settle on the hillside. "This next question doesn't imply any reflection upon you. But why didn't you shoot?" she said.

"I'm a ranch hand. Shooting people ain't in my job description."

"We can find you at Albert Hollister's?"

"I got no reason to go anywhere else."

"You're sure about that?" she said.

"What's that mean?" he asked.

But she walked away without replying, and J. D. Gribble wondered if he had wandered into an outdoor mental asylum.

Two Ravalli County sheriff's deputies were interviewing Clete Purcel. He was sitting on the floor of the ambulance, the back doors open, his legs hanging over the bumper. He had taken off his shoes and socks and gasoline-soaked clothes and had put on a big smock given to him by the paramedics. His bare feet looked strangely white and clean in contrast to his face and hair, both of which were streaked with soot and the cleansing cream the paramedics had used on him.

"Give us a minute?" the FBI agent said to the deputies.

After they had walked off, she stepped into the box of light created by the interior of the ambulance. "What did the guy in the mask have to say to you?" she asked.

"Not much. He said he was having fun."

"Just like that, 'having fun'?"

"I asked him why he was doing it. He said, 'It's fun.' "

"What else did he say?"

"I tried to keep him talking and turn his thoughts on himself. I thought maybe I could buy a little time. He thought that was funny. He said, 'No cigar.' "

"That's all of it?"

"He said, 'No cigar, fat man.' "

"You told the deputies he blew smoke in your face?"

"From a cigarette. I could tell by the smoke. You find a butt?"

"No. Gribble said he picked it up from the ground. The guy was evidently sanitizing the crime scene before he set you on fire."

The image her words created made Clete glance up at her face. "The FBI was still following me?"

"No, we got a call from the Ravalli County Sheriff's Office."

"What have you found so far?"

"The tie cuffs and the tape he used on your eyes. We've got his gas can, too. Maybe we can trace it back to the vendor."

"I heard machinery up the hill, steel treads and a clanking sound."

"It's a front-end loader with a claw bucket on it. He hot-wired it."

"Why was he digging on the side of the hill?"

"I think he was going to cook you and put you in a grave."

"We finished here?"

"You ought to go to the hospital."

"I need a drink. Thanks for your time."

"Thanks for my time? Your vehicle is evidence. It's going to be towed into Missoula. You're not driving anywhere."

"Then I'll walk."

She looked at the flashlights and emergency flashers burning in the mist, one hip cocked, a holstered Glock on her gunbelt. Her dark hair looked clean and full of tiny lights. "Go sit in my car with Mr. Gribble. I'll take you home in a few minutes."

"I didn't ask for a ride home. I told you I need a drink. How do I get that across?"

"We can stop at a store on the highway," she said. "I'd like to tell you something on a personal level, Mr. Purcel."

He waited for her to go on.

"You deserve better treatment than you've gotten. I think Sally Dee and his men died because of an engine failure. If the airplane crash wasn't an accident, I still say good riddance," she said. "We're going to find the guy who did this to you. But you're going to have to help us, and that means you need to take care of yourself."

"The guy knows heavy equipment. He had the burial site set up. He also knows a cigarette butt is a source for DNA. I think he's done this lots of times."

Alicia Rosecrans made no comment. Clete looked at her left hand and the absence of a ring on it.

"I'm gay," she said.

REVEREND SONNY CLICK didn't think anybody's luck could be this bad. First those two plainclothes roaches had come to his house asking questions about a double homicide, then they'd indicated he was a molester they were going to throw into his own airplane propeller. His stomach was flip-flopping for an hour. He smoked a joint down on the river to calm his nerves and rebuild his mental fortifications, then threw his suitcase in his twin-engine and fired it up. He blew out his breath, resolving to put the two plainclothes snerds out of his mind, and eased the throttle forward, gaining speed down the pale green runway that had been mowed out of a hayfield.

In seconds he would be climbing above the Clark Fork River on his way to East Oregon, where that evening he would address a rural audience that treated him like a rock star. Enough with the polyester jerk-offs and their threats.

Except his port engine began leaking oil across the wing, and the propeller locked in place and the plane spun sideways on the strip.

Now it was Monday morning, and he was still stuck in Missoula, having canceled out in East Oregon and Winnemucca, wondering if those cops would be back again, asking questions about a pair of dead kids he wished he had never seen.

An SUV came down the service road and turned onto his property, two people in it, a woman in the passenger seat and a tall man behind the steering wheel. No, "tall" wasn't the word. "Huge" was more like it.

They parked on the edge of his lawn and got out of the vehicle, glancing at the dry grass and the dead flowers in his window boxes. The woman wore a black cowboy shirt that was unsnapped to expose her cleavage and the tattoos on the tops of her breasts. Just what he needed showing up at his house when cops were sniffing around him for a possible molestation beef. But it was not the woman who bothered the Reverend Sonny Click, it was the man. He wore a short-brim Stetson slanted on his head and mirror shades and spit-polished needle-nosed boots. His posture and the fluidity of his walk and the grin at the corner of his mouth reminded Click of John Wayne.

"My name is Troyce Nix, Reverend. Candace and me caught your revival on the res. Hope you don't mind us dropping by," he said. "You got you a fine place here."

"It's all right," Sonny Click said, his voice hollow, the way it got when he felt the presence of danger. "Just passing by, are you?"

"Not really," Troyce said.

Sonny waited for the tall man to explain the contradiction in what he had just said. But he didn't. "What do you mean?" Click asked.

"Wonder if you can do us a favor."

"I'm waiting on a mechanic. My plane engine froze up." Click wondered why he was offering excuses to a person he didn't know, a man who kept his eyes hidden behind mirrors. This was *his* property. Who was this guy, and who was the woman hanging her tattooed melons in his face? "So I'd better get back to my obligations."

"The favor I need is an introduction," Nix said. "I'm sure you don't mind giving folks an introduction."

Sonny Click cut his head, a gesture he had learned from watching both Ronald Reagan and Jerry Falwell, one that indicated humility and tolerance but benevolent contention at the same time. "I'd like to help out a fellow southerner, but I'm supposed to be on a mercy mission this afternoon."

"You're from Ohio, Reverend. You went to Bible college in Indiana. I like your accent, though. You want to drive with us up to Swan Lake? I think you should."

Sonny tried to hold his eyes on Nix's face, but his mouth was becoming dry, his throat constricted. He folded his arms on his chest, clearing his throat, pretending he had an allergy, knowing that his dignity was being pulled from him like a handkerchief from his pocket. *Get the subject off me,* he thought. "This got something to do with her?" he said, nodding toward the woman with the flowery jugs.

"Miss Candace is my lady. We both want to meet Jamie Sue Wellstone. I also want to introduce Wellstone Ministries to a couple of religious foundations I'm associated with in West Texas and New Mexico."

"Then why don't you call them up?" Click replied.

Troyce Nix reached out and rested his big hand on the top of Sonny Click's left shoulder. He tightened his grip, the grin never leaving the corner of his mouth. "'Cause we like having a man of the cloth along," he said.

When Click looked at the distorted reflection in Troyce Nix's mirrored glasses, he saw the face of a frightened little man he hardly recognized.

Candace Sweeney had never been inside a grand home, particularly one that looked out upon red barns with white trim and emerald-green pastures full of bison and longhorn cattle. The deep carpets and recessed floors in some of the rooms and the French doors with gold handles and the chandeliers hanging over the entrance area and in the dining room gave her a strange sense of discomfort and awkwardness, like she was someone else, not Candace Sweeney, somehow less than what she had been before she had entered the house. The feeling reminded her of a dream she used to have in adolescence. In the dream, she would see herself walking nude into a cathedral, her body lit by the sunlight that filtered through stained-glass windows, and she would be filled with shame. Now, in this grand house that cost millions to build, she unconsciously fastened the top button on her cowboy shirt, wondering why she and Troyce were there, why Troyce had turned the screws on Sonny Click to get an introduction to people who wouldn't spit in Candace's or Troyce's mouth if they were dying of thirst.

The two brothers had come into the living room first, one horribly mutilated by fire, the other on aluminum braces, followed by Jamie Sue Wellstone. They sat and listened politely while Troyce talked about the religious foundations he was connected with, the number of churches the foundations subsidized in the Southwest, the number of congregants who wanted to support patriotic, family-oriented political candidates.

Why was he saying all this crap?

Sonny Click sat by the French doors on a straight-back antique chair, one that had a little velvet cushion tied on the seat, and didn't say a word. Even weirder was the fact that the guy who had given Candace a bad time at the filling station was driving a lawn mower across the side yard, his face bruised up as if a horse had kicked it.

When Troyce finished his spiel, a Hispanic woman in a maid's uniform served mint juleps off a silver tray. The man who walked on aluminum braces—Ridley was his name—said, "So you want to put us in touch with your friends? That's why you got Click to bring y'all out here?"

"The Reverend Click was all for it," Troyce said.

"And you did this out of the goodness of your heart?" the man with the burned face said. His name was Leslie, and his eyes had a way of lingering on Candace that made her skin crawl.

"I'm also a longtime fan of Miss Jamie Sue," Troyce said.

"We're flattered, Mr. Nix, but our friend Reverend Click over there looks seasick," Leslie said. "You didn't upset him in some way, did you? We'd be lost without his sonorous voice floating out to the multitudes."

Troyce was standing by the mantel, a relaxed grin on his face, inured to mockery and to amateurs who might try to take him over the hurdles. Above him was a signed painting by Andy Warhol. "I used to know a carnival man turned preacher who said the key to his success was understanding the people of what he called Snake's Navel, Arkansas. He said in Snake's Navel, the biggest thing going on Saturday night was the Dairy Queen. He said you could get the people there to do damn near anything—pollute their own water, work at five-dollar-an-hour jobs, drive fifty miles to a health clinic—as long as you packaged it right. That meant you gave them a light show and faith healings and blow-down-the-walls gospel music with a whole row of American flags across the stage. He said what they liked best, though—what really got them to pissing all over themselves—was to be told it was other people going to hell and not them. He said people in Snake's Navel wasn't real fond of homosexuals and Arabs and Hollywood Jews, although he didn't use them kinds of terms in his sermons."

Leslie Wellstone was wearing a red smoking jacket and slacks and Roman sandals, one leg crossed on his knee, one hand clenched on his ankle. He took a sip from his julep. The coldness of the ice and bourbon and water turned his lips a darker purple. "You seem to be a man of great social insight. But why is it I don't believe anything you're telling us?" he said. "Why is it I think you're a duplicitous man, Mr. Nix?"

Troyce's gaze drifted to Jamie Sue and remained there for a beat. "I'm a founding company officer in a corporation that builds contract prisons. Right now I'm on medical leave from my job. But that don't mean I'm necessarily off the clock," he said. "I think we've got what some call commonalities of interest."

"I think I've had all of this I can stand," Jamie Sue said. She set down her drink and walked out of the room.

La-de-da, Miss Poopah, Candace said to herself.

Ridley Wellstone lifted himself up on his braces and looked at his brother. "You clean this up," he said, and clanked down a hallway toward a study filled with shelves of books.

Now only Candace, Troyce, Sonny Click, and Leslie Wellstone remained in the room. "Sonny, would you wait outside?" Leslie said.

"Beg pardon?" Click said.

"Outside," Leslie repeated. "There's a rainbow up in the hills. See, right up there where it's green from the rain. Why don't you go into the yard and enjoy the view?"

"The man said he was hooked up with a lot of money down in Texas. What was I supposed to say? 'Wipe your horse's ass with it'?" Sonny Click said.

"You did exactly the right thing. You run along now, and don't worry about a thing."

Click got up from his chair, shame-faced, the top of his forehead shiny with hair oil. He opened the French doors and stepped onto the patio, trying to appear composed and natural.

Leslie Wellstone took a peppermint from a glass container on the coffee table and stuck it in his mouth. He did not offer one to Candace or Troyce. He cracked the mint on his molars. "Care to tell me the true nature of your errand?"

Troyce lifted one finger toward the French doors. "That fellow driving the mower across your lawn? It was me what busted up his face on the rim of a toilet bowl," he said.

"My," Leslie said.

"I done that 'cause he was disrespectful to Miss Candace. He also told me he might take me down in pieces. He don't strike me as overly religious in nature."

"What's the purpose of your visit, sir?"

Troyce removed the booking-room photo of Jimmy Dale Greenwood from his shirt pocket and handed it to Leslie Wellstone. "You know this old boy?"

"Oh, yes," Leslie said.

"He's around here somewhere, ain't he?"

"Possibly," Leslie said, returning the photo to Troyce.

"Either he is or he ain't."

"What do you plan to do with him?" Leslie asked.

Troyce kept his eyes locked on Wellstone's and didn't answer.

"You're that serious about him?" Leslie said.

"We got us a mutual interest, is the way I see it."

"I don't believe that's the case at all. What do you think, Ms. Sweeney? You seem like a nice young woman. Do you understand what Mr. Nix is suggesting?"

"No," she said.

"You don't?" he said.

"It's not my business."

His eyes roved over her face, her mouth and throat, dropping briefly to her breasts. "Well, it's been a pleasure meeting you all. Perhaps you can come back another time. We're having friends over for a late lunch."

"I was looking at your painting," she said.

"Yes?"

"It reminds me of a billboard on the highway just south of Portland. Did the guy who painted this ever do billboards?"

Leslie Wellstone looked at her for a long time. Candace did not believe she had ever seen eyes like his. They seemed to exist like a separate and disconnected entity behind the burned shell that constituted his face.

"A billboard south of Portland?" Wellstone replied. "I'll have to check that out and let you know."

"Can I use your bathroom?" she asked.

He paused, then gestured with an open palm toward the hallway.

A few minutes later, she came back out of the bathroom. Troyce was alone in the living room.

"Where is everyone?" she asked.

"I think they'd rather we let ourselves out," he said. "They'll probably count the ashtrays when we're gone."

They walked down the flagstone steps to the SUV, where Sonny Click was waiting for them. Troyce was touching at his pockets.

"You forget your *Cool Hand Luke* shades?" Candace said.

"Yep."

"Know why you're always forgetting your glasses? It's 'cause you don't need them. It's 'cause you use them to hide the real person you are."

"Stay away from them self-help books, Candace," he said.

Troyce returned to the doorway. He started to push the bell, then noticed that the lock had not clicked back into place. He eased the door open and stepped inside. Leslie Wellstone was standing by the hallway that led to the bathroom Candace had used. He was talking to the Hispanic maid.

"Spray every surface with Lysol and hand-wipe it with paper towels and clean rags," he said. "Be especially attentive to the lavatory, the handles on the faucets, the toilet bowl and the rim and the toilet seat, everything she might have touched. When you're done, put the rags and soiled paper towels and your cleaning gloves in a paper bag and burn them in the incinerator."

"Yes sir," the maid said, her eyes focusing on Troyce.

Wellstone turned around.

"I forgot my sunglasses," Troyce said, picking them up from the coffee table.

"I see. So now you have them."

Troyce slipped his shades into his shirt pocket and chewed on the corner of his lip. "You asked me what I aimed to do to Jimmy Dale Greenwood if I got hold of him," he said. "The real question here is what I should do to a cripple man what just insulted the best person who probably ever come in his house. I feel like slapping your brains out, Mr. Wellstone. But I don't think I could bring myself to touch you. It's not your disfigurement, either. It's what you are. I've knowed your kind since I was a boy. You're in a category that ain't got no name. Stay clear of us, partner. Next time around, I'll forget my Christian upbringing."

With that, he went outside and got into the SUV, Sonny Click in back, Candace behind the wheel. Troyce looked at the rainbow up in the hills, his hands relaxed between his legs, and waited for Candace to start the engine. His face contained the benign expression it always took on when he went to a private place in his mind that he didn't allow others to enter.

"Something go wrong in there?" Candace said.

"Not a thing. Let's drop off the reverend."

"Then what are we gonna do?" she asked.

"Go up to the res and buy you the prettiest Indian jewelry in West Montana," he replied. "Then have a couple of them buffalo burgers and huckleberry milk shakes."

He put his big hand on the nape of her neck and brushed the stiffness of her hair against her scalp, like he was stroking the clipped mane on a pony.

CLETE PURCEL HAD given up on sleep, at least since he had been sapped with a blackjack, wrist-cuffed to the base of a pine tree, and forced to listen to a machine scrape his grave out of a hillside. He kept his night-light on and his piece under his pillow and slept in fitful increments. The trick was not to set the bar too high. If you thought of sleep in terms of minutes rather than hours, you could always keep ahead of the game. In a tropical country years ago, Bed-Check Charlie had arched blooker rounds through the canopy at odd intervals during the night, blowing geysers of dirt and foliage into the air, ensuring that Clete's squad would be exhausted at sunrise when they resumed humping sixty-pound packs in heat and humidity that felt like damp wool wrapped on the skin. Then Clete would hear the throbbing sound of a Cobra coming in low over the canopy and a Gatling gun rattling inside the downdraft of the helicopter blades, and in the silence that followed, he would rest one meaty arm across his eyes and tell himself that Bed-Check Charlie had been put out of business, that all he had to do was sleep for the next twenty minutes and not think about tomorrow. The fact that Sir Charles was down in a spider hole waiting to set up again was irrelevant. You copped twenty minutes of Z's and trusted the angels until you woke again.

But the images from the hillside in the Bitterroot Valley were worse than those from the war. As soon as Clete dropped off to sleep, he was powerless over the man with the sloshing gas can in his hand. He could hear the man whistling a tune behind his mask, gathering sticks and leaves, raining them on Clete's head, dusting off his palms, taking an immense pleasure in the systematic deconstruction of someone's soul.

Clete sat up in bed at two A.M., his eyes wide, his throat thick with phlegm. Three deer had just walked through Albert's yard and knocked over the water sprinkler. Clete got up and removed a carton of milk from the icebox and drank it in a deep chair that looked out on the valley. He could see the outcroppings of rock and the silhouette of the trees on the hilltops, the wind bending the trees against the starlight. But the windswept loveliness of the night sky and the alpine topography were of no help to him. He put his face in his hands, and when he drew in his breath, it sounded as ragged as a fish bone in his throat.

When he woke in the morning, he was wired to the eyes, a pressure band tightening across one side of his head. The clinical term for the syndrome is "psychoneurotic anxiety." It's almost untreatable, because its causes are armor-plated and deep-seated down in the bottom of the id. The level of tension is not unlike what you feel at the exact moment you realize you have stepped on a pressure-activated antipersonnel mine. Or if you have to open the door on an abandoned refrigerator in a vacant lot five days after a child has disappeared from the neighborhood. Or if your job requires you to climb out on a fourteenth-story ledge in order to dissuade a jumper who is determined to take her infant child with her. The analogies are not exaggerated. The tension is such that at one time patients who suffered from it were lobotomized with their full consent.

But Clete already knew all these things, and he also knew, waking at nine A.M., that understanding the mechanisms of fear and buried memories did nothing to get rid of the problem. VA dope didn't help, either, or vodka and orange juice for breakfast and weed and downers for lunch. He had already mortgaged too many tomorrows to get through the present day. Eventually there would be no more tomorrows to mortgage, and the day would come when he would find himself drawing an X through the last empty square on his calendar.

What he needed to do was find the dude with the gas can and look into his face, he thought. What all predators hated most was to be made accountable. It wasn't death that they feared. Death was what they sought, onstage, with the attention of the world focused upon them. But when you took away their weapons and their instruments of bondage and torture, when you pulled the gloves off their hands and the masks off their face, every one of them was a pathetic child. They were terrified of their mother and became sycophantic around uniformed men. The fact they were reviled by other felons and that cops would not touch them without wearing polyethylene gloves was not lost on them.

But how do you get your hands on a guy who has probably been killing people for years, in several states, leaving no viable clues, threading his way in and out of normal society? How do you find a sadist who probably looks and acts just like your next-door neighbor?

Clete fried up a ham-and-egg sandwich for breakfast and ate it in his skivvies and tried to keep his mind free of memories from the hillside. Through the window he saw a four-door silver Dodge come up the dirt road and turn under the arch over Albert's driveway, an Amerasian woman behind the wheel.

SPECIAL AGENT ALICIA Rosecrans was not an easy woman to read. Clete figured she was a dutiful federal agent and inflexible on most issues of principle, but he also suspected she was a private person with her own code and one day would be in trouble because of it. For Clete, bureaucracy and mediocrity were synonymous. Alicia Rosecrans probably wouldn't hit a glass ceiling. It would get dropped on her.

She was good to look at, the way she wore her jeans loosely on her hips, her shirt hanging over her firearm. She had just had her hair cut, and the freshly clipped ends lay in a curve under her cheekbones. But it was the self-contained look of intelligence in her face that intrigued Clete most. How many female cops did you meet who were so confident that they didn't need to compete with their male colleagues? Answer: somewhere between not many and none.

Clete had put on his slacks when he saw her coming up the walk and was combing his hair in the mirror over the lavatory when she knocked on the door. He washed his face and wiped it off with a towel, buttoning his shirt at the same time, wondering at his own preoccupation with his appearance because a federal agent was knocking on his door.

As soon as she was inside, the first thing out of his mouth was an apology for the messy state of his living room and kitchenette. Why was he acting like this? He was probably thirty years older than she was and looked it, from his girth to his fire-hydrant neck and the hypertension flush in his cheeks. She sat down on the stuffed couch backed against a bank of windows and unzipped a folder on her lap. When she looked up at him, he noticed how little lipstick she used and the fact that its absence made her look even more attractive and confident.

"We've interviewed the people we thought might bear you a grudge," she said. "Because you almost beat Lyle Hobbs to death, we started with him. He says he was shopping at Costco in Missoula Saturday night. He has an AmEx receipt that shows he was there. Except Costco closes at six. So in effect, he doesn't have an alibi. You think Hobbs could be our guy?"

Her choice of language contained implications that were hard to track and tie together, and Clete could not tell if his confusion was because of his sleepless night and the booze in his system or because Alicia Rosecrans just wanted to put thumbtacks in his head. At first she had mentioned his almost killing Lyle Hobbs, as though incriminating Clete, then she had talked about "our" guy, indicating that the two of them were on the same side. He sat down at the breakfast table, three feet from her, and paused before he spoke.

"In my view, Hobbs is capable of anything," he said. "But let's straighten out something here. If I'd wanted to beat him to death, he wouldn't be walking around. Second of all, Hobbs is a child molester and should have had his wiring ripped out long ago."

"Right," she said, looking down at the papers in her lap. "We also interviewed Quince Whitley. He says he was in a motel outside Superior on Saturday night. He says he picked up a woman in a bar there, and she was in the motel with him. He says he paid cash for the room because the motel doesn't take credit cards. Unfortunately for him, he doesn't remember the woman's last name or know where she lives."

"Does he have a receipt for the room?"

"No, but the owner remembers him because of the damage some-one had done to his face."

"Yeah, this guy Troyce Nix worked him over in a convenience store or something?"

"Here's the short version. Quince Whitley rented the motel room, and maybe he even took a woman there. But there's no proof he was in the room at the time you were abducted. He has a pronounced south-ern accent. You heard the abductor's voice. Could it be Whitley's?"

"The guy who sapped me was whispering. According to Gribble, he was wearing a mask. That probably explains why I could hardly hear his words. Look, this is what I don't get. My eyes were taped, my wrists cuffed behind the trunk of a tree. Why would he need to wear a mask?"

"The perpetrator loses his own identity and takes on the self-manufactured image of a terrifying figure that can reduce his enemies to trembling bowls of pudding," she said. "Also, if he decides to take the tape off his victim's eyes, the impersonality of the abuse increases the humiliation and emotional pain of the victim. The perpetrator retains his option of ratcheting up the victim's suffering and stays high on several different levels. It's all about control."

"You learned this at Quantico?"

"In Sociology 102 at Imperial Valley College."

"I think you're looking at the wrong guys. Hobbs and Whitley are hired help. Whatever they do, they do for money. Their kind seldom if ever act on their own."

"Maybe they had permission. There must have been two guys on that hillside—one to drive Albert Hollister's truck with you in it, and one to drive the getaway car."

"I was with the perp on a very personal level. He blew his cigarette smoke on my skin. When he said he burned people for fun, he meant it."

She studied Clete's face, her eyes unblinking behind her small glasses. "Who do you think we should be looking at?"

"A guy who wants other people to suffer as bad as he has. Maybe a guy who's been burned up in a French tank. I wouldn't exclude the sheriff."

"You're serious? Joe Bim Higgins?"

"Half his face got fried with a phosphorous shell. I think I'm not one of his favorite people, either. Listen, the person who will kill you is the one who'll be at your throat before you ever know what hits you."

"You don't think much of us, do you?"

"The feds? They treat other cops like they're from Dogpatch. The problem's not mine, it's theirs. Maybe you're different. You said you're gay. You thought I was putting moves on you? Why am I the guy under the magnifying glass? That's what arrogance is. The feds always think the other guys have the problem."

"You're an unbelievable person. You have more arrests than most recidivists do. You dropped a Teamster out of a hotel window into a dry swimming pool. You actually shot and killed a federal informant and got away with it."

"I was having a bad day when those things happened."

"Maybe it's time to lose the Bozo the Clown routine. I'd like to help you. But frankly, you act like an idiot."

Clete felt himself swallow. "Was your dad a GI?"

"None of your business."

"I was in the Central Highlands. That's where I got wounded and sent home. That's the only reason I asked. I thought Vietnam was a beautiful country. I thought what happened there was a tragedy."

She crimped her lips together and looked down at her lap. "My father was a marine. He was captured by the Vietcong and held seven weeks before he escaped. He killed himself when I was twelve."

"Sorry."

"What were we talking about, Mr. Purcel?"

"I don't know. The shitbag who sapped me."

"Yes, the shitbag."

"You don't connect him with the Wellstone entourage?"

"I can't concentrate now," she said.

"Once before, you said his MO was like a guy or guys operating along the interstates."

"A rest stop coming off Wolf Creek Pass, a campground at Donner Pass. Some other places, too. Where did you say you were in Vietnam?"

"I got my second Heart in the Central Highlands. But I was in Force Recon and on the Cambodian border, too. We were picking up LURPs who'd gone into Cambodia, except nobody has ever admitted they were in Cambodia. What was your old man's name?"

"Joe Rosecrans."

"No, I don't think I knew him. You want some coffee?"

She didn't answer.

"Look, Dave says I got the finesse of a junkyard falling down a staircase," Clete said. "I didn't mean to knock your organization. I'm just not totally comfortable with guys who smell like mouthwash. You ever been around undertakers? Every one of them smells like he just gargled with Listerine."

"I have to go."

"Don't," he said.

"Why shouldn't I?"

"Because you're different."

"Mr. Purcel, you're the most inept, outrageous person I've ever met."

"It's part of my rationality deficit disorder. It's called RDD. There's a lot of it going around. I'll fix some eats for us. Then we can take a drive up to Lolo Peak. There's still snow back in the trees. We can talk about the dude who almost lit me up."

"Your rationality deficit disorder? RDD?"

"My shrink is a pioneer in the field," he said.

"Goodbye. I'll call you when we develop more information."

He tried to hide his disappointment. "Yeah, anytime," he said. "Tell the guys you work with I'm not the problem in their lives."

From the window, he watched her get in her car and back it around and head down the driveway and under the arch. He watched her drive down the road along the rail fence while Albert's Foxtrotters raced beside her in the pasture. He watched her reach the south end of Albert's ranch, marked by a grove of cottonwood trees. He watched her car disappear inside the leafy shade of the grove, the leaves flickering like thousands of green butterflies in the breeze. Then, a moment later, he saw the car reemerge, pointed back toward the house. He watched it coming up the road, the horses, all colts, running with it. He watched the car slow, the turn indicator blinking, although no other vehicles were on the road. He watched it turn under the arch and come up the driveway and stop by the garage, beyond his line of vision. He heard the driver's door open and slam shut.

She came down the flagstone steps to his door and arrived just as he was opening it, his mouth agape.

"I left my ballpoint," she said.

"Oh."

"My roommate at Quantico gave it to me."

"Yeah, I can relate to that."

She opened her eyes wide and blew out her breath. "You up for this, chief?" she asked.

For Clete, the next few moments could be described only in terms of skyrockets bursting in the heavens or the Marine Corps band blaring out "From the Halls of Montezuma" or, on a less dramatic level, his morning angst dissolving into the sound of a lawn sprinkler fanning against his bedroom window, the smell of flowers opening in a damp garden, the throaty rush of wind in the trees, or perhaps an Asian mermaid swimming through a rainbow that arched across the entirety of the landscape.

CHAPTER
15

THAT SAME MORNING I went to the post office to pick up our mail, then into Missoula to buy new tires for my pickup. On the way back, I stopped at the cabin where J. D. Gribble lived, just over the mountain from Albert's house. I had been there twice since Gribble had woken up in the back of Albert's truck and had seen the man in the mask pouring gasoline on Clete Purcel. In both instances, Gribble had not been home or anywhere on the property that I could see. This time, when I parked my pickup by his cabin, I heard music, first the tail end of "Cimarron" and then "Madison Blues."

Gribble's door was open, and I could see him sitting in a straight-back chair, three steel picks on his right hand, a Dobro stretched across his lap. The Dobro was inset with a chrome-plated resonator, and Gribble was accompanying his chord progressions with a kazoo that he blew like a saxophone, leaning into it, totally absorbed inside his music, one booted foot patting up and down on the plank floor. His face jerked when he saw me, and he lifted the steel picks from the strings.

"Not many guys can do both Bob Wills and Elmore James," I said.

"It was Leon McAuliffe that was the big influence. White or black, they all got their styles from him, no matter what they claim," he said.

"I wanted to thank you for saving Clete's life. I came up here yesterday but didn't see you around."

"A cougar or a bear busted the wire on the back fence, and some of the horses wandered up the hill. That deal concerning Mr. Purcel is something I'd rather not revisit."

"Why's that?"

"'Cause it scared the hell out of me. That FBI woman has done talked it to death, anyway. I don't know who that guy in the mask was, and I ain't interested in finding out. I'd just like to get shut of the whole business."

He set the Dobro on his table and looked around, as though his exasperation were a means to confront spirits or voices that hung on the edges of his vision.

"What I'm trying to tell you is Clete and I are in your debt. You need a favor or help of some kind, we're your guys," I said.

He sucked in his cheeks and stared into space. "Mr. Purcel said you was in Vietnam."

"A few months."

"You come back with some spiders in your head?"

"A couple."

"You spend a whole lot of time talking about it with other people?"

"No."

"How come?"

"Because it's not something they care to hear about or would understand."

The sun had gone behind clouds, and it was dark and cool inside the cabin. Gribble pulled the steel picks from his fingers and dropped them in a tobacco can. He wore a denim shirt buttoned at the wrists. He brushed at his nose with his shirt cuff, his gaze turned inward. He waited a long time before he spoke. His manner, his mind-set, the opaqueness of his expression made me think of hill people I had known, or company-town millworkers, or people who did stoop labor or bucked bales or worked for decades at jobs in which a certain meanness of spirit allowed them to survive.

"I come out here to be let alone," he said. "That's all I ever wanted. That and my music and a woman I used to love and our Airstream trailer and the life of a rodeo man. You reckon that's a lot to ask?"

Not seventy-five years ago, it wouldn't have been, I thought. But I kept my own counsel. "How much does a Dobro like that cost?" I asked.

"I don't remember," he replied, drumming the pads of his fingers on the tabletop. When I didn't speak, he shifted his eyes onto mine. "Something else?"

"Yeah. Can you play 'Cimarron' again?"

MOLLY WAS SPRINKLING the flowers in the window boxes with a watering can when I got back to our cabin. To the south, rain was falling in the valley, and in the sunlight it looked like spun glass on the trees that grew along the slopes. "I just tried to thank J. D. Gribble for saving Clete's life. He wasn't interested," I said.

"Maybe he's a humble man," she said.

"He owns an antique Dobro. It must be worth thousands of dollars. You ought to hear him sing. His voice is beautiful. Why's a guy like that shoveling horse flop in Lolo, Montana?"

"Did you see Clete?" she asked, changing the subject.

"No, why?"

"I just wondered," she said.

I waited. She moved the watering can back and forth over the pansies in the window boxes, her face empty.

"What's he done now?" I asked.

"I didn't say he'd done anything. Besides, it's time to stop micromanaging his life, Dave."

"Will you stop this?"

"That FBI woman was there. She left and then came back. His secretary in New Orleans couldn't reach him, so she called me on my cell. I went down to his apartment. No answer to the knock. Nobody in the living room or the kitchenette. As quietly as possible, I walked back here and didn't look over my shoulder. Later, the two of them drove off in her car. Is that detailed enough?"

"You're kidding?"

"It's his life. We need to butt out, troop."

"In the sack with the FBI? While she's on duty? I can't believe it."

"Remind me not to have this type of conversation with you again," she said.

But Molly didn't get it. The problem wasn't Clete's romantic entanglement with a federal agent; the problem was the long-dormant investigation into the plane crash that had killed Sally Dio and his fellow lowlifes. In the eyes of some, Clete was still a suspect, and he had just managed to swim back onto the radar in the most annoying fashion he could think up.

"*What?*" she said, setting down the watering can on the porch. She was wearing a sundress, and in the shade, her freckled skin had a pale, powdery luminescence that made my heart quicken.

I smiled at her. "Clete is just Clete, isn't he?" I said.

"Dave, you're so crazy," she replied.

I went inside and put on a pair of gym shorts, my running shoes, and a T-shirt, then jogged down the road toward the highway. The sun shower had stopped and the air smelled cool and fresh, like mowed hay. A family of wild turkeys was drinking from the horse tank in Albert's pasture, the male and female fluttering up on the aluminum rim with their chicks, the horses watching the show.

I hit it hard for half a mile, running through the dappled shade of cottonwoods, chipmunks skittering in the rocks up on the hillside, the great hulking presence of Lolo Peak rising into the sky by the Idaho line. It was a grand morning, the kind that makes you feel you shouldn't look beyond the day you have, that it's enough simply to be at work and play in the fields of the Lord. But I could not rid myself of my worries about Clete Purcel, nor could I stop thinking about the ordeal he had suffered on the mountainside Saturday night down in the Bitterroots.

Who was the culprit? God only knew. I've known sadists, sexual predators, and serial killers of every stripe. In my opinion, no matter what behavioral psychologists say, none of them fits a profile with any appreciable degree of exactitude or predictability. Searching their backgrounds for environmental explanations is a waste of time. Deprivation, abuse in the home, and alcoholism and drug addiction in the family may be factors, but they're not the cause. Turn the situation around. In the Western world, who were the worst monsters of the twentieth century? Who tortured with glee and murdered with indifference? Stalin was an ex-seminarian. The people who fired the ovens in Auschwitz were baptized Christians.

The truth is, no one knows what makes psychopaths. They don't share their secrets. Nor do they ever confess their crimes in their entirety, lest the confessions rob them of their deeds and the power over others those deeds have given them.

I had no doubt the man in the mask was out there, biding his time, waiting to catch Clete in an unguarded moment or vulnerable situation. Sadists and serial killers feed on trust and naïveté and do not like to be undone by their adversaries. As long as Clete remained alive, he would represent failure to the man who had tried to burn him to death.

I rounded a bend in the road and slowed to a walk in the shade of cottonwoods, my skin cool and glazed with sweat, my heart steady, my breath coming easy in my lungs. The wind was ruffling through the canopy, the sky an immaculate translucent blue, as bright and flawless as silk. I didn't want to think any more about serial killers, about violent men and cupidity and the manipulation for political ends of uneducated and poor people whose religion was expropriated and used to hurt them. I only wanted to disconnect from the world as it is, or at least as I have come to know it.

Just when I had convinced myself that it was possible to live inside the moment, that neither the past nor the future should be allowed to lay claim to it, I saw an SUV headed toward me, a tall man in a pearl-gray western hat in the passenger seat, a woman driving.

The woman lifted a hand in recognition as they passed, then continued up the road and turned in to Albert's driveway. The man wore a grin at the corner of his mouth, a bit like John Wayne.

ALBERT HOLLISTER KEPT his office on the main floor of his home, with a view that looked out on his barn and northern pasture and an arroyo behind the house. His bookshelves extended from the floor to the ceiling. The shelves by his writing desk were littered with Indian arrowheads and pottery shards, fifty-eight-caliber minié balls, a milk-glass doorknob from the bathroom of Boss Tweed, switchblade and trench knives, a tomahawk, nineteenth-century telegraph transformers, an IWW button, goatskin wine bags from Pamplona, and a deactivated World War II hand grenade. The office also contained a glass case for his published books and short stories and another case for his guns, which included an M16, a twelve-gauge pump, an '03 Springfield, a '94 lever-action Winchester, and a half-dozen sidearms.

When the couple parked the SUV by the side door, Albert was writing a short story in longhand, his thoughts deep inside the Texas City disaster of 1947. In his mind, he saw a mushroom cloud of smoke and flame rise from the Monsanto chemical plant, generating heat so great that the water in the harbor boiled. He saw liquid flame rain down in umbrella fashion on an oil field, setting off wellheads and natural-gas storage tanks like strings of firecrackers. Then the man and woman from the SUV knocked on the French doors, peering at him through the glass, the man shading the glare with one hand so he could see more clearly into Albert's office. When Albert didn't rise from his writing desk, the man tapped a knuckle on the glass.

"What do you want?" Albert said, getting up and opening the door.

"My name is Troyce Nix," the man said. "We're looking for a man by the name of Jimmy Dale Greenwood."

"I've never heard of him," Albert said.

"Can we come in a minute?" the man asked.

"What for?"

"I just told you," Nix said.

"It's obvious I'm busy."

"It's important, Mr. Hollister."

Albert hesitated, glancing at the woman, looking back at the man, the western clothes, the grainy skin, the long sideburns, the mirrored sunglasses protruding from his shirt pocket. The man's physical stature and his posture and manner conjured up memories in Albert that were like someone scratching a match across his stomach lining. *Deal with it now, not later. Don't let a guy like this get behind you,* he heard a voice say inside his head.

"Go around front," he said, and closed the door. A moment later, he let Nix and the woman into the living room, both of them a bit awed by the elevated view of the Bitterroot Mountains, massive and blue-green and strung with clouds.

"You got you a nice place," Nix said.

"Who sent you out here?" Albert said.

"I'm looking for this man here," Nix replied, handing a photograph to Albert, ignoring the question.

"What makes you think I know him?" Albert said, not looking at the photo.

"Folks here'bouts say you help out guys on the drift or people that's down and out."

"The bottom of this photograph has been cut off," Albert said.

"Have you seen Greenwood? He's a breed. Wiry guy with a soft voice."

"Why is the bottom of this picture cut off?"

"It had more information on it than people need to see. I just want to know where the man is at and talk with him."

"I don't know him," Albert said, returning the mug shot to Troyce Nix.

"You didn't look at it."

"I don't have to. I don't know anybody named Jimmy Dale Greenwood."

"You want to know what he did?"

"It's not my business."

"I guess we disturbed you in your work. Sorry about that," Nix said.

"No, you're not."

"Say again?"

"If you were sorry, you wouldn't have come out without ringing me first."

Nix grinned. "I heard you were a crusty one. Can Candace have a glass of water?"

Regardless of the transparency of Nix's attempt at manipulation, Albert filled a glass at the kitchen tap for the woman and put ice in it and brought it back into the living room.

"That's maple in your floor?" she said.

Albert said it was.

"The way it catches the light is pretty," she said. "Did your wife put all the flowers on the mantel?"

"My wife died three years ago. She used to put flowers there, in front of the mirror and on the breakfast table, too. So now I do it for her."

Candace Sweeney lowered her eyes, her cheeks coloring. Then she looked out the window at the mountains again, the long slope of the meadow dipping into the distance. "This valley is a paradise. Are there a lot of wild animals here?"

"Elk and white-tail and some mule deer. A few cougars up on the ridge. A few wild turkeys. A moose comes down occasionally."

"You hunt the animals?" she said, a line creasing across her brow.

"I don't allow hunters on the property. Not any kind, not under any circumstances," Albert said, shifting his eyes onto Troyce Nix.

"I read a couple of your books. I thought they were pretty good," Troyce said.

Albert nodded but didn't reply.

"You never asked me what I do for a living," Troyce said.

"I already know what you do."

"Oh?"

"You're not a lawman, or you would have rolled a badge on me. But you're connected to the law, at least in some fashion. From the look of you, I'd say you're a gunbull, or you used to be. Maybe you were an MP or a chaser in the Marine Corps. But you've been a hack someplace."

"Not many people use terms like 'hack' or 'gunbull,' " Troyce said.

"I know them because I served time on a Florida road gang when I was eighteen. Most of the gunbulls weren't bad men. They'd work the hell out of us, but that was about all. A couple of them were otherwise, men who were cruel and sexually perverse."

Troyce Nix had never looked into a pair of eyes that were as intense as Albert Hollister's. He took a business card from his pocket and wrote on the back of it. "I'm leaving you my cell number in case Jimmy Dale Greenwood should knock at your door. I'm putting down the name of our motel, too."

"Give it to somebody who has need of it."

Nix twirled his hat one revolution on his index finger, then his eyes crinkled at the corners. "Thanks for the glass of water," he said. He set his business card down on a table.

"You don't need to thank me for anything," Albert replied.

He opened the heavy oak door for Nix to leave. Without saying goodbye or shaking hands or watching Nix and the woman leave, he walked back into the kitchen, hoping that somehow the world that his two visitors represented would exit from his life as easily as they had walked into it. He heard the lock click shut in the jamb, the wall vibrate slightly with the weight of the door swinging into place. He propped his arms on the marble counter and stared at the mountains at the south end of the valley, wondering why his age seemed to bring him neither wisdom nor peace. A moment later, the door chimes rang. He opened the door again and looked into Candace Sweeney's face. With her tattoos and her jeans that were too tight, the pant legs stuffed in a pair of cowboy boots, she reminded him of the girls he had known years ago when he was on the drift, riding flat-wheelers, sleeping in oil-field flophouses, bucking bales and harvesting beets and hops.

"We're sorry we bothered you," she said. "Troyce got hurt real bad down in Texas and almost died. His wounds still bleed, and he has trouble sleeping. Sometimes he gets an edge on."

"What are you trying to tell me?" he asked.

She looked over her shoulder at the driveway, then back at Albert. "I told Troyce I just wanted to apologize for disturbing you at work. But that's not why I came back."

Albert waited for her to go on.

"If that fellow Jimmy Dale Greenwood comes around here?" she said.

"Yes?"

"Forget we were here. Forget you heard about any of this. You don't need to pass on any information to Troyce or me. Maybe you won't believe this, but Troyce is a good man."

Albert continued to look at her without replying. Her hair was tousling in the wind, her black cowboy shirt with purple and red roses sewn on it puffing with air.

"You're not going to say anything?" she said.

"With a gal like you, he'd damn well better be a good man," Albert said.

Her face suddenly went soft, like a flower opening in the shade.

As soon as I got back from my run, I showered and walked up to Albert's house. He was behind the back steps, a tank of Tordon and 2,4-D strapped to his back, spraying leafy spurge and knapweed on a grassy slope that led into shade and fir trees. The air smelled like it had been rinsed in a chemical factory. I tried to find out why Troyce Nix and Candace Sweeney had come to his house. Albert's response to my questions was to widen the circle of his spray, whipping the applicator back and forth, hosing down everything in sight, letting the mist drift back into my face.

"Will you stop that?" I said.

"I have to finish this before the wind comes up," he replied.

"When I first saw Troyce Nix, he was showing a photo to people at the revival on the res. He was about to show it to me until his girl-friend mentioned I was a cop. What's that tell you, Albert?"

"Nothing."

"It tells you he's here on a personal mission, and the mission is to do the guy in the photo some serious damage."

"That might be."

"Does this have something to do with J. D. Gribble?"

"A man's past ends at my front gate, Dave."

"Good way to get your throat cut."

Albert's eyes looked like small blue lights inside the softness of his skin. "Would you kindly take yourself someplace else?" he said.

"Is Gribble a fugitive?" I asked.

"Don't know and don't give a shit."

"Is Gribble the man in that photo?"

"I gave Nix back his photo without looking at it. I suspect Nix is up to no good. The woman seems like a good person. Why she's with the likes of him is beyond me. Case closed, conversation over."

How did Albert Hollister remain functional inside an academic bureaucracy? Why was he not beaten to death by his colleagues?

You got me.

I WALKED BACK up to the cabin and tried to think. J. D. Gribble's possible status as a fugitive was an issue between Albert and Gribble. Troyce Nix's possible beef with Gribble was Gribble and Nix's grief and none of my own. The only relevant issue for me was Clete Purcel and the decades he had invested in being my closest friend. A deviant had attempted to burn him alive and in all probability would take another run at it, possibly with different methods but with the same depraved intentions. Gribble had told the FBI he had heard a car or truck engine in the darkness, then the sound of the vehicle's door slamming. Alicia Rosecrans, the FBI agent, had concluded that perhaps two perpetrators were involved, the driver and the man in the mask. But the man in the mask may have opened the vehicle's door, started the engine, then slammed the door later. Or Gribble could have simply been mixed up.

I needed to concentrate on the man in the mask. I was convinced he was the same man who had abducted and murdered the college kids on the mountainside behind the university and killed the California couple in the highway rest stop. It wasn't a matter of forensics; it was a matter of mathematical possibility. How many men like Clete's tormentor could be living in the same sparsely populated area?

Unfortunately, there were precedents that went against the math. The Hillside Strangler was actually not one man but a team of two cousins, both of whom seemed to have souls that were fashioned in a furnace. What is the probability that two monsters, with little in their background that would explain the depth of their cruelty to innocent and trusting young women, could come from the same family?

Years ago, in a midwestern city whose collective ethos was heavily influenced by the humanitarian culture of abolitionists and of Mennonites, I attended twelve-step meetings with some of the best people I ever knew. Most of them were teachers and clerics and blue-collar workers in the aircraft industry. They were drunks, like me, but by and large their sins were the theological equivalent of 3.2 beer. The meetings were small, the content of the discussions restrained, the mention of sexual indiscretions infrequent. Two ex-felons, recently discharged from the state pen, were required to attend the meeting by their PO. They sat quietly in the back of the room, deferential, neatly dressed, and polite. They were well liked and gradually were considered twelve-step success stories in the making. I became accustomed to seeing one of them sitting in front of me at Sunday-morning Mass, his wife and two children next to him in the pew.

Then the two of them were busted ninety miles to the north of us, in a wheat-farming town where the biggest social event of the season was the John Deere exhibition at the high school gym. The charge was homicide, but that convenient abstract term didn't come close to what these men had done to their victims. They had lain in wait for girls leaving bars by themselves at two A.M., offering them rides, maybe a toke or two of some Acapulco gold or a steak at an all-night café. Once the two ex-felons got their hands on their victims, they raped and tortured them for hours, degrading and humiliating them and putting them through every ordeal imaginable before snuffing out their lives.

The people at the meeting I had been attending were stunned. No one could deal with it, explain it, or reconcile himself to his own naïveté. What are the odds of two men like this finding each other at a small, family-oriented twelve-step meeting in a city associated with Toto, Dorothy, and the yellow brick road? What are the odds that all of us, including me, would be taken in by them? What are the odds that one of them would sit with his family in front of me at Sunday Mass?

The answer that presents itself is not a pleasant one: There are more of them out there than we think, and they recognize one another when we do not. If you doubt this, check the statistics on the number of children who disappear each year and are never seen or heard from again.

But the attack on Clete Purcel was not random. When people kill one another, it's always for reasons of money, sex, and power. I suspected that whoever was behind the attack on Clete was driven by all three.

I called the sheriff of Iberia Parish, Helen Soileau. She had worked her way up from meter maid to patrolwoman at the NOPD, and later had become my plainclothes partner at the Sheriff's Department in New Iberia. She was an attractive, enigmatic woman, and I was convinced several personalities lived inside her. She was the subject of an IA investigation after she had an affair with a confidential female informant. She also had an affair with Clete Purcel. She was the only cop in the area he allowed to bust and hook him up after he had destroyed a saloon in St. Martinsville and almost killed three outlaw bikers with a pool cue.

On occasion her eyes would turn warm and linger on mine, as though one of the women who lived inside her was having thoughts about straying. But I never questioned her integrity or challenged her authority, and I always respected her courage and the grace with which she conducted her life. I also learned that anyone who mocked or treated her disrespectfully did so only once. When our former sheriff retired and Helen took his place, Helen won the hearts of the entire community, and no one publicly discussed her sexual persuasion.

I called her and asked if she could run Leslie and Ridley Wellstone for me.

"The oil and natural-gas guys?" she said.

"Right," I replied. But I knew what was coming.

"Is there a pattern here?"

"Sorry?"

"You have trouble with rich people, Streak. Entertain the trout and let Montana take care of its own problems."

Then I told her what had happened to Clete Purcel.

"I'll get back to you in two hours," she said.

Her phone calls produced a surprise.

CHAPTER
16

I HAD EXPECTED HELEN to find compromising material on the patriarch of the family, Oliver Wellstone, or on Leslie, the Berkeley-educated humanist who had given up on the flower children and gone to the Sudan, where his features had been melted off his face like wax on a candlestick.

But it was Ridley, the over-the-hill cowboy, the stoic, laboring painfully on his aluminum forearm crutches, whose name had figured in a double-homicide investigation many years ago. The case had almost been forgotten and written off by everyone except a Houston homicide detective who had worked on it for a decade before he was found asphyxiated in his garage, his car motor running for twenty-four hours in the middle of July. He left no suicide note and, according to his friends and colleagues, had shown no signs of depression or worry in the days leading up to his death.

But the homicide detective had left behind a case file bursting with notes and transcriptions of interviews with people who occupied every stratum of Houston society.

Thirty-one years ago, Ridley had met a salesclerk by the name of Barbara Vogel in a Galleria jewelry store. She was approaching middle age, but her suntanned skin was as smooth as tallow, her chestnut hair cut like a young girl's, giving her an appearance that was both asexual and yet strangely erotic. But it was her brown eyes that made Ridley return to the store twice, finding excuses to talk about jewelry, finally asking her to have dinner with him at the River Oaks country club, the same club that had excluded his parents from membership years before. Barbara Vogel's eyes were warm and guileless and seemingly intrigued by everything Ridley had to say. Her body had the firmness of an athlete's, and she could talk about any subject and had experience far beyond that of a salesclerk. She said she had been a barrel-racing rodeo queen in Dalhart, the owner of a boutique in Fort Worth, and an insurance appraiser in Beaumont. She also knew quail hunting, the price of slaughter beef, and the depth a drill rig was expected to hit a pay sand in a certain offshore quadrant. She also hinted that she was part owner of the jewelry store.

They got married after making a spontaneous champagne-soaked flight on his private jet into Juárez. Barbara Vogel didn't bother to tell Ridley that she had been married twice already and her first husband had gone to prison for embezzlement. She also didn't bother to tell him about her outstanding debts, her love of charge accounts, and her friendship with a collection of white trash who hung at a notorious bar in North Houston once known as the Bloody Bucket. Ridley got to meet a few of the latter when she bought a motor home the size of the Taj Mahal, loaded her friends into it, and drove to a Waylon and Willie concert in Austin. When she and her friends returned to the Wellstones' sprawling estate, they were wiped out on reds and weed and purple acid and could hardly stand up in the yard. Most of them went to sleep on the lawn furniture and didn't wake up until Ridley turned on the sprinkler system.

Ridley also discovered his wife's affection for unusual fashion. She favored skintight riding pants, push-up bras, and western shirts unsnapped at the top that exposed both her cleavage and a diamond cluster that spelled out RICH BITCH.

Two years into the marriage, Barbara's teenage daughter showed up, fresh out of rehab, her hormones blinking in red neon. She hung paper all over town and threw a roach in a horse stall, setting the barn on fire. She also got caught screwing her former high school drama teacher on his desk. The kicker for Ridley was the night both Barbara and her daughter piled his collector's Rolls into a live-oak tree by Rice University. They not only left the scene, they told the cops later that they had not been driving the car, implying that Ridley was the man the cops needed to question.

The divorce should have gone smoothly. Ridley's attorneys offered Barbara a three-million-dollar settlement. Barbara's attorneys sued for seventy million and the house. They also indicated their hired psychiatric consultant had noted definite signs of sexual abuse in Barbara's daughter and that nobody was ruling out criminal charges being filed against Ridley, with as much attendant publicity as Barbara's attorneys could generate.

The double homicide took place on a humid September night in a quasi-rural area dotted with oak trees and split-level ranch houses. The spacious grounds surrounding Barbara's house were bordered by a piked iron fence, the gates electronically locked, the hedges and gazebo and gravel walkways monitored by security cameras. The underwater lamps in the swimming pool automatically clicked on at sunset, creating a brilliant patch of blue light in the backyard, turning the flowers and umbrella and banana trees into a Gauguin painting. Fall was at hand, and the languid air was tinged with the odor of chrysanthemums and charcoal starter flaring on a grill. No one in the neighborhood paid particular attention to the visitor who arrived at Barbara's house in a yellow cab.

He was tall and wore gloves, a raincoat, and a slouch hat, although the thunder in the clouds was dry and the local meteorologist had said there was little chance of rain that evening. The visitor punched in the security numbers on the gate and entered the grounds as the cab turned around in the lane, then parked under a tree.

The visitor's weapon of choice was a cut-down pump twelve-gauge, loaded with double-aught bucks, hanging from his shoulder on a looped cord under his coat. While a neighbor broiling steaks stared aghast, the visitor walked poolside and paused in front of the recliner where Barbara's daughter lay in a bikini, a movie magazine on her lap, her face lifted in either disdain or annoyance. The visitor raised the shotgun and squeezed the trigger six inches from her forehead. Behind him, the visitor heard Barbara drop a tray with two cream-cheese sandwiches on it and try to run for the patio door. He pumped the spent shell casing onto the tile and caught her with a wide pattern across the back of her blouse. He crossed the St. Augustine grass, ejecting the casing, and looked down at his handiwork. He touched her once with the tip of his shoe, then buttoned his coat over his shotgun and got into the back of the waiting cab.

The two homicides had all the signs of the classical hit. The cut-down twelve-gauge pump and the dispassionate execution of the victims were marks of a professional killer. The gloves and raincoat ensured that no fingerprints would be left at the crime scene and the killer would not have blood splatter on his clothes. The stolen cab was a perfect getaway vehicle—commonplace and innocuous and easily dumped in a restaurant parking lot five minutes from the crime scene.

But how did the killer acquire Barbara's security code? The electronic gate had been installed only six days before the night of the homicides. She would have had no motivation to give the code to her estranged husband. The cops pulled in an ex-convict whose wife ran a bar on Jensen Drive. His words were "A rich guy put out an open whack for fifteen grand on the Wellstone bitch and her daughter. I wouldn't touch it with a pole, man."

"Why is that?" a cop asked.

"Those oil-and-gas fuckers don't pay their bills," the ex-convict replied.

But the ex-convict was also known as a pathological liar, and he later tried to sell his story to a detective magazine.

Houston PD and the Harris County Sheriff's Office questioned two men Barbara Wellstone had carried on affairs with. They also questioned an Australian porn actor the daughter had informed on after she had been pinched with a brick of his marijuana. That the shooter had sought her out first may have indicated she was the target rather than the mother.

But nobody was sure. Neither Barbara Wellstone nor her daughter was a sympathetic victim, and many people had motive to murder either or both of them. After a couple of years, media interest waned, the homicide detectives assigned to the investigation gradually moved on, and Barbara and her daughter became interesting mounds in a treeless cemetery outside Dalhart, Texas.

The only remaining problem for the killers was the homicide detective who had continued to work on the case long after everyone else had given up. Was his death a suicide? Or was he getting too close to the wrong people?

I knew those questions would probably never be answered. Not unless someone got the Wellstones into the iron cage where I thought they belonged.

THAT AFTERNOON I drove into the Swan Valley. The day had warmed precipitously, and in the distance I could see a single column of smoke rising from a dark green stand of timber on a mountain slope. June is the wet month in Montana, but this year the rains in the lowlands and the snows in the high country had been less than they should have been. I hoped wildfires would not have their way, as they had in the years 2000 and 2003. I hoped that Montana would remain the fine place that it was, a window into America's pristine magnificence. But as I looked through the windshield of my truck, the signs of change were everywhere. Maybe that's just in the nature of things, but who says you have to like it?

Better yet, who says you have to accept the presence of those who would turn the earth into a sludge pit? The minions of the Wellstones were hired cretins, men like Lyle Hobbs and Quince Whitley. Their kind attach themselves to an authority figure, one who pays them not to think, and then they go about hurting other people with the idle detachment of someone clipping his nails. Putting them in penitentiaries provides jobs for correctional officers and makes everyone feel better about our justice system, but in reality, it does little to change the way things work. The enlisted people who were punished for crimes inside the Abu Ghraib prison wouldn't drop their pants in a latrine without permission. If Hobbs and Whitley were involved in the attack on Clete, they had not acted on their own. But the problem lay in the very fact that they were windups—lacking credibility, fearful of retaliation, ultimately dispensable.

It was time to take a different tack. The convergence of so many disparate elements at Albert's ranch was too much for coincidence. Clete had trespassed accidentally onto the Wellstone ranch, setting off a reaction by the Wellstone employees and then the Wellstones themselves. A college kid with ties to the Wellstone Ministries had been abducted and murdered on the ridge behind Albert's house. Later, a drifter with a Texas accent who looked part Indian and called himself J. D. Gribble had shown up at Albert's secondary pasture, claiming to be a down-and-out rodeo man but with a singing voice like Jimmie Rodgers. In the meantime, a drifter who looked a lot like J. D. Gribble had been hanging around the Swan Lake café and nightclub where Jamie Sue Wellstone often stopped in for a drink. Last, Troyce Nix, also from Texas, had appeared on the scene, looking for a man who had put a shiv in him, a man I thought Albert knew was his newly hired hand, J. D. Gribble.

I had gotten Jamie Sue Wellstone's cell number from Clete before I drove in to the Swan. I parked in front of the nightclub on the lake and punched her number into my cell, wondering at the levels of unhappiness people could visit upon themselves, usually over things that were only symbols for the things they actually wanted. But the fate and choices of others were not my business. The attack on Clete Purcel was.

After the seventh ring, I got Jamie Sue's voice mail. I left my name and told her I would like to talk with her, at any time or any place of her choosing. I did not tell her where I was. Nor did I expect her to call me back. I had already placed Jamie Sue Wellstone in a categorical shoe box, that of opportunist and user of other people. However, I was about to relearn an old lesson, namely that our judgments about our fellow human beings are usually wrong.

My cell vibrated while I was eating in the café. I flipped it open and placed it against my ear. "Hello?" I said.

"Mr. Robicheaux?" the voice said.

"Yes?" I replied.

"This is Jamie Sue Wellstone. What is it you want?"

Go right to it, I told myself. "To talk about a guy by the name of J. D. Gribble."

I could hear her breathing in the silence. "Is he all right?" she asked.

"As far as I know. When can we talk?"

There was a long pause. "Where are you?"

"At the café on Swan Lake."

"Are you a Christian?"

"Beg your pardon?"

"You'd better not deceive me, Mr. Robicheaux."

How strange can it get?

Fifteen minutes later, she turned out of the late-afternoon shadows on the highway and parked in front of the nightclub. Her little boy was strapped into the child seat in back. She walked into the café holding him against her shoulder, a diaper bag hooked around her waist. She looked through the front window, then studied the vehicles parked in the side lot. I pulled out a chair for her, but she ignored the gesture and asked the waitress for a high chair, then walked through the bead curtain and checked to see who was inside the bar. When she sat down, her expression was circumspect, her frown like a tiny stitch between her eyebrows. She had not spoken a word.

"That's a handsome little boy you have there," I said.

Still she didn't speak. Her eyes were busy with thought, as though she was reconsidering the wisdom of meeting with me.

"What was Gribble down for?" I said.

She didn't understand.

"He doesn't deny he's done time," I said. "He just doesn't say what for."

"He tried to help someone."

"You're seeing him?"

"I came here for one reason only, Mr. Robicheaux. Somebody has to help J.D. before he gets hurt. That female FBI agent was out to our house again. She talked about you."

"FBI agents don't do that."

"She said you were an ex-drunk but an honest man. I took her at her word. I'm taking you at yours. A man named Troyce Nix came to our house. He'll kill J.D. if he catches him."

"Why don't you tell J.D. this?"

"J.D. wants both me and his son back. He won't leave unless we go with him."

"I think your friend is a fugitive, but I'll say this anyway. If I were you two, I'd take my little boy and get a lot of gone between me and the Wellstone family."

"You don't know them."

"I don't want to."

"They won't let me go. I know too much. The Wellstone Ministries aren't a scam about money. They're not interested in money. They don't even preach politics. They focus on the family, on family values, all that kind of stuff. They've won over millions of people that way. Toward election time, the message goes out: If you believe in the family, vote against gay marriage and abortion. Vote against the people who believe in them. The Ministries don't get you to vote for people, they get you to vote against them. All they need is about four percent of the electorate. They're hooked in with some of the most powerful people in the country."

"Who cares? Get away from them."

"They'll find J.D. No one will know what happened to him. No one will find a body. No one will find a witness. You think I'm making this up?"

No, I didn't. But I had no solution for her predicament or the sorrow and regret that I suspected characterized her daily life. "Who killed those two college kids?"

"I don't know. I don't like to think about it," she replied.

"I doubt their parents do, either."

Wrong choice.

"You hear me on this, Mr. Robicheaux. I just wanted a good life for my child. I also wanted to get his father out of prison. That's why I married Leslie. He came to a club where I was playing. He was a gentleman, and he was kind and well mannered. He's good to little Dale. He treats him like his own son. But I—" She took a butter knife out of her child's hand and gave him a ring of car keys to play with. "I made a mistake when I married him. Leslie is not to blame, I am." She hesitated again. "I was attracted by his wealth, too. I have to live with that knowledge about myself, and it's not pleasant. I don't know who murdered those kids. Probably the same person who killed that poor couple from California. But I'm not the person to ask."

"The attack on Clete Purcel was not random," I said. "The attacker is a sadist whose targets are given to him by someone else. Who has that level of hatred for Clete, Ms. Wellstone? Who has the motivation? You're a smart woman. Don't tell me you don't know the answer to that question."

"Leslie is too proud and vain."

"I don't understand," I said.

"He believes in nothing except his own disillusionment with the world. He thinks his war injuries are such that he's above any pain others can inflict upon him. He thinks of revenge as a mark of mediocrity."

"You've already said he and his brother are capable of having J.D. killed."

"You weren't listening. They do nothing in a direct way. When somebody gets in their way, they bring up the problem with their attorneys or a man who runs their computer systems or the head of a security agency in Dallas. Without their ever knowing what happens, somebody's life becomes a nightmare, or he just disappears."

"Somebody broke into Seymour Bell's house. He and his girlfriend, Cindy, had evidence of some kind about the Wellstones. What was it?"

"They were just kids. What could they have that could hurt Leslie and Ridley?"

"That's the point. They were rural Montana kids. What did they have in their possession that would make someone kill them?"

"It's not how Ridley and Leslie operate," she said, more to herself than to me, her eyes searching in space.

I was beginning to lose patience with her introspection and perhaps disingenuousness. "Then how *do* they operate?" I asked.

"There's a great darkness in both of them. I don't know how

to describe it. They don't love evil, but they're not disturbed by it, either. Evil is a tool. They use it when they need to. Otherwise, they live their lives just like the rest of us."

Through the window, I could see a second column of smoke rising from the timber across the lake, a helicopter with a giant water bucket slung under its airframe trying to extinguish the fire before it spread. I walked out of the café into the lengthening shadows in the parking lot, into the cooling of the day, the trout dimpling the surface of the lake like raindrops. For reasons I couldn't quite explain to myself, I remembered a Jewish lady I had once known. She had survived Bergen-Belsen, although her parents and siblings had died there. When asked by a friend of mine whether she still believed in God, she replied that she did. When my friend asked her where God was when her family died, she replied, "Looking down from above, wondering at what His children had done."

CHAPTER
17

ONCE, IN SEATTLE'S Pioneer Square, Candace Sweeney had passed by a blind preacher ranting at a bunch of drunks by the homeless mission. The preacher's eyes had no pupils and were the color of peeled hard-boiled eggs that have turned blue inside a refrigerator. His voice and words were cacophonous, threaded with rage at either his audience or his own misspent life. In the middle of his incoherence, he said something Candace never forgot: "Hell is a black box that's got locks all over it. Kick the door and you'll hear them rattle, but it won't do you no good. You don't die to get to hell. You're already there."

She had come to wonder if the preacher had been talking about Troyce.

During the night, she could feel his great weight turning on the mattress and hear his breath coming hard in his chest, as though he were inside a capsule that was sucking the oxygen from his lungs. He wore only his skivvies, and when she touched his bare skin, she could feel it twitch under her fingers. She stroked his hair, and for just a moment he was quiet. Then he cried out and his head jerked up from the pillow, his eyes wide, his face limned by the pink glow from the neon sign outside the motel.

"What is it, baby?" she asked.

"Nothing. A dream," he replied.

He sat on the side of the bed, his shoulders rounded, looking into the shadows, listening for sounds that were not there. When she placed her palm on his back, his muscles were as hard as iron.

"You called out somebody's name. You said, 'Don't do that.' Then you said the name."

Troyce turned around. His eyes were a washed-out blue, and in the semidarkness, they looked as though they had been snipped out of paper and glued on his face. "I did?"

"Other nights you've said this same name. Is this somebody you knew in Iraq?"

He shook his head, cupping his big hands on his knees, rocking on his buttocks.

"What'd you do, Troyce? What bothers you?"

"This wasn't in Abu Ghraib. But we done things at this other place that got out of control, just like at the prison outside Baghdad. Some contract intelligence personnel wanted this one guy prepped. That's what they called it. Like softened up, before they interrogated him. The guy was a hard case. We called him Cujo 'cause he had jaws like a big dog. He'd been tortured in Egypt and showed off his scars like they was badges of honor. He told us we couldn't hurt him 'cause he wasn't like us, that he didn't eat God in a Communion wafer, that he lived inside Allah just like those Bedouins live inside the desert. He said Allah was as big as the desert, and once you were in Allah's belly, you became part of him and nobody could touch you, not even death. He told all this to guys who was going to cuff him to a bed frame and wrap a wet towel around his face and keep pouring water into his nose and mouth till he near drowned."

Candace had propped herself on her knees behind Troyce, one hand resting on his shoulder. His skin was as cold as stone. She could see both her reflection and Troyce's in the wall mirror, and she tried to keep her face empty of the sick feeling his words were creating inside her.

"I told him, 'Don't do it, Cujo. Don't try to be stand-up. Give these assholes what they want.' I liked Cujo, but maybe not in a good way, get my meaning?" Troyce said. He turned and looked into her face to see if she understood. There was a dry click in his throat when he swallowed. "When Cujo told them to go fuck themselves, he said 'Go fouk yourself,' that's the way he said it, I felt myself getting madder and madder at him, like he was better than me, like he was braver, like no matter what they done to him, he would always be the same man and I wasn't as good as him, I was small somehow. And I thought about what my uncle and his friends done to me when I was a boy and how maybe I let it happen, how maybe I could have stopped it if I'd fought back, maybe it was my fault after all and I'd brought it on myself somehow, and I hated Cujo for being better than me and for the way maybe secretly I had feelings for him an American man don't have for an Arab terrorist."

Troyce stopped, his hands still cupped on his knees, his eyes staring down at his feet. Candace could feel a warm slick of perspiration forming between her palm and the smooth contour of Troyce's shoulder. "What did you do, Troyce?" she said, almost in a whisper.

"I joined in with the intel guys. For just a second the towel slipped, and Cujo looked straight into my face with one eye. He couldn't talk 'cause he was strangling, but he was looking at me, not at nobody else. He didn't care about the contract intel guys. I was the Judas. I saw it in his eye. He died right then. He made sure I knew that he knew, and he died."

Candace took a deep, almost ragged breath and rested her forehead on top of Troyce's head, her knees tucked against his buttocks. He continued to look straight ahead, unsure what his revelation had done to Candace's perception of him.

"That's behind you now, honey," she said. "You're sorry for what you did. That's all a person can do sometimes, just say he's sorry. I think people can forgive us from the grave. We've just got to ask them. Cujo knows you're sorry, doesn't he? Why don't you give him credit?"

"One of those contract intel guys had three cases of hot beer in his truck. We drove out in the desert and drank it. We smoked some dope and got drunk. These guys was talking about trout fishing in South Dakota. I kept pretending I was listening, but I knowed even then I wasn't ever gonna be the same."

She rearranged herself and sat next to him on the side of the bed. "Give it up, baby."

"Words don't bring back dead people. When people are in the grave, their mouths and their ears are full of dirt. They don't talk and they don't hear. I had a dream, that's all it was. I shouldn't have told you about it."

She got up from the mattress and worked her nightshirt off her shoulders and head, then spread herself across his thighs, something she had never done before. "You tell me to stop and I will," she said.

She held his head between her breasts, then picked up his phallus and placed it inside her. She felt her own eyes close and a quickening in her heart and a surge in her loins, then his hands were on her back and he was rising from the bed so he could lay her down on the mattress while he remained on top of her.

She became lost in the smell of his skin and hair, in the hardness of his sex deep inside her, in the laboring of his hips between her thighs, and she wondered if indeed she and Troyce were still lying in the pink glow of the motel neon, in a bed that thudded against the wall, or if the ferocity of his need had transported both of them to a desert where his jaws had become coated with grit and carrion birds made cawing sounds above their heads.

I GOT UP early Wednesday morning and made ham-and-onion sandwiches and packed cold drinks in an ice chest for Clete and me, then put my creel and fly vest and fly rod and hip waders in the back of my truck and knocked on his door before the sun had risen above the mountain. He said he was tied up and couldn't fish with me, that he had to see Alicia Rosecrans that day, that he had to run down a lead on Quince Whitley, that he had to talk long-distance with his former employers, Wee Willie Bimstine and Nig Rosewater, that Wee Willie and Nig's clients were skipping their bail all over Orleans Parish and Clete needed to do something about it.

"How about the pope? You need to chat him up today?" I said.

"I can't take another lecture," he said.

"I'll give you the keys. You don't like how things are going, you can drive back to town and leave me on the stream."

He gave me a long look, the kind he rarely gave anyone, one that indicated surrender to stubbornness that was worse than his own. We drove through Missoula to Bonner, then headed up the Blackfoot River to a spot an army friend had introduced me to when he and I were just back from Vietnam. It was one of those places that call to mind Hemingway's statement that the world is a fine place and well worth the fighting for. Clete and I parked on a pebbly strip of sand at the entrance to a box canyon threaded by the river. The morning was still cool, but the sun was shining on the flooded grass and exposed rocks in the shallows, and flies were hatching in the sunlight and drifting out onto a long green riffle that undulated over boulders that were as big as cars.

I promised to myself that I would keep my word and not lecture Clete, nor give him any more grief or worry than he already had to bear. We fished upstream with dry flies, working our way around a bend with high canyon walls and woods on either side of us, staying fifty yards apart so one of us would not ruin the fishing for the other. The German browns would not spawn until fall, but the rainbow and the cutthroat were hitting on a Renegade fly, whose wings float high up on the riffle and imitate the configuration and appearance of several different insects. It was grand to be on this particular stretch of the Blackfoot, not unlike entering a Renaissance cathedral. The canyon was full of wind and filtered light, and magical transformations seemed to take place constantly in the water that hummed around our thighs. It was the type of moment you do not want to give up, because you know intuitively that it is irreplaceable and even sacred in ways you don't try to describe to others.

But I believed Clete was on a collision track with a train, and as his friend, I had to say something to him, if only to share information I possessed and he did not.

Just before noon, when the sun was high above the canyon, we got out of the riffle and unsnapped our waders and sat on a cottonwood log that was sculpted as white and smooth as bone by years of spring runoff. We ate the ham-and-onion sandwiches I had made, and drank the soda I had packed in ice, and listened to the rocks creak under the heavy pull of the current.

"I went up to Swan Lake yesterday and talked with Jamie Sue Wellstone," I said.

He continued eating, watching an osprey sail above the cotton-woods. He seemed to take no note of my words.

"I believe she's a lot better person than I gave her credit for," I said.

"Glad to hear you say that, big mon."

"I learned some other things, too. The guy who calls himself J. D. Gribble is probably her boyfriend and the father of her child. Gribble is likely also a fugitive."

This time I got his attention. "Wait a minute," he said, shaking one hand in the air as though warding off flies. "The ranch hand is her ex-lover?"

"I don't know if 'ex' is the right prefix."

"The night I got sapped, when Gribble and I were drinking, I told him I got it on with Jamie Sue."

"That's not your fault. I mean, you didn't know Gribble was her boyfriend."

"I slept with one woman and cuckolded two guys. How can one guy manage that?"

"Maybe that's what both those guys deserved."

I couldn't believe what I had just said. Once again, I had slipped into my old role as Clete's enabler. He put down his sandwich on a square of waxed paper on top of the log and screwed an index finger into each temple. "What are you trying to do to my head?"

"Listen to me, Cletus. This gunbull, Troyce Nix, was at Albert's looking for a guy who probably cut some holes in him. Albert isn't saying, but I think the guy is Gribble."

"What has this got to do with the guy who tried to light me up?"

"I don't know. But you're involved with Alicia Rosecrans now. Think about what that means."

Clete Purcel was a man of large physical appetites and a propensity for violence and mayhem when the situation required it. He also had a propensity for violence and mayhem when the situation did not require it. But he was also one of the most intelligent men I have ever known. It didn't take long for the connections to come together in his eyes.

"The guy who saved me from getting burned to death may have a warrant on him, and I know this, but I'm not going to tell Alicia Rosecrans about it?"

"If you're copacetic with that, no problem. If not—"

He folded the waxed paper around his sandwich and placed the sandwich in a paper trash sack I had brought along. He stared at the stream and the froth curling around a beaver dam where I had told him some large cutthroats were holed up. "I'd better head on back," he said.

"Let's fish the dam, Clete. There'll be another hatch soon. I got a two-pounder out of there once."

"Another day," he said. He peeled off his hip waders one at a time and kicked them high in the air toward the truck, standing in his socks on the strip of pebbly beach, indifferent to the rocks cutting into his feet, his mouth hooked down at the corners, his green eyes clouded with a special kind of sadness.

QUINCE WHITLEY COULD not believe how badly he had messed up. No, that wasn't correct. Quince could not believe how badly other people had messed *him* up. He had worshipped Jamie Sue Wellstone, had told her how everybody dug her music back in Mississippi, how he had listened to her songs on the jukebox and on the late-night country broadcast from Memphis, same station that had first broadcast Jerry Lee Lewis's recordings at Sun Records, doing all this for a woman who had turned around and treated him like he was toe jam.

Then, while he's fueling up at the convenience store, minding his own business, Miss White Trash of 2007 starts staring at him like somebody upwind just passed gas. He says, "Can I help you?" and she dimes him with her swinging-dick boyfriend, this guy pretending he's a Texas lawman who then smashes Quince's face on the toilet-bowl rim because he offers the guy an honest business deal.

What happens as a result? Nothing. People outside the crapper are buying picnic supplies while Quince's bridge and a half-cup of his blood are sliding down the bowl. You hurt, fella? Of course not,

I always walk around with wads of toilet paper shoved up my nostrils.

"The difference between the black and white races?" his daddy used to say. "There ain't none. It's a state of mind, not a matter of pigmentation. Let rich people treat you like a nigra, you are one."

Quince believed what his daddy said. Folks look at you the wrong way, their nostrils thin and white around the rims like the air has gone bad, their eyes not seeing you when you look back at them, you educate them regarding the potential of a man who's been treated with a lack of respect. Back in the 1960s, Quince's uncle had been a city marshal in a little town nobody would take time to wipe his ass on. He pulled over a homegrown black boy and two white boys from up north for driving five miles above the speed limit. When their bodies were dug out of an earthen dam, everyone thought they had died because they were registering black voters. Maybe part of that was true, but it wasn't the real cause. The driver, this smart-ass Jewish college boy, had called Quince's uncle "man." Not "sir," not "constable," not even "mister." Just "man."

The legacy of violence in Quince's family was as natural in their daily lives as the bitterness and sense of failure that greeted them with each sunrise. The Whitleys nursed their resentments and carried their reputation for lethality with them, using it as a silent weapon against their enemies, in the same way the dried sweat on their skin assailed the sensibilities of others and dared them to show any objection to it.

But living vicariously through the stories of lynchings and castrations Quince had heard as a child did nothing to relieve him of his anger. He had put in five years with the Wellstones, after an adult lifetime of working in a pesticide plant and hauling hogs to Chicago and breathing granary dust in a place called Texline on the New Mexico border. He had not only found a comfortable job and home, he had come to think of himself as an extension of the Wellstone estate. He always used the term "Wellstone estate" when he was asked where he worked. It rang with a sound and cadence like gold coin bouncing off a plate.

When Leslie Wellstone had brought Jamie Sue Stapleton home

as his wife, Quince felt that starshine had been dusted on his own shoulders. Leslie Wellstone might have been educated and rich, and Leslie Wellstone might have fought in foreign wars over issues Quince knew nothing about, but Quince understood the world of country music and hardscrabble farms and picking cotton until the tips of his fingers bled. You didn't learn those kinds of things at a snooty eastern university. Jamie Sue recognized one of her own as soon as she laid eyes on him, Quince told himself. In his own mind, he had become Jamie Sue's blue-collar knight errant and personal adviser. Yes sir, Quince Whitley, a sharecropper's son, was the bodyguard and friend in need of the most beautiful woman who had ever walked out on the Opry stage. He wondered what his old friends working at the roach-paste factory would have to say about that.

Now it was all blown to hell. He had tried to sell out the Wellstones to the hick with the big dick from Bumfuck, Texas, and had gotten his ass kicked in the process. Then he'd gone back on the job at the Wellstone compound, cutting grass, pretending to run off tree huggers who, if truth be known, didn't exist, and driving Jamie Sue to the bar on Swan Lake so she could get enough brew in her to forget whom she had married.

Here he was on Thursday afternoon, driving the lawn mower across eighteen acres of yard the Wellstones and their friends played croquet and badminton on, the air hot and dry in ways it shouldn't have been, columns of smoke rising from the timber on a distant mountain. The heat made him think of Mississippi and the burnt-out end of summer days when the sky was bitten with dust blowing out of the fields. Why did he feel that everything in his life was ending, that his life had been a long elliptical path that would take him back to the same world he had tried to flee?

The weather itself seemed to plot against him. He had come to the Big Sky for the big score, not for hot days that smelled of fires and reminded him of Mississippi, not to cut people's grass, either, with clouds of grasshoppers lifting from the yellowed edges of the yard. He could feel a balloon of anger rising in his chest, one that actually pushed bile into his mouth and caused him to spit. Back home, people learned quick you didn't dump on a Whitley. Your anger was a friend, a flag under which you conducted yourself and which made other people cross the street when they saw you coming. But now he had no one to vent his anger upon, and it was consuming him as though he had swallowed a chemical agent.

Just this morning Jamie Sue had taken off for the day, the Hispanic woman carrying her baby for her, the two of them walking past Quince like he wasn't there. Quince wondered if she was still pumping it with that fat shit from New Orleans or if she was slipping off to meet this convict on the run, Jimmy Dale Greenwood. Maybe that was what galled him worst, he thought. Jamie Sue had an eye for anything in pants except Quince Whitley, the one person who had always admired and treated her with respect. That's what he got for his loyalty, the switch of the hips while she passed him on the flagstones, her lower body silhouetted through her dress against the early sun, her nose lifted in the breeze, just like that bitch at the gas pump.

The tractor-mower throbbed between Quince's thighs, calling up thoughts about other women in his life, some of them white, some black, but all of them aware you didn't dump on a Whitley, by God.

His memories of the way he had dealt with other challenges to his pride earlier in life had almost set him free from his present misery when a rock exploded from the mower blade and smacked like a rifle shot against the picture-glass window in Leslie Wellstone's study.

Leslie stepped out on the porch and motioned for Quince to cut the engine.

"Sorry about that, Mr. Wellstone," Quince said.

"It might be a good idea to rake the lawn before you run the mower past the windows," Leslie said.

"I did that, Mr. Wellstone," Quince lied. "But I'll do it again."

"Maybe use a better rake, one with finer tines."

Quince had gotten the point. Why was Wellstone pushing it? Because he liked rubbing his shit in Quince's hair, Quince told himself.

"Maria went into Missoula with Ms. Wellstone. I need you to round up the garbage and tidy up," Wellstone said.

"Sir?"

"The plastic bags are in the pantry. Empty all the wastebaskets in leaf bags, put plastic ties on them, and put fresh white bags inside the baskets. Make sure you get all the bathrooms. Take some Ajax and Windex and rags and clean the counters and mirrors and basins. Can you handle that?"

Quince could hear the wind blowing through the shrubbery. A grasshopper struck his eye and caused it to tear.

"Are you listening?" Leslie asked.

"That ain't exactly what I usually do."

"Then perhaps it's time to expand your horizons." Leslie smiled, showing his teeth.

"You got it, Mr. Wellstone," Quince replied, restarting the engine. "Just soon as I make this last cut here." Then he added under his breath, "Yassuh, boss, I's sure on it."

"What was that?"

"Said I'll be right in there, Mr. Wellstone," Quince replied above the roar of the engine, wheeling the mower away so Leslie could not see his expression.

Ten minutes later, Quince entered the back of the house through the attached garage and was told by the chef to remove his boots and to put plastic covers, like those a surgeon would wear, over his sock feet. Then he was given a huge black leaf bag and a handful of smaller white plastic bags threaded with red drawstrings and was told to begin his trash pickup under the kitchen sink, where a pile of pungent shrimp husks and spoiled potato salad waited for him.

He dragged his leaf bag throughout the mansion, filling it with all the residue and discarded material that filtered from farms and factories and stock brokerages throughout the nation into the daily lives of the Wellstones, feeding them, entertaining them, keeping them comfortable and satiated, and making them richer by the minute.

In Leslie Wellstone's office, Quince emptied a tall plastic wastebasket filled with shredded strips of paper. But some of the pages Leslie had sent through the shredder were partially intact and Quince could see the name Vanguard Group at the top and columns of tax-sheltered municipal bond accounts that ran into double-digit millions. On Ridley Wellstone's upstairs balcony, Quince emptied a champagne bucket filled with the chewed butts of illegal Havana cigars. In the bottom of Ridley's bathroom wastebasket was a used rubber. The Hispanic maid must be putting in some overtime, Quince thought. But actually, he could live with picking up the detritus of the rich and tolerating their hypocrisy. Why? Because he had been onto their secrets for a long time. The rich were no smarter than he was, no better at dealing with the world, no more worthy of their wealth than the people they hired to clean up after them. He knew things about survival they couldn't guess at. The only difference between him and the Wellstones was the difference between good luck and bad luck. The rich screwed down and married up. People like the Whitleys just got screwed.

What tore it for Quince was cleaning up in Jamie Sue's bathroom. A small straw basket was filled with lipstick-smeared Kleenex. A plastic receptacle by the toilet contained her used tampons. Her fingernail clippings lay in a spray on the black marble countertop. Strands of her hair had to be pulled out of the drain with his fingers. A Q-tip blackened with eyeliner was stuck to the base of the toilet stool.

The chef had given Quince plastic covers for his feet but none for his hands. *Thanks a lot, motherfucker.*

When he finished cleaning Jamie Sue's bathroom, he pulled the laden leaf bag down the back stairs, the garbage inside thudding heavily on each step. He opened the iron lid on the Dumpster and dropped the bag inside, a cloud of gnats and the smell of a week's rotting produce rising with the heat into his face. He slammed the lid down as loudly as he could, hoping the sound reverberated through the wall into the house.

But his wishes were fulfilled in a way he hadn't foreseen. When he turned around, Leslie Wellstone was staring at him, a frosted mint julep clutched in his right hand. "You out of sorts about something, Quince?" he said.

Quince could feel words forming in his mind that he had never spoken to a man of Leslie Wellstone's background, words requiring an intimacy and a reciprocity of trust that he realized, for the first time in his life, he actually feared.

"Speak up. Are you not feeling well?" Leslie said.

"What would you do if folks spit on you, Mr. Wellstone? If they treated you like a nigra or white trash or like you didn't have any dignity in their eyes?"

"Me? That's a good question. Let me think on it a minute. Why, I don't really know, Quince. It must be awful when somebody does that to a person," Leslie replied.

You don't even know what I'm asking you, do you? Quince said to himself. *Shows how goddamn smart any of y'all are.*

"I'd like to help you, Quince, but you got into it with that big fellow from Texas on your own," Leslie said. "Why not just file charges against him? You're not afraid of him, are you? That couldn't be the case, could it?" Leslie Wellstone lifted his julep glass to his mouth and drank, his eyes brightening.

"Nobody disrespects a Whitley and gets away with it," Quince said.

But Leslie Wellstone had lost interest in the conversation, and he went back into the house without replying. When he pulled the door into place behind him, the rubber seal along the jamb hissed from the compression of air inside. A fire had broken out above Swan Lake, and the bottoms of the clouds along the mountaintop had turned a soft red from the flames' updraft. Quince felt as though ants were crawling across his brain.

Hurt them all, one by one, in ways they've never been hurt before, a voice inside him said. *Get to Mr. Leslie Wellstone last, the way you save out a dessert. See if he's got that smirk on his mouth then.*

But where to start?

Quince walked toward the garage apartment he shared with Lyle Hobbs. What did the man from West Texas own that he couldn't bear to lose?

Quince's answer to his own question created an image in his mind that made him close his eyes and wet his lips, like a hungry man about to begin a fine meal.

CHAPTER 18

Late the next afternoon, Candace Sweeney dressed by the bed while Troyce was showering. Through the open door, she could see his used bandages in the wastebasket. They were dry, unspotted by blood, and had been that way for three days. For the first time she began to believe that Troyce would heal in both body and spirit and that an opportunity was at hand for the two of them to simply step through a door into a life that would have no connection to their pasts.

"You believe in karma?" she said through the door.

He turned off the water and began drying himself on top of the bath mat. His body was pink from the shower heat, the hard contours of his chest and ribs and the flatness of his stomach a study in power and masculinity, his wounds like black zippers on his skin.

"Karma is for people looking for excuses, if you ask me," he said.

"There's different kinds of karma," Candace said. "It's like people's lives are supposed to intersect, but not because that's their fate. The intersection is the place where they make the choice that results in their fate. See?"

"No."

"It means a certain kind of fate doesn't have to be ours. It means there are people we're destined to meet. It's them that lets us choose the door we're supposed to walk through."

"Where'd you get all this stuff?" he said, smiling, wiping at his hair with the towel.

"From a guy who used to smoke dope with us in Pioneer Courthouse Square in Portland."

"You're cute," he said.

"You don't take me seriously sometimes, Troyce."

"Always," he said, placing a towel on the bedspread, then sitting down nude next to her. He put his arm around her shoulders. "You've got the prettiest-shaped face of any woman I ever knowed. I love your tattoos, too. Not many women look good tattooed, but you do."

She placed her hand on his thigh. She could smell the clean odor of his hair and feel the heat his skin gave off. "We could just go away. Pack it up and start all over," she said.

"Where?"

"Washington or Oregon. We could open a café in the Cascades for tourists and loggers. I'm a good cook, Troyce. I know everything there is about food service. The key to a café's success is having a good cook and making sure your suppliers aren't cheating you. You'd be good at managing a café. You ever been to the Cascades?"

"I don't see that happening right now."

She thought a long time before she spoke again. "Troyce?"

"What is it, you little honey bunny?"

"You're in over your head."

"Not to my mind, I ain't."

"Messing with rich people like the Wellstones? Think you're gonna come up here and write the rules with people like that?"

"You ain't got to tell me about the likes of the Wellstones. I knowed their kind all my life."

"Your wounds are healing up now. Isn't that a sign?"

"Of what?"

"Those choices I was talking about. The fate that's waiting for us if we'll just reach out and take it."

"The choice right now is what kind of steak we're gonna order at that club up yonder."

He patted her on the back, then slipped on his boxer shorts and began combing his hair in front of the mirror.

"You want me to put on fresh bandages for you?" she asked, her face blank now, all of her arguments used up.

"Don't worry about them rich people. They ain't interested in folks like us. We ain't got nothing they want," Troyce said.

"We went to their house. We told them we know their business. You told them you beat up one of their employees. They won't forget it," she said.

He stopped combing his hair and looked at her reflection in the mirror.

Ten minutes later, when they were about to leave, someone with a heavy fist knocked hard on the door. Candace peeked through the window curtain. A man with sandy blond hair and a scar that ran through one eyebrow waited in front of the door. He wore a porkpie hat and a Hawaiian shirt that was almost bursting at the shoulders. A semi passed on the road, and the man turned and watched it disappear around a bend. The back of his neck was oily and pockmarked. His whole body seemed to be supercharged by energies that it could barely contain.

"Who is it?" Troyce said to Candace.

"A guy who looks like a cop or a bill collector," she replied.

"Let him in. It's been a dull day," Troyce said.

CLETE PURCEL OPENED his badge holder when he entered the room and introduced himself. The room smelled of aftershave and hair tonic. "Albert Hollister gave me the name of your motel," he said. "He says you're interested in finding a guy by the name of Jimmy Dale Greenwood. An Indian, I think."

"More like a breed," Troyce said. "Know where he's at?"

"Can't say I do. You know who Ridley and Leslie Wellstone are?"

Clete saw the young woman's eyes shift onto Nix's face.

"I know they're probably the richest people in the state of Texas," Nix replied.

Clete studied Nix's expression. It was relaxed and confident, even good-natured. Clete said, "Somebody tried to light me up, Mr. Nix. Problem is, I got no idea who. But one way or another—"

"Light you up?" the woman said.

"A man in a mask sapped me with a blackjack and tied me to a tree and poured gasoline on me and tried to burn me alive. I don't know who this dude is, but one way or another, I think he's involved with the Wellstones. You have any opinion on that, Mr. Nix?"

"Not really. Jimmy Dale Greenwood is a fugitive from the law. He escaped while in the custody of a contract prison which I'm a founding officer of. He was also the boyfriend of Jamie Sue Wellstone, formerly Jamie Sue Stapleton. Does that clear things up for you, Mr. Purcel?"

"There're people who think you kicked the shit out of a guy by the name of Quince Whitley. Why would you do a thing like that, Mr. Nix?"

"Troyce hasn't done anything wrong," the woman said. "I think you need to spend more time at Weight Watchers and quit bothering people who haven't bothered you."

Clete saw Nix suppress a laugh. The woman was three feet from Clete, her thumbs hooked in her back pockets, her chin and her boobs pointed at him. She wore a Mexican blouse and black jeans and had a small Irish mouth and bangs like a little girl's.

"I had a friend run Quince Whitley's sheet," Clete said to Nix. "Guess what. He doesn't have one. Does it seem reasonable to you that a dude like that wouldn't have a sheet?"

"I'm not interested in this fellow you're talking about," Nix replied.

"You should be. I made a couple of calls to the county in Mississippi where he grew up. Quince put out a girl's eye with a BB gun when he was ten. A retired sheriff told me he thought Quince and two of his friends dropped a log from a railroad overpass through the windshield of an automobile. They almost killed the driver, a black man from Memphis. But the log and any prints on it disappeared the same night. Quince's uncle was in charge of the investigation. The uncle was also an officer in the Ku Klux Klan. That's why

Quince doesn't have a sheet. Are you going to bother my friend Mr. Hollister again?"

"I couldn't care less about your friend, Mr. Purcel. Second of all, I don't think that's why you're here. You've got a bug up your ass about either the Wellstone family or Jimmy Dale Greenwood. Which is it, or is it both?"

"Two college kids were abducted from the hillside behind the university and murdered. One of them wore a wood cross. It was of a kind that kids in the Wellstone ministry program are given. Then a California couple who had been drinking in a saloon on Swan Lake with Jamie Sue Wellstone were murdered in a rest stop on the interstate west of Missoula. The woman was set on fire in the toilet stall. I think the guy who committed these murders is the same guy who tried to turn me into a candle. If I find out you're holding back on me, Mr. Nix, you and I will be shooting the breeze again."

"Listen, lard ass, nobody invited you here," the woman said. "Go to a blubber farm or get your stomach stapled. Just go somewhere else. Think about changing your brand of deodorant while you're at it."

Clete gave Nix and his girlfriend a long look. Nix was laughing under his breath while the girlfriend stared up into Clete's face with what seemed to be barely restrained outrage. Except Clete was convinced her emotions were manufactured.

"Thanks for your time. Welcome to Montana. It's a real tolerant place," Clete said.

He went outside into the twilight and got into his Caddy. He let out his breath and started the engine, revving it up senselessly. What had he accomplished? he asked himself. Nothing, except perhaps to indicate to Troyce Nix that Nix had gotten close to finding Jimmy Dale Greenwood, also known as J. D. Gribble. Clete shifted the transmission into reverse. The convertible top was down and the air was cool, the hills along the winding two-lane road already purple with shadow. Just as he began to back onto the asphalt, he heard footsteps on the gravel.

Troyce Nix's girlfriend cupped both of her hands on top of the passenger door. Her eyes were glistening. "Were you saying this guy Quince Whitley might be the one who killed all those people?" she asked.

"Ask your bozo boyfriend," Clete said, and gunned the Caddy onto the highway.

As he sped away, the young woman grew smaller in his rearview mirror, his dust drifting back into her face. *Way to go, Purcel,* he thought. *Next time out, beat up on a cerebral palsy victim.*

THE SUNSET HAD died on the far side of the mountain when Candace Sweeney and Troyce Nix pulled into the club up the road from their motel. The bottom of the valley was dark with shadow, but the sky overhead was still blue, tinged with the pink afterglow of the sun, the moon as thin as a wafer over the mountains that jutted straight up from the south banks of the Clark Fork River. The day was cooling rapidly, the eastern sky starting to grow dark, like the color of a bruise. Candace could smell smoke blowing from a fire up in the Swans. The smell seemed to hang in the air, to wrap itself around her skin and seep into her lungs. She wondered if it was an omen.

"It's too early in the season for fires," she said. "June is always wet. There're no serious fires here till August."

"Well, they're not burning here," Troyce said, walking beside her toward the club's entrance.

"You ever been to Portland or Vancouver?" she asked.

"Nope."

"You'd like it out there, the fishing and outdoors and all. It's green all year round, like down south. Like Miami, except with rain and cool weather."

He was still wearing his shades, even though the sun had set. He pulled them off and slipped them in a leather case. He pinched the bridge of his nose and blinked. "We can check it out," he said. "In the meantime, ain't nobody running us off. That ain't our way."

She didn't pursue it.

The inside of the club was crowded, the country band located on the far side of the dance floor, the tables filled with people who were

drinking pitcher beer and eating fried chicken and pork-chop sandwiches and steaks ordered from the truck-stop café that adjoined the
main building. Candace and Troyce had to take a table by the entrance, one that gave them a poor view of the bandstand and dance
floor. Troyce kept trying to get the waiter's eye.

"This is gonna take all night. I'll get a pitcher from the bar and
order direct from next door," he said, getting up from his chair.
"Don't run off with no movie stars."

"What movie stars?" she said, looking up at him.

"Look yonder at the end of the bar."

A man with rugged good looks was buying a round for a half-
dozen people who were gathered around him, much like candle
moths hovering around a flame inside a glass chimney.

"He's in that new western," Candace said.

"And he was looking at you, darlin'. Tell him you're taken."

"That's silly," she said.

But after Troyce left, she realized the actor *was* looking at her
with a faint smile while he pretended to listen to the conversation
going on around him. He set his glass down and approached her
table. She studied the tops of her hands. When she looked up again
the actor was standing two feet from her, his fingers resting on the
back of Troyce's empty chair.

"I wondered if you and your friend would like to join us," he
said.

"We just ordered dinner," she replied.

"After you eat, come over to the bar for a drink."

He was of medium height but extremely handsome in the way
that some men can be handsome without trying, his dark hair freshly
barbered, his skin clear, his dress shirt and gray slacks loose on his
athletic frame.

"Thank you, but we just came here to eat." She glanced toward
the doorway that led into the truck stop. "We're probably not staying long."

"You ought to. They got a great band. There's a guy sitting in
with them who's really good."

"Thanks for the invitation. We're just going to eat."

"You ever do any film work?"

"No. I don't know anything about it."

"I'd like to talk to you about it. Your friend, too. He's got an unusual face. Was he in an accident of some kind?"

"I'm a cook. Listen, I love your movies, but you're talking to the wrong person." She tried to smile. She looked toward the entrance to the truck stop again. "I think my friend is coming back with our food."

"It's nice meeting you," the actor said. "What's your name?"

"It's Candace. Excuse me, I got to go to the restroom."

"Where do you live?"

"In a motel up the road. No, I'm kidding. Troyce and me own half of Beverly Hills. We eat in dumps like this for kicks."

"If you change your mind, Candace, we'll be at the bar. I'm not hitting on you. I meant what I said."

When Candace returned from the restroom, her heart was still pounding. Troyce was sitting at the table, a foaming pitcher and two glasses in front of him.

"I was right, wasn't I?" he said.

"About what?"

"That guy had his eye on you."

"He wanted to invite us for a drink. He said maybe both of us could work in films. I think he was just being a nice guy, that's all."

"Yeah?" he said, grinning. "What'd you tell him?"

"That we were having dinner. You're not gonna do anything, are you?"

"You know better than that," he said playfully. "I ordered your steak medium well done, with a baked potato and double melted butter and a salad with buttermilk dressing. That's what you wanted, right?"

But she realized she *didn't* know better than that. In his dreams, Troyce traveled to places she could never enter, and he saw things and heard sounds inside closed rooms that she refused to let herself think about. When she watched the news about a distant war where American soldiers trudged through biscuit-colored villages blown with flies and garbage, she tried to imagine Troyce as one of them, brave, uncomplaining, his uniform stiff with salt, his skin gray with dust, like a Roman legionnaire coming out of a sandstorm. But all she could think of was Troyce in a closed room while a man with a towel wrapped around his face was being drowned.

Out of the corner of her eye, she saw the actor take a mixed drink from the bartender and place it in the hand of a windburned, dark-featured man who wore jeans and a denim jacket and whose un-shaved face was the same as that of the man in the jailhouse photo that Troyce carried in his billfold. Her beer glass trembled in her hand.

"That fellow eyeballing you again?" Troyce said.

"No," she said, taking his wrist, keeping his eyes on hers. "Troyce, let's go over to the Cascades. We can stop for the night in Coeur d'Alene and go on in the morning. I'll show you the place where we can start up our café. We can have a good life there."

"I declare if you're not a puzzle," he replied.

WITHOUT TROYCE NIX'S ever noticing, a diesel-powered fire-engine-red pickup truck with oversize tires and headlights that sparkled had followed him from the motel to the club. Now the driver of the pickup sat in the cab in the parking lot, gazing through the windshield at the front of the club, wondering about his next move. The driver was wearing neatly pressed navy blue work pants and a wide belt with a big chrome buckle and a magenta shirt that changed colors in the light. He also wore a black vest, with a silk back, like a nineteenth-century gunfighter or a riverboat gambler might wear. He had shaved and gotten a haircut that afternoon and had showered and washed his hair. He had put on a Resistol hat and a new pair of Acme pointy-toed boots. Looking at himself in the mirror before he left his garage apartment on the Wellstone estate, he hardly recognized his reflection. He had drawn all his money out of the bank and had put eight one-hundred-dollar bills in his wallet, clipped by a chain onto his belt. He had also dropped a clasp knife with a hooked blade for cutting thick twine into his trouser pocket.

Somehow, in surrendering himself to the deeds he was about to commit, Quince Whitley had discovered he possessed a persona he had never thought would be his, namely that of a Mississippi farm boy who had become the debonair scourge of God. That thought caused a surge in his blood that was like his first time with a black girl, way back when it was exciting, back before he stopped keeping count.

"Getting your ashes hauled tonight?" Lyle Hobbs had asked him.

Quince had just finished combing his hair. He blew the dandruff out of the comb's leather case and slipped the comb inside. "That's one way to put it. Except the lady doesn't necessarily know what's on her dance card yet," Quince had said.

In the silence, Lyle had seemed to look at Quince in a different light.

Now Quince sat tapping his hands on the steering wheel, staring whimsically at the split-log facade of the club and the strings of tiny white lights that framed the windows and the dark shadow of the mountain that lifted into the sky just beyond the rear of the building. He could hear the music of a country band, a clatter of dishware, and a balloon of voices when a door opened and closed. He could play the situation several ways, but he knew Quince Whitley's time had come around at last, and all the people who had hurt him, including that burned freak and his wife up at Swan Lake, were going to get their buckwheats. You just don't dump on a Whitley, bubba, whether it's in Mississippi or Montana or Blow Me, North Dakota.

He removed a twenty-five-caliber automatic from under the dashboard and Velcro-strapped it to his right ankle. From under the seat he removed a small brown plastic-capped bottle of sulfuric acid, wrapped it carefully in a handkerchief, and slipped it into his pants pocket. Then he walked around behind the club and entered through the back door so he could sit in a dark area where the bar curved into the wall and watch the band and the dancers on the floor and the people eating at the tables in the front of the building.

• • •

TROYCE WAS ENJOYING his T-bone, forking meat and french fries into his mouth with his left hand. He drank from his beer and winked at Candace. "Don't be worrying, little darlin'. People like us is forever," he said.

"You're willful and hardheaded, Troyce."

"If you don't find your enemies, your enemies will find you."

"My father's nickname was Smilin' Jack. He had impractical dreams. He thought he was gonna find gold in the Cascades," she said.

"Yeah?" Troyce said, not understanding.

"I don't know if he found his gold or not. If he did, he probably died doing it. He never came out of the mountains. But he believed in his dreams."

"Your meaning is I don't?"

"You don't know how to dream. You're caught up in a mission. You're like a bat trying to find its hole in the daylight."

"Wish you wouldn't talk that way."

"You break my heart," she said.

He crossed his knife and fork on his plate and rested his hands on the table. "I thought you wanted to come here," he said. "What the hell is going on?"

She stared at nothing, her face wan.

"I bet your old man was a good guy," Troyce said. "It's too bad he went away. But everybody gets hurt. Life's a sonofabitch, then you die. In the meantime, you don't let people run you over."

She thought about leaving and walking back to the motel. But if she did that, eventually she would have to tell Troyce why—namely that she had recognized the man he had come to Montana to find. "The food is real good. I'm glad we came here," she said. "After we eat, I'd like to go back to the motel, though. I'm not feeling too good."

He picked up his knife and fork and began eating again. A few minutes later, up on the bandstand, the dark-skinned man in jeans and a denim jacket sat down in a straight-back chair and placed a Dobro across his thighs. Another musician lowered a microphone so it would pick up the notes from the Dobro's resonator. The man in the denim jacket slipped three steel picks on his left hand and slid a chrome-plated bar along the guitar's neck, the resonator picking up the steel hum of the strings, a sustained tremolo like the vibration in the blade of a saw. The band and the man in the denim jacket began to play in earnest. Troyce kept eating, seemingly unmindful of the music, his face empty.

Then he looked up from his plate and smiled. "What's the name of that piece?" he asked.

She shook her head.

"It's a Bob Wills number, ain't it?" he said.

"I don't know, Troyce," she replied.

" 'Cimarron,' that's what it is," he said.

"I got to go to the restroom. I really don't feel good."

But Troyce had spent a lifetime reading lies in other people's faces. "Did that actor upset you? Tell me the truth. I'm not gonna hurt him. You got my word. But tell me what's going on here."

"I got the headspins, that's all. I don't know what it is."

She got up unsteadily from the table and walked between the dance floor and the groups of people drinking at the bar. The actor was facing the bar, talking to his friends. When he saw her approach, he stepped away from them into her path. "Decide to join us?" he said.

"Tell the guy playing the bottle-neck guitar that Troyce Nix is here. Tell him to get his ass out the back door," Candace said.

"That's J. D. Gribble. He's a quiet, gentle guy. I think you've got him mistaken for somebody else."

"I don't know his name. If you like your friend, take him somewhere else, you hear me?" she said.

"What'd he do?"

"You asked if Troyce was in an accident. The accident was the guy up there on the bandstand."

The actor raised his eyebrows and set his drink on the bar. His cheeks were slightly sunken, his jaw well defined, his eyes clear as he looked at her. "I'd like to help," he said. "But it's not my business."

She walked away, not surprised by the actor's unwillingness to involve himself in the plight of another, but oddly depressed just the same. When she returned from the restroom, the actor was still looking at her. "I did it," he said.

"Did what?"

"What you said. I did it. But I don't think J.D. could hear me over the noise. He was toking on a jay earlier. I tried. What's your last name?"

"Why?"

"You're fucking beautiful is why."

"It's my tattoos and the pits in my skin that turn men on," she replied.

When she sat back down with Troyce, he was looking at her strangely. "Were you talking with that actor again?"

"He said I was beautiful."

"He's got good judgment."

"My stomach's not right. I'd like to go back to the motel," she said.

"You're jerking me around about something. I just don't know what it is," he replied.

"You ever hear of Looney Larry Lewis?"

"No."

"He was a black roller-derby star in Miami. He told me I was the only girl he ever met who was as crazy as he was. He meant it as a compliment. I can't finish my food."

Troyce put down his knife and fork and sat back in his chair. He wiped his mouth with a paper towel and dropped the towel on the table. "I'll get a box," he said.

CLETE PURCEL CALLED me on his cell phone just after nine P.M. I had not seen him all day. Since he had become involved with Special Agent Rosecrans, which in Clete's case meant in the sack and in trouble, I had seen less and less of him.

"I'm in the parking lot of a joint on the two-lane in East Missoula. I could use some backup," he said.

"What's the deal?" I asked.

"I interviewed this prison guard Troyce Nix and his girlfriend at their motel, then decided to follow them later, just to see what might develop. So I ended up at this juke joint where—"

"Why are you following Nix?"

"Because both he and his girlfriend are hinky."

"In what way?"

"The guy who tried to fry me had a mask on. I don't think it was because he's seen too many chain-saw movies. I think his face is deformed, like Nix's or the sheriff's or Leslie Wellstone's."

"We've talked about this before."

"Quince Whitley is here, too."

"Where?"

"At the juke joint. Are you listening to anything I say?"

"Anything else going on?"

"Yeah, J. D. Gribble is up on the bandstand. How's that for a perfecta? Jesus—"

"What?"

"I'm outside. Gribble just came out the back door with this actor and some other people. What's that actor's name, the guy in that new western? They're smoking dope."

QUINCE WHITLEY WAS getting sick of watching this collection of Hollywood characters down the bar from him. Who were *they*, anyway? They all thought their shit was chocolate ice cream, but probably not one of them had ever heard of Tammy Wynette or Marty Stuart or knew they came from Mississippi, or knew that Marty Stuart was from Neshoba County, where those civil rights workers got killed back in the 1960s, because that racial crap was all they cared about, not the fact that a celebrity like Elvis grew up in Tupelo. One guy had even been hitting on Troyce Nix's punch, keeping his eyes level with hers, like he wasn't aware of her tattooed bongos sticking out of the top of her blouse. For just a second Quince entertained a fantasy in which he was a movie director, orchestrating the deaths of Nix, the girl, and the actor, turning the three of them into a bloody swatch across a camera lens. *Now, that would be a movie worth seeing,* he thought.

From his bar stool in the shadows, he had a wide view of the building's interior, with enough people between him and Nix and the girl so they wouldn't take particular notice of him. Also, he realized that his new persona—clean-shaved, immaculately dressed, his sideburns trimmed, the Resistol low on his brow—was not cosmetic. Quince had become somebody else, on his own, no longer taking orders from the Wellstones. He was the captain of his soul, with the power to arbitrarily decide whom he would leave his mark on.

"See that couple eating at the table by the door?" he said to the bartender.

"What about them?" the bartender said, looking at Quince, not the doorway.

"Send them some Champale or a beer and a shot or whatever they're drinking. Just don't tell them who sent it over."

"Somebody's birthday?" the bartender asked.

"Something like that."

"I'm a mixologist. Talk to the table waiter."

"I should have known that. I can see this is an uptown joint," Quince said.

The band had taken a break, and the actor who had been scoping out Nix's girl was going in and out of the back door with one of the guitar players, a guy who looked familiar for some reason. The guitar player had put his Dobro in a case and carried it outside with him; he was evidently through playing for the evening. He looked like a Mexican or an Indian. Where had Quince seen him? Was he the guy the Wellstones were looking for, the one who had been putting the wood to Jamie Sue down in Texas? No, it couldn't be. Not unless the guy had a death wish or wanted to go back to prison.

Whenever the back door opened and closed, Quince could smell an odor like leaves and damp moss burning on a winter day. Those Hollywood douche bags were smoking dope in full view in a state that still officially employed a hangman. *What a bunch of idiots,* he thought. Then he glanced toward the front of the building. Troyce Nix was boxing up his girlfriend's food, preparing to leave.

Quince swallowed the rest of his beer and went out the back door, ignoring the dope smokers and the breed with the guitar case. How

was Quince going to play it with Nix and the girl? Answer: any way
he felt like it. The "new" Quince was in control, dealing the play,
doing what *he* wanted to his victims, every moment of their fate in
his hands. His victims didn't have any kick coming, either. The girl
had dissed him at the gas pump up in the Swan, and Nix had attacked him without provocation in the can, smashing his head into
the rubber machine, breaking his mouth and bridge apart on the rim
of the bowl. Maybe he should take down Nix and the girl in an iso-
lated place where he could make each of them watch the fate of the
other. The thought made his colon constrict and his genitalia hum
like a nest of bees. This was a payback he was going to savor.

The question was one of method and how to make it hurt as long
as possible. He stood at the corner of the building and watched
Nix and the girl emerge from the front door and walk toward their
SUV. The mountainsides were black with shadow, the trees hardly
distinguishable, the sky purple, Venus twinkling in the west. Quince
watched Nix open the passenger door for his girl, then hand her the
boxed remnants of her supper.

Take both Nix and the girl down at once? Or pop Nix with the
twenty-five and get the girl into the truck?

Bad idea. Gunfire would draw witnesses. Quince's concept of revenge did not include doing time in Deer Lodge. The challenge was
to get Nix out of the way so he could mess up the girl proper. He
wondered how Nix would like her without a nose or with eyes that
had been burned out of their sockets.

Nix shut the passenger door and started around the front of the
vehicle. Then he touched his shirt pocket. The girl rolled down the
window and stuck her head out. "What is it?" she said.

"Guess," he said.

"I saw them on the table," she said.

"I'll be right back," Nix said.

Quince couldn't believe his luck. Nix was headed back inside
the nightclub, and the girl with the muskmelon boobs had gotten
out of the SUV and propped her ass against the headlight while she
watched a Forest Service slurry bomber approach the airport.

The girl first, then Nix later, Quince thought. So Nix would have the opportunity to see what happened when you tried to dump on a Whitley.

THE MAN WHO called himself J. D. Gribble took a final hit off the roach clips being passed around the circle, hefted up his Dobro case, and said good night to his newly acquired friends.

"Come see me in the Palisades," the actor said. "I really dig your voice. You sound like Ben Johnson. I could cast you in a minute."

"Who's Ben Johnson?" J.D. asked.

J.D.'s new friends grinned, pretty sure he was kidding. J.D. walked along the side of the nightclub into the main parking lot. He never did well with booze or weed, and he could not explain why he used either one. But use them he did. This evening he'd drunk four beers and smoked dope on top of them, and now the high he had experienced had been replaced by feelings of both corpulence and carnality, as though his metabolism had been systemically invaded by weevil worms. He paused and took a breath under a cone of light emanating from a pole above his head. The air was heavy and damp and stained with smoke from fires that were breaking out north of Seeley Lake. Then he proceeded toward Albert Hollister's pickup truck, which he had borrowed for the evening. But something was happening on the periphery of his vision, something that was out of place or wrong or nonsensical, like a broken shard of memory that had tangled itself on the corner of his eye.

A man in a cowboy hat and western vest like a gunfighter would wear was walking toward an SUV. J.D. thought he had seen the same man outside the café on Swan Lake, sitting behind the wheel of Jamie Sue Wellstone's Mercedes, waiting patiently for her to leave the saloon next door. Even in that innocuous setting, J.D. had made Jamie Sue's driver as a violent man for hire. But why would he be here? Had Leslie Wellstone finally run J.D. to ground and sicced his dogs on him?

A girl was leaning against the front end of the SUV, watching a large plane descend through the valley toward the airport. Her back was turned to the man in the vest.

J.D. stepped out of the cone of light and let his eyes adjust to the gloom. The man in the vest held a brown pill bottle in his right hand and was unscrewing the cap as he walked. His trousers were tight on his hips, the bottoms tucked into his cowboy boots. A fat wallet on a chain protruded from his back pocket. The silk back of his vest glowed like dull tin when a pair of car lights flashed across it. He moved mechanically, his torso rigid, his stiff hat jiggling on his head. J.D. saw him hold the uncapped bottle away from his body, his fingers pinched hard against the glass, careful not to spill the contents on his skin. The girl heard the sound of feet on the gravel and turned around. She was smiling, as though she expected to see a friend.

My cell rang at 9:21 p.m. "What's your ten-twenty? There's some weird shit going down," Clete said.

"There's been an accident on Brooks. What weird shit?" I said.

"Gribble and Whitley are both in the parking lot. So is Nix's girl. Dave—"

The connection went dead.

Quince Whitley could smell the fumes rising from the bottle in his hand. He had wanted to bring a paper cup of water with him and throw it in the girl's face before he hit her with the acid. His uncle the Klansman had told him sulfuric acid and water produced a devastating combination on human tissue, but there hadn't been time to plan. Well, that's just the way it was. No worry, though. Pitching the acid directly into her eyes would do the job, and it was doubtful that the girl would ever be identifying her attacker in a lineup.

She had been smiling when he approached her, but now she was staring at him curiously, not recognizing him, the smile starting to die on her mouth. It took all of Quince's self-restraint not to tell her who he was before he stole her sight and destroyed her face.

"Hey, you! What the hell you doin'?" a voice called out.

Quince's head jerked sideways, and he almost spilled the acid on himself. The musician he had seen on the bandstand was running at him, his guitar case swinging out in front of him, like a man trying to catch a train.

Do it now, Quince thought. *Then drop the breed and bag ass. Do it, do it, do it.*

He flung the acid at the girl's face. But the breed lifted his guitar case in front of her, and the acid flattened against its top and foamed on the plastic and cardboard and filled the air with a stench like rotten eggs. Some of the splatter also landed on Quince's hand and wrist and cheek, and the pain was like someone touching his skin with a soldering iron.

But his ordeal was not over. The breed smashed him in the face with the end of the guitar case, knocking him backward onto the gravel. Quince tried to make sense out of what was happening to him. Only seconds earlier, he had been the "new" Quince Whitley, in control, dressed like a gunfighter, painted with magic, the giver of death. Now he lay in a parking lot, his skin burning, far from the place of his birth, a girl—no, a bitch—and a half-breed staring down at him, their faces dour with disgust and loathing, not because of what he had tried to do but because of what he was—a failure, unwanted in the womb, despised at birth, raised in a world where every day he had to prove he was better than a black person.

What does a Whitley do when he doesn't have anything else to lose?

He could almost hear his uncle's voice: "That one's easy, boy. Leave hair on the walls."

Quince got to his feet, pulling the twenty-five auto from the Velcro-strapped holster on his ankle. "Suck on this, all y'all, starting with you, sweetheart," he said. He felt his finger tighten inside the trigger guard. He aimed carefully so the first round would take the girl in the mouth.

That was when Clete Purcel came out of nowhere and lifted his thirty-eight revolver with both hands and blew Quince Whitley's skullcap and brains all over Troyce Nix's windshield.

CHAPTER
19

CITY AND COUNTY emergency vehicles were already at the scene when I arrived. Clete was sitting in the passenger seat of a cruiser, the door open, his feet outside on the gravel, while a plainclothes investigator interviewed him. His face looked poached, pale around the eyes. He was looking up at the investigator, who stood outside the cruiser. I could see Clete's chest rising and falling under his oversize Hawaiian shirt. He reminded me of a guppy seeking oxygen at the top of a polluted aquarium. The paramedics had just zipped up a body bag on a corpse and were pushing the gurney toward the back of an ambulance. There was a stench in the air like smoke from burning garbage or a dead fire. The overhead lights in the parking lot glowed with a greasy iridescence inside the humidity, buzzing with a sound that made me think of blowflies. The two-lane highway the club was on threaded its way back through a place called Hellgate Canyon. The only good thing I could see in the entire scene was the absence of cuffs on Clete's wrists.

I had to work my way through a large crowd of onlookers that had gathered behind the crime-scene tape, and show my Iberia Parish badge to a uniformed deputy to gain access to the sheriff, Joe Bim Higgins. The sheriff was not in a good mood.

"What are you doing here?" he said.

"Clete Purcel called me for backup," I replied.

"He inserts himself into a criminal investigation and calls you instead of 911 just before he kills a man? That's interesting. Is this the way you do business in Louisiana?"

"If Clete shot somebody, it was for a reason."

"I've seen Purcel's sheet. Your friend is rolling chaos. The victim is Quince Whitley, a guy your friend had a grudge against. Now Whitley's brains are glued to a windshield. You think there might be a problem here?"

"Can I talk to Clete?" I asked.

"When my investigator is through with him."

"Thank you."

"Don't get the wrong impression. I'm fed up with both you guys."

The ambulance made its way through the crowd and headed back through Hellgate Canyon, its siren off, its emergency lights pulsing in the darkness. I saw Candace Sweeney and Troyce sitting in the back of another cruiser, talking to a deputy in the front seat. The interior light was on, and I could see blood splatter like tiny rose petals on Candace's blouse. Five minutes later, the investigator who had been questioning Clete put away his notepad and rejoined the sheriff. Clete walked toward me, his face empty, his green eyes locked on mine, like a drunk man who thinks the ground might cave under him at any moment.

"What happened?" I said.

"Whitley was going to toss acid in the girl's face. J. D. Gribble threw his guitar case in front of her. Whitley pulled a hideaway and was about to drop her. So I parked one above his ear." He widened his eyes briefly, as though his words were floating in front of him.

"Where's Gribble?"

"He took off in Albert's truck."

"He doesn't want to be a hero again?"

"He saw Troyce Nix coming out of the club. I think Gribble is the dude Nix has been looking for."

"We need to get you a lawyer."

"I'm clean on this one, Dave. The girl saw what happened. So did Nix. Gribble left his guitar case behind. There's acid all over it. I've got a permit for the piece in five states, including Montana."

"Higgins is pissed off. Don't empower him. You made your statement. From this moment on, you're deaf, dumb, and don't know."

"Forget Higgins. I need a drink."

"You're serious?"

"I just splattered a guy's grits all over an SUV. So it's time for a double Jack and a beer back, and that's the way it is." He started to walk away, then stopped and turned around. "You want a Diet Doc?"

"Tell Higgins where you're going."

"He's got my piece and my keys. I can't go anywhere. The way I see it, I'm the injured party here, not Higgins, not the dirt bag I just smoked. What's the matter with you, Dave? You know the score. The locals can't clean up their own shit, and they're putting it on us. We were locking up the skells when these guys were in the 4-H Club."

You're wrong, Cletus, I thought. But I didn't want to argue with him. For a lifetime, violence and the shedding of blood had been our addiction and bane. We had traded off our youth for Vietnam and had brought back a legacy of gall and vinegar that we could not rinse out of dreams. We had learned little from the past and were condemned to recommit most of its mistakes. This parking lot was perhaps just another stopping-off place in our odyssey toward the destruction of everything we loved. Clete's cavalier attitude was a poor disguise for the ethos of blood and the heart-pounding adrenaline high of burnt cordite we had chosen for ourselves. Unfortunately, illusion is sometimes the only element that keeps us sane, and you don't rob others of it when they need it most.

What's the point? You don't have to drink alcohol to stay drunk.

I saw two deputies finishing a search of the diesel-powered truck Quince Whitley had driven to the nightclub. I also saw Special Agent Alicia Rosecrans talking to them. She was not wearing the customary blue windbreaker with yellow lettering on the back that she and her colleagues usually wore when they investigated a crime scene, and she was obviously agitated by the way things were going. She made a call on her cell phone, then snapped it shut when the deputies tried to hook Whitley's pickup to a tow truck.

"What's the trouble?" I said, walking up to the three of them.

"Who are you?" one of the deputies asked.

"Dave Robicheaux," I said. I already had my badge holder in my hand. I opened and closed it before he could take a good look at it. "What'd y'all come up with?"

He held up a bone-colored mask inside a large Ziploc bag. The mask was made of plastic and was shiny and ribbed with streaks of blue when the light struck its angular surfaces. "I think we may have our guy," the deputy said.

"Which guy?" I said.

"The one who's been killing people around here. You're not working with Joe Bim?" the deputy said.

"I have. I'm here to help in any way I can," I said.

"You were conducting the search without gloves, you idiot," Alicia Rosecrans said to the deputy. "You didn't try to obtain a telephone warrant, either. You may have already queered the evidence."

The deputy had a brush mustache and salt-and-pepper hair. He shook his head and looked at me. "You know her?" he asked.

"Do you want to say something to me?" Alicia Rosecrans asked.

"No ma'am," the deputy replied. He laughed to himself and looked at his partner.

"Then you'd better change your fucking attitude," she said.

"What else did you guys find?" I asked.

"A transfer of ownership in the glove box. It looks like this guy just bought his truck from somebody named Leslie Wellstone."

"Where was the mask?" I asked.

"Under the backseat, wrapped in an old shirt."

"I don't want to break in on all you swinging dicks here, but none of you are to put your hands on that truck," Alicia Rosecrans said. "We have jurisdiction on this investigation, and as of this moment you're out of it. In about five minutes, three people who talk like me are going to be kicking a telephone pole up your ass."

"Yes ma'am. Whatever you say. We got it. We're here to please. So sayonara or *hasta la vista,* whichever you prefer," the deputy said, bowing slightly, his hands pressed together in prayerful fashion. "When you're at the Asian Garden restaurant, you and your fellow agents have a big plate of shiitake on us."

"What did you say? *What* did you say?" she asked.

Both deputies walked off without replying, glancing absently at the smoke that was beginning to veil the stars, and I was left alone with Special Agent Alicia Rosecrans. Her small wire-framed glasses were full of light.

"You like sexist and racist humor, Mr. Robicheaux?"

"They were out of line, but they're not bad guys. The feds talk down to them. So they get defensive."

"How grand and kind. I wish I had that level of humanity. It must bring you great comfort."

Don't take the bait, I told myself. "You had Whitley under surveillance?"

She paused as though deciding whether I was worth continuing a conversation with. "We got a report off the police band. I was a few blocks away."

I didn't believe her, but I let it go. "You think Whitley is the guy who tried to burn Clete?"

"Maybe. What has Clete Purcel told you?"

The fact that she didn't refer to Clete in the familiar wasn't insignificant. "You haven't talked with him?" I asked.

"Someone else will be doing that." She was looking toward the cruiser where Troyce Nix and Candace Sweeney were sitting, her eyes not meeting mine.

"Clete's personal relationships have nothing to do with what happened here tonight," I said. "Clete hasn't done anything wrong. I don't think you have, either."

"I noticed the religious chain and medal around your neck. Are you Catholic, Mr. Robicheaux?"

"Yeah, why?"

"Have you ever considered taking a Trappist vow of silence?" she asked.

I went inside the club to find Clete. He was standing at the far end of the bar, knocking back shots from a bottle of Jack Daniel's, chasing it with a can of Bud. The customers who had come back into the club were avoiding him, and so was the bartender.

"Pouring your own drinks these days?" I said.

"Yeah, suddenly I'm butt crust."

"Did you see your girlfriend?"

"Alicia's here?"

"Amerasian, likes to call county cops 'swinging dicks'? I think that might be her."

"She get in your face about something?"

"Let's get you out of here before the feds arrive in force."

"What'd Alicia say to you?"

"Nothing. I think you're nuts, that's all."

"I get this from you every time I meet a new woman."

"Yeah, I think that's what Henry the Eighth said to his confessor once."

"*What?*"

I saw a red smear on the back of Clete's thumb. I wiped it off with a paper napkin and crumpled the napkin and dropped it on the floor. He looked dumbly at the spot I had cleaned. "He fell on top of his piece. I took it out of his hand so his weight wouldn't discharge it," he said.

"You did everything you had to do, Clete. You saved the girl's life and probably Gribble's, too. No matter how this plays out, you're the best."

But my words were probably too late and too few. He sat down on the bar stool like an elephant that has tired of its own performance and has decided to sit down on a small chair in the middle of the ring. I could almost hear a wheeze of air from his chest. His shot glass was half empty. There was a smear of salt on his lip from his beer chaser. His eyes looked scorched in the glow of the beer sign behind the bar. "You think the feds might use this to get me for the Sally Dio plane crash?"

"Who knows? They've got their own agenda. They don't share knowledge of it with others. We brass it out."

He pinched his temples and closed and opened his eyes. "Some life, huh?"

I cupped my hand on the back of his neck. It was as hot as a sunburn. "Going up or coming down, it's only rock and roll," I said.

But we both knew better.

CHAPTER
20

At sunrise the next day, Albert Hollister found his truck in his driveway but did not see J. D. Gribble. Nor did he find J.D. at his cabin on the other side of the ridge. At noon, while I was out in the yard, I saw Alicia Rosecrans drive past the arch over Albert's driveway and turn in to the dirt lane that led to our cabin, north of the barn.

I wasn't anxious to see her again. She and Clete had created a problematic personal relationship that could cause her to lose her career. Second, Clete knew that Gribble was probably a fugitive from the law and had not yet told her. Who said you should never go to bed with a woman who has more problems than you? Actually, it doesn't matter who said it, because the admonition was not one I could have passed on to Clete. Why is that? Because I've never met a woman who had more problems than he did.

"Have you seen J. D. Gribble?" she said.

"No, I haven't," I replied.

"I called Mr. Hollister earlier. He said Gribble left his pickup in the driveway before dawn. He said he thinks Gribble may be in town."

"Could be."

"Mr. Robicheaux, I seem to get one of two responses from you. You're either handing out moral observations, or you're the laconic Spartan who has trouble putting two words together."

"I guess that's the way it flushes sometimes," I said.

"Clete Purcel's fingerprints are on the twenty-five auto that was found next to Quince Whitley's body."

"Whitley fell on top of his gun. Clete removed it from his hand so it wouldn't discharge and hit somebody in the parking lot. What difference does it make? There were eyewitnesses. Candace Sweeney was there, and so was Nix."

"Candace Sweeney has an arrest record for possession of heroin."

"So what? She saw what happened. Why should she lie about it?"

"I don't think she's lying. She says after Whitley threw acid at her, she crouched in front of the SUV. She thinks Gribble knocked Whitley down with his guitar case. When she got up, somebody's headlights were shining in her eyes. She says she started to run and heard Whitley say something, then the headlights went out of her eyes and she saw Clete aim his weapon with both hands and blow Whitley's brains out. She was close enough to him that blood splattered on her blouse. But she didn't see a gun in Whitley's hand."

"What did Nix see?"

"He was just coming out of the club when he heard the gunshot. He says he heard the gunshot, but he couldn't see what was happening on the far side of the SUV."

"One of the paramedics told me Whitley had a holster strapped on his ankle."

"That doesn't put the gun in Whitley's hand. It also won't make Clete's prints go away."

"You ran the twenty-five?"

"It was boosted in a home invasion in New Orleans six years ago."

How bad could Clete's luck be? What were the odds of Whitley ending up with a weapon that had been stolen in Clete's hometown? "I don't buy this stuff. Clete probably saved two people's lives. Everything you've told me is based on the worst kind of conjecture. Are some of your colleagues trying to put Clete in the cook pot?"

I saw the beat in her eyes before she spoke. "Clete killed a government witness years ago. A lowlife by the name of Starkweather. Some people might see that as a precedent."

It took a second before I realized what she was telling me. "Whitley was an informant?" I said.

"We need Gribble as a witness, Mr. Robicheaux, unless you want to see Clete jammed up real bad."

A time comes in every human situation when you finally decide to stop protecting people from others and themselves. A time comes when you simply have to tell the truth and let the dice create their own arithmetic. But in this case, no matter how you cut it, the fallout for Clete was probably going to be treys, boxcars, and snake-eyes.

"I think Gribble may be an escapee from a contract prison in West Texas," I said, holding my eyes on her. "I think his real name may be Jimmy Dale Greenwood. I think Troyce Nix came to Montana to find him."

"How long have you had this information?"

"I'm not sure I know any of this with certitude."

"Take the marbles out of your mouth, Mr. Robicheaux."

"Call me Dave or call me Detective Robicheaux, but stop patronizing me, please."

"You and Clete both knew this man was probably an interstate fugitive?"

"I can only speak for myself."

"Stop lying. Clete knew Gribble's background but protected him because Gribble saved his life. Is that fair to say? Don't just stare at me. Answer my question."

"Sorry, I'm all out of gas."

"How would you like to go to lockup for aiding and abetting?"

I heard Molly open the screen door and step out on the porch. "How would you like to take yourself to hell and gone down the road?" Molly said.

"It's all right," I said.

"No, it's not all right, Detective Robicheaux. You deceived me, and so did Clete Purcel." Alicia Rosecrans raised a finger at me, her little glasses wobbling with light. "I won't forget it, either."

• • •

JAMIE SUE WELLSTONE'S favorite time of day had become the hour between false dawn and the first glow of blue light on the walled garden behind the main house. Even when the garden was still cold and speckled with night damp, she would take the morning newspaper from the cylinder out front and read it and drink coffee at the mosaic-tile table just inside the garden's back gate, which allowed her a view of the sun when it first broke above the mountaintop and lit the hillsides on the far end of the valley.

This morning the lead story in the paper was about a shooting death in East Missoula. She started to skip over the story, then saw names inside the type that seemed as sharp in relief as lettering on a headstone. Quince Whitley was dead, killed instantly by a visiting private investigator from New Orleans, Louisiana. According to the story, Whitley had tried to throw acid in the face of a woman by the name of Candace Sweeney. A man named J. D. Gribble had thrown his guitar case in front of the woman when she was attacked by Whitley. Then Gribble had disappeared. The shooting was under investigation, and by press time no one had been charged or taken into custody. In the last paragraph, the article stated that Whitley was thought to be an employee of the Wellstone ranch in the Swan Lake area.

The sun had just broken above the mountaintop, shining through the trees on the crest. A shadow fell across the front page of the newspaper as Jamie Sue was reading it.

"The sheriff's office called late last night," Leslie said, standing behind her in a purple robe and slippers and a warm scarf wrapped around his throat. "The phone didn't wake you, sleepyhead?"

"No, it didn't," she replied.

"I explained that we had to fire Quince yesterday. Poor fellow, it must have sent him over the edge."

"Fire him?"

"I thought I told you. He'd become so ill tempered and disrespectful, I decided it was time we let him go. Are you coming upstairs?"

"I was going to have some dry toast."

"Cook can bring it up. Would you like an egg-white omelet?"

"I really don't feel well."

"That's too bad. Must be the weather. Fire season upon us again and all that. Looks like your fellow Mr. Purcel earned himself some ink this morning."

She rested her forehead on her fingers. The print on the newspaper was swimming before her eyes.

"That's quite a story, isn't it? Wonder why this Gribble fellow ran away. You think he'd want to hang around and receive some gratitude for his good deed," Leslie said. He stared at the back of her head. He waited a long time for her to reply, but she didn't. "Nix came to Montana to catch up on old times with Jimmy Dale Greenwood. You think this J. D. Gribble fellow might be Jimmy Dale?"

"I don't know, Leslie."

"Sure you wouldn't like to come upstairs?"

"It's my stomach. The veal we had last night tasted strange," she said. "I couldn't sleep."

"You think the pitcher of martinis might have had something to do with it?" he said. He waited. "No? I'm sure it was the veal, then. Maybe you haven't quite developed a taste for it. Did you and Jimmy Dale eat very much of it?"

When she looked up at the burned mask that was Leslie's face, his eyes seemed filled with concern, perhaps even pity. Then he patted her on the shoulder and went back into the house. Was he trying to drive her mad?

She sat for a long time inside a rectangle of cold sunlight, the sound of her own blood whirring in her ears. When she shut her eyes, she remembered a field of bluebonnets in Yoakum, Texas, and saw the wind denting the grass and the flowers, spinning the blades of a windmill while well water gushed out of an iron pipe into an aluminum tank. She wondered how the paintless house in the background, where her blind mother was hanging wash, could have become the most heartbreaking symbol of loss she could imagine.

She went upstairs and showered in her bathroom, locking the door before she undressed. After she dried off, she wrapped herself in the towel and went into her bedroom, keeping her eye on the door that opened into Leslie's bedroom. She went into her walk-in closet and dressed in a pair of old jeans and a flannel shirt and suede boots lined with sheep's wool. She sat on the side of her bed and looked at the heavy black guitar case propped against her desk. Inside it was the HD-28 Martin guitar Jimmy Dale Greenwood had given her. She started to open the case, then hesitated. Through the door she could hear Leslie moving around in his bedroom. He had disabled the lock when she had first moved into the house, claiming that she should have more than one exit in case of fire. But in one fashion or another, he always let her know that her privacy was subject to his consent.

She took a gold-leaf book from the shelf above her desk and opened the French doors onto the balcony and sat on a scrolled-iron chair that stayed there year-round, even when the balcony was banked with snow, so that the cushion on the seat had become dry and bleached of color and she could feel the hard frame of the chair against her buttocks. She opened the book on her lap and began to read. The temperature had dipped into the high thirties during the night, and the sunlight still had not penetrated the shade on the west side of the house. Down by the barn, there was frost on the spigot above the horse tank and steam was rising off the coats of the horses. It was hard to believe that fires were breaking out in the hills, started by either dry lightning or a bottle thrown on the ground by a careless hiker. How had this beautiful piece of countryside become harsh and cold and fouled by the smell of fire all at the same time, as though the season were out of sync with itself?

"I haven't seen you read your Bible in a while," Leslie said behind her.

She turned in her chair, and her mouth parted slightly. "What are you doing with that gun?" she said.

"This? It's a single-action Ruger Buntline. It has interchangeable cylinders. One for twenty-two long-rifles, one for twenty-two Magnums. The Magnums will make you deaf. So I don't use them a lot. Here, hold it in your hand."

"No."

"It's a beautiful piece. It penetrates cleanly, but with a hollow-point, it can do some very effective damage." He opened the loading gate and slowly rotated the cylinder, clicking each loaded chamber past the opened gate. "I can break a beer bottle at ninety yards with it, although I have to prop my arm across a tree limb when I do. I bet you'd be a fine shot with a little training. A Texas ranch girl and all that sort of stuff."

He looked out across the yard and down the slope at a sugar maple whose leaves were so dark they were almost purple. A robin had built its nest in the fork of the tree, and a shaft of sunlight shone directly on the nest and the bird sitting atop its eggs.

"You reading from Psalms?" he said.

"I just flipped open the pages. I wasn't—"

"You seem quite concentrated. What did you find that's so revelatory in nature?"

" 'I'm the alpha and the omega. I am the beginning and the end. I am he who makes all things new.' "

"My father used to say, 'When you see a man run for his Bible, he's usually in the situation of a track crew trying to build a trestle over a canyon after the locomotive has gone over the cliff.' I don't think you would have liked my father. He wasn't a likable man. There was a story that he beat a man to death with his fists. But I never believed it. Yes, that's quite a quotation. But when I was having my face rebuilt, it didn't strike me as altogether convincing."

She heard Leslie pull back the hammer on the pistol. She breathed through her mouth and looked straight ahead, trying to concentrate on the symmetry of the countryside, the snow high up on Swan Peak, the normalcy of the world beyond the Wellstone compound. She could feel a tic begin to form in the skin under her left eye. "What are you doing?" she said.

"Setting the hammer on an empty chamber. That's the safest way to carry a revolver. If I should drop it, there's no way it can fire. See, a revolver doesn't have a safety. I always set the hammer on an empty chamber so I don't have to worry. Worry is like guilt—it can drain a person, can't it, Jamie Sue?"

"Please don't stand behind me with that gun."

"A revolver is a pistol, not a gun."

He stepped within her line of vision and propped one hand on the balcony's rail. Something had frightened the robin. It flew to the barn roof, perched briefly on the apex, and seconds later, returned to the nest. "Would you like to fire a round?" Leslie said.

"It'll frighten the animals."

"I doubt it. They're hardy fellows. Besides, I don't have the Magnum cylinder in the frame. The twenty-two long-rifle doesn't make much noise. Just a little *pop*. Give it a try."

"I don't want to."

He studied the sugar maple, then lifted the revolver and pointed it out in front of him, closing one eye as he aimed. "Either you take a shot or I do," he said.

"Don't do this, Leslie."

"Just one shot. I don't miss. But you just might. Give it a try. You might like it. Women do it once and sometimes fall in love with it. I think it's a guilty pleasure with them."

"Why are you so cruel?"

He notched back the hammer to full cock with his thumb. "Last chance. If I can bust a beer bottle at ninety yards, I should be able to pot a robin."

"You're sickening and hateful. You make everyone over in your image. You're like a virus that spreads from one person to the next," she said, closing the Bible, getting up from her chair, her blood draining into her stomach.

The corner of Leslie's mouth flexed in a smile, exposing a canine tooth. He lowered the pistol and reset the hammer on half-cock, then rotated the cylinder to an empty chamber again. He eased the hammer softly onto the firing pin, locking the cylinder back into place, effectively disarming the pistol. "I just wanted you to say it. Your husband both sickens and inspires loathing in you. But tell me, Jamie Sue, do you think you might be guilty of marrying up and screwing down? I think that's the term for it. Is it possible the blight is on your soul and not just on the face of your disfigured spouse?"

LATER ON SATURDAY, Clete walked up to our cabin but did not knock. Instead, he sat down heavily in a wood chair, propped his hands on his knees, and watched a flock of wild turkeys pecking in the grass across the dirt road. I opened the front door and looked at the back of his head. "Want to come in?" I said.

"Not particularly," he said. His porkpie hat was slanted on his forehead, his shoulders rounded like the back on a whale. The truck was gone, so he knew Molly was not at home. "You dimed me with Alicia?"

"You mean did I tell her you and I both thought Gribble was using an alias and that he was a fugitive? Yeah, I did."

"You want to explain why you took that upon yourself?"

"The guy is a material witness in a homicide, specifically a homicide you committed. In case you haven't heard, the person whose life you saved, Candace Sweeney, didn't see a gun on Whitley. We need Gribble or Greenwood or whatever his name is to clear you."

"I know all about that, Dave. You should have let me talk to Alicia."

"You seem to be taking your time in getting around to it."

"She accused me of being a sexual Benedict Arnold. She said I'd deceived and made a fool out of her. She said she might have to tell her supervisor she's been getting it on with me. Her career might be flushed."

"Did she bother to tell you Whitley was an FBI informant?"

He turned around in the chair, his eyes on mine. "You're not putting me on?"

"The feds aren't pissed at you for taking out Sally Dio. They're still pissed because you capped that guy Starkweather in '85. The way they see it, you punched the ticket on two guys the government probably worked years to flip."

"So that's why Whitley doesn't have a sheet," he said. He fiddled with his hands, cracking his knuckles, rubbing his palms together with a sound that was like sandpaper. "You think the feds are investigating Wellstone Ministries?"

"Maybe."

"Then they put a guy like Whitley on the payroll, and he turns out to be a serial killer?"

"You think he's the guy?"

"Not sure. Whitley wasn't that smart. He was the kind of guy other people use. But any way you cut it, the feds have a pile of shit on their hands. They flipped him, and now they have to deal with the fact that he had a mask in his truck like the geek who almost did me."

"But Alicia Rosecrans didn't bother to tell you any of this?"

He made a face, going into his old pattern of defending the indefensible whenever women hurt him. "She can't give up the identity of an informant to someone outside the Bureau," he said.

"But she can call you deceitful because you didn't throw Gribble or Greenwood or whatever to the wolves—a guy who saved you from being burned to death?"

Clete got up and took off his hat and combed his hair. He watched the turkeys feeding in the grass. They were fanned out in a straight line, working their way up a slope, their feathers puffing in the wind. I knew he was reconstructing his defense system and was not going to give up his relationship with Alicia Rosecrans, no matter how much it hurt him.

"When Alicia first questioned me about the guy in the mask, she kept asking if I thought he could be Whitley," he said. "She must have had her suspicions about him from the jump. Maybe she was trying to tell me something."

"Lose the sentiment. The feds are covering their butt."

He put an unlit cigarette in his mouth. I removed it and flipped it out into the dirt.

"Why'd you do that?" he said.

"Because you don't know how to take care of yourself. Because you're unteachable."

"You'll never change."

"*I* won't change?"

"You've got an anvil for a head, Dave. Everybody knows that except you. If it weren't for me, your life would be a mess. I have to screw up for both of us. It's a big job."

Try to argue with a mind-set like that.

KNOW WHY THE FBI write down car tag numbers at Mafia funerals? Because all the players are there, including the ones who put the deceased in the box.

On Monday a funeral notice for Quince Whitley was printed in the *Missoulian*. The service was to be held the next day in a small Protestant church just south of Swan Lake. On Tuesday afternoon Clete and I drove in my pickup to the church and parked about three hundred feet away, in a grove of cottonwood trees where a family of Indians was selling cherries out of a flatbed truck.

Clete and I stood back in the shade and used my Russian military binoculars to watch one of the strangest assemblages of contradiction I have ever witnessed. The setting and the mourners were a study in juxtaposition. Jamie Sue and the Wellstone brothers arrived at the clapboard building in their white limo, chauffeured by Lyle Hobbs. Jamie Sue wore a white suit and dark glasses and a gray mantilla. The mixed message her choice of clothing sent could have been deliberate or even hostile. Or possibly it meant nothing at all. The Reverend Sonny Click had on yellow-tinted aviator glasses and was wearing a blue polyester suit that, in the sunlight, seemed to have lubricant on it. The faces of Hobbs, Jamie Sue, Sonny Click, and the Wellstone brothers were as opaque as glazed ceramic. The faces of Quince Whitley's family, who arrived in a rental car, were another matter.

The Whitley family not only resembled one another, they looked as though they had all descended from the same impaired seed. Their skin was the color of dust. Their expressions seemed incapable of showing either joy or grief. Briefly, one of the women looked at Jamie Sue with indignation, as though Jamie Sue were perhaps the cause of Quince's death. Their ages gave no clue to their relationship with the deceased. An unkind observer might have said they possessed all the characteristics of livestock milling around in a feeder lot, waiting for their roles in the world to be imposed upon them.

The hearse from the funeral home arrived late, and Lyle Hobbs and the Whitley men lifted up the coffin and carried it inside. Five minutes later, we could hear the voice of Sonny Click booming from the church's interior. In the slanting rays of the sun on the pines and the dilapidated shingle roof of the building, the scene was like a photograph taken in an earlier time, perhaps during World War II, when death came much more violently and prematurely to us than it does today, and disparate elements of the country were drawn together in humble surroundings to mourn the loss of a much admired man or woman. But the scene Clete and I were watching was quite different. Quince Whitley had probably been a misogynist, if not a misanthrope, and his mourners represented elements in our culture whose existence we either deny or whose origins we have difficulty explaining. But maybe what appeared to be myriad contradictions in the mourning ritual we witnessed that afternoon had more to do with the presence or absence of money in our lives than it did anything else.

For Whitley's people, life and hardship and struggle were interchangeable concepts. Man was born in sin and corruption and delivered bloody and terrified from the womb. The devil was more real than God, and the flames of perdition roared right under the plank floor of the church house. The man with the power to shut down a mill or evict a tenant farmer's family lived in a white house on the hill. But the enemy was the black man who came ragged and hungry into the poor whites' domain and asked for part of what the white man had been told was his by birth. When people talk about class war, they're dead wrong. The war was never between the classes. It was between the have-nots and the have-nots. The people in the house on the hill watched it from afar when they watched it at all.

Or at least that's the way things were in the South during the era when I grew up.

After the service, the hearse drove to a cemetery four miles away, with the limo and the Whitley rental cars in tow. The grave had already been dug, the dirt piled on one side, a rolled mat of artificial grass dropped nonchalantly on top of it. The sun sliced through the pines and maples. In the spangled light, motes of dust and pieces of desiccated leaves floated like gilded insects. Clete had said few words in the last hour, and I wondered if he was reliving the moments before he had sighted on the side of Quince Whitley's head and pulled the trigger.

"We haven't learned a lot here. You want to wrap it up?" I said.

"Let's see it through," he said.

We had parked the truck not over fifty yards up the road from the cemetery, but so far the mourners had either not taken notice of us or didn't care whether we were there or not. Regardless, I didn't want to see Clete forced to confront Whitley's family. Sonny Click read from a Bible over the coffin, then the mourners held hands and lowered their heads while Click led them in prayer. Through the binoculars, I saw Leslie Wellstone fight to keep from yawning.

Then the mourners got into their vehicles and began leaving, while the funeral attendants waited to lower the casket into the grave.

"I'll buy you supper," I said.

"Hold on," Clete said, pointing down the road with his chin.

A dark SUV had approached the cemetery from the other end and parked in the trees. When the last of the mourners had left, a big man got out of the SUV and walked to the grave site. A long-necked bottle of beer protruded from his right pants pocket.

"It's what's-his-name, the bartender from the club on the lake," I said.

"Harold Waxman, the blue-collar suck-up guy."

"Wait here," I said.

"What for?"

I walked away without offering an explanation. The afternoon sun was waning, which meant Clete's need for alcohol and the irritability that went with it were growing by the minute. As I entered the cemetery, the funeral attendants were lowering the casket on the motor-operated pulley. Harold Waxman said something to them, then twisted off the cap on his beer bottle and poured the beer on top of the coffin.

"Buying Whitley a last round?" I said.

He looked at me indifferently. "I'm taking over his job. I figured he deserved one for the road," he replied.

"You'll be working for the Wellstones?"

"Just for Ms. Wellstone. She doesn't have a personal driver right now." He looked past me at Clete, who was standing in the shade by my truck. "Your friend up there is the one who capped him?"

"No, my friend is the one who stopped Whitley from shooting an unarmed woman."

"Some kill. Whitley couldn't hit the ground with his hat." Harold Waxman tossed the beer bottle into the grave. It clanked and rolled off the rounded top of the casket and landed with a thud in the dirt.

CHAPTER
21

After Jimmy Dale Greenwood had recognized Troyce Nix coming out of the nightclub, he had driven straight to his cabin, packed his duffel bag, and stuffed his twenty-two Remington rifle inside. Then he dropped off Albert's truck in the driveway, and under a gunmetal sky sprinkled with stars that smoked like dry ice, he hitched a ride over Lolo Pass into Idaho.

He should have kept going and beat his way on a two-lane back road up through the Idaho Panhandle into Canada. The international frontier was a sieve, and everyone knew it. All he had to do was get into British Columbia and go on the drift again. In Canada, logging was subsidized, and the exportation of lumber to the United States was booming. If he got tired of whittling trees, he could catch the wheat harvest in Alberta, or work the cod and salmon trawlers on the coast, or beat his way on up to Alaska. There were still streams in Alaska that had float gold in them, and veins in the mountains that a pick had never glazed. The choices were his. If he just stayed in motion, that was the trick.

Stay in E-major overdrive and don't think, he told himself. Flat-wheelers and hotshots were still free, the world of the side-door Pullman no different than it was in 1931. The only real crime for a bum in the United States was not to have a destination. If you stayed in motion, cops and yard bulls left you alone. Tell one of them you planned to stay in town for a few days, and you'd find yourself on the way to the can. Whether riding the spines or the blinds on the Burlington or the Northern Pacific, or traveling free on the old SP, all of North America and its infinite promise waited for him. Woody had said it a long time ago: This land was made for you and me. You claimed it with a thumb out on the highway or running alongside an open boxcar, a guitar strung on your back.

Except he didn't have a guitar. He had left it in the parking lot in front of the nightclub, sulfuric acid eating into its case. What he did have was a head full of snakes. He knew Troyce Nix would eventually find and kill him. He also knew he would never have any peace of mind until he got Jamie Sue back, and not only Jamie Sue but his little boy as well.

There were still places where people could live off the computer, he told himself, mountain drainages right off the highway, up in the high country on the Idaho-Montana line. He knew a town in northern Nevada, at seven thousand feet elevation, where everyone got his mail at general delivery and did nothing but play cards and catch trout in a river that was so cold the rainbows had a dark purple stripe along their sides. A rodeo friend of his, a rough stock handler, owned a lettuce farm in Imperial Valley and had always said Jimmy Dale could buy into it, paying on the deed with the work he put in. Or up in eastern Utah he could chicken-ranch, bust rescued mustangs, contract Mexican farm labor, or build an irrigation system that could make a desert bloom. Just him and Jamie Sue and little Dale.

Woody Guthrie had believed the country was a grand song. Jimmy Dale believed it still was. If you jumped a flat-wheeler headed through West Kansas, all in one day you could see silos silhouetted against a storm-black sky, oceans of green wheat thrashing in the wind, then sagebrush hills in eastern Colorado and the Rockies rising up out of the sun's hot shimmer on the hardpan—blue and snowcapped and strung with clouds. That same night your boxcar would be sliding down the other side of the Grand Divide, the wheels locked and squealing on rails that rang with cold in the moonlight. It was just a matter of choice. How had his old cellmate Beeville Hicks put it? "Everybody stacks time. You just got to decide where you want to stack it at."

In spite of all his poetic visions about a future with Jamie Sue and little Dale, one irrevocable fact stayed with him like a thorn driven under the fingernail: Troyce Nix was still out there, his wounds still green, his ferocious energies unabated and hungry for revenge.

Jimmy Dale still couldn't figure out exactly what had happened in the parking lot. He had accidentally stumbled into a situation involving one of the Wellstones' lowlifes and a girl he had never seen before. But how had Nix shown up at exactly that moment? Why was the private detective following this greasebag Quince Whitley around? Why was Nix in the club? Thinking about it all made Jimmy Dale's head hurt.

Regardless of what had happened, the dice were out of the cup. Jimmy Dale could head for Canada or turn his life around. He decided on the latter, but not in the way a preacher would necessarily recommend.

On Tuesday night he boosted a gas-guzzler from a used-car lot in Sand Point, Idaho, switched the plates in Superior, Montana, and on Wednesday morning walked into a gun store in Missoula.

"I'd like a box of them twenty-two long-rifle hollow-points," he said to the clerk.

CANDACE SWEENEY COULD never figure out what was going on in Troyce's head. Only last night he had started acting weird, telling her that he had to be gone for a while, he had to run errands around Missoula, did she want anything from the grocery store?

"A thermometer. So I can take your temperature," she had replied.

Then early this morning he had gotten up and met a man outside who was driving a new Ford pickup, one with an extended cab. She had watched through a crack in the curtains while Troyce took everything he owned from the SUV, plus a cake box and a big paper bag from Albertsons, and put it in the truck.

"Get dressed. We're going up Rock Creek," he said.

"What for?"

"It's that kind of day."

"Where'd the truck come from?"

"Bought it."

"Why?"

"'Cause an SUV is a big box on wheels that carries air around inside itself and don't have no other purpose."

"Troyce, has this got anything to do with—"

"With what, little darlin'?"

"That man you been chasing—Jimmy Dale Greenwood. He saved me from getting acid thrown in my face. Doesn't that count for something?"

"Get in the truck, you little honey bunny."

"Stop calling me dumb names."

"They ain't dumb. They're from the heart, too."

"You do it when you don't want to talk about things."

"If you ain't Venus de Milo on skates."

She shook her head in dismay.

They drove through Hellgate Canyon and crossed the Blackfoot River and followed the Clark Fork for another ten miles, then entered a spectacular mountain drainage called Rock Creek. The mountains on either side of the valley were thickly timbered and rose straight up into the sky, and the creek down below ran fast and clear over a bed of green and purple and apricot pebbles, the riffle undulating out of boulders marked with water-worn troughs like creases in elephant hide.

Troyce parked the truck in a grove of aspens and cottonwoods and dropped the tailgate. The wind was cool and fluttered the leaves in the grove and smelled of wood smoke from a log house set back in a meadow. "I want to show you something," he said. He removed an antler-handled knife from the scabbard threaded on his belt. He gripped the blade between the tips of his fingers and his thumb, the handle pointed down. His whole body became motionless, the veins in his forearms as thick as soda straws. "You watching?"

"What are you doing, Troyce?"

He kept his eyes straight ahead. Then he flung the knife sideways, end over end, into a cottonwood trunk ten feet away. The blade embedded cleanly in the bark, the handle quivering with tension.

"Why'd you do that?" she asked.

"To show you what I can do in a fair fight. Except the man who busted off a shank in my chest don't fight fair."

"I'm not saying he does. I'm just saying sometimes you got to let the past go, no matter what people do to you."

He pulled the knife from the tree trunk and wiped the blade on a square of paper towel he took from the grocery bag. "Would you get a fire started?"

He didn't tell her; he asked.

He untied the leather thong on a canvas rucksack and removed two GI mess kits from it. Then he began slicing tomatoes and onions on a chopping board, his eyes darting sideways as she hunted for sticks and pinecones to place inside an old fire ring. "You like ham-and-cheese omelets?" he asked.

"Everybody does."

"You like strawberry cake and ice cream that's been put on dry ice?"

"What's the occasion?"

"It's your birthday."

"No, it's not."

"We're celebrating your last birthday a little late or the upcoming one a little early. So that makes today your birthday. I used the Internet at the public library."

But she didn't make the connection and had no idea what he was talking about. She dropped a pile of kindling into the fire ring and dusted her hands. "The Internet?" she said.

"I downloaded a bunch of information and printed it up. Get that manila folder out of the glove box. I thought we might need this truck. If you live rural, you got to own a truck."

She got the manila folder from the box and opened it on the truck's hood. "You downloaded this from a real estate Web site in Washington?"

"They got acreage for sale all up through the Cascades. I done talked to the agent already. Look at that sheet of notepaper in there."

She lifted up a piece of lined paper that had been torn from a spiral notebook. On it was a long list of figures.

"That's my total assets. I'm selling off my stock in the prison. That'll give us a hundred and sixty-eight thousand dollars. I got twenty-three thousand in an Ameritrade account, and a couple of commercial lots in El Paso. Way I see it, we can build us one of those log-kit houses on land that comes at about ten grand an acre. We can get a mortgage on the house and land and still have money left over for that café you was talking about."

She felt her eyes moistening. "I'm not contributing very much, Troyce."

He picked her up, high on his chest, his arms propped under her rump. She held on to his neck, her breasts pressed into his face, her cheek against his hair.

"I ain't sure there's a God, but I suspect there is or I wouldn't have you," he said. "And I'll call you all the silly names I want."

THAT SAME MORNING Jimmy Dale Greenwood parked his boosted gas-guzzler at a truck stop just outside the sawmill town of Bonner and dropped several coins into a pay phone. Even as he punched in the cell number given to him by the young actor at the nightclub, his hand hesitated. There was still time to back out. He was a half-continent away from the prison he had broken out of. Had he come all this way to step irrevocably across a line, one that had less to do with the law than with the image of the man he believed himself to be? He had never been a violent man and had originally gone to jail for stopping an assault on a prostitute. Even when he had cut up Troyce Nix, he had done so only because all his other selections had been used up.

Then he thought about Nix again and the labored hoarseness of his voice in Jimmy Dale's ear and his fingers seeking purchase on Jimmy Dale's hip bone. The memory of it caused the cars and trucks out on the interstate to blur and shimmer for a moment. He clicked the rest of the actor's phone number into the telephone pad, his heart beating.

"G'day," a voice said.

"It's J.D. You said call you if I need a favor. You sound like an Australian."

"I'm rehearsing for my new picture. Where you been, bud? You're a hero."

"I cain't figure out what was going on in the parking lot Friday night. Who was the woman that guy was trying to throw acid on?"

"I told you about her when you were on the bandstand. But you couldn't hear me over the noise. I think my friends' weed had herbicide on it, too."

"Told me what?"

"She said some guy named Nixon was after you. I told her she probably had the wrong guy."

"You mean Nix? She was with Troyce Nix?"

"Yeah, that was the name. She said they were staying at a motel down the road. Look, if you're in L.A., give me a call. I'll hook you up, man. This place is dangerous. J.D., you still there?"

For the next half hour, Jimmy Dale cruised up and down the highway, checking out the motels in Hellgate Canyon and on East Broadway. Some were upscale, some were dumps. He guessed Nix would stay in a place that was clean and squared away, located by a restaurant that served steaks. A trusty in records back at the prison had said Nix was kicked out of the army for something he did in Iraq, but Nix still had a military tuck in all his clothes and hated dirt and disorganization, and on the hard road he knew where every man and shovel and machine was at any given moment.

But Jimmy Dale didn't know what kind of vehicle Nix was driving, so his knowledge about the man's habits was of little value to him. Also, he was sweating inside his clothes, his mouth was dry, and the unmistakable odor of fear was rising from his armpits. He ordered a big take-out meal at the McDonald's drive-through window on East Broadway and tried to eat it in the park across the river. The hamburger tasted like wood pulp, and when he drank the milk shake too fast, he had a brain-freeze that made him double over on the picnic bench.

A little girl at the next table pointed at him and said, "Mommy, look, the funny man has ice cream coming out his nose."

He stuffed his food in a trash can and got back in his gas-guzzler. His duffel bag with the twenty-two pump inside lay on the backseat.

His heart was racing, his thoughts like lines of centipedes crawling around inside his head. He could not remember ever being this afraid. But why? Because he didn't have the guts to kill Troyce Nix, a man who had sodomized Jimmy Dale and come all the way to Montana to make his life even more miserable than it already was? Maybe Nix had recognized Jimmy Dale early on for the punk he had always been. Maybe he deserved what had happened to him back at the prison.

As he drove out of the university district and headed back through Hellgate Canyon again, he secretly hoped that fate would intervene and he would not find Troyce Nix. Then, almost as though a malevolent prankster were orchestrating a script that controlled his life, Jimmy Dale looked through the windshield at a dark blue truck turning out of traffic into a motel that was only a few hundred yards from the club where Quince Whitley had died. There was no mistaking the woman in the passenger seat. She was the one whose life he had saved. There was also no mistaking the chiseled profile and big chest and shoulders of the man behind the wheel, or the way he wore his Stetson at a jaunty angle or the way he grinned at the corner of his mouth when he told a joke. Jimmy Dale felt like he had just swallowed a cupful of diesel fuel.

He drove past the motel and pulled in behind a truck stop where he could watch Nix and his girlfriend getting out of their pickup.

Okay, you found out where they're at, he told himself. *But you cain't do anything sitting here except get yourself busted. Come back later, when they're going to dinner or to a movie or to wherever in Montana psycho gunbulls and tattooed women hang out at. You don't have to prove anything.*

He was lying and he knew it. He was scared of Troyce Nix, and he was scared of going back to the joint, and he was scared his friends outside of prison would learn what Troyce Nix had done to him. In fact, Jimmy Dale Greenwood wanted to chamber a round in the Remington, slide the muzzle over his teeth, and drive a hollow-point through the roof of his mouth into his own brain.

Maybe he had always been a loser from the jump, he thought.

Most of his life, he had lived within a few hours' drive of Austin, the same place Willie Nelson and Jerry Jeff Walker and a dozen like them had started out. But Jimmy Dale had never made it to Austin, convincing himself that a real artist played shithole beer joints and didn't compromise his music for commercial success. How about Mac Davis and Buddy Holly and Waylon Jennings and Jimmy Dean? All of them had grown up within spitting distance of Lubbock, all of them poor and without much education, or at least as poor as Jimmy Dale's family had been, but today their names were known all over the world.

Jimmy Dale always told others that if you're a rodeo man, "you ride it to the buzzer." But in truth he had never ridden it to the buzzer and had set himself up to fail. One lesson you learned quickly in prison: Once inside, time stopped, and you didn't have to make comparisons. Outside the walls or the fences topped with coils of razor wire, you had to keep score. Inside the system, the reflection you saw in a mirror was no problem. Everybody around you was a loser. The big score of the day was to get high on pruno or nutmeg and black coffee or have a punk free of AIDS delivered to your cell.

Jimmy Dale could feel tears welling in his eyes. *Screw Troyce Nix,* he thought. *I cain't shoot the guy in the middle of town. It ain't supposed to happen. I give it my best and I'm out and that's it.*

He fired up his stolen car, a gush of oily smoke bursting from the exhaust pipe, and waited for a tractor-trailer to clear the diesel pumps so he could pull back on the two-lane. Then he saw Troyce Nix and his girlfriend emerge from their motel room and walk toward their pickup truck, chatting with each other, the sunlight warm on their faces.

You gonna do Nix or let him do you? What's it gonna be, waddie? a voice inside him said.

Jimmy Dale hit his fist on the steering wheel. When Nix was in the traffic, Jimmy Dale pulled onto the two-lane, three cars behind Nix, hating all the forces that had made him the driven man he was.

• • •

TROYCE AND CANDACE bought camping supplies and warmer clothes at Bob Wards, and groceries and gasoline at Costco, then drove through an underpass into North Missoula and parked their truck at a recreation area in a poor neighborhood where a chapter of Narcotics Anonymous was holding a five-fifteen meeting and a potluck supper.

Troyce didn't understand why Candace wasted her time with a bunch of addicts, since she didn't use dope anymore or have any of the dependent characteristics that he associated with junkies. But live and let live, he thought, and carried a paper plate of fried chicken and potato salad to a lone table among maple trees behind the baseball diamond backstop. Through the wire screen, he could see the whole panorama of the park: worn base paths, the patches of yellow grass in the outfield, an empty swing set in the distance, houses along the street that had no fences between them, and gardens where vegetables grew rather than flowers.

Most poor neighborhoods didn't have fences, he thought. The porches had gliders on them and sometimes stuffed couches. On one corner there was a small grocery store with a neon bread ad in the window. An ancient brick firehouse, painted lead-gray, stood on another corner. Unlike in subdivision neighborhoods, sidewalks connected the houses. A kid was flying a kite emblazoned with the image of the comic-book hero Captain America, the kite stiffening in the wind, rising higher and higher into a perfect blue sky.

How had he, Troyce Nix, ended up in both the Abu Ghraib prison and this working-class neighborhood in the northern Rockies? He was the same man and had the same hair, skin, eyes, bone, and sinew that had defined him in the mirror many years ago. How had he gone from the winter-green palm-dotted alluvial floodplains of the Rio Grande Valley to an Iraqi prison whose floors during the regime of Saddam Hussein had been stained by fluids that had become part of the stone and could not be scrubbed out? And from there to a contract jail where, in many ways, he had stacked time inside the machinations and perversity he had helped create and to which he had given legitimacy?

Now, on a breezy, warm afternoon in a town that was ringed by mountains and traversed by three rivers, he was eating by himself at a picnic table carved with names and initials and hearts and arrows, like petroglyphs left by ancient people on a cave wall, while one hundred feet away a woman he had come to love sat among junkies, ex-prostitutes, and petty boosters, waving at him, her face full of joy and expectation, her faith and belief in him like that of a child.

Beyond the baseball diamond, a gas-guzzler was parked in the shade, its paint pocked with blisters. Had he seen the same vehicle at Bob Wards or at Costco? There were shadows on the windshield, and Troyce could not tell if anyone was behind the steering wheel. A city groundskeeper was driving a mower along the swale, the discharge from the blades firing sideways against the parked vehicle, pinging the metal with chopped-up pinecones, blowing a cloud of dust and grass cuttings through the open window.

Troyce bit into a drumstick and turned his attention back to the dancing kite emblazoned with the shield and winged helmet and masked face of Captain America. For some reason, backdropped by a blue sky, it seemed the most beautiful piece of art he had ever seen.

THE GRINDING AND pinging sounds of the mower were like slivers of glass in Jimmy Dale's ears. He waited until the driver had threaded his machine around a couple of trees and had turned onto the swale on the park's far side, then he got into the backseat and slid the Remington pump from the duffel bag.

Now he was in a perfect shooter's position. His vehicle was inside dark shade, the rifle easily concealed below the level of the passenger window, his target lit by spangled sunlight on the other side of the ball diamond. By propping the rifle over the right front seat, he could fire at an angle out the passenger window, hiding the muzzle flash, perhaps even muffling the report. He could probably get off two shots before anyone realized what had happened.

He pumped a round into the Remington's chamber and sighted on Troyce Nix's yellow-tinted aviator glasses. Even if he missed, the round would strike the side of a parked truck, so he was not endangering an innocent person. There was no excuse for not taking Nix out. He'd be doing Nix a favor, pocking one right through the lens, following it up for good measure with a second one in the forehead, putting him out of his perverted misery, maybe saving somebody else from being raped at another contract prison.

Then a kid pulling a kite string ran across Jimmy Dale's line of vision. The wind had dropped, and the kite was dipping precariously close to the tops of the maple trees that bordered the park. Jimmy Dale lowered the rifle, easing the hammer down on the firing pin with his thumb, and watched the kid coiling up his string, running backward, lifting the kite's tail across the top branches of a maple. Jimmy Dale let out his breath and felt his heart slow and his pulse stop jumping in his neck, as though someone had declared a temporary truce in his war with Troyce Nix, just so everyone could watch a young boy save his kite from crashing into a treetop.

Then the wind gusted across the baseball diamond, blowing a cloud of fine dust from the base paths, and the kite rattled against its stick frame again and rose steadily into the sky. Now the kid and his kite were safely out of the way, and Jimmy Dale's view of his target was unobstructed, his choices clear. He raised the rifle, thumbed back the hammer, and sighted on Troyce Nix's face, his pulse beating in his throat.

The mowing machine was headed down the swale toward Jimmy Dale's vehicle, the engine roaring louder and louder, rocks splintering sideways off the blades. Jimmy Dale looked through the back window, the rifle balanced across the top of the passenger seat. The groundskeeper was turning the mower around, cutting a clean swath through blue fescue back toward the far curb. Jimmy Dale threw the rifle stock to his shoulder, put Nix's mouth squarely in the steel notch on the rifle barrel, and slowly tightened his index finger on the trigger.

I'm gonna blow your cranberries, Cap. This is for every guy you sodomized back at the joint. Hope you find a shady spot in the flames.

Then something snapped inside his head, like a wound-up rubber band breaking behind his eyes. His breath exploded from his chest.

He jerked his hand free of the trigger guard and jacked open the chamber, ejecting the unfired round on the car seat. Outside the car, the mowing machine scotched the top of a tree root into pulp.

Once again, Jimmy Dale had failed. But this time he didn't care. He wasn't a killer, no matter what Troyce Nix or the world or the prison system had done to him. Then he realized all the sound had gone out of his ears. The entire park seemed empty of voices or bird-song or the rattle of a kite in the wind or the roar of a grass-cutting machine. He opened and closed his mouth as though he were inside the cabin of a plane losing pressure at high altitude.

The problem was not with his hearing. The groundskeeper had hit the kill button on his machine and was staring through the back window of Jimmy Dale's vehicle. "That man's got a gun!" he shouted, his finger pointing frantically.

Jimmy Dale piled into the front seat, fired up his stolen gas-guzzler, and left a cloud of blue smoke behind him.

When Candace Sweeney got to Troyce Nix's side, he was staring at the now empty street and the elevated interstate the street fed into.

"It was him, wasn't it?" she said.

"That boy just don't learn. He's a real hardhead is what he is."

She waited for him to go on, but he didn't. "We're leaving tonight, though?" she said. "Right, Troyce? Nothing has changed."

"I think we might have to put things on hold a little bit," he replied. He removed his shades and pinched his eyes, as he always did when he did not want her to see the thoughts he was thinking.

CHAPTER
22

THURSDAY MORNING I made an appointment to meet with Special Agent Alicia Rosecrans in the federal building on Broadway in Missoula. I had many things to say to her, or to ask her, some of it about Clete, some of it not. Unfortunately, because of my desire to protect Clete, my relationship with her had become adversarial when it should not have been. Regardless, I needed her help, and as a visitor to Montana with no legal authority in the state, I was taking on the role of a beggar inside the legal system. If she wanted to rub my face in it, now was her opportunity.

When I entered her office, her hands were folded primly on her desk blotter, her lean face turned upward like a blade. The last time I had seen her, she had told me she would not forget that I had deceived her regarding my suspicions about J. D. Gribble's identity and the fact that he was an interstate fugitive. The truth was, I could not forget her accusing me of duplicity.

"Before you say anything, Mr. Robicheaux, please be aware that I'm speaking to you only because you're an officer of the law in the state of Louisiana," she said. "I've spoken to your sheriff, and she tells me you're an honest man. But so far that hasn't been my impression of either you or Clete Purcel. I don't like being lied to."

I felt a wave of heat bloom in my chest. I started to speak, but she raised one finger. "No, it's time for you to listen," she said. "You and Clete Purcel seem to think you can decide what other people need to know or don't need to know. Does that strike you as a bit arrogant?"

"If you put it that way, I guess it does."

"If I put it that way?"

"No, as you say, it's arrogant," I replied.

"Why are you here?"

"May I sit down?"

Her face was tight and white around the mouth. I could see her nostrils dilating when she breathed. I sat down without waiting for her to give me permission. "What did you guys find out about the mask in Quince Whitley's truck?"

I could see the pause in her eyes, as if she was deciding whether or not she should continue our meeting. "It probably came from a store in Denver or Seattle or Salt Lake," she said. "Actually, it could have come from anywhere. It's no help. There were no prints on it at all, not even Whitley's."

"But y'all are still looking at him for the attack on Clete?"

"We know Whitley filled a two-gallon gas container at a convenience store near Swan Lake on the day of the attack. Whitley worked as a truck driver over the years. We can put him in the general area where a number of homicides remain unsolved, all of them similar in some way to the homicides we're dealing with here. I think I've probably told you enough."

But I could tell she had not told me enough and that she was bothered in the same way I was about elements in the case that were not getting looked at squarely, for whatever reasons. "We're talking about a lot more here than just the death of a possible serial killer, aren't we?" I said.

"I looked at the bodies of those two college kids in the morgue," she said. "I don't mind admitting I have nightmares about them. I think the day you can say you sleep well in this job is the day you should leave it. I think those kids had information or evidence of some kind that someone wanted from them. I don't think the primary motivation for their deaths was simply sadistic, although that was clearly part of it."

I thought back upon the burglary of Seymour Bell's house. "After

Bell was killed, an intruder took a throwaway camera from his room. The camera was in full view. But the intruder tore up the whole house. So he was after something else as well," I said.

"Go on," she said.

"I think the Wellstones are big players in this. But I don't know what a kid could have in his possession that could endanger people as powerful as they are."

Her eyes were glued on mine, fraught with both meaning and conflict. She had just lectured me on the arrogance of an individual deciding what others should or should not know. I believed she was caught inside her own admonition. Her stare broke, then she knitted her fingers and swallowed and looked at a place just to the right of my face.

"What is it?" I asked.

"When Sally Dio's plane crashed into a mountainside, it exploded in a ball of flame. Everybody inside was badly burned. Some of the identification was speculative in nature. But maybe one man survived. The Indians found him and took him to a hospital in Kalispell. Then he disappeared."

"Who was he?"

"We don't know. But the Wellstones had ties with casino and hotel interests in Vegas and Reno. They've also been tied up with casinos on Indian reservations, particularly in your home state. Are you following my drift here, Mr. Robicheaux?"

"Maybe."

"The Bureau has hit a giant dead end on this case. It's not because we're inept or corrupt or arrogant or any of the things our critics like to say about us. It's because we spend most of our time following around foreign students who are thinking about math tests and getting laid and not hijacking airplanes so they can fly them into the administration building."

"You're saying maybe Sally Dio survived the crash?"

"No, I'm saying don't ever lie to a federal agent again. Anything else on your mind?"

"Yeah, Clete Purcel is outside in my truck. He's the best cop I've ever known. He's a recipient of two Purple Hearts, the Silver Star, and the Navy Cross. He also happens to have enormous affection and respect for you. Why don't you give him a break?"

AT A CERTAIN time in your life, you think about death in a serious way, and you think about it often. You see your eyes and mouth impacted by dirt, your clothes a moldy receptacle for water leaking through the topsoil. You see a frozen mound backlit by a wintry sky, a plain of brown grass with tumbleweed bouncing across it. Inside the mound, if your ears could hear, they would tell you the shovel that raises you into light again will do so only for reasons of scientific curiosity.

When you see these images in your sleep or experience them in your waking day, you know they do not represent a negotiable fate. The images are indeed your future, and no exception will be made for you.

During these moments, when you try to push away these images from the edges of your vision, you have one urge only, and that is to somehow leave behind a gesture, a cipher carved on a rock, a good deed, some visible scratch on history that will tell others you were here and that you tried to make the world a better place.

The great joke is that any wisdom most of us acquire can seldom be passed on to others. I suspect this reality is at the heart of most old people's anger.

What does this have to do with the murder of the two college kids and the attack on Clete and perhaps the murder of the Los Angeles tourists west of Missoula?

Everything.

Because anger is what I felt that afternoon when I looked at the television monitor attached to the StairMaster I was working out on in the health club on the Bitterroot highway. Reverend Sonny Click was evidently moving up in the world and had become the host of a televangelical daytime show featuring—guess who—the Reverend Sonny Click.

The aggressiveness of his overture to the audience was as naked as it was meretricious. "Out there right now someone is debating whether they should send in that one-thousand-dollar seed-of-faith gift to our crusade. I can hear your thoughts, the fury of the debate raging inside your heart. 'Is it worth it? Is this what God wants me to do?' I'll tell you what Our Lord has told me to tell you."

He looked earnestly into the camera, handsome in his tailored dark suit and starched white shirt and luminescent pink necktie. "If you pledge your seed-of-faith one-thousand-dollar gift, you will immediately be joined with God in all your endeavors. Your adversaries will become His adversaries. Your economic burdens will become His economic burdens. The physical illnesses in your life, the turmoil in your home, the unkindness with which the world has treated you will all be transferred into His hands.

"You will not become God's partner. God will become your partner. That's what the seed of faith does. It allows God to take every hardship and every enemy in your life from you and to reduce them to dust in His palm."

The camera panned on a choir of college-age kids who looked like they had been scrubbed with wire brushes, all of them clapping and singing, their faces seemingly lit by ethereal forces.

I showered and changed into fresh clothes at the health club, then drove out to the home of Reverend Sonny Click, east of Rock Creek. His Mercury was in the driveway, and his twin-engine plane was on the runway he had mowed in the pasture. His house was built of logs that had never been debarked. With its shady front porch and riparian backdrop, it should have resembled a sport fisherman's rustic cottage in an advertisement for western real estate. But to my mind, the yellow lawn and the dead flowers in the window boxes and a cluster of plastic cups under the steps told a different story about Sonny Click. He was one of those who did not have geographical ties. He floated on the wind, as all predator birds do, searching out his prey, the bead of light in his eyes as steady and unrelenting as the sun, his hunger never quite satiated.

When he answered the door, I could hear a teakettle whistling in the kitchen. "I told you not to come around here again," he said.

"Is that college girl with you?" I asked.

"No, she's not. Now get out of here."

"Not a smart answer," I said, and pushed him in the chest as I stepped inside.

His mouth dropped open. "Are you crazy?"

"No, I often experience visions of mortality," I said, pushing him in the chest again, back toward the kitchen. "Know what that means? I don't give a rat's ass what people do to me or think about me. If I can hose a skid mark like you off the bowl before I catch the bus, I figure I'm way ahead of the game." I glanced through the open door of the bedroom. "Where's the girl I met here before?"

"I don't know. I don't keep track of her."

"There's a woman's nightgown on your dresser."

"I'm not going to put up with this," he said.

From the counter, I picked up an empty tin pot by the handle and swung it against the side of his head. His face quivered with both shock and disbelief. I hit him with it again, this time harder. A small cry broke from his throat, and he cupped one hand over his nose, blood leaking down his wrist.

"I don't have any mercy on a man like you, Mr. Click," I said. "The last time I was here, I told you I'd shove you into an airplane propeller if I caught you sexually abusing that young woman. I'm not sure if that's the case here or not. But I do know you lied to me about Seymour Bell and Cindy Kershaw. You held their pictures in your hand. You studied them. Then you looked me straight in the face and told me you'd never seen them before. Those kids died terrible deaths. But when they needed you to speak up for them, to help us find their killers, you put your own interests first and denied knowing them. It takes a special kind of coward to do that, Mr. Click."

I could see the fear growing in his eyes as he looked at my expression and heard my words and realized that all the rules of constraint and procedure and protocol that had always kept him safe had just been vacuumed out of his life. He backed against the stove, the spout of the teakettle touching his spine, sending a tremor through his body. He wiped the blood from his nose with the flat of his hand, then tried to wipe it off with the other palm, smearing it on both hands. The texture of his face looked coarse, ingrained with dirt somehow, as though the personae he had presented to the world were melting off his skin like makeup under a heat lamp.

"I need to turn off the burner," he said.

"No, you need to tell me why those two kids died. What did they have on the Wellstones?"

"I don't know about those things. I'm a preacher. If you're saying I'm tempted by the flesh, then I'm guilty. But I didn't kill or hurt anybody."

I cannot offer an adequate explanation for what happened next. Maybe it was Click's disingenuousness; maybe it was the fact that he used the teachings of Jesus to deceive and betray the young people who trusted him; or maybe it was just the bloodlust that had lived inside me for most of my adult life.

The manifestation was always the same. It was like an alcoholic blackout, except the kind of blackout I'm describing occurred most often when I was not drinking. A red-black balloon would fill the inside of my head, and I would hear sounds like trains passing or high winds blowing among cresting waves, and I would experience a coppery taste in the back of my throat like pennies or the acidic taste in your saliva when your gums are bleeding. My age, my service overseas, my attempts to repudiate violence in my life, my membership in Alcoholics Anonymous, and my participation in my church community would have no influence on the events that would follow.

Clete had saved me from myself in many instances. But this time he was not around.

I drove my fist into Sonny Click's face and felt his upper lip split against his teeth. Then I hit him in the stomach, doubling him over. I'm not sure of the exact order of the things I did to him next. I could hear the teakettle screaming and feel its steam boiling my cheek and neck as I pulled open the oven door and shoved his head and shoulders inside. I turned on the gas and smelled its raw odor gush from the unlit jets below the grill. When he struggled, I kicked him in the back of the thigh, collapsing his purchase on the floor, and held him down tighter against the grill.

"Why did those kids die?" I asked.

"The burner's on," he said, the side of his face wedged into the steel wires, his nostrils flecked with blood around the rims. "The room will explode."

"Answer my question. Why did they die?"

"Things happen inside the Wellstone house that nobody knows about. The girl, Cindy, tried to tell me something. I didn't want to hear it. I was afraid. I hope she'll forgive me."

I tightened my hold on his neck and shoved his head harder into the grill. I could feel an even more dangerous level of anger rising inside me. "Don't pretend you're a repentant man. You molested that girl who was here, didn't you?"

"She's of legal age."

I raised his head slightly and smashed it again into the grill.

"Yes, I slept with her," he said. "I'm sorry for what I did. The gas is going to ignite and we're going to die. Don't do this. I'll make it right. I'll go away and you'll never see me again. Whatever you want, just tell me and I'll do it."

I pulled him from the oven and turned off the gas feed to both the oven and the burner under the teakettle. Click was crying, his face trembling, tears coursing down his cheeks. A dark stain had spread through the crotch of his slacks.

"Get up," I said.

When he didn't move, I lifted him by the front of his shirt and threw him in a chair. "Who burglarized Seymour Bell's house in Bonner?"

"I don't know anything about that."

There was a long silence. Outside, I could see the wind blowing in the trees that grew on a slope across the river. Sonny Click's eyes followed my hand as I placed it behind my back. "What are you doing?" he asked.

"Cops call this kind of gun a 'drop.' The numbers are acid-burned. It has no prints on it. It can't be traced back to me. What did the intruder take from Seymour Bell's house?"

He looked at me blankly, his mouth a round O. I forced the barrel of the thirty-two over his teeth and pulled back the hammer. His eyes bulged from their sockets as he stared up into my face. Then he began to tremble all over, his teeth clicking on the steel.

I said, "If you make me jerk the trigger, the round will punch a hole through the base of your skull."

But by now he was shaking so badly he had to grip the sides of the chair to keep his upper torso stationary. He tried to speak and gagged on his words.

"Say it again," I said, removing the pistol from his mouth.

"Nobody told me about a burglary. If you don't believe me, go ahead and shoot me," he said. "What kind of man are you? What kind of man would do this?"

"Somebody who's too old and tired to care. Sayonara, Mr. Click. If you see me coming, cross the street."

I walked back outside and let the door slam behind me. I could smell smoke from a forest fire in the wind and dust blowing out of a rain squall farther down the Clark Fork gorge. Had Click lied? Did he know more than he had told me? I doubted it. But it was his question to me that I couldn't let go of. What kind of man was I? he had asked. My answer to him had been both facile and cynical. The fact was, in moments like these, I had no idea who actually lived inside my skin.

I FOUND AN A.A. meeting that afternoon in Missoula, but I did not introduce myself when the woman leading the meeting asked out-of-town visitors to do so. Nor did I speak during the meeting or afterward. I got caught in a traffic detour downtown and passed Stockman's bar and a place called the Oxford and another bar called Charlie B's and one called the Silver Dollar by the railroad tracks. Two Indians were sitting on a curb in front of the Silver Dollar, drinking from a flat-sided bottle wrapped tightly in a paper sack. They were half in shadow and half in sunlight, squinting up into the brightness of the afternoon, the reddish-amber tint of the liquor glinting like the flash of a stained diamond whenever they tilted the bottle to their lips.

I cleared my throat and swallowed and took a candy bar from the glove box and bit into it. Then I drove into the university district and parked in front of the church where Molly and I attended Mass when we were in Missoula. The priest was my age and had grown up in the smelter town of Anaconda. His ancestors had worked in the mines and had been members of the Molly Maguires and the IWW in an era when Irish working people had paid back in kind, sometimes with dynamite dropped in the bottom of the hole. We went into his office, one that looked out upon maple trees and shady lawns and big stone houses with huge blue spruces in the yards. I told him what I had done to the Reverend Sonny Click, sparing nothing, including the systematic degradation I had put Click through.

The priest was a tall, raw-boned man with an aquiline profile and a taciturn manner that belied his strong feelings, particularly about social justice. I thought I might get a free ride.

Wrong.

"I think you're leaving something out," he said.

"Pardon?"

"You've described what you did, but you haven't talked about why you did it, Dave."

"Click is a charlatan. He preys on young girls. He lied about knowing those two kids who were killed. He belongs to the bunch that Jesus recommended millstones for."

Good try.

"Is that the only reason?" the priest asked.

I scratched my arm and looked out the window. "I wanted to tear him apart. Maybe I wanted to kill him. I don't know what else to say, Father. I've done these kinds of things before. It's an old problem."

"What do you think the cause is?"

I did not want to answer the question. He waited a long time, then gave it up. "Well, neither of us is a psychiatrist." He started to give me his absolution.

"I did it because I want to drink," I said. "The desire is always there—in my sleep, in the middle of a fine day, in the middle of a rainstorm. It doesn't matter, it's always there."

He nodded, his face empty, his eyes directed away from mine. The silence was such that my ears were ringing.

• • •

BUT MY EXPERIENCE with the Reverend Sonny Click wasn't over. I had turned my cell phone off at the A.A. meeting and had left it off until I drove away from the church. When I turned it back on, I had a voice mail from Sheriff Joe Bim Higgins: "Call me when you get this message. This isn't a request, either." The message had been left only ten minutes earlier.

I punched in his callback number. "This is Dave Robicheaux," I said.

"Where are you?" Higgins said.

"In my truck. By Christ the King Church."

"I'm on my way to Rock Creek. I'll meet you at Sonny Click's house."

"What for?"

"You'd better be there in twenty minutes, or you'll be under arrest."

I took him at his word. When I turned in to the Rock Creek drainage, I could see two Missoula County Sheriff's Department cruisers parked in front of Click's house. I also saw an ambulance parked on the yellow grass in the side yard.

Joe Bim Higgins walked toward me, his trousers stuffed inside his cowboy boots, his suit flecked with chaff blowing out of the field. The burned side of his face made me think of plaster that has dried unevenly on a wall. "What time were you out here?" he asked.

"Who says I was?"

"You want to be a smart-ass?"

"Midday."

"What time, exactly?" he asked.

"Somewhere around one-thirty. I'm not sure."

"The mailman says a guy answering your description left here at about a quarter to two. Would you say that's correct?"

"I just told you."

"Did you come back later in the afternoon?"

"No, I didn't."

"What'd you do to him?"

"Ask Click."

"You want a lawyer? I think you and your friend Purcel should have a team of them to follow you around."

"I lost control. If you want the details, get them from the good reverend. While you're at it, ask him why he lied during a murder investigation."

"I thought I had seen the whole cast of characters, but you and your fat friend take the cake."

"I'm getting a little tired of this, Sheriff."

"You are? I bet Click is, too."

"I have no idea what you're talking about."

"We're still waiting on the coroner. Come inside and tell me what you think." He handed me a pad and a pencil. "Jot down every place you've been this afternoon, Mr. Robicheaux, and the names of people who saw you there. How about your friend Purcel? Know where he's been? Seems like when one of you tracks pig flop on the rug, the other one is right behind. You don't have mad cow disease in Louisiana, do you? That's what we're afraid of in Montana. At least until you guys arrived. I've never been to Louisiana. Me and the old woman got to visit there someday."

I followed him inside the house. Two plainclothes cops were in the bedroom. They wore polyethylene gloves and were taking everything out of Click's dresser drawers. A straw-bottom chair lay on its side in front of an open closet.

"The wind knocked down a tree on the power line. A lineman looked through the side window and saw Click. He was still warm when we got here. That's the only reason you're not in handcuffs."

Click had been suspended from horse reins that were looped over a rafter at the top of the closet. They had been wrapped around his throat and were knotted tightly under the carotid artery. His loafers had fallen from his feet. The purple discoloration had not left his face, and he wore the strange, lidded, downcast expression of a man who has accepted that he has gone permanently into deep shade. His neck did not look broken, and I suspected he had strangled to death.

When the coroner arrived, he and a deputy cut Click down with a pocketknife. I walked outside and stood in the wind. Afternoon fishermen were headed up Rock Creek Road and soon would be casting flies on sunlit riffles. I could see mountain goats high up on one side of the canyon, and down below, penned horses inside the afternoon shadows and a man splitting wood and stacking it inside a pole shed. I saw all these normal and beautiful things while I waited for Joe Bim Higgins to come out of the house.

"The coroner thinks Click bailed off the chair. He also says somebody put some serious hurt on him," Higgins said. "You got any problem of conscience about that?"

"Guys like Click don't kill themselves because of guys like me," I said.

"You're saying this is a homicide?"

"I think he was unconscious when he was dropped from the rafter."

"Why's that?"

"His hands were free. He was an able-bodied man. He could have pulled himself up."

"Yeah, if he wanted to. But suicide victims don't want to save themselves. That's why they commit suicide."

"You want me to come down to the department and make a statement?" I asked.

"No, what I would really like is for you and your friend to get off the planet," he replied.

CHAPTER
23

THE BEST RESTAURANT in Missoula was called the Pearl Café. The walls were salmon-colored and hung with pastel paintings inside gnarled wood frames. The tablecloths and silver and crystal settings glowed with clarity and light; the waitstaff was dressed as formally as waiters and waitresses and bartenders in fine New York restaurants, and they had the same degree of manners and professionalism. Alicia Rosecrans had selected the Pearl, not Clete Purcel, who normally ate in saloons or working-class cafés where the food was deep-fried in grease that could lubricate locomotive wheels. Clete's objection was not the ambience but his belief that Alicia Rosecrans's career would be compromised by her being seen in public with him.

Nonetheless, he had consented to go there with her and had put. on a new powder-blue sport coat and gray slacks, shined loafers, and a soft gray fedora that he had recently purchased at a fashion store in Spokane. He had ordered iced tea rather than wine with his dinner, and hadn't broached the subject of what they might do or where they might go later in the evening or, for that matter, tomorrow or the day after that or the day after that. The truth was, Clete didn't even know where Alicia lived. When she was in Missoula, she stayed in a motel. That day she had been in both Billings and Great Falls, and she was vague about where she would be the following day.

"You're pretty tired?" he said.

"I think in the next two months I might be transferred to San Diego," she replied.

"Yeah?" he said.

"You've been there?"

"When I was at Pendleton. It's a nice city, the ocean and all."

The waitress set a loaf of hot sourdough bread wrapped in a napkin on the table and went away. Alicia removed her glasses and put them in a case and snapped the case shut. For some reason, the indentations where the glasses fitted on the bridge of her nose made her look disarmed and vulnerable, as if she had chosen to look that way.

"You like West Coast living? Starbucks and jogging on the beach and surf fishing with old guys, that kind of stuff?" she said.

"Yeah, I can dig that. Any place where it's warm and there's water and a few palm trees. I spend most of my time now in New Iberia, where Dave lives."

"I don't understand," she said.

"Because New Orleans isn't New Orleans anymore."

"It's being rebuilt, isn't it?"

"They won't rebuild the place I grew up in. They don't know how to. They weren't there. Back then every day was a party. I don't mean horns blowing and people getting drunk on their balconies. It was the way you woke up in the morning. Everything was green and gold, and the oaks were full of birds. Every afternoon it rained at three o'clock, and the whole sky would turn pink and purple and you could smell the salt in the wind. No matter where you went, you'd hear music—from radios and cafés and dance orchestras on the rooftops downtown. You could have all of it for the price of the ride on the St. Charles streetcar."

"You're going back there, aren't you?"

"No, I like the idea of the West Coast," he said. "See, I remember the way New Orleans used to be. If I didn't remember the way it used to be, I could go back and live there. Sometimes good memories mess you up. What I mean is I dig the coast. A guy like me can always adjust."

She looked at him a long time, as though staring at a man through a pane of thick glass she would never be able to penetrate. When their food was served, she barely spoke. If prescience was a gift, it did not show as such on her face.

Later that night, after he left her motel room, he thought he smelled flowers and the smell of salt spray on the wind. Then he realized it was her perfume and the smell of her skin and not a night-blooming garden in the neighborhood where he had grown up, or waves crashing on a beach in a place where he might live in the future, and he felt more alone and lost than he had ever felt in his life.

TWO HOURS LATER, while Clete was trying to go to sleep, his cell phone vibrated under his pillow. The caller ID was blocked. "Clete?" a woman's voice said.

It was not a voice he wanted to hear. "What's the haps, Jamie Sue?" he said.

"We've got to get a message to this man Troyce Nix," she said.

We?

He sat up in bed and adjusted the cell phone to his ear, wondering at the lack of judgment that seemed to characterize everything he did. "Why don't *you* call Nix up? I'll give you the name of his motel," Clete said.

"I don't have credibility with him. Neither does Jimmy Dale."

"Jimmy Dale doesn't have credibility with me, either. He hauled ass and left me to explain why I parked a round in Quince Whitley's head. I may end up on a homicide beef because of Jimmy Dale, or J.D., or whatever his name is."

"You've got it wrong, Clete. Jimmy Dale called the sheriff yesterday and told him what happened at the nightclub. He told the sheriff you saved the girl's life and probably his own, too."

She knew how to set the hook. "Yeah, but he didn't make a formal statement, and he's not going to, is he?" Clete said. "So my witness has the legal value of an anonymous phone caller."

"You've got to help us. Jimmy Dale made a big mistake, and he doesn't know how to correct it."

Don't bite, he told himself. *It's their problem, their karma, their bullshit.* "What mistake?" he asked.

"Jimmy Dale thought Nix was here to kill him. So he decided to do it to him first."

"Do what?"

"Shoot Nix. It was in the park. He couldn't go through with it. But Nix saw him and doesn't understand what happened. Can't you help us?"

"Are you running off with Jimmy Dale?"

"I can't live with Leslie any longer. I can't take his hate and his sickness and his cruelty. He's not going to poison my little boy with it."

"Is Sally Dio alive?"

"The gangster? Why should I know about him?"

"Because the FBI thinks he or one of his men survived a plane crash he should have gotten fried in. Because the Wellstones were mixed up in casino interests in Reno. Because a guy who worked for Sal is also working for your husband."

"My husband is a lizard. You don't know the things he does. Have you been drinking?"

Clete couldn't put together the disconnect in her thinking. "I'll call Troyce Nix for you, Jamie Sue. But I'm done with this doodah. You tell Jimmy Dale he and I are square, all sins forgiven, all debts paid. That means I want miles of track between me and y'all's problems. We clear on this?"

"You're a sweet man."

"Anybody who says that doesn't know anything about me," Clete replied.

He closed his cell phone and flipped it over his shoulder onto the bed. If ever reincarnated, he vowed, he would live in a stone hut on top of a mountain in Tibet, thousands of miles away from people whose lives were modeled on the lyrics of country-and-western songs.

THAT SAME NIGHT I lay beside Molly in our cabin north of Albert's barn. The moon was down, and the sky was black and channeled with stars that looked like the tailings of galaxies. Our windows were open, and inside the wind and rumble of heat lightning, I could hear Albert's horses nickering in the darkness.

We're the blue marble in the solar system, wrapped by water and vapor but also by stars. The same ones I could see outside the window shone down on all of us—Clete Purcel and Alicia Rosecrans, wherever they were that night, Sonny Click on a slab, the Wellstone brothers and Jamie Sue and Lyle Hobbs in their compound north of Swan Peak, Quince Whitley awaiting the worms to violate his coffin, the improbable couple made up of a Texas gunbull and a young woman with chains of flowers tattooed on her breasts, the pair of them hunting down a hapless creature like Jimmy Dale Greenwood, whose only desire in life was to play his guitar and follow the rodeo circuit with Jamie Sue and his little boy.

All the players were out there, the children of light and the children of darkness, the blessed and the malformed, those who were made different in the womb and those who cursed the day they were born and those to whom every daybreak was filled with expectation. The stars enveloped the entirety of the planet, blanketing a desert where people killed one another in the name of God, while oil fires burned on the horizon and other people sloshed gasoline into their SUVs and believed in their innocence that the earth and its resources were inexhaustible.

What a grand deception and folly it was, I thought, and could not rid my mind of the bitterness in my own words.

I sat on the side of the mattress, my hands cupped on my knees, a chill shuddering through my body, as though my old friend the malarial mosquito had taken on new life inside my blood. I felt Molly's hand touch my back.

"You have a bad dream?" she said.

"No," I replied.

"You blame yourself for Sonny Click's death?"

"No, he was an evil man, and I'm glad he's dead. But I think something very bad is about to happen. It's a feeling I can never explain. My nerves are wired, my skin crawls, my stomach starts churning. My spit tastes like battery acid. It's like the feeling you have when you hear the popping of small-arms fire and you know something a whole lot worse is coming down the pike."

She sat beside me and took my hand in hers. In the starlight I could see the freckles powdered on her shoulders. Her skin was still warm from sleep. "It's Clete, isn't it?" she said.

"He's going to get himself killed. He won't listen to me about anything. I wish I hadn't brought him up here. This whole place is full of ghosts."

"You're talking about Sally Dio?"

"Chief Joseph and the Nez Perce came down that ridge right behind us and were wiped out on the Big Hole. The Blackfeet Indians got massacred on the Marias River the same way. The army burned their tents and blankets and left the wounded and the old people and the children to freeze to death. That's the history that seldom gets written."

She placed her hand on my forehead, then looked into my eyes. "I think you have a fever."

"So what? That doesn't change what I said."

"Dave, let go of it."

"Let go of what?"

"Everything. You can't change the world."

"Why did you work in El Salvador and Guatemala?" I said.

"So the world wouldn't change me. There's a big difference."

"Your friends were killed down there, and few people cared. There's no way to put a good hat on it, Molly. You ever see the media interview a GI who comes back on the spike?"

"That's just the way it is. You give unto Caesar and hope he chokes on it. Like Clete says, good guys forever, and fuck the rest of it."

"You don't need to use language like that to make your point."

"Under it all, you're a priest, Dave. But that's all right. I love you just the same."

She ran her fingernails up through my hair. Then, as though conceding that her words would never be enough to argue against the rage and violence and thirst for alcohol that burned inside me, she exhaled and hit her fists on the mattress.

"Don't be like that," I said.

"Nothing I do helps. Nothing, nothing, nothing." She pulled up her gown and spread her knees on my thighs, pressing my head into her breasts, her desperation and her own secret despair and need perhaps greater than mine. But if a momentary erotic impulse was driving her, she hid it well. She hit me again and again in the back, refusing to show me her face, her breath coming in angry gasps.

THE NEXT MORNING Candace Sweeney and Troyce Nix ate breakfast downtown, then returned to the motel and saw the red message light blinking on their telephone. Candace called the front desk. She wrote down a number and a name on a notepad and replaced the receiver in the cradle.

"Who was it?" Troyce asked.

"That cop, that guy Purcel," she replied.

"He's a PI, not a cop. Most PIs are guys who got thrown off the force, usually for drinking or 'cause they were on a pad."

"What do you think he wants?"

"To do his job, whatever it is. Most of those guys are bums and liars, so nothing they say means anything anyway. Tear up his number." Then his face brightened. "I cain't get over that line you used on him. 'Change your deodorant.' You're a beaut."

"I want to leave, Troyce. To eighty-six this crap and go ahead with our plans. Just a few hours' drive, and we can start a whole new life."

"I know, darlin', but I cain't have Jimmy Dale sneaking up on us when we're in the Cascades, blindsiding us, maybe hurting you 'cause he cain't get at me."

"The cops or the FBI will catch up with him sooner or later."

"Maybe they will. But 'later' ain't much help when you're dead."

Troyce was combing his hair in the door mirror. The early-morning hours had been cold, and he had put on a long-sleeved gray shirt with white snap buttons, and his shoulders and arms looked huge inside the heavy fabric. He saw the disappointment in her face and stopped combing his hair.

"Jimmy Dale's got an edge," he said. "He ain't a criminal. He's committed crimes, but that don't make him a criminal. He don't think like and act like one. Cops don't catch his kind. Maybe his kind catch themselves, but cops don't do it. When you have trouble with a guy like Jimmy Dale, I'm talking about a breed with a resentment, you got to take him off at the neck, 'cause he'll fix you if he has to spend the rest of his life doing it."

"There's something you never told me, Troyce."

"What's that?" he said, looking at his reflection again.

"If he's not a criminal, why'd he cut you up? Why's he hate you so much?"

"You got to ask that of a smarter man than me," he replied. He turned away from her and brushed his teeth in the lavatory, although she was almost sure he had brushed them only a few minutes earlier.

Just after lunch, when Troyce went to buy a new battery for his cell phone, Candace punched in the number Clete Purcel had left with the front desk. "This is Candace Sweeney," she said. "What do you want?"

"Where's your boyfriend?" Clete asked.

"Troyce isn't here."

"When he is there, tell him to call me."

"Why are you bothering us, fatso?"

"I think you're insulting the wrong person. The last time I saw you, I prevented a peckerwood asswipe by the name of Quince Whitley from putting a bullet in you. You paid back the favor by telling the sheriff you didn't see Whitley with a gun."

"I told the sheriff the truth."

"Glad to hear you're keeping the standards up. In the meantime, I'm being looked at for a possible homicide beef. Tell Nix I got a message for him from Jamie Sue Wellstone. Also tell him I checked him out. He has a BCD from the army for his activities at Abu Ghraib. He seems not to have overcome his problems at that contract prison he worked at in Texas, either."

"What message?" she said, her face burning. But she didn't wait for Clete to reply. "You listen, you bucket of whale sperm, you couldn't carry Troyce's jockstrap."

"I tell you what, here's the message. Tell Mr. Nix he doesn't need to call me back. Neither do you. Jamie Sue Wellstone says Jimmy Dale Greenwood thought your friend was going to take him out. Jimmy Dale tried to cap your friend first. Except he couldn't go through with it. Why is that? you ask. Because as probably anyone with more than two brain cells could realize, Jimmy Dale Greenwood is not a killer. This is the message: Why don't you leave the poor fuck alone? This is Clete Purcel signing off. You and your boyfriend have a great life, and please stay out of mine."

The line went dead.

THE PREVIOUS NIGHT Jimmy Dale had abandoned the boosted car up by Ravalli, on the Flathead Indian Reservation, and buried the hot plates in a hillside and hitched a ride to a ranch a short distance from the Jocko River. The ranch was owned by a Salish shaman who was married to an aging hippie white woman. The couple sold jewelry on the powwow circuit and belonged to that group of non-ethnically defined gypsies who still wander the West and somehow manage to live inside its past rather than its present. Jimmy Dale slept in their barn that night without ever notifying them he was there, and in the morning they welcomed him into their clapboard house as though it was perfectly natural for someone to knock on their back door at five-thirty A.M.

Their water came from an overflowing cistern elevated on stilts behind the house. Most of their vegetables came from a half-acre garden whose wire fence was strung with aluminum-foil pie plates and tin cans to keep out the deer. The barn was a two-story desiccated shell, the faded red planks glowing magically when the early sun broke through the cracks. The house and the wide gallery were buried amid poplar, willow, and apple trees. The valley where the house was located was a long alluvial slit among greenish-brown mountains on which there were no other structures. The entire valley, as far as the eye could see, was unmarked by human activity, except for the two-lane state road and a train track on which a freight went through every evening at seven o'clock. In the false dawn, just before the stars faded over the hills, just before the breeze stopped blowing in the cottonwoods along the river, Jimmy Dale believed he was standing on a stretch of America that hadn't changed in seventy-five years.

He showered and shaved in the couple's bathroom and put on fresh underwear and socks and clean blue jeans and a purple-and-white-checked cowboy shirt with puffed sleeves and red stars brocaded on the shoulders. Then he and the couple ate a breakfast of pork chops and fried eggs and talked about an upcoming rodeo in Reno, one in Calgary, the big dance down in Vegas, and a half-dozen powwows strung across the Southwest.

His hosts were kind and gentle people and spoke with him as though the three of them shared the same future. But in truth, they knew his future was not theirs and perhaps not anyone else's except Jimmy Dale's. The shaman was an overweight, jolly man who wore his hair in pigtails and clearly did not like to speak of harsh realities in front of his wife, who still believed the year was 1968 and the flower children had never ceased dancing on the edges of San Francisco Bay.

"You need some money, Jimmy Dale?" the shaman asked.

"No, I been working pretty reg'lar. I just needed a place to sleep and freshen up before I get on my way," Jimmy Dale said.

"Where might that be?" the shaman asked.

"You know me, just a rolling stone."

"I ever tell you I spent two years in Deer Lodge when I was a kid?" the shaman said.

"Wasn't aware of that," Jimmy Dale said.

"Always swore they'd never get me again."

"Yeah, them jailhouses ain't no fun."

"A man can develop certain attitudes about jail. It's either the worst thing in life or it's not. I'd hate to go back, but I'd probably let them do it to me if they wanted. What about you?"

"I don't study on it."

"I guess that's a good way to be."

"Is there cutthroat and rainbow in that stream out there?" Jimmy Dale asked.

"It's full of them," the shaman said. "Come back and we'll throw a worm in. Make sure you come back, Jimmy Dale."

"Yessirree," he replied.

Two hours later, Jimmy Dale had hitched a ride on a flatbed truck boomed down with big bales of green hay, and was riding north up the side of Flathead Lake, past cherry orchards and expanses of shimmering blue water so vast they could easily be mistaken for part of the Pacific Ocean. The Swan Valley was to the east, just over the mountain, and soon he would have to make choices that would place him in immediate jeopardy. The Wellstones' hirelings would have no qualms about killing him if they were ordered to do so, and if the cops got their hands on him again, he would be on his way back to Texas, where he would get an extra five years for running and probably another twenty for the attempted murder of Troyce Nix, all of it to be served under mounted gunbulls at Huntsville prison.

The shaman had asked Jimmy Dale his thoughts on a man returning to jail. No, that wasn't correct. He had asked Jimmy Dale his thoughts on an Indian going back to jail. When Jimmy Dale said he had given the question no study, he had answered truthfully. For him, the question had never been up for debate. Before he'd do time again, he'd eat a Gatling gun.

CHAPTER 24

Troyce told Candace they were moving their "situation," as he called it, up to the Swan, where he'd worked out an arrangement with some people who owned time-share units on the shores of the lake. The cottages had been built of stone and gray-painted shingles during the Depression, on thirty-six acres that sloped down through birch trees to a shoreline that offered a magnificent view of Swan Peak. In the hottest days of summer, the thirty-six acres were always cool and breezy inside the shade of the birch trees, and guests played tennis on a court stained by leaves that had stayed wet and gold under winter snow.

It was a grand place to vacation, and that its grandeur had in part been created by impoverished craftsmen hired by people with Midas levels of wealth seemed of little significance today. But Candace could not keep her mind on the loveliness of the setting or its arcane history or Troyce's endless conversation about pike fishing and the fact that this was a glacial lake and right beneath the water's surface were the peaks of mountains that could slice the bottom out of an aluminum boat.

"Will you shut up?" she said as they pulled into the shale driveway of the cottage he had rented.

"You shouldn't ought to talk to me like that," he said, cutting the engine.

"You shouldn't ought to lie."

"Lie about what?"

"Why we're here, why you're set on ruining all our plans."

"If I don't deal with Jimmy Dale now, I'll have to deal with him when we get our café. It ain't me what's writing up the itinerary. He's gonna come for Ms. Wellstone, and I'm gonna be waiting for him. Maybe they done took off already, but at least I can say I give it my best."

"I believe what she said. Jimmy Dale doesn't want to hurt you, Troyce. If he did, he would have pulled the trigger in the park. He stopped Quince Whitley from throwing acid on me. But that doesn't mean anything to you, does it?"

"Of course it does."

"But not enough. You know why? Because you won't face up to what's driving you. You did something awful to Jimmy Dale to make him cut you up the way he did."

"How about what *he* done? Like open my face when I was unarmed and bust off a shank in my chest?"

"What did you do to him?"

Troyce's hands rested on the bottom of the steering wheel. All she could see was the side of his face, but in his right eye was an intensity that she could compare only with a bee trapped inside a glass. "I had certain kinds of sexual problems for a long time, least till I met you. When I try to sort them out in my head, I always think back on Cujo and the towel we wrapped around his face and the water we poured from a bucket into his nose and mouth. There was gasoline in the water, and when I think of Cujo and the towel and the water breaking across his face, I can smell gasoline, just like I could smell it on them men that raped me when I was little.

"Out in the desert, after we killed him and everybody was drinking beer and smoking dope, I could hear these vultures up in the sky. Their sounds was just like the gurgling sounds Cujo made before he died. Other people might hear mockingbirds in the morning, but I hear them vultures."

She stared out the passenger window at the lake. An elderly man was showing a little boy, probably his grandson, how to spin-cast off the end of the dock. The water looked blue and deep and cold, and in his concentration, the little boy seemed about to fall in, until the elderly man steadied him and pulled him back by the hand.

"You hurt Jimmy Dale Greenwood because of your own guilt, Troyce. Till you own up on that, it's gonna keep eating on you, just like a tumor growing inside your chest. It'll squeeze everything good out of you till one day none of the good man I know will be left."

She went inside the cottage with her suitcase and began unpacking in the bedroom, throwing her things onto shelves, not bothering to pick them up when they fell on the floor.

"Maybe I got another reason for being up here," Troyce said from the doorway. "Maybe you don't know the whole story about everything."

"I'm not the one hurting all our plans just so he can get even for something he caused to happen."

"When we went up to talk to the Wellstones? When I left my shades inside and had to go back inside for them?" he said.

"What about it?"

"The door was still partly open, so I went in the living room and got my shades without knocking. Leslie Wellstone was telling the Spanish woman to wipe down everything you touched in the bathroom and to put all the tissues and cleaning towels in a bag along with the cleaning gloves and burn them in the incinerator. He's a cripple man, or I would have twisted that ugly head of his off the stem and stuck it on a pike."

Candace thought she would not be vulnerable to Troyce's re-creation of Leslie Wellstone's insult, but the images Troyce's words conjured up in her imagination caused the blood to drain from her cheeks and her eyes to water. She jerked open a dresser drawer, dumped the rest of her clothes on the bedspread, and began sorting out her underthings, unsure exactly what she was doing.

"Who cares what Leslie Wellstone said?" she said impotently. "Besides, what does that have to do with Jimmy Dale Greenwood?"

"Maybe that fellow Quince Whitley wasn't after you with a bottle of acid just 'cause I give him a beating in a convenience-store restroom. Maybe he had permission from Leslie Wellstone to do that. Or Leslie Wellstone's wife, the one who's telling you to leave Jimmy

Dale alone. A guy like Whitley don't use the toilet less'n somebody gives him permission."

"I think that's crap," she replied.

"Maybe it is. But that Wellstone woman ain't no good. She dumped Jimmy Dale when he went to jail, and now she's using him to escape that freak she married. Bet you as soon as they're in Canada, she'll get shut of Jimmy Dale again and find another hard-up rich guy who cain't keep his big-boy in his britches."

Candace shoved the rest of her garments in a dresser drawer and now had no other place to put her hands except the back pockets of her jeans.

"Are you trying to say something?" Troyce asked.

"Yeah, I guess I am. I just didn't think I could."

"What are you trying to tell me, little darlin'?"

"That if you hurt that guy, that Indian, Jimmy Dale Greenwood, I swear to God I won't be around anymore," she replied.

CLETE PURCEL DROVE his Caddy down to our cabin and got out and looked at its maroon finish reflectively. He removed a soft cloth from the glove box and wiped dust off one fender, wetting a finger and touching a spot on the chrome molding around the headlight. But his attention did not seem concentrated on his vehicle.

I stepped out on the porch. The sun was shining through the trees on the mountaintop, and Clete had to squint to look at me.

"What are you thinking about?" I asked.

"Alicia told me the feds and the Sheriff's Department found a box of Halloween masks in Sonny Click's basement," he replied. "They all look just like the one they found in Quince Whitley's truck. They also found a photo in a scrapbook at Click's place. It shows a bunch of college-age kids wearing the masks at a party two years ago. Alicia said the DNA inside the mask from Whitley's truck isn't from Whitley."

"The feds have a vested interest in Whitley's role as a CI. I wouldn't blow him off as a suspect," I said. "Remember that case in Boston when one of their CIs was doing contract hits?"

Clete shook his head as though a fly were buzzing around his face.

"Yeah, I think Whitley is involved on one level or another. The Wellstones didn't hire him just to shovel horse turds. A guy like that is a weapon you point at other people."

"You want to have another talk with the Wellstones?"

He chewed at a piece of skin on the ball of his thumb. "Yeah, then we start over. We missed something. It's real simple, too. Know why we haven't seen it?"

"No, but tell me."

He gave me a look. "The main players all have normal roles," he said. "They're not skells or grifters or junkies or porn addicts. They don't have rap sheets. They don't get picked up in shooting galleries or at cathouses or live-sex shows. They don't give us the edge."

"But sooner or later, they all go down, Cletus, edge or no edge."

"That's why neither one of us ever developed drinking problems," he replied.

When Cletus was at the plate, your best slider usually came back at you like a BB in the forehead.

WE HEADED UP to the Swan Valley in Clete's Caddy. An hour and a half later, we were rebuffed at the Wellstones' front gate by none other than Lyle Hobbs. Even though Clete had ripped out Hobbs's wiring at the park in Missoula, Hobbs was oddly detached and self-possessed. His recessed eye, the one looped by a chain of tiny scars, still looked as dead as a lead ball but no more lacking in expression than his other eye. "The Wellstones aren't receiving guests right now," he said. "You can come back tomorrow or the next day."

Through the electronically locked gate, I could see the fortress-like structure the Wellstones called home at the end of the driveway. Deer were feeding on the lawn, their coats golden in the sunlight, like decorative ornaments. I got out of the Caddy and closed the door behind me, indicating physically that my presence was going to be a problem that wouldn't disappear easily. "How about calling up to your boss and asking?" I said.

"They're not to be bothered," Hobbs replied, his expression flat, his gaze fixed on the mountains.

"Would you tell Ms. Wellstone I'd like to speak with her?" I said.

"She's not here right now," he replied.

"Do you know when she'll return?" I asked.

"No sir, I don't."

"Would you know where she is?"

"With the driver and the maid and the little boy. Shopping, maybe. She's real good at shopping."

"You think your buddy Quince Whitley got a raw deal?" I asked.

Hobbs's mouth was pinched, as though he were sucking in his cheeks. His dry, uncombed hair blew in the wind, his untucked short-sleeve shirt loose on his thin frame. "The way I hear it, Quince dealt the play. He wasn't a bad guy. But he made mistakes in judgment sometimes," Hobbs said. "I don't play another man's hand, if that's what you're trying to make me do."

"You think Reverend Sonny Click offed himself," I said.

This time his eyes found mine. "That's what happened, right?" he said.

"I think he was unconscious when somebody strung him up," I said. "I think somebody thought he was the weak sister in the chain. You're a smart guy, Lyle. You were Mobbed up and in the life when the Wellstone brothers were getting blow jobs with their daddy's credit card. What do you think is going to happen to you when you're no longer useful?"

Clete leaned over to the passenger window. "Hey, Lyle, remember what Sally Dee used to always say: 'There're kings and queens, and then there're worker bees.' Did you know Sally read Machiavelli and Hitler in jail? Glad you're not working for him anymore."

Lyle Hobbs stared blankly at both of us. Nobody knew the skells better than Clete Purcel, and nobody was better at pressing thumbtacks into their heads.

LATER THAT AFTERNOON Candace Sweeney and Troyce Nix were eating in the café that adjoined the nightclub on the lake when a long white limo pulled in and the daytime bartender, Harold, got out and went inside. He placed a take-out order for hamburgers and fries at the counter, then went into the nightclub and began fixing a drink with a blender behind the bar. The curtains were partially closed on the café's front window in order to keep out the glare, but through a crack, Candace could see the extravagant full length of the limo and its charcoal-tinted windows, its bulk and mass and power a visible rejection of all those who set limitations on their own lives. The engine was running, the air-conditioning units on, the charcoal windows damp from the coldness inside.

"Why would people with money like that want to eat in a greasy skillet like this?" Candace asked.

"So they can pretend they're like the rest of us," Troyce replied.

"Why do they want to pretend to be like us?"

"So they can make us feel bad about ourselves. So they can tell us they made it but we didn't." Then he grinned at her in his old way, at the corner of the mouth, like the Duke. "Or maybe there just ain't another place here'bouts to get good food."

Candace felt like a clock was running faster and faster inside her, its wheels and cogs starting to shear, its hands spinning in a blur. "There's still gold up in the Cascades, places where nobody ever found the mother lode," she said. "My father swore it was there, up in the high country, up in the snow line. All those years it was washing down into the creeks, telling the panners down below where it was, but nobody was interested. Think of it, Troyce, maybe a vein three inches thick running through the face of a cliff you just have to sweep the snow off of."

Troyce looked at her peculiarly. "Bet you and me could find it," he said.

She waited for him to finish.

"Soon as we tie up things here," he said.

He forked down the last of his chicken-fried steak and mashed potatoes and peas and took a final sip from his coffee. "I need to talk to that old boy in the saloon a minute."

Candace realized who was in the white limo. "Leave them alone, Troyce."

"Don't worry. It's them what better look out for us," he said.

• • •

WHEN TROYCE ENTERED the nightclub, Harold Waxman was pouring a daiquiri into a stemmed glass, wrapping a towel around the bottom to catch the overflow.

"Remember me?" Troyce said.

Harold lifted his eyes from his work. "I'm on my own time right now. If you want a drink, order from the other bartender," he said.

"I'm a businessman. I don't drink during the day," Troyce said.

Harold Waxman wore black slacks and a black leather belt and a long-sleeve dress shirt that was so white it had a blue tint. Every hair on his head was combed neatly into place, with no attempt to disguise his growing baldness or advancing age. A toothpick protruded from the corner of his mouth. "The state of Texas hires businessmen as prison guards?" he said.

"I'm empowered to offer a reward for this escaped felon Jimmy Dale Greenwood," Troyce said. "The reward pays upon custody rather than conviction. I'm talking about five thousand dollars."

Harold Waxman propped his hands on the bar and stared at the video poker machines lined up against the far wall. "Number one, I don't know any escaped felons. Number two, if I did, I'd call the Sheriff's Department. Number three, this is the second time you've come in here pestering people. I'm hoping it's the last."

He looked at the young woman who had entered the saloon and was standing behind Troyce. "You want a drink, miss, you need to order from the man down the bar. I'm off the clock," he said.

"I'm with him," Candace said, nodding toward Troyce.

"My offer still stands," Troyce said to Harold.

Harold let his eyes go flat and rolled his toothpick to the other side of his mouth. He poured the rest of the daiquiri from its pitcher into a large thermos. He did not look up again until Troyce and Candace were gone.

While Troyce paid the check in the café, the limo drove away with the bartender behind the wheel, the charcoal windows still closed to the heat outside.

"Why were you talking to that guy?" Candace asked.

"'Cause he's hinky. 'Cause he's working for the Wellstones now."

"Hinky?" she said. "He's a cop."

"Maybe he used to be, but not now."

"A cop's a cop. I can always tell one. That guy's a cop, Troyce," she said.

"If he is, he's for sale. I know a dishonest man when I see one."

ONE HOUR'S CROOKED drive to the north, up by the Canadian line, Jimmy Dale Greenwood entered a phone booth by a filling station at a crossroads, where a single traffic light hung suspended from cables over the intersection. He began feeding pocket change into the coin slot. Through the scratched plastic panels in the booth, he could see the wind blowing clouds of dust out of a wheat field, hills that had started to go brown in the summer heat, a windmill ginning on the horizon, a dead Angus bull swollen under a willow tree whose canopy looked like an enormous stack of green hay. A gas-guzzler loaded with Indian teenagers went through the red light and disappeared down the asphalt, a beer can bouncing end over end in its wake.

No answer. Jimmy Dale hung up the receiver and checked the heel of his hand where he had written Jamie Sue's cell phone number. He dialed the number a second time.

"Hello," she said.

"Hey, hon," he replied.

"Where are you?"

"Up on the Blackfeet res. I can see Canada from here. Where are *you?*"

"In the garden. Leslie is looking down at me from the window. I'll call you back in five minutes." She clicked off.

He left his duffel and rolled sleeping bag by the phone booth and went inside the filling station and bought a soft drink. He drank it outside by the booth, the wind blowing hot across the fields. To the west, past the undulating golden plains that had once been carpeted by buffalo, he could see the translucent smoky-blue outline of the northern Rockies and the eastern boundary of Glacier National Park. The phone rang inside the booth. His heart was beating when he picked up the receiver. "Hello," he said.

"I'm on the other side of the stable. Leslie can't see me. But I can't talk long," she said.

He told her where he was and described how she could get there, how to skirt the southeast corner of Glacier and to cross the Continental Divide at Marias Pass and to keep going through Blackfeet country all the way to the Milk River. He felt as though his words were actually creating her and Dale's journey, drawing them closer as he spoke.

But she wasn't hearing him. "Listen to me, Jimmy Dale!" she said. "I can't drive up there. I don't have a car. Leslie watches me all the time. There's another way."

"No, just get out of there."

"You know how you ended up in jail? You don't listen to anybody. With you, it's always full throttle and fuck it, no matter who gets hurt."

He felt his hand squeeze tight on the receiver. He had left the door to the phone booth open, and he could hear the wind blowing through the ocean of dry grass that surrounded him. He cleared his throat.

"Are you still there?" she asked.

"Yeah, I'm here," he replied. "I'm definitely way-to-hell-and-gone up *here*."

She ignored the implication. "A man is going to help us. I'm buying a used Toyota. He'll drop it in Arlee with the keys under the fender. There'll be money and a cell phone in the dash compartment. The car should be ready tomorrow."

"I don't want Leslie Wellstone's car, and I don't want his money, either."

"It's not Leslie's. I'm buying it with my money. You get rid of that stubborn attitude, Jimmy Dale."

He pressed the heel of his hand against his forehead and realized he was rubbing her cell number off his skin.

"What's wrong?" she said.

"Everything. I thought you and me and little Dale was gonna be together today. I thought we'd be highballing up into Alberta. I know people who can take us across on a dirt road with no customs check. I thought we'd go plumb to Calgary."

"We will. We just got to do it right. You don't know what Leslie and Ridley are like. They own people. They suck the life out of them."

He took the ballpoint from his shirt pocket and, pressing the phone receiver against his ear with his shoulder, tore a piece of paper loose from the phone directory and wrote out her cell number on it. Then he thumbed the piece of paper into his watch pocket. "I keep thinking we're gonna get blown away in the wind, like leaves that go bouncing across a field. It's the feeling I had in prison. That no matter what I tried to do, I was gonna be buried alive and wouldn't ever see y'all again. You never come to visit me, Jamie Sue."

"I couldn't. But I'm going to make up for that," she said.

He wanted to believe her. He wanted to believe her real bad. In the silence, a cluster of newspaper scudded across the concrete and broke apart in the air. He watched the pages lift above an irrigation ditch and float like broken wings inside a dust devil. "How's little Dale?" he asked.

"He's wonderful. You're going to love him."

"I already do."

"I know that, Jimmy Dale."

"Who's this guy helping out with the car?"

"He just started driving for me. But I knew him from before. He'd do anything for me."

"What's his name?"

"Harold Waxman, the daytime bartender at the nightclub on the lake," she replied.

AFTER CLETE AND I left the Wellstone compound, we drove down to the edge of Swan Lake and parked in a grove of cottonwoods. We ate some sandwiches and drank soda that Clete had put in his ice chest. I had started the trip up to the Wellstone manor with a sense of optimism, but my spirits had begun to sink, and I wondered if we would ever find the people who had killed the two college students, Cindy Kershaw and Seymour Bell, or the sadist who had tried to burn Clete alive.

The soda had been in the cooler for days and was ice-cold and for some reason made me think of fishing trips with my father during the 1940s. Clete got out of the Caddy and walked farther down the shore and began skipping stones across the water. It was breezy and warm inside the trees, and I reclined the leather seat and thought I would rest my eyes for a few moments. In seconds I was fast asleep, and I had one of those daytime dreams that tell you more about your life than you wish to learn.

I thought the images were from a tropical forest in a Southeast Asian country. Mist hung in the trees, and the ground was white or gray with compacted layers of winter-killed leaves. Air vines hung in the columns of tea-colored light that penetrated the canopy. But the backdrop for the dream was not Vietnam; it was the Louisiana of my youth. The trees were all old growth, the trunks as hard as iron, the roots as big as a man's torso, gnarled and brown and bursting through the earth. In the midst of the forest was a clearing, and inside the clearing was a freshly dug grave. An M16 rifle with an unsheathed bayonet affixed to the muzzle had been upended and driven solidly into the mound above the grave. A steel pot had been balanced atop the rifle butt, with a chain and a set of dog tags draped around the circumference. The cloth cover was rotted, blowing in cottony wisps, the inked turkey-track peace symbol barely visible. I could hear the dog tags tinkling in the breeze and see the soldier's name and serial number stamped into the metal. I felt my mouth go dry and my heart expand to the size of a small pumpkin.

I woke up suddenly, unsure where I was. Clete was standing on the lakeshore, a smile on his face, a flat red stone poised in his hand. "Come throw a few with me," he said.

"Throw what?" I said, my eyes blinking at the glare on the water out beyond the shade of the cottonwoods.

"Stones. I'm heck on pike."

"Sure," I said, getting out of the Caddy, my mind still inside the dream.

"You nod off for a while?"

"I saw a marker left by the graves detail. Except it was in Louisiana, not 'Nam. My tags were wrapped around my steel pot."

He let the stone drop from his hand onto the bank. He walked up the slope and fitted his big hand around the back of his neck. I could smell the piece of peppermint candy in his jaw. I could see the texture in his facial skin and the lidless intensity of his green eyes. I could also see pity and love in them, and the terrible knowledge that for some situations there are no words that can help, no anodyne that will make facing our greatest ordeal less than it is.

I rubbed the back of my wrist against my mouth. I knew at that moment I would have swallowed a razor blade for four fingers of Jack on cracked ice, and that realization filled me with shame. When I saw a caravan coming through the trees, I was glad for the danger it represented.

CHAPTER
25

CLETE PURCEL HAD descended from a Celtic ancestry that was more pagan than Christian. His forebears had ridden the coffin ships in the 1840s and had been reviled by Nativists and consigned to urban sewers like Five Points in New York and the Irish Channel in New Orleans. Arguably, they had been treated as subhuman. The upshot was they developed the ethos of people like Clete, whose admonition in dealing with skells and other people who give you trouble was always the same: "Dust 'em or bust 'em, noble mon" or "Take it to them with tongs."

Maybe that isn't a bad way to go. But sometimes when you disengage from your adversaries and isolate them and leave them to deal with their own hostilities and fears, sealing the worst elements in their personalities inside their skins, with no form of release, you condemn them to a nongeographical form of solitary confinement that is like steel blades whirling inside the viscera. Better yet, sometimes you accomplish this without even trying.

Three waxed and buffed new vehicles came down the winding access road through the trees and stopped up the slope from where Clete and I stood on the water's edge. The sun was in the west, the sky ribbed with blue-black clouds that gave no offer of rain, and shadows had pooled on the front windshields of the three vehicles so we couldn't see inside them. The moment reminded me of Clete's original encounter with the Wellstones' minions.

The vehicle in the lead was a black Mercedes. Lyle Hobbs opened the back door for Leslie Wellstone. When Wellstone stepped out on the edge of the beach, the windows of the other two vehicles rolled down on their electric motors. I could see the humped shapes of men inside, all of them watching us, two or three of them wearing shades although the vehicles were parked in shadow.

"You got your piece?" Clete said.

"Nope," I said.

Leslie Wellstone approached us, a flash of white teeth showing at the corner of his mouth, his eyes never quite resting on ours, as though he wished to be deferential and courteous. "On a fishing trip, are we?" he said.

"It's the place for it," I said.

"Mr. Hobbs said you wanted to see me."

"Mr. Hobbs told us to beat it," I said.

"The door is always open for you gentlemen. Particularly for Mr. Purcel," Wellstone said.

"Let's get something straight, Jack," Clete said. "I got on your marital turf. I'm sorry that happened. But it's on me, not on your wife, not on Dave here. So fuck me. If you got issues with that, let's get it out on the table now."

"You're a direct man," Wellstone said.

"I get that way when a psychopath soaks me in gasoline," Clete said.

"I see. But you didn't get to have the complete experience, did you? Did you know that at a certain point your sensory system dumps into your blood and your nerve endings go dead? You feel as though you're inside a blue tongue of flame that gives no heat."

Clete cupped his hands on his lighter and lit a cigarette. I took the cigarette from his mouth and threw it in the water. Wellstone watched this as though he were a spectator at a Guignol.

"Somebody locked you down in an oven and cooked you alive," Clete said. "But sometimes that happens when you join the shake-and-bake brigade. Most of the original members in my platoon didn't come back, at least not with all their parts. Most of the ones who came home wake up every day with their heads in the Mixmaster. So how about getting off other people's backs?"

The rise in the pitch of Clete's voice caused two of Wellstone's employees to step out of their vehicles.

"Mr. Wellstone, we didn't ask to get involved in your family's business affairs or your personal lives," I said. "You brought the trouble to us. In the meantime, two college kids died terrible deaths. I think your house is about to come down on your head. But Clete and I didn't do it to you. Quince Whitley was a federal informant. I suspect he screwed you good with the feds before he cashed in."

I could see the attention grow in Wellstone's eyes. "Who was Whitley's best friend?" I asked. "None other than Mr. Hobbs over there. You taking good care of Mr. Hobbs?"

"Questioning the altruism of my employees, are you?" Wellstone said.

"No, I'm questioning the loyalty of everybody around you, including your wife," I said. "How about Sonny Click, man of the cloth that he was? Guys like Click don't bounce themselves off a rafter. I think he was about to do some serious damage to your reputation, and he got taken off the board. I think it's got something to do with sex."

"You have a nasty tongue on you, Mr. Robicheaux," Wellstone said.

Clete just had to do it. "We also know your entourage of gumballs here isn't entirely about us," he said. "You think Jimmy Dale Greenwood is out there climbing your old lady. If that's true, it's because you made her life purely awful. I think you've got the same problem I have, Mr. Wellstone. It's called the reverse King Midas touch. Everything we put our hands on turns to shit."

Leslie Wellstone stepped closer to me. I could feel his breath on my skin and smell an odor, perhaps imagined, perhaps not, that was like the afterburn of kerosene. His eyes stared like a lizard's out of his encrusted face. They were liquid, as though fluid from a systemic malignancy had pooled inside them. His voice became a hiss. "You read Shakespeare, Mr. Robicheaux? The Prince of Darkness is a gentleman. But don't underestimate his power."

Involuntarily I stepped back from him, the lip of the lake touching my shoe.

He turned and walked away, his men falling in beside him.

"Keep your wick dry, Sally," Clete said at his back.

But if Leslie Wellstone was Sally Dio, he didn't take the bait. Instead, he kept walking toward his Mercedes, his gaze lifted to the hooded blue jays in the tree branches overhead.

Then I gave it a try. *"Comment va votre famille à Galveston?"*

This time Wellstone turned around. *"Bien, merci,"* he replied.

Got you, motherfucker, I thought.

But Leslie Wellstone wasn't one to be easily undone. "We have relatives in Galveston, Mr. Robicheaux. I'm sure that's whom you were referring to," he said.

WE DROVE BACK to Albert's ranch, west of Lolo, and I made another call to Sheriff Helen Soileau, my boss down in New Iberia. "I think some heavy stuff is about to go down here," I said.

"Why now?"

"This escaped convict, Jimmy Dale Greenwood, is probably planning to run off with Leslie Wellstone's wife."

"What do you need?" she said, barely able to hide the fatigue in her voice.

"We're looking at four open homicide cases and one questionable suicide," I replied. "I think they're all related, but I can't fit one net over all five of them. I think the motivation has to do with sex, but I'm not sure."

"Money buys sex. It also buys power. I'd follow the money, Streak."

"That's why I'm calling. You remember when you gave me the background on the murder of Ridley Wellstone's ex-wife and stepdaughter? You said the Harris County Sheriff's Office and Houston PD thought the target might have been the stepdaughter rather than the wife, because the daughter had dropped the dime on an Australian porn actor after she got pinched holding a brick of marijuana."

"You have to forgive me if the details are a little vague," she said.

"One of the homicide victims up here was a porn film producer from Malibu. Maybe it's just coincidence."

"Could be," she said.

I couldn't blame her for her level of response. She had enough to do in the post-Katrina, post-Rita world of southern Louisiana, a place that had once been an almost Edenic paradise. Now I was calling from thousands of miles away and, like the obsessed man railing in sackcloth, expecting others to rally to my cause.

"Run a guy by the name of Harold Waxman for me," I said. "He's a bartender and a seasonal truck driver."

"You're calling him a person of interest?"

"I don't know what he is. Maybe he's just a bartender and part-time truck driver. None of this stuff makes any sense. Remember the name of Sally Dio?"

"From Galveston?"

"There's a possibility he's still alive and posing as Leslie Wellstone. I asked him in French how his family in Galveston was doing. He said fine, in French, but maybe he didn't hear the entirety of my question."

Whatever degree of interest she'd had was now totally gone. "How's Clete?" she asked.

"He says he might move to California."

"*Right,*" she replied.

That was the best statement I'd heard all day.

THAT EVENING JIMMY Dale Greenwood camped in a grove of pine trees on Flathead Lake. He created a tent by tying a cord between two tree trunks and hanging his poncho over it, then he spread his sleeping bag under the poncho and started a fire inside a ring of stones he had gathered from the water's edge. When the fire was hot and had begun to crumble into ash, flaring with even greater heat under the blackened logs, he opened a can of pork and beans and set it to bubbling on a flat stone. Then he made two cheese sandwiches and toasted them inside a sheet of foil that he curled up on the sides.

While his food cooked, he drank a soda and watched the sun burn into a spark on the far side of the lake.

Down the beach, someone was playing a guitar. Jimmy Dale rested his head on his duffel bag and could feel the stiff outline of the Remington pump inside the cloth.

Tomorrow would be the day that decided the rest of his life, he thought. He could say in all honesty he did not fear death. Once born, you were already inside eternity, not preparing for it. Existence was a deep pasture that had no fence across it. Jimmy Dale's grandfather, who had been a shaman, had said that embarking upon the Ghost Trail was not a passage as much as a sharpening of his vision. Unfortunately, being unafraid of death was not the same as being brave.

If you were indeed brave, you had to face your greatest fear and overcome it. Jimmy Dale had no doubt what his greatest fear was. But he was not going back to prison to overcome it. If others wished to be buried under concrete and steel to demonstrate their spiritual courage, they could have at it.

The first stars were twinkling in the sky. If he died tomorrow, he died tomorrow, and to hell with the white man's jail. Perhaps death was nothing more than drifting like ash among the stars, or living inside the rain and wind, or being part of a celestial being that could never be locked inside a cage.

Chief Joseph, before he was sent in chains to Oklahoma, said, "I will be where I am." You just have to remember words like those, Jimmy Dale told himself.

He balanced his can of soda on his forehead as he stared up at the sky. He placed his arms straight out at his sides and felt like he was floating through space, in control, beyond the grasp of men like Troyce Nix and Leslie Wellstone.

Tomorrow he would hitch a ride into Arlee, on the Flathead res, and go to a bar where Jamie Sue had told him he would find a used Toyota with the keys in a magnetized box under the left fender. Then he would pick up her and Dale outside a department store in Kalispell at exactly seven P.M.

It would all happen tomorrow. Alberta and British Columbia

waited for the three of them, the chains of lakes through the Canadian Rockies like giant blue teardrops backdropped by mountains whose peaks rose through the clouds.

The wind gusted off the lake, showering pine needles down on his face, and he felt the soda can tilt on his forehead. Before he could catch it, it fell on his chest, its contents pooling in the folds of his shirt.

ON SATURDAY I woke in the early A.M. It was black outside, and the air was dense and humid, stained with the stench of a fire over in Idaho. I could hear the horses in the dark, clattering against the railed fence, a shoed hoof sparking on a flat rock.

I didn't want to think about fire in the hills or the fire that could have consumed Clete Purcel. I didn't want to think about the events unfolding around us. But I did, and I got up from the bed while Molly was still in a deep slumber. I turned on the reading lamp in our small living room and pulled the magazine from my forty-five and cleaned and oiled all the parts and ran a bore brush through the barrel, then inserted a folded scrap of white paper in the chamber to reflect the lamp's glow through the rifling, which was now clean and unnicked in appearance and spiraling with an oily light.

One by one, I thumbed the rounds free from the magazine, tested the tension in the spring, and pressed each round down against the spring again, until the last round notched tight under the steel lip at the top of the magazine. I released the slide before I pushed the magazine into the butt of the gun so the chamber would remain empty, then I put the gun in its leather holster and snapped the strap across the hammer and set the holstered gun on the table and looked at it.

My 1911-model army forty-five had never let me down. As a second lieutenant in Vietnam, I had carried one that was official-issue, and the one I brought home I had purchased from a Vietcong prostitute in Saigon's Bring Cash Alley. For years I slept with a gun under my bed. So did Audie Murphy. He once said for every day on the firing line, you have to spend five days in the normal world before you can sleep again. Because he had been in combat for almost four years, he believed he had been condemned to twenty years of sleeplessness. His gambling addiction cost him two million dollars but did not purchase him one hour's rest. He put a bed in his garage and spent his nights there because his wife could not sleep with an armed man wired for sounds that no one else could hear.

All of that made perfect sense to me.

I picked up the forty-five and rested it on my knee. It was heavy and cool in my hand, an old friend that represented power and control over one's environment and the ability to call down lightning and fire on one's enemies. Do not go gently into that good night, the poet said. Rage against your fate and protest it to death's door. Don't buy into the lie that the good die in bed, either. A dying man's bed is stained with phlegm and urine and feces and the pus leaking from his sores. Doc Holliday coughed his lungs into a nun's cupped hands, his guns hanging in a closet, his last sight of the earth a wind-swept Colorado plateau that could have been moonscape. I doubt that he would have recommended his fate to others.

I touched my hand to my head. My skin seemed to be on fire. Heat lightning flared in the sky, and I heard horses' hooves thudding across the pasture, muffled inside the grass. I wished the sounds were human, not those of animals. I wished my enemies were out there so I could lock down on them with iron sights and blow them all over the serviceberry trees. I wished Death himself would confront me and release me from his taunts and allow me to deal on equal terms with him. Like the fool in a medieval morality play, I wanted the rules of mortality rewritten for me.

At sunup Molly and I went for breakfast in town. When we came back to the cabin, I had a message waiting on the machine from Helen Soileau. "Give me a call, Dave. I'm at home. I'm a little confused about what I've found on your bartender friend," she said.

I punched in her number. "You found out something about Waxman?" I said.

"Dave?" she said.

"Yeah."

"You sound funny. You all right up there?"

"Always."

"A guy by that name shows up in lots of places. If they're all the same guy, he's been a long-haul truck driver for the last ten years or so. He's also worked as a heavy-equipment mechanic and a bartender and restaurant manager. The Waxman with that Social Security number doesn't have a criminal or military history. An H. T. Waxman was a cop thirty years ago in Conroe, Texas. But I don't know if that's the same Waxman, because I couldn't confirm the cop's Social Security number."

"Your message said you'd found something you weren't clear about."

"Waxman has long periods without an earnings history. That's not completely unusual, but your guy seems to have licenses and skills that would give him more computer-generated visibility."

"Where was he a truck driver?"

"He worked out of Sacramento, Seattle, and Denver. Wait a minute." I heard her rustling pages, as though turning them on a legal pad. "He also drove for a grain company of some kind in Dumas, Texas. Where's Dumas?"

"In the Panhandle," I said.

"Your guy doesn't fit a profile. The defectives always leave shit prints. But your guy has no jacket of any kind. What are you looking at him for?"

"Conroe is forty-five minutes north of Houston. Funny he was around there at about the same time the Wellstones were."

"God forgive me, I have to ask you a question," she said.

"What?"

"I love you, Pops, so don't hold it against me."

"Say it."

"Did you have a slip? Are you back on the dirty boogie? Tell me the truth."

LYLE HOBBS WASN'T the brightest bulb in the box. He was a southern street rat and mean-spirited peckerwood descended from the kind of white people who, in an earlier time, had worked as paddy rollers and assistant overseers. But unlike his friend Quince, he had the ability to think and looked upon passion and anger and delusions about human fidelity as forms of self-indulgence that only the rich could afford.

As a consequence, he had never stacked serious time. In short, he was a survivor. He was also what investigative cops call "a weak sister." The latter is the frail link in the chain, the conscript looking over his shoulder at the fort, the sycophant trying to guess which way the political wind is about to blow. If there is only one life raft on board a ship, and if seawater is flooding up through the ruptured hull and waves are washing over the gunwales, you can bet that someone of Lyle Hobbs's ilk will already have the life raft strapped on his back.

He was driving an old Japanese car when he came up the dirt road, the windows down, the dust funneling back inside. He drove past the archway in front of Albert's house and turned in to the lane that led to our cabin, his eyes switching from the rearview mirror to the side window, checking to see if his nemesis Clete Purcel was anywhere in sight.

His shirt was open, and I could see the iridescent shine of sweat on his chest. His skin and eyebrows and hair were gray with dust, his eyes bright, as though he'd had a couple of hits of crystal. When he cut the engine, the sun was baking on his car, a cloud of grasshoppers swarming past his window. There were two suitcases in the backseat, one piled on top of the other, the two of them roped together.

"What's the haps, Lyle?" I said.

He looked up at me, his mouth slightly open, his recessed eye somehow lower than the other. "I didn't sign on to take somebody else's bounce. I do security. I chauffeur people's automobiles. That's all I do. Where's Purcel?" he said.

"Not here," I lied.

"I thought I saw his Caddy behind Albert Hollister's house."

I glanced at my watch. "I'm kind of busy right now. What's on your mind?"

"Sorry to get in your space."

"I didn't invite you here, bud. Take your bullshit someplace else." I started to walk away.

"I tried to get aholt of that Vietnamese woman."

"Alicia Rosecrans?"

"Nobody would return my calls."

I kept walking toward the cabin. I heard him get out of the car and slam the door. When I turned around, I thought he was going to hit me.

"I was there the morning that college boy gave it to Ridley Wellstone," he said. "The kid was bent out of shape. He came there by himself. He didn't use his head. Maybe it was pride, like before he went to the cops, he had to confront Mr. Wellstone and shame him for what he tried to do to the girl. It's the kind of dumb thing a kid would do. That's kids, right? But it was dumb. The kid's parents ought to have taught him better. You don't let your pride push you into situations you got to bluff your way out of."

"You want a drink of water? You look a little hot."

Lyle Hobbs glanced back at Albert's house. Clete's Caddy was parked in the shade. A large raven was standing on the convertible top, cawing at the trees. Hobbs touched at his mouth and widened his eyes, as though trying to see more clearly into the shade.

"I could hear him talking loud in Mr. Wellstone's office, all wired up, like he could deal with somebody like Mr. Wellstone on equal terms."

"Seymour Bell went to the Wellstones' compound? That's what you're telling me?" I said.

"Mr. Wellstone has an office upstairs. Bell went straight upstairs and told Mr. Wellstone he'd propositioned his girlfriend, what's-her-name."

"Cindy Kershaw," I said.

"She worked as a janitor at the health club where he was getting therapy for his sciatica. Sonny Click tried to get it on with her. She came up to Swan Lake to tell Mr. Wellstone. Except he tried to put moves on her himself. When she didn't go for it, he must have got a little rough, maybe feeling her up or something. Or at least that was what Bell was saying to him. Mr. Wellstone told him to file a report with the Sheriff's Department, because he knew the kid didn't have diddly-squat to support his story. That's when Bell tried to one-up him."

"What do you mean?" I said.

"He told Mr. Wellstone the girl had a digital recorder in her purse, that she had turned it on and caught the whole thing, everything about the ministry and Click seducing young girls and Mr. Wellstone trying to get into Cindy's pants. I heard a chair scraping. I think Mr. Wellstone must have gotten up and tried to push the kid out of his office. Except it didn't work out that way. Bell said he was gonna dime Sonny Click and Mr. Wellstone and show them up for the frauds they were. Then he shoved Mr. Wellstone down the stairs. He looked like a pile of broken sticks at the bottom of the steps."

"When did this happen?" I asked.

"The same day those kids got killed."

"Who did it to them, Hobbs?"

"Not me. I drive people's cars. That's it. You tell that Asian cunt what I said."

"I think maybe you're still working for Sally Dio. I think maybe Sally is still alive. One guy survived that air crash. It was Sal, wasn't it? Where is he, Lyle?"

"Sally always said you were stupid."

"Could be," I said. I smiled at him, my thumbs hooked on the sides of my belt, my eyes roving over his face. "Just a footnote to all this. If you ever refer to a woman like that in my presence again, using that particular word, I'm going to pick up a ball-peen hammer and break out all your teeth."

I walked up to the main house and told Clete of Hobbs's visit. Then I got Alicia Rosecrans's cell phone number from him and went back to the cabin and called her. I told her everything Hobbs had said, excluding the insult.

"Where's Hobbs now?" she asked.

"Probably headed for Reno or Vegas."

"Seymour Bell told Ridley Wellstone he had recorded evidence against both him and Sonny Click? That the Kershaw girl had a digital recorder in her purse?"

"That's correct, at least according to Hobbs."

"But Bell was bluffing?"

"That's right," I replied.

"Ridley Wellstone couldn't figure that out? Kershaw came from a poor family. She worked as a janitor to go to college. Where would she get money for a digital recorder? Those kids died for nothing."

"Yeah, they did," I said.

"I thought I had more objectivity about this case, but this really pisses me off. Hobbs wouldn't say who abducted Bell and Kershaw?"

"No. But Quince Whitley has got to be a player in this."

"How about the California couple? What's the connection?"

"I'm not sure."

"That's a long way from 'don't know,' Mr. Robicheaux."

"Thirty-one years ago Ridley Wellstone's stepdaughter was mixed up with a porn actor. She and her mother were both murdered. The murder remains unsolved."

"Where's Clete?"

"In his apartment, up at the main house."

"You guys stay out of this."

"I'd love to. Would you pass on your sentiments to the Wellstones?" I replied.

CHAPTER
26

THE PREVIOUS AFTERNOON, after Troyce had talked to the bartender at the nightclub, he had been silent all the way back to the cottage. Then he had left Candace by herself and gone away for three hours, claiming he had to get the truck serviced and to buy pike-fish tackle at Seeley Lake. This morning he had gotten up in the false dawn and had showered in cold water because the pilot had gone out on the tank; in the frigid temperature of the kitchen, without shoes or a shirt on, he had fixed breakfast for both of them but had left most of his uneaten on the plate. Minutes later, without explanation, he had driven off in the first pink touch of sunrise on the birch trees, leaving her a fifty-dollar bill to buy lunch in case he wasn't back by noon.

But he returned four hours later, a lump of cartilage working in his jaw, the armpits of his red shirt dark with sweat. He clenched his stomach, his face white around the mouth with discomfort.

"You sick?" she said.

"I got to go to the can," he replied.

Ten minutes later, he came out of the bathroom, drying his hands on a towel, blowing out his breath. "I feel like I was poisoned. What'd I eat last night?"

"What you always do—steak."

"Anyway, I'm okay now. Let's pack it up," he said.

"We just got here."

"That's right. We been here. So let's go see some other place."

"Like where?"

"Glacier Park, then all points west. Next stop, the Cascade Mountains. How would you like that?"

"Where have you been, Troyce?"

"Here and yon, taking care of this and that. Come on, gal, let's head 'em up and move 'em out."

"Were you following that guy?"

"Which guy?"

"The bartender, the one that looks like he's got strands of black wire combed across his head."

"I just been taking care of business, that's all. You don't take care of business, somebody will take care of it for you, and that don't usually work out too good."

Fifteen minutes later, through the windshield of the truck, she watched the sun-spangled canopy of birches sweeping by overhead, the shadows of their leaves netting the dashboard and her skin and clothes, the ethereal blue-gray beauty of the lake and Swan Peak disappearing behind the truck. She looked at Troyce's chiseled profile and cupped her hand on the point of his shoulder and tightened her fingers on the bone and muscle. But she didn't speak, not at first, because she couldn't find the vocabulary that would make Troyce understand her sense of apprehension.

"You fixing to tell me something?" he asked.

"No, because I haven't figured it all out. When I do, I'll tell you," she replied.

"How am I supposed to read that, Candace?"

"I never had any understanding of the big mysteries and why things happen and why people get hurt and do the things they do to each other. I don't think figuring it out comes with age, either. Otherwise we'd want to listen to old people. But we don't, because most of them act selfish and childish and have to be tolerated and taken care of. I can't even figure out us, much less anything that's bigger than us."

His eyes crinkled at the corners as though he was either amused by her words or honestly trying to understand them. He blew his horn and swung around a truck on the two-lane, pressing the accelerator to the floor, barely getting back in before he hit the double yellow warning lines. "You're too deep for the likes of me," he said.

"I made you a promise, but I'm not keeping it," she said.

"What promise?"

"That I wouldn't be here if you tried to hurt that man."

"You talking about Jimmy Dale Greenwood?"

"I don't want you to even use his name to me. Don't say it. Don't tell me why he's so important to you, don't tell me any of your lies. You make me resent myself, Troyce. That's the worst thing somebody can do to somebody else."

He looked at her, the pickup drifting across the center stripe, his face clouding. "'Cause of a guy like that, you'd throw everything we got out the window?"

She stared at the long tunnel of shadow and light and pines and fir trees and cottonwoods that seemed to be racing past the truck. She didn't know if Troyce was being disingenuous or if he truly could not understand what she was saying to him. She rolled down the window and let the road's trapped heat blow into her face, whipping her hair, stinging her skin with invisible pieces of grit.

Her adolescent and adult life had been spent proving her lack of dependence on others—hustling as a street kid in Portland, body-blocking other women senseless on the roller-derby circuit, cooking at hunting lodges for corporate executives who made jokes about learning from the Indians, namely how to do it dog-style in the great outdoors, wheezing while they told their jokes, their faces flushed and porcine above their drinks.

But the truth about Candace's relationship with the world was otherwise. The defining moment in her life, the passageway that forever changed her, one that was like an arc of dark light across the sky, was the day Smilin' Jack left her behind and entered the Cascades, his head full of dreams about the mother lode buried somewhere inside the clouds, his whole body full of love and energy and physical courage, smelling of aftershave lotion and pipe tobacco and the Lifebuoy soap he bathed in, full of everything except concern for the little girl he had abandoned.

Candace and Troyce spoke about little of consequence during the ride through Bigfork and down the two-lane that bordered the eastern shore of Flathead Lake. The day was bright, the wind drowsy and warm, the surface of the lake a hot blue, the highway full of vacationers on their way to Glacier Park.

"I think maybe you ought to drop me at the bus depot," she said. "Time I fired myself as your number one douche bag and box of Valium."

"Okay, here it is, little darlin'. I told you that bartender was a Judas of some kind, that he put me in mind of an egg-sucking dog hanging around a brooder house?" he said. "I followed him yesterday and today and was about to give up. Then I went into the café at the lake and had coffee. This waitress in there who tried to come on to me before says, 'You still want to drive me home, Tex?' I go, 'I thought the bartender or your husband drove you home.' She goes, 'My husband is drunk, and Harold is running errands for Ms. Wellstone down at Arlee or something.' "

"You're telling me you tried to pick up a waitress?" Candace said.

"*Nooo,*" he said, drawing out the word. "I'm not saying that at all. I was trying to get information from her. The waitress told me this guy Harold Waxman—that's the bartender—was delivering a car to a bar in Arlee this afternoon, and she didn't have a ride home from work. That car is for Jimmy Dale Greenwood. He's blowing the country, and maybe he's taking the Wellstone woman and his kid with him."

"So all this time you've been talking about Glacier Park and the Cascades and starting up our café, you've really been planning on getting even with this guy? I think this pretty much does it for me, Troyce."

"You're not listening," he said. "I'm going down to Arlee for one reason. It's to look Jimmy Dale in the face and tell him I wouldn't dirty my hands by giving him the beating he deserves. If I don't do that, I'll never have no peace."

"You're not gonna have any peace till you admit something else, either."

"Like what?"

"That you made that guy's life awful."

"You still want to go to the depot?"

"Maybe," she replied.

He glanced sideways at her, the right front wheel of the truck skidding rocks off the embankment into the water far below.

"No, I don't want to go to the depot. You have a cinder block for a head, but you're a good man. Your problem is, you don't believe in the one person who tells you that," she said. "That's how come you hurt me."

She saw the confusion in his expression. Then his face emptied and he looked straight ahead at the road, as though a solitary thought dominated all his senses and gave him a respite from the sounds constantly grinding inside his head. "People like us ain't supposed to be apart, Candace. If you ever run off from me, I won't never be the same, and I won't never find nobody like you. That's the way it is. After today, we're gonna have the perfect life. I promise. I ain't gonna hurt that man. You'll see."

MOLLY HAD PICKED a bouquet of lupine, Indian paintbrush, asters, harebells, wild roses, and mock orange and placed them in a glass pitcher of water in the kitchen window. She was washing her hands at the sink, and the wind was blowing across the meadow, swelling the curtains, tousling her hair. She dried her hands and turned around. "Why are you looking at me like that?" she said.

"It's a strange day. There're locusts all over the pasture. I could hear them hitting on the screens this morning," I replied.

"July is a dry month," she said.

"Maybe," I said. But how do you tell someone the light is wrong, that it's too bright, that the glare is of a kind you associate with a desert, with heat that dries mud bricks into powder and makes rocks sharper than they should be and burning to the touch?

"You want to go downtown today? The street market is open by the train station," she said.

"If you'd like to," I said.

"What is it, Dave? What bothers you all the time?"

Nothing other than an oblong black hole, one that waits for all of us.

"Nothing. I'm fine," I said.

"Why did you get up in the middle of the night and oil your gun?"

"Primitive people believed they could drive evil spirits from the grave by firing arrows at them. Oiling a sidearm under a reading lamp in the dark makes about as much sense."

I saw a question mark form on her face, then dissolve into an expression of loss and incomprehension. I saw her chest rise and fall, her eyes go away from me and return. "For good or bad, no matter what happens, we're in it together," she said.

"You're a stand-up guy, Molly."

"A guy?"

But I wasn't interested in rhetoric or verbal assurances or defining myself or my relationship with my wife or even trying to explain how the measure of one's life finally reduces itself to the possession of the moment, then the moment after that, moving through each of them in sequence from day to day, letting go of yesterday and asking nothing from the future except to be there for it.

"Good guys forever," I said.

"Pardon?" she said.

I locked my hands around her back and lifted her into the air and walked with her into the bedroom, the bottoms of her bare feet touching the tops of my shoes.

"What you doing, cap'n?" she said.

I pulled her dress over the top of her head and kissed her on the mouth. She sat down on the side of the bed, wearing only her panties and a bra. She glanced toward the window. The curtains were billowing in the wind, and dust was rising from the field and we could see the shadows of ravens racing across the tips of the grass. "You hear a clock ticking, Dave?" she said.

I looked around the room as though I didn't quite understand.

"You know what I mean," she said.

"Hemingway once said three days can be worth a lifetime if you live them right," I said.

"Hemingway shot himself," she replied.

"He left behind books that people will read as long as there are books," I said.

"But maybe no one told him that. Or he didn't listen to them when they did." She lifted her eyes to mine.

"No one knows what goes on in the mind of a suicide, Molly. They don't come back to tell us."

The room was silent.

She finished undressing and lay down and waited for me, indifferent to the fact that someone might walk up on the porch, or that a recreational rider might come down a trail on the hillside, or perhaps, more important, no longer worried about the lack of resolution in our discussion or a lack of resolution in the latter part of our lives.

When I was inside Molly, I saw images behind my eyelids that seemed to have little to do with marital congress. I saw gossamer fans floating inside a coral cave, a field of red poppies hard by the sea, a glistening porpoise sliding through a wave. I could feel her heart beating against my chest, her breath puffing against my ear. I could smell her hair and the heat in her skin, like a fragrance of flowers at first light. But Molly's greatest gift to me during those erotic moments was simply her touch, the presence of her body under me, the grace of her thighs, the tightness of her arm across my back, the steady pressure of her hand at the base of my spine.

There are occasions in this world when you're allowed to step inside a sonnet, when clocks stop, and you don't worry about time's winged chariot and hands that beckon to you from the shadows.

Then I felt a sensation that was like a fissure splintering down the face of a stone dam, spreading through my loins, collapsing my insides, draining my heart, pushing the light out of my eyes. I tried to stop it from happening, to make it last longer, to bring Molly inside the intensity of the moment with me, but she tightened her thighs and drew me deeper inside her and bit my neck and made a sound perhaps like the Sirens did when they lay atop rocks jutting from an ancient sea.

When it was over, I could hear no sound other than the wind in the grass outside and the hammering of my blood in my ears. When I kissed her again on the mouth, her fingers were wrapped in my hair, her body damp with sweat, our bedsheets imprinted with a moment I never wanted to leave.

That was when Albert knocked on the door and shouted that I'd had a phone call up at the main house.

"Who from?" I said from the bedroom as Molly drew the sheet over her breasts.

"She didn't say. She said she'd call back in ten minutes," he called through the screen. "She had an accent like a twanging bobby pin. She also sounded a little bit hysterical. Caller ID blocked. I'd leave her the hell alone. Message delivered. Adios."

I dressed and went up to the main house. The phone rang in the kitchen just as Albert opened the front door. He went back to his office, and I picked up the receiver.

"Hello?" I said.

"Mr. Robicheaux?" a woman's voice asked.

"What can I do for you, Ms. Wellstone?" I said.

"It's Jamie Sue," she replied, either correcting or not hearing me. "We're in terrible trouble."

"Who's the 'we'?"

"I think I've been betrayed. I think my husband found out."

"About what?"

She hesitated. "I was supposed to meet Jimmy Dale. I bought a car for us and had it delivered by somebody I trusted. But I can't leave the compound. All our cars are gone. Ridley and Leslie's security men won't take me anywhere, either."

"Call 911," I said.

"And tell them I'm meeting an escaped convict?"

"I can't help you."

"They've set up a trap. Clete doesn't answer his cell. They're going to kidnap or kill Jimmy Dale."

"Where did you have the car delivered?"

She gave me the name of a bar on the Flathead res and described the vehicle.

"You said someone betrayed you."

"I paid Harold Waxman to buy the car and park it at the bar in Arlee," she said.

"You paid the bartender at the club on the lake, the man now working for your husband?"

"I thought he was my friend. It's not my fault. I thought he was loyal. I can't believe he sold us out."

"What do you know about Waxman?"

"Nothing. He was a fan and an admirer. Maybe I'm wrong about him. Maybe Lyle Hobbs followed him. Maybe Harold is innocent. I don't know what I'm saying anymore."

I couldn't help but wonder if her sense of betrayal had less to do with an individual than her discovery that fame and celebrity are cheap currency and seldom purchase loyalty in others. I wanted to ask why she hadn't stuck by Jimmy Dale when he went to prison and why she had married into a collection of scum like the Wellstones. I wanted to ask if she ever felt remorse because she'd helped deceive the audiences who had bought in to Reverend Sonny Click's charlatanism. I wanted to ask if she had ever thought about the suffering Seymour Bell and Cindy Kershaw had gone through before they died. But I already knew the answers I would get. Andy Warhol was dead wrong when he said every American is allowed fifteen minutes of fame. Fame comes to very few, and when it does, it takes on the properties of a narcotic and puts into abeyance our fears about our own mortality. Anyone who acquires a drug that potent does not give it up easily.

"Are you there?" she said.

"Clete knows nothing about your plan to run off with Jimmy Dale?" I said.

"No. Are you going to ask him to help?"

"Tell me, Ms. Wellstone, does it bother you at all that you're asking a man you slept with to help you leave your husband and run off with a third man? No, let me rephrase that. Does anything at all bother you except the fact that you screwed up your life?"

"Yes, quite a few things bother me, Mr. Robicheaux. I deserted Jimmy Dale when he needed me most, and I married a monster. Now I have a little boy who may fall into the hands of the most evil people I've ever known. If you condemn me for it, I've earned every bit of your scorn and then some."

The side of my face felt as though it had been stung by a bee when I replaced the receiver in the cradle.

"You sure this is the place?" Candace asked as she and Troyce pulled off the narrow asphalt road in the middle of the Jocko Valley. A bar built of logs and topped with a peaked red roof was set back from the road, a few vehicles parked in front, the windows lit with neon beer signs.

"It's got to be. There's only one or two bars here," he said.

"How do you know what the car looks like?"

"The waitress told me. The bartender came by the café with it."

Troyce drove the pickup around the back of the log building, leaning forward to see beyond a parked tractor rig. His face was gray under his hat, the skin around his eyes whiter than it should have been. He cleared his throat and spit out the window.

Candace touched his cheek with the back of her wrist. "You're sick," she said.

He didn't argue. All the way from Swan Lake, a pain like a shard of glass had been working its way through his viscera, causing him on a couple of occasions to suck in his breath as though his skin had been touched with a hot wire.

He pointed through the windshield. "Look yonder—a white Camry, just like she said."

Candace had hoped they wouldn't find it, that Troyce would give up his anger and pride and stubbornness and let go of his obsession with a man who perhaps someday he would meet on the street and smile at and shake hands with and feel neither ashamed nor resentful about. Candace looked around at the great empty bowl of the valley they were in, the Mission Mountains rising straight up into the sky, leviathan and green and so massive she thought they would crack the earth where they stood. The sun had reddened behind the smoke from forest fires and the thunderclouds building in the west, and the air smelled of dust and chaff blowing out of the fields. She thought she could smell rain in the air, too, although only an hour earlier, the sky had been clear and hot, the treetops glazed with heat. Now a shadow seemed to be slipping across the land from one end of the Jocko Valley to the other.

"This doesn't feel right, Troyce," she said.

"What don't?"

"Everything—this place, that car, the way the light is changing, those dark clouds moving across the valley."

"It's probably just one of them dry electric storms. All snap, crackle, and pop, and not one drop of rain."

"What do you know about that bartender? You said you knew a dishonest man when you saw one. Why do you trust what the waitress says? You like her boobs?"

"Cut that stuff out."

"Then start thinking about what we're doing."

"It ain't that complicated, darlin'. Jamie Sue Wellstone got that idiot to help her run away with an escaped felon. That makes the idiot a felon, too. But he ain't figured that out yet. You know why criminals are criminals? It's 'cause most of them majored in dumb."

Troyce parked the truck thirty yards from the Camry and cut the engine. He closed and opened his eyes as though he were dropping through an elevator shaft.

"We need to take you to a hospital," she said.

"I just need to hit the can. Come inside."

"No."

"Why not?"

"Sitting at the bar by myself in a joint on the res on Saturday afternoon? *Duh!*"

She watched him enter the back of the bar. Two Indian men who looked like father and son came out the side door. Both of them wore braided pigtails on their shoulders. They got into the cab of a flatbed and drove away, neither of them looking directly at her. She watched their vehicle disappear down the highway, over a rise, dipping into the sun, straw blowing off the bed of the truck. She wondered if they were going home to a Saturday-evening meal with the members of their family gathered around the table, an unwatched television set playing in the living room, the mountains gold and purple against the sunset. She wondered if a time would come when the simplest activities of others would not make her covetous.

The wind was picking up, and a solitary drop of rain struck her face like a BB just below the eye. She turned, wiping the wetness off her skin, just as a bus stopped on the road and a dark-complexioned man carrying a duffel and a rolled sleeping bag stepped down on the gravel in a whoosh of air.

He walked into the parking lot, carrying his bag on his shoulder, a shapeless, sweat-rimmed hat low on his brow. He was unshaved, his denim jacket tied by the arms around his waist. But incongruously, he wore an immaculate white long-sleeve cowboy shirt, one with pearl-gray snap buttons and a silver thread woven into the fabric.

He stopped and stared at the white car, then surveyed the parking lot and looked over his shoulder at the bar. His eyes seemed to linger on Candace's for a moment, as though he recognized her, but the sun's refracted glare was like a heliograph's on the windshield, and it was obvious he could not make out her features. Oddly, without thinking, Candace had started to raise her hand from her lap and wave at him, as though they were old friends.

Jimmy Dale Greenwood set his duffel and rolled sleeping bag on the hood of the Camry and began fishing under the fender with one hand. When he could not find what he was looking for, he squatted on one haunch and put his arm deeper under the fender's recesses.

Then a black cargo van backed up from the far side of the bar, not hurriedly, not in a dramatic fashion, merely creeping across the gravel as though the driver wished to create a wide arc in order to turn around. But when the vehicle stopped and the driver and two passengers got out, stepping down almost gently on the ground,

Candace knew her premonitions were as they had always been—true and destined to be disbelieved by others.

The three men were not large; they were simply physical. They were the kind of men whose stare was always invasive, whose teeth were too big for their mouths, whose hard bodies were genetic and not earned, whose hands could be like the claws on a crab.

Where was Troyce? Why did he have to get sick now? Why had she not gone inside with him?

Jimmy Dale stood up from the Camry's fender, his expression empty. The engine of the cargo van was running, the sliding side door open. The three men from the van formed a circle around him. One of them lit a cigarette and blew the smoke at an upward angle, as though he had stopped to shoot the breeze with a friend who was having car trouble. There was no one else in the parking lot. Candace could feel her ears popping and hear the wind whistling through the open windows of the pickup. The men from the van were smiling, touching Jimmy Dale on the arms, patting his back, picking up his duffel and sleeping bag for him, nodding reassuringly.

The sun dipped behind a cloud, and she saw Jimmy Dale's eyes look through the pickup's windshield and lock on her own. This time it was obvious he recognized her as the woman he had rescued from Quince Whitley in a Missoula parking lot. His expression was that of a man who knows he's been tricked and lied to, taken over the hurdles again, treated for the fool he has always been. No, worse, it was the expression of a man who thinks he deserves his fate, who thinks the role of victim and loser is one he began earning from the moment of his birth.

He started to fight with the three men, kicking impotently while they held his wrists, their smiles still in place, as though they were protecting a drunk friend from himself.

Troyce, for God's sake, get out here, she thought.

But the cavalry was in the can, and Candace Sweeney was on her own.

She reached under the seat and felt the cold touch of the lug wrench Troyce kept there. He had said, "Don't let them bust you for carrying a concealed firearm. Carry a baseball bat or a lug wrench.

Ain't nothing like a wrench or a ball bat to make Christians out of unwanted presences."

She clasped her fingers around the wrench's shank and pulled it clanking from under the seat and opened the door and stepped out on the gravel, the wind cold on her face. The wrench was heavy in her hand, weighted with a rough-edged, thick steel socket welded on the tip. She began walking toward the Camry and the three men who held Jimmy Dale by his arms. The great green-gray density of the mountains seemed to tilt on the horizon. She felt small inside the vastness of the landscape, even smaller inside the wind that seemed to finger her blouse open, exposing her tattoos and her sagging breasts. In fact, she felt the entire valley was empty of people except her and Jimmy Dale Greenwood and the three men who had already started pushing him inside the van.

"Leave him alone," she heard herself say.

"What's that you're saying?" one man asked. He was blond and chewing gum. He had green eyes that were like drills and biceps the size of softballs and an upper torso that was too long for his short height. There was an electric anticipation in his face, like that of a man riding on the crest of a wave. "Want a drink?" he said. "Let me get our friend in the car, and I'll buy you a drink."

"I said let him go. He hasn't done you any harm."

Jimmy Dale began to fight again, driving his boot heel into one man's foot, spitting in another man's face, dropping his weight down on his suspended arms to spear-kick the blond man in the groin.

"Get her out of here," one of the other men said.

The blond man shoved her in the chest. "You heard him. Hoof it, sweet thing," he said. "Our friend is plastered. You deaf? I said you haul your gash out of—"

She swung the lug wrench at him, tearing skin, breaking something, maybe his nose, maybe the ridge above his eye, but something that smeared blood and shock across his face.

"You stupid—" he said, holding one hand to his wound. Then he let out a sound like an animal whose foot was caught in a trap, except it was a grinding noise, one of personal offense and not pain.

She heard a brief buzzing sound, similar to downed power lines arcing in a puddle of water. Then something exploded in her chest, like steel tongs cutting deep inside her, expanding into places she did not know existed. Her knees buckled, a plaintive cry rose involuntarily from her throat, and she felt herself being thrown headlong into the cargo van, side by side with Jimmy Dale Greenwood, like two slabs of spoiled beef on their way to the acid pit.

CHAPTER
27

THERE HAD BEEN a three-car pileup on Evaro Hill, the narrow pass that leads up to the plateau on which the Jocko Valley is geologically located, and vacationer traffic had been backed up to the interstate. Clete had tried to work his way through a number of cars, then had clamped an emergency flasher on the dash—one he was not legally empowered to use—and had swung out on the shoulder and driven over the pass onto the Flathead reservation.

When we arrived at the bar, the first person we saw was Troyce Nix, wandering in the rear of the parking area, looking in all directions, raindrops spotting his hat. Clete pulled up abreast of him, rolling down the window. "What's going on?" he said.

"She's gone," Nix replied.

"Who's gone?" Clete said.

"Candace is. I went inside to use the restroom, and I come out, and she was gone," Nix said.

"What are you all doing here?" Clete said.

"Looking for Jimmy Dale Greenwood."

"How'd you know Greenwood was going to be here?" Clete said.

"I followed the bartender from Swan Lake, a guy by the name of Harold Waxman. What are y'all doing here?"

"Same thing you are. Start over again," Clete said.

But Troyce Nix wasn't faring too well. He wandered about in a daze, staring at the tire marks next to the white Camry, staring at the two-lane road that led through the valley and up a rise into mountains that seemed stacked higher and higher against the western sun. I got out of the Caddy and placed my hand on his shoulder. When he turned and looked at me, I could see a sense of loss and bewilderment in his eyes that I did not associate with a man of his size and physical strength.

"Nobody saw anything?" I said.

"I went back inside. Nobody was interested. It's Saturday on the res," he replied.

"You didn't see a suspicious vehicle in the parking lot?" I asked.

"I told you, I didn't see anything. I wouldn't have left her out here if I'd seen something. What are you trying to say to me?"

"I was just asking you a question, partner. Why would somebody take your girlfriend?"

I could see a thought working in his eyes. "The bartender inside said a couple of Indian guys left. Then he said the bus stopped outside."

"Who were the Indian guys?"

"Just guys, feed growers. They drink here reg'lar. It's not them."

"Somebody got off the bus?"

"I asked the bartender that. He didn't see nobody. He said it stops there sometimes to pick up people. They stand by the road, and the bus picks them up."

I wasn't getting anywhere with Troyce Nix. I flipped open my cell phone. No service. I went to the Camry and searched under the fenders for a magnetized key box. If one was there, I couldn't find it.

"Come over here, Dave," Clete said.

He was standing by the Camry. He pointed at the ground. There were fresh divots in it, funnel-shaped tracks like those of someone who had been wearing cowboy boots, someone who had been struggling. "Look over there," he said.

Next to a set of fresh tire imprints were a half-dozen drops of blood on the gravel, each of them star-pointed around the edges. Clete squatted down and touched the blood with his ballpoint pen. "It's still wet," he said.

"What do you want to do?" I said.

"Why ask me?" he said.

"You're the guy that bozo tried to light up."

"You think we're getting set up?" he said.

"No, but I think Jimmy Dale Greenwood was DOA before he ever got here. There's no key under any of the Camry's fenders. I have a feeling the Sweeney woman saw what happened, and the guys who grabbed Greenwood took her along with them."

Clete opened his cell and started to punch in a number, then realized he didn't have a signal. "I'm going to use the phone inside and call Alicia," he said.

"Then what?" I said.

"In for a penny, in for a pound."

"What about Troyce Nix?"

"That's one dude we can do without."

"He may not read it that way."

"That's his problem."

We went inside the bar, and Clete used the pay phone to leave a message for Alicia Rosecrans. I used it to call Jamie Sue Wellstone's cell, but she didn't pick up. When we drove back onto the two-lane and headed toward the Swan Valley by way of Flathead Lake, Troyce Nix was standing in the middle of the parking lot, our dust drifting back across his hat.

FOR CANDACE SWEENEY, time was an odyssey in a wood-wheeled wagon down a broken road, each jolt forming another threadlike crack in a piece of bone here, a piece of connective tissue there. Even after her mouth and eyes and ankles were wrapped with duct tape, and her wrists fastened with plastic ligatures behind her, she knew her physical presence still represented a threat to the three men who had abducted her and Jimmy Dale Greenwood. Inside the rocking shell of the van, she could almost smell the self-centered fear that governed their lives and their immediate situation. And if she didn't smell it, she could hear it in their conversation.

"This wasn't supposed to happen, man. We were supposed to

grab the guy and deliver the freight. In and out. Let that fucking geek handle the rest."

"Why you looking at me? I didn't do it." It was the voice of the blond man.

"You didn't do it? You let a dimwit broad with tats on her tits bust open your face. You don't call that doing it?"

"I told you this deal sucked from the start. You don't take down somebody in broad daylight on Saturday afternoon behind a bar on the res," the blond man replied.

"The key word there is 'res,' Layne. Committing a crime on a federal reservation isn't the way it was supposed to be. The blood is on the rocks back there."

"Listen, you guys, we stay with the plan," a third voice said. "We deliver the guy. We were just giving him a ride, that's all. Then he started fighting with us 'cause he's on meth or something. We drop the guy off, and that's the end of it."

"What about the gash?"

"Same thing. She was with the guy. She attacked us. What the geek does with them ain't our business. We're just doing a job. Look, nobody saw what happened back there. Only one story comes out of this deal. You just heard the story. *That's* the story. That's what history is, right? History is the story that survives."

"Yeah, but I got one more message for our girlfriend," Layne said. "Hand it to me."

"That's sick, man."

"Yeah? Take a look at my face."

"Some might call it an improvement." There was a long silence inside the van. "Okay, man, but I think you ought to get some help."

Candace heard someone turn around in the front seat, as though handing something to the man named Layne. She had little doubt about what was coming next. The blond man had already beaten her with his fists after she had been put in the van, uttering the same insatiable grinding sound he had made earlier.

The Taser arced into her back with a level of penetration and pain that seemed to radiate out through her muscles like hundreds of yellow jackets stinging her simultaneously.

"How do you like it, girlie?" Layne said.

"Maybe you should team up with the geek," the driver said.

"The gash asked for it. The geek don't need a reason. Give me that box of Kleenex. I can't stop bleeding."

Somehow, perhaps because of the convulsion she had experienced on the floor of the van when the Taser struck her back, a piece of tape had loosened enough from one eye so she could see Jimmy Dale Greenwood lying next to her. He was bound hand and foot, just as she was, the tape wound so tightly around his eyes that she could see the outline of his skull against his skin. But his captors had used tape on his wrists instead of ligatures, and Candace could see him twisting his balled fists back and forth, stretching the elasticity of the tape with each movement.

"You want to stop at a drive-through for some eats?" the blond man said.

"What about *them*?" the passenger in front said.

"I'll throw a blanket over them."

"We got food at the cabin. You two shut the fuck up," the driver said.

CLETE FLOORED THE Caddy up through Ravalli and Ronan, the Mission Mountains so high in the sky that the waterfalls at the top were still braided with ice. Then we were headed north along the shore of Flathead Lake, passing cherry stands and homes built of stone by the water and sailboats that had given up and were coming out of the rain. The Caddy shook as we went into the turns, drifting slightly in the slick, on one occasion sucking past an oncoming camper with perhaps only three inches to spare.

I opened my cell phone and saw that I had a signal. I punched in Jamie Wellstone's number. She answered on the third ring.

"Ms. Wellstone, it's Dave Robicheaux," I said.

"Where's Jimmy Dale?" she asked.

"We're not sure. The Camry is still at the bar."

"I don't know what you're saying. The Camry is at the bar but Jimmy Dale is not? Maybe he hasn't arrived."

"No, we think he's been abducted. We think a woman by the name of Candace Sweeney may have been abducted with him."

"What is *she* doing there?"

Perhaps trying to save your boyfriend's life, I said to myself. "Does your husband own a camp, a cabin, a boathouse, a place only he goes to?"

"Leslie's here, inside the house."

"Would you answer the question, please?"

"I'm trying to think. No, he doesn't have a place like that. Where are you? Where is Clete? Put him on."

My sympathies with Jamie Sue Wellstone's problems were quickly dissipating. "Has anyone called your house in the last hour?"

"How would I know that? I'm outside in the barn. I'm afraid to go inside my own house. Why are you asking about callers?"

That she had used the possessive pronoun in mentioning the Wellstone manor did not strike me as insignificant.

"If some men working for your husband or his brother kidnapped Jimmy Dale, I'd assume they'd pass on the information to their employer," I said.

"Just after the turn from Bigfork, there's a dirt road that leads into a peninsula. Leslie and Ridley are building a lodge way back in the timber. You can barely see it from Swan Lake."

"What's at the lodge?" I asked.

"It's not really a lodge. It's just in progress."

"What's there, Ms. Wellstone?"

"Nothing, just a bunch of debarked logs and a backhoe and stuff like that," she replied. "Harold Waxman was helping with the foundation for the garage. He used to be a heavy-equipment operator."

"If we get lost, I'll call you back," I said. I closed my cell phone and set it on my thigh, waiting for Clete to ask what Jamie Sue Wellstone had said. Instead, he was staring intently into the rearview mirror.

I looked through the back window but couldn't see anything.

"It's Troyce Nix," Clete said. "He just melted back into the traffic. If I ever get out of this, I'm buying a charter fishing boat in Baja. Let all these people drown in their own shit. You're looking at the new marlin king of the Pacific Coast."

He grinned at me like an albino ape, his porkpie hat pulled down tightly on his brow. Then he went into a slick bend on the road, high above the water, never easing up on the gas, a truck horn blaring past us from the opposite direction.

CANDACE SWEENEY FELT the cargo van slow and make a sharp turn off the asphalt onto a rough road pocked with divots that slammed the van down on its springs, rocking her hard against Jimmy Dale Greenwood. For the last few miles, the abductors had grown tired of their own conversation and all the banality that seemed to constitute their frame of reference. But when the van began bouncing down the dirt road, they came alive again, irritably, blaming one another for their bad luck that day, complaining about the road and the lousy food they had to eat and someone they referred to as "the geek."

She assumed the geek was Leslie Wellstone.

The one who complained most was her blond tormentor. "Look, man, maybe I should have finessed her better back there on the res, but I'm like y'all, we shouldn't be here for the main gig. There's no percentage in it. We're security guys. We fly back to Houston and forget everything that happened here. Do you know how much you can make working Arab security at the Ritz-Carlton? I worked the penthouse at the Ritz out by River Oaks. A whole bunch of Bedouins took up the entire floor. The old guys were wearing striped robes and floppy pink slippers with bunny ears on them. They cooked in their rooms and were always taking showers and asking for more soap, like they'd bathed in camel shit most of their lives."

For the first time, all three men laughed. So the blond man, encouraged, continued his monologue. "A couple of the young guys wanted to see some tits and ass, so I took them to this skin joint on Richmond. This one broad had a pair of jugs that could knock your eyeballs out of their sockets. She not only had big knockers, she had a voice that had the two Bedouins creaming in their Calvin Kleins. One of them asked if he could buy her and take her back to Dubai or whatever sand trap his family is in charge of. I go, 'You can't buy women in this country.' He goes, 'Why not? I bought a Kentucky racehorse. This one on the stage has a tattoo on her rear end. My horse doesn't. The horse doesn't shit in the house, either. The woman does. Which is the more dignified creature?' "

The three laughed uproariously, so hard the driver lost his concentration and hit a pothole that bounced Candace into the air.

"Here's the rest of it," the blond man said. "You know who the broad was?"

"Your mother?" the driver said.

"Jamie Sue Wellstone. Except that wasn't her name then. Small world, huh? I saw her sing later. Same broad, still selling the same tits. I wonder if Mr. Wellstone knows her history."

Candace realized the men had not been referring to Leslie Wellstone when they had mentioned the geek. That thought filled her with a new fear, one that made her insides turn to water. In her mind's eye, she saw a faceless silhouette, a black-suited, humped, and spiritually deformed creature whose existence was confined to nightmares and who was supposed to disappear at first light. When the van hit another pothole—this time with such violence that the frame actually slammed into the ground—she was jolted once more into the air. A moan broke from her throat, muffling against the tape.

"What's going on back there?" the driver asked.

"Nothing," the blond man said.

"No more rough stuff," the driver said. "It ain't our way. We dump 'em, and then this place is a memory."

"What if Mr. Wellstone says different?" the blond man said.

"This state injects," the driver said. "We didn't sign on to ride the needle for fraternity guys who can't manage their poontang. We eighty-six the sticks, and we're down and outbound for Houstontown. Twenty-four hours from now, we're gonna be drinking margaritas and eating Mexican food at Pappasito's."

"What do you think the geek has got planned?" the blond man said.

"Show some respect, Layne," the man in the front passenger seat said.

Through the crack in the tape, Candace saw him gesture at her and Jimmy Dale.

AT THE NORTHERN end of Flathead Lake, in the town called Bigfork, Clete turned east and drove through a break in the mountains. Just before we reached a bridge at the Swan River, we saw the dirt road that accessed the peninsula on the west side of Swan Lake. The sun had broken through the rain clouds in the west and was the reddish-yellow of an egg yolk. But another front was moving toward us, a separate weather system, this one ugly and mean. It was gray and swirling with rain, pelting the lake, and when we drove onto the dirt road, the trees on either side of us were already bending in the wind, shredding cascades of pine needles across the windshield. The light had almost disappeared inside the timber, and the front end of the Caddy was bouncing hard in the potholes, patterning the windshield with more mud than the wipers could clean off.

"I feel like I'm sitting on sandbags in a six-by, waiting for Sir Charles to pop one through my windshield," Clete said. A downed limb broke in half under a front tire and clanged against the oil pan. "My transmission's not up to this. Check your cell."

"What for?" I said.

"To call Alicia again. I think we might be firing in the well. I think Jamie Sue might have given us a bum lead. My engine is about to come off the mounts."

"She didn't exactly give us a lead."

"Want to explain that?"

"I asked if her husband had a private place where he went. This is the only place she could think of."

"That's it?" he said.

"That's it."

"I thought I had obsessions. You know what your problem is? You're like those biblical fundamentalists. They believe if one part of the Bible is not literally correct, the rest of it is no good, either.

Except with you, it's people. You got to prove everybody is on the square, or the whole human race is no good."

"Pretty sharp thinking, Clete. Except it's not me who couldn't keep his johnson in his pants when he met Jamie Sue Wellstone."

He laughed, looking at me sideways, the Caddy dipping into a huge hole, shuddering the frame, throwing both of us against our seat straps. "What was I supposed to do? Hurt her feelings?"

"Don't ever go into analysis," I said.

"Why not?"

"Your psychiatrist will shoot himself."

But he was smiling at me, not listening, not caring what I said one way or another, indifferent to all the minutiae that had gone into the ebb and flow of our lives, remembering only the bond we had shared over the decades, the wounds we had suffered and survived together, the flags under which we had fought and the causes we had served, many of which were no longer considered of import by others.

"We painted our names on the wall, didn't we?" he said.

"You'd better believe it, Cletus," I replied.

I looked through the back window and thought I saw headlights glimmering in the trees. Then they disappeared. The rain swept westward across the timber, bending the canopy, channeling serpentine rivulets in the road.

We were high enough that I could make out lights on the far side of Swan Lake, like beacons inside ocean fog. I suspected the lights came from the nightclub on the shore, but I couldn't be sure. I thought of the photograph of Bugsy Siegel and Virginia Hill mounted on the wall behind the club's bar, and I wondered why such criminals beckoned to us from the past, why they were able to lay such a strong romantic claim upon us. Was it because secretly we wanted to emulate them, to possess their power, to burn that brightly inside the mist, incandescent as they pursued all the trappings of the American dream, just as we did? Was it because the art deco world of 1940s Hollywood and the sweet sewer it represented were as much a part of our culture as the graves of Shiloh?

Clete rolled down his window halfway, and the rain blew inside. "Listen," he said.

"What?" I said, waking from my reverie.

"I thought I heard a piece of heavy equipment working. You hear it?"

"No," I replied.

"Maybe I'm going nuts. I still hear that motherfucker who tried to set fire to me."

I rolled down my window and looked at our headlight beams bouncing off the tree trunks, but I could not see anything unusual or hear any sound except the wind sharking through the canopy and a solitary peal of thunder across the sky.

JAMIE SUE COULD not understand her own thoughts. She had stayed in the barn, her cell phone in her jeans, grooming the horses, listening to the rip of thunder across the skies and the rain mixed with hail that was clattering on the barn's metal roof. Leslie or one of the servants carrying out his orders had removed all the vehicle keys from the hooks in the mudroom. His and Ridley's security personnel had tripled in number in the last week, men who dressed neatly and were barbered and clean-shaved and were deferential but, she guessed, also more professionally criminal than either Quince Whitley or Lyle Hobbs. In retrospect, Lyle seemed like an amateur, perhaps another Judas for sale, blowing the compound with whiskey on his breath and a tic in his eyes like that of a crystal addict, but by comparison, a bumbling amateur.

Jamie Sue had never understood why Leslie had hired Lyle. It seemed to have something to do with their common experience in Vegas or Reno, or other marginal enterprises the Wellstones dabbled in as part of the price they paid for doing business in what they considered a corrupt culture.

She had taken little Dale into the barn with her and unrolled a plastic tarp on the floor for him to play on. But the two of them were trapped, with no means of escape, and she had no idea where Jimmy Dale was or the fate that might be awaiting him if he had been abducted by Ridley and Leslie's goons. She felt a terrible sense of urgency, as though she were drowning in full view of others and no one on the bank could hear her voice. Or was that just her melo-dramatic daytime-television mentality kicking into gear?

No, time was running out, and not simply on this situation on this particular Saturday in the summer of 2007, she thought.

The choices she had made over the years all had a consequence and a cost, and the bills were coming due. She should have toughed it out by herself when Jimmy Dale went to jail, staying loyal to him and accepting privation as her lot, just as her blind mother and dis-abled father had. What would have been the worst thing to happen if she had gone it on her own? Second-class-celebrity status as an aging honky-tonk performer? Living in a trailer? Putting up with over-the-hill, drunk truck drivers who wanted her to sing "Dim Lights, Thick Smoke (And Loud, Loud Music)"?

The list of things she should not have done was long. She shouldn't have married her community-college English professor and used his alcoholism to sue him in divorce court for almost everything he owned. She shouldn't have posed as a religious woman and deceived the crowds who flocked to Sonny Click's revivals. She shouldn't have used her sexuality to manipulate uneducated family men who trusted her. She shouldn't have used Leslie, and she shouldn't have pretended she had married him in order to care for Dale.

It was the last thought that bothered her most. Everything she'd done had been a justification for her own agenda. She had even used her little boy as an excuse, when in reality, she had loved all the benefits of marriage to a man like Leslie Wellstone—the limos and luxury cars and private planes, the palatial estates, the servants who attended her every need, the awe and respect and diffidence she cre-ated with her presence wherever she went. In the meantime, she had lost her music, the one element in her life she had treated as a votive gift and had not compromised for the sake of either celebrity or commercial success. In her earlier career, she had continued to sing in the traditions of Skeeter Davis and Kitty Wells while everybody else in Nashville was going uptown, then somewhere along the way, she had forgotten who she was and what she was and had taken the gift for granted and used it to manipulate people into voting against their own interests.

She remembered a statement that Keith Richards once made regarding a famous R&B musician whose hostility to his own audience hid just beneath his skin: "Chuck's tragedy is he doesn't realize how much joy he brings to other people."

Her head was dizzy, her hands dry and hard to close.

She began brushing a mahogany-black gelding in his stall, raking burrs out of his mane and forelock, rubbing him under the jaw, touching the graceful line and smoothness of his neck, talking in a reassuring voice in his ear. The gelding was four now but still hot-wired and subject to spooking and rearing in dry mustard weed, and neither Ridley nor Leslie would ride him. But Jamie Sue could and did, sometimes without a saddle, using only a hackamore to rein him.

Ownership of a fine horse came with ability, not legal title, Jimmy Dale always said. He said no one owned the sunrise or the rain, or mesas and mountains, or the bluebonnets of South Texas. Your claim to ownership of the earth was based on the six feet of dirt that went into your face. The rest of it was a grand playground that God had given to all His children. At least that was what Jimmy Dale and his peyote-soaked friends said.

She wondered if her thoughts amounted to what a theologian would call contrition. She decided they probably did not. But perhaps they were a start.

She picked up Dale from the tarp and set him like a clothespin on the gelding's back, keeping her arm around his waist to steady him. "I'm going to get you your own pony one day," she said. "Maybe back in Texas, where your grandma and granddaddy used to live and your mama grew up."

"Just when do you plan on doing that, Jamie Sue?" a voice said behind her.

She turned and looked into her husband's face. "What have you done with Jimmy Dale?" she asked.

"*I* haven't done anything with him. I've never even had the pleasure of meeting him. But tell me, why is it you think I might have harmed him? You weren't planning on going somewhere with him today, were you? You haven't been screwing him in the bushes, have you?"

She had stepped into his trap. "I've never understood your mean-spiritedness, Leslie. Your brother orders things done to his enemies, but only when he's forced to. You enjoy offending and hurting people just for the sake of hurting them. Maybe the war did that to you. Maybe it's because you married someone who doesn't love you. But you're a sad man and an object of pity. Not because of your deformity, either. You're pitied by others because of what you are, and that's what you've never understood about yourself."

She lifted Dale off the horse and set his weight on her hip, momentarily shifting her attention away from Leslie. When she looked at him again, his head was tilted sideways, the shriveled skin alongside one cheek and his neck stretched free of wrinkles, like a large piece of smooth rubber.

"I have the sense you're at a point of decision in your life," he said. "Standing at the crossroads, wading across the Jordan, that kind of thing. You know, Scarlett O'Hara gazing out upon the wastes?"

"What decision? How can I make decisions? You've fixed it so I can't go anywhere."

"Would you like to go for a late dinner tonight? I'll have Harold drive us in the limo to Bigfork or Yellow Bay."

"Who lives inside you, Leslie? Who are you?"

"Not interested in dinner tonight? The lake is lovely when the rain is falling on it. Last chance, Jamie Sue. I wouldn't ignore the importance of the choice you're about to make. There are maybe three or four choices we make in our lives that determine our fate. A random turn off a freeway into the wrong neighborhood, buying a burnt-out sweet-potato patch that sits on top of an oil pool, taking off the night chain because we trust the Fuller Brush man. You took a chance and married a man who is physically repellent to you. Want to back out? I don't mind. Want to roll the dice and see what happens? Tell me. Tell me now."

"What do you mean?" she asked, her voice dropping in register, a cold hand squeezing at her heart.

"It's all a matter of choice. You want to believe you can walk away with half of our wealth. You also want to believe you can walk away with all your knowledge about how things really work, how we jerk around others, how our enterprises are nothing like they seem. Pick up the dice and drop them in the cup. Everyone should have a second chance. It's easy enough. You're a brave girl. Shake the cup and rattle them out on the felt."

She looked into the moral vacuity of his eyes and for the first time felt genuine mortal fear of the man she had married. She started to speak, but her words caught in her throat.

"A country-and-western band should be entertaining the folk at Yellow Bay," Leslie said. "We can watch the folk at work and play in the fields of the Lord. It's Saturday night for the folk, and their messianic songstress will be there to brighten their lives."

"I think you're going to hell," she said.

"We already live there, my dear. You just haven't realized it."

He reached out with his mutilated hand and touched little Dale's cheek.

CHAPTER
28

AFTER THE CARGO van stopped, someone slid open the side door, and Candace felt a rush of cool air and mist in her face. Through the loose space in the tape, she saw a framed-up two-story building, half of it walled with logs. A yellow backhoe was parked in the trees, its lights on, a pile of dirt glistening by the steel bucket. A work-booted man in a rumpled black suit walked heavily across the clearing and grabbed Jimmy Dale Greenwood by the shirt and the back of his belt and dragged him across the ground to the edge of a pit. Then he used one foot to shove him over the edge.

The three men who had kidnapped and bound Candace were still inside the vehicle, smoking cigarettes, uncomfortable with what they were becoming witness to, trying to figure out a way to extricate themselves and still get paid by their employer.

"Put her in the house," the driver said.

"What for?" Layne, the blond man, said.

"We don't know what for. That's the point," the driver said. "Let's put her in the house and get out of here. We delivered the Indian. That was our job. We didn't see the rest of it. The girl brought herself here. It's not on us."

"What about el geeko?" Layne said.

"What about him?" the driver asked.

"We just gonna drive off?" Layne said.

Candace could hear the men in front turning around in their seats to visually confirm the naked fear they had heard in Layne's question. The man in the front passenger seat said, "Yeah, just drive off. What, you worried about our friend's feelings out there?"

"I'm for it if you guys are," Layne said. "I was just saying . . ."

"Saying what?" the driver asked.

"That guy has got a long memory."

Candace could hear no sound in the van except the drumming of the rain on the roof.

"Put her in the house, Layne," the driver said.

"Me?" Layne said. "Put her in there yourself. I ain't touching her."

But their argument was moot. The man in the rumpled suit returned to the van and lifted Candace up like a bale of hay by the twine. He carried her to the edge of the pit and swung her out into space, where for a moment she saw the sheen of the fir and pine trees in the lights of the backhoe, just before she plummeted into the pit.

She thudded on top of another body, her bones jarring inside her. She thought she had landed on Jimmy Dale Greenwood, but he was lying against the wall of the pit, his face turned from her, his hands jerking furiously against the tape that was still cinched around his wrists. Then she realized a third person, someone she didn't know, was in the pit with them.

The mist was drifting down into the excavation in the lights of the backhoe. The person she had landed on was a man. His face was staring straight into hers, and neither his eyes nor his mouth were taped. His hair was brown and shaggy, like dark straw piled on a scarecrow's head. She was perhaps six inches from him, and she kept expecting him to blink, to send her a signal of some kind, to show recognition of their common humanity and plight, maybe even to give her a glimmer of hope.

Then she saw the dark hole in his hairline, and she realized his eyes hadn't blinked, that his slack jaw and his parted mouth were not those of a man preparing to whisper a secret to her. Below one of his eyes was a chain of scar tissue, the socket recessed, mashed back into the skull. Where had she seen him?

At the Wellstones' front gate, she told herself. They had killed their own security guard.

"We figure we'll head on out," she heard Layne say.

"No, you won't," the black-suited figure standing by the lip of the pit replied.

"Our work is done, bub," Layne said.

"What'd you call me?"

"Nothing."

"You're saying I'm nothing?"

"No, I didn't say that."

"Then what did you say?"

"I called you 'bub.' It's just a word."

"Then you won't mind taking it back."

"So I take it back. It's just a word. No offense meant."

"Where's that leave you now?"

"Say again?"

"It leaves you back where you started when you were telling me you're about to head out. Is that where you are? You're heading out?"

"Not necessarily."

"That's what I thought. What's my name?"

"I don't know your name."

"So you thought that gave you the right to call me 'bub'? . . . Don't turn your back on me. What's my name?"

"It's 'sir,' if that's what you want."

"No, what's my name?"

"It's 'sir.' "

"You'd better get out of the rain. You're going to catch cold. Your nose is already running."

The dirt under the dark-suited man's boots sifted down on top of Candace's head. She stared helplessly at Jimmy Dale Greenwood's back. He had stretched the tape on his wrists to the point where he could get an index finger under the adhesive and start working it down over one thumb. High above her, she saw lightning flare inside the thunderheads, like a match igniting a pool of white gasoline.

• • •

CLETE AND I should have taken my pickup truck and not the Caddy. Most hillside roads in Montana were cut years ago by logging companies and left unseeded and at the mercy of the elements. With the passage of time, they had become potholed, eroded, strewn with rocks and boulders and sometimes fire-blackened trees that had washed out of the slopes. The Caddy bounced into a hole and went down on the transmission. When Clete tried to shift into reverse, we heard a sound like Coca-Cola bottles clanking and breaking inside a steel box. The Caddy would not budge in reverse and was high-centered and couldn't get out of the hole by going forward.

Clete looked glumly through the windshield. The road wound higher and higher through the trees, with water rilling down the incline. We saw no sign of a structure of any kind, much less a lodge under construction.

"What a mess," he said. "Maybe this isn't even the right road."

"When we first turned off, I thought I saw headlights behind us. Maybe it was Troyce Nix," I said.

"If it's Nix, he's coming up the road on the braille system. There're no headlights behind us."

"I saw them, Clete."

"Okay, you saw them. We shouldn't have listened to Jamie Sue. This is three monkeys fucking a football."

"Why don't you get out of your bad mood?" I said.

"My bad mood? Look at my car. It's probably impaled. The transmission is frozen in low. My paint job probably looks like a herd of cats used it for a scratching post."

"We'll get the jack out and bounce the car out of the hole. We'll just keep bouncing it in a circle until we can point it back down the road."

"What about Greenwood and the Sweeney woman?"

"We'll walk to the top of the mountain. That's all we can do. It's my fault, Cletus. I don't see any other tire tracks. I think it's a bum lead."

"No, the tracks could be washed out. Let's bounce it out of the hole and go all the way up with the car. If we're on the right road, there should be enough space by the lodge to drive the Caddy in a circle so we can head back down."

We got the jack out of the trunk, fitted it under the frame, and raised the Caddy high enough so that when we pushed it off the jack, it fell sideways, partially clear of the hole the wheel had sunk into. We repeated the process three times, filling in the hole each time with rocks and mud and rotted timber that was as soft as old cork. Our clothes were soaked with rainwater and splattered with mud. Clete's porkpie hat looked like a wilted blue flower on his head.

"What are you grinning at?" I asked.

"Us."

"What for?"

"Broads and booze, that's what has always gotten us in trouble. Every time. I can't think of one exception."

"Speak for yourself," I said.

The Caddy's engine was still running, and the headlights were on. I could see the whiteness of Clete's teeth and his chest shaking while he laughed without sound. This time he was not going to reply to the ridiculous nature of my denial.

"Look down the road," I said, my hand slowing on the jack handle.

"What?"

"Headlights," I said.

Clete raised up so he could see beyond the length of the Caddy. "It's Troyce Nix," he said.

"You're sure?"

"It's a blue Ford pickup with an extended cab. It's Nix. What's the Jewish expression? 'A good deed by a Cossack is still a good deed'?" he said. "I didn't think I'd ever be glad to see a dickhead like that."

No, it's not blue. It's purple, I thought. I remember thinking that distinctly. But the jack was starting to slip, the Caddy yawing inward on it, back toward the deepest part of the hole, the steel shaft arching slightly with the tension. I forgot about the color of the truck. "Clete, get away from the jack," I said.

But typical of Clete, he didn't listen. He went around behind me and dug one foot into the mud and shoved his shoulder against the fender, pushing the Caddy's weight back against the jack. "Come on, pump it, big mon. One more bounce and we're out."

He was right. I ratcheted up the jack three more notches, then we pushed the Caddy sideways until it teetered briefly and fell clear of the hole. Clete's face was happy and beaded with raindrops in the headlights. He stared into the high beams of the pickup, blinking against the glare. Inside the sound of the wind and the rain in the trees, I thought I heard a sound I'd heard before, one that didn't fit the place and the situation. It was a rhythmic clanking and thudding sound, accompanied by labored breathing—a thudding clank, a hard breath, another thudding clank.

I rose to my feet. My forty-five was on the car seat, and Clete's thirty-eight was on the dash. Ridley Wellstone worked his aluminum braces over a rut in the road and stood by the passenger door of the Caddy, his arms held stiffly inside the metal half-moon guides of his braces. He wore a Stetson that had long since lost its shape to rainwater and sweat. He even looked handsome and patriarchal in it, rain running in strings off the brim and dissolving in the wind, his face craggy like that of a trail boss in a western painting.

"You fellows having a little car trouble?" he asked.

I shielded my eyes from the glare of the pickup's high beams. Behind Ridley Wellstone was a man I didn't know. He was holding a Mac-10 with a suppressor attached to it. Leslie Wellstone opened the door of the pickup, turning on the inside light. Behind the rain-beaded glass in the extended cab, I saw a third man and the pinched and resentful face of Jamie Sue Wellstone with an expression on it that had more to do with resignation than with fear.

"We've already informed the FBI of where we are," I said.

"Then why are you here? Why aren't you having a drink some-where, watching the light show in the sky, minding your own busi-ness?" Ridley said.

"Use your head, sir. You can't airbrush all of us off the planet," I said.

"Perhaps you're right. Then again, perhaps you're not," Ridley said. "You did this to yourself, Mr. Robicheaux. I have a feeling

most people who know you have long considered your fate a fore-
gone conclusion."

"Don't talk to these cocksuckers, Dave," Clete said. "They
wouldn't be out here if they weren't scared shitless."

"You're wrong about that, Clete," Leslie Wellstone said.

"Where do you get off calling me by my first name?" Clete said,
already knowing the answer.

"Excuse me, Mr. Purcel," Leslie Wellstone said. "I forgot what a
civilized individual you are. Do you mind walking ahead of us, Mr.
Purcel? It's not far. Just over a couple of rises and you'll see a happy
gathering. You'll be joining up with them. You'll like it."

Our weapons remained a few feet away, inside the Caddy, as useless to us as pieces of scrap iron. The man with the Mac-10 pushed
us both against the car hood and shook us down, while the other
man from the pickup truck held a cut-down pump on us. The man
with the Mac-10 was especially invasive toward Clete. After he
found a switchblade Velcro-strapped to Clete's ankle, he felt inside
his thighs, working his hand hard into Clete's scrotum.

Clete twisted his head around, his legs spread, his arms stretched
on the hood. "When this is over, I'm going to be looking you up,"
he said.

"They're clean," the man with the Mac-10 said to Leslie, ignoring
Clete's remark.

"Clasp your fingers behind your heads and let's take a walk,
gentlemen," Leslie said.

And that's what we did, like humiliated prisoners of war, walking
up the incline, the pickup following behind us with Ridley and Jamie
Sue inside. I couldn't believe how our fortunes had turned around so
quickly. Was it stupidity, naïveté, professional incompetence, or just
bad luck? No, you don't try to jack up a Cadillac convertible and
turn it in a circle on an uphill slope in an electric storm with a heavy
gun like a 1911-model forty-five auto stuck in your belt or a thirty-
eight shoulder harness wrapped around your chest and shoulders.
We simply screwed up on the identification of Troyce Nix's vehicle.
In the bad light, the dark blue of Nix's truck resembled the purple
paint job on the Wellstone vehicle. It happens. We called Vietnam

the "sorry-about-that war." I just hated to have a repeat of the experience on a hillside above a lake in an electric storm in western Montana.

But where was Troyce Nix? He had followed us all the way up the highway along the side of Flathead Lake, then had disappeared. As we trudged up the slope through the trees, I knew Clete was thinking the same thoughts.

"We got to get them distracted," he said under his breath. "Nix is out there somewhere."

"How do you know?" I said.

"The girl. He won't rest till he gets the girl back," Clete said.

"Shut up, fat man," the man with the Mac-10 said.

"Blow me, you prick," Clete replied.

The man with the Mac-10 walked closer to Clete, leaning forward slightly, his professional restraint slipping for the first time. His body was hard and compact, like that of a gymnast, his hair mowed military-style, balding through the pate. His skin seemed luminescent in the shadows created by the headlights of the pickup following us, his lips taking on a purplish cast. "For me, it's usually just business. But I'm gonna enjoy this one," he said.

"I think I know you," Clete said.

"Yeah? From where?"

"A hot-pillow joint for losers in Honolulu. You were standing in line to screw your mother. I'm sure of it."

"Tell me that joke again in about fifteen minutes," the man with the Mac-10 replied.

JIMMY DALE GREENWOOD could smell the rawness of the freshly dug pit in which he lay, the severed tree roots, the water leaking out of the scalped sides, the cold odor of broken stone, and he knew, even though his eyes were taped, that his greatest fear, the one that had pursued him all his life, was about to be realized: In the next few minutes, he would be buried alive.

He kept twisting and jerking at the tape that bound his wrists, but it was wound deeply into the skin, cutting off the blood in the veins, numbing his fingers and palms. Troyce Nix's woman lay next to him, but there was a third person in the pit, and Jimmy Dale had no idea who the person was or why he or she had been put there. He could hear the voices of the men who had abducted him in the cargo van, and the voice of the man who had dragged him from the van and flung him into the pit. He could also smell the stench of diesel exhaust and the odor of electric lights smoking in the mist.

He tried to reach inside himself for the strength to accept whatever ordeal lay in store for him. He remembered all the great challenges in his life that in one way or another he had mastered and come out on the other side of: a horse named Bad Whiskey that he rode to the buzzer in Vegas with two broken ribs; his first appearance on a stage, at an amateur competition in Bandera, Texas, when he was so frightened his voice broke and his fingers shook on the frets but he finished the song regardless and won a third-place ribbon; the time he tied himself down with a suicide wrap on a bull that slung him into the boards and whipped two extra inches on his height; and the biggest crossroads of all, the day he decided to get a shank and end the abuse visited upon him by Troyce Nix.

But all those milestones in his life, or the degree of victory over fear they may have represented, had been of no help in overcoming his nightmares about premature burial. Now the nightmare was about to become a reality. Once, in a beery fog at a roach motel outside Elko, Nevada, he had flicked on the television set and inadvertently started watching a documentary about the atrocities committed during the Chinese civil war between the nationalists and the communists. Peasants with their hands bound behind them had been laid out in rows and were being buried alive, a shovelful at a time, the dirt striking their faces while they pleaded in vain for mercy.

Jimmy Dale had never rid himself of that image, and now he was at the bottom of a pit, waiting to become one of the images he had seen in that grainy black-and-white film years ago.

He felt a hand touch his wrist and pull against the tape. It was the woman; she had gotten her fingers on the tip of the tape and was peeling back a long strand from his wrist.

"Can you hear me?" she whispered.

"Yes," he said, the word barely audible behind the tape that covered his mouth.

"Don't move, don't talk. I'll get you loose," she said.

He heard footsteps and other voices by the pit, and he felt the woman's hand go limp.

"You're putting a mask on?" Layne said.

"What about it?"

"Why do you put on a mask if we all know what you look like?"

"Because I like to."

"Each to his own, huh?"

"You seem to have a lot of comments to make about what other people do."

"No sir, I don't. I'm sorry if I gave that impression."

"You're sorry, all right. You don't know how sorry you really are."

Layne was obviously not sure what he was being told. Nor did he seem to know how to respond. "There's some lights coming up the road," he said.

"You figured that out, did you?"

"I got nothing else to say to you, man."

"You were watching the girl, weren't you, thinking about what's going to happen to her?"

"I was gonna have a smoke."

"No, you were imagining her fate. But you don't have the courage to make that fate happen, do you?"

"Buddy, I won't say another word to you. I got no issue with what you do."

"No issue? You mimic the language of people who don't have brains."

The speaker walked away, his footsteps heavy, booted, a man whose movements and speech were all in exact measure to his purpose. Jimmy Dale heard Layne exhale.

WE CAME OVER a knoll and walked down into a depression that was flanked on either side by fir and larch trees. Ahead, the road climbed again, and just beyond the spot where it peaked, I could see a glow shining upward through the trees, and I knew this was the place where all the roads Clete and I had followed for a lifetime had finally converged. Leslie Wellstone and the man with the Mac kept behind us, their shoes padding softly on the layer of wet pine needles that carpeted the ground, the truck with Jamie Sue and Ridley Wellstone and the other hired man bringing up the rear.

At the corner of my vision, I saw a movement in the trees. Or at least I thought I did. Perhaps it had been wishful thinking, I told myself. But I saw Clete's eyes glance sideways, too. A moment later, the wind blew in a violent gust across Swan Lake and swept up the side of the mountain, shaking the trees, filling the air with pine needles and a smell like water and humus and cold stone. Have you ever been in a nocturnal environment where snipers lurk inside the foliage? The wind becomes your indispensable ally. When the trees and undergrowth and sometimes the elephant grass begin to thrash, the object that does not move or the shadow that remains like a tin cutout becomes the entity that is out there in the darkness, preparing to take your life.

Except in this case, the presence on our perimeter, among the fir and larch and pine trees, was our friend and not our enemy.

Nix was a military man and knew what to do when wind or a pistol flare threatened to reveal his position. He settled himself quickly into the undergrowth, his arms freezing into sticks, his face downturned so as not to reflect light. But I had seen him, and I knew Clete had seen him, too.

Neither Leslie Wellstone nor the man with the Mac had taken their eyes off us. Wellstone obviously had noticed something in our manner that was making him suspicious.

Clete had told me to keep them distracted.

"There're too many loose ends," I said. "You guys won't get away with this."

"Your lack of both wisdom and judgment never ceases to amaze me, Mr. Robicheaux," Wellstone said.

"I majored in low expectations," I replied.

"That's not bad. I'll have to remember that," he said.

"Remember this," Clete said. "Every one of these morons working for you is for sale. You don't think the feds are going to start squeezing them? Who are they going to roll over on?"

"God, you two guys are slow on the uptake," Wellstone said. "You know why most crimes go unsolved? Because most cops have IQs of minus eight. Those are the smart ones."

For a moment the supercilious accent and manner were gone, and I heard the clipped ethnic speech that I used to associate with only two crime families—one in Orleans Parish, one in Galveston, Texas.

"You think the FBI is stupid, too, Sal?" Clete said.

"What'd you call me?"

"You're Sally Dee, right?" Clete said.

"What's he talking about, Mr. Wellstone?" the man with the Mac asked.

"Nothing. Mr. Purcel is a noisy fat man who's having a hard time accepting that he ruined his career and his life and that his options are quickly running out. Is that fair to say, Mr. Purcel?"

"No matter how it plays out, you're still a french fry, Sal. And I'm the dude who did it to you."

Shut up, Clete, I thought.

"Well, maybe someone is arranging a special event for you tonight. The gentleman who will be taking care of it is quite imaginative," Leslie Wellstone said.

"Sal, you were a pretentious douche bag twenty years ago, and you're a pretentious douche bag now. In the joint, you were a sissy and a cunt. Your old man sent you out to Reno because you couldn't even run one of his whorehouses on your own. After your plane crashed, a couple of your ex-punches told me you were a needle dick your skanks laughed at behind your back."

"You want me to shut him up?" the man with the Mac asked.

"Mr. Purcel is a frightened man, Billy. Frightened people talk a lot."

"The guy you're working for is a cheap punk from Galveston by the name of Sally Dio," Clete said to the man with the Mac. "He ran the skim for his family out in Vegas and Reno. He'll rat-fuck his friends, and he'll rat-fuck you. He used to put on speed-bag gloves and hang up his hookers on doorframes and beat them unconscious. Don't believe me? Ask him."

The man with the Mac was looking strangely at Leslie Wellstone.

"Something wrong, Billy?" Wellstone said.

"Yeah, why we putting up with this guy?"

"Because we're kind to those who have Charon's boat waiting for them," Wellstone said.

Billy looked confused. Wellstone's smile sent ice water through my veins.

We topped the rise in the road and walked down the other side into a clearing that was lit by the lights on a backhoe, a battery-powered lantern on the ground, and the headlights of a cargo van. In the background were a partially completed log building and a machine for planing the bark off logs. Three men I had never seen were sitting inside the van, the sliding door open wide.

A man in a black suit was standing between the van and an open pit. He wore a full-face mask whose plastic contortions imitated the expression of the screaming man in the famous painting by Edvard Munch. His suit was spotted with gray mud that had dried in crusted patterns like tailed amphibians. He wore a denim shirt that was buttoned at the throat, and heavy lace-up steel-toed work boots. He was pulling on a pair of rawhide gloves, his eyes staring at us from behind the mask.

"I want you to meet an old friend, Clete," Leslie Wellstone said.

TROYCE NIX HAD gotten caught behind several cars as he had followed the Caddy up the lakeside highway, finally losing sight of it south of Bigfork. At Bigfork he had swung off the two-lane highway and crossed the bridge over the Swan River. When he had not seen the Caddy anywhere around the Swan Lake area, he had reversed his direction and retraced his route back across the bridge, his frustration and anger and helplessness growing by the minute. Then, standing in front of a café, wondering what he should do next, he saw the Wellstone pickup truck roar past him and turn onto the dirt road that accessed the peninsula on the west side of Swan Lake. He jumped in his truck and followed.

He cut his headlights when he entered the dirt road, then chose to continue on foot rather than risk blowing the edge he had accidentally gained on the Wellstone brothers. He parked his truck amid trees, locked the doors, and set out walking on the road, his nine-millimeter stuck in the back of his belt, his leather-sewn, lead-weighted blackjack in his pants pocket, an aluminum baseball bat gripped in his right hand.

When the Wellstones' pickup had passed him out on the highway while he was standing in front of the café, he had recognized Ridley and Leslie inside, but he had not been sure who else was in the cab. He was convinced the agenda of the Wellstones was a simple one: They wanted revenge against Jimmy Dale Greenwood for the infidelity of Jamie Sue. Candace had blundered into the middle of the abduction, and the Wellstones' hired goons had taken her along with Jimmy Dale to keep her from dropping the dime on their operation and preventing them from getting back to Leslie Wellstone with the freight.

Wellstone didn't like being a cuckold. He wanted revenge, and he wanted his wife taught an object lesson. It wasn't an unnatural reaction. But if the only issue were revenge, at least of a conventional kind—a thorough beating of the lover, a few broken bones, maybe— why hadn't the goons simply given Candace a warning about keeping her mouth shut? Why hadn't they dropped her off on the road somewhere, given her a few bucks, and said they were sorry, they were straightening out a breed who didn't know how to keep his twanger in his Levi's?

Because they planned to kill Jimmy Dale Greenwood, and they planned to kill the witness who could finger them for his abduction, Troyce thought. Something else was going down, too. The Wellstones were religious frauds, and their house was about to collapse on their heads. Maybe they were tidying up on a large scale, washing the blackboard clean and starting over. Or maybe a freak like Leslie Wellstone enjoyed hurting people. Troyce could not forget Wellstone's instructions to his Hispanic housekeeper about the surfaces Candace had touched. Troyce wished he had settled the account right there in Wellstone's living room.

Up ahead, he saw the Caddy owned by Clete Purcel. It had been abandoned at an odd angle in the middle of the road. An elevated jack and its stand lay in the mud by the front bumper. The doors of the Caddy were open, the keys still hanging in the ignition, the interior light manually set on "off." Troyce looked in the glove box and under the seats for weapons but found none. He concluded that the interior of the vehicle had been rifled, which meant its occupants probably had not deserted the car of their own accord.

He walked over a knoll and saw headlights progressing slowly down the road and two figures walking inside the beams with their hands clasped behind their necks. He went deeper into the woods and kept walking parallel to the road, his bowels like water, his rectum constricting, his head as light as a helium-filled balloon. Ahead he could see other lights down in a depression or a clearing, and he thought he smelled diesel exhaust and heard the sound of a heavy machine idling, one without a muffler.

The wind gusted off the lake below and swept up through the timber, pattering raindrops on Troyce's hat, the air blooming with a smell like fresh oxygen. He knelt down in the second growth, tilting his face toward the ground, freezing behind the trunk of a huge pine. A procession of people on foot, with the pickup behind them, wound its way up the road. Through the rain-beaded side window of the truck, Troyce thought he could make out the face of Jamie Sue Wellstone.

What was she doing here? he asked himself. Where was Candace? Where was Jimmy Dale? Had Troyce made a terrible mistake and followed the wrong vehicle and the wrong group of people? Was Candace somewhere else, depending on him, waiting helplessly for him to save her from the men who had stolen her out of the parking lot behind the bar? The possibility that he had screwed up and let her down when she needed him most made him almost insane with anger at himself. Was this punishment for what he had done to Cujo in Iraq? Was this punishment for what he had done to Jimmy Dale?

He wanted to rush the Wellstone vehicle and tear both brothers apart and do as much damage as possible to their hired help as well.

No, "damage" wasn't the word. As always, when Troyce felt a red balloon of anger blossom in his chest, he smelled an odor like stale sweat and machinist grease and gasoline soaked into coarse fabric. He felt a man's whiskers on his face, a soiled hand unbuttoning his pants, a man's labored whiskey breath working its way across his skin. In these moments Troyce knew why men could kill other men as easily as they did.

In his mind's eye, he saw himself swinging the bat, doing amounts of bone-breaking injury to the Wellstones for which they would never find medical remedy.

CLETE AND I stared dumbly at the man in the mask. Ridley and Jamie Sue Wellstone and the man with the cut-down pump were climbing out of the purple pickup. The man with the cut-down pump was wiping his cheek on his sleeve. He wore a damp dark blue tropical shirt that looked like Kleenex wrapped on his muscular torso.

"Problem?" Leslie said to him.

"She slapped my face," the man said. "She cut the skin with her nails."

Leslie laughed. "Put it on my tab."

"I don't like a woman hitting me, Mr. Wellstone," the gunman said.

"It could be worse. She could be your wife," Leslie said.

"Let's finish it," Ridley said, propped on his braces, a flicker of pain in his expression from the ride down the potholed road.

"I think the Dio family clap has finally climbed from your dick up into your brain, Sal," Clete said. "Look around you. You think all these people are going to forget what they see here?"

Leslie Wellstone walked toward Clete, a nine-millimeter hanging from his left hand. He was no longer smiling. I saw him whisper in Clete's ear and then step back, his eyes glinting with whatever sliver of glass or ounce of poison he had managed to put inside Clete's system.

"Why don't you share it with me, Sal?" I said.

"I look like a dead Italian?" he said.

"Yeah, you're Sally Dio," I said. "Punks can read books and hire speech coaches, but you're still the same punk who pretended he was a blues musician or whatever else was in style at the time. You're a gutter rat, Sal. It's in your genes."

"Know what I was telling Clete, Dave? That both of you are about to be dead for a long time. But it's going to come to you in pieces. Mr. Waxman over there loves his work. There are anonymous mounds all over this country that are silent tributes to his skill."

"He's the guy who killed Ridley Wellstone's wife and stepdaughter, isn't he?" I said.

"When you're in the ground, you won't be dead, Dave. You'll be choking on dirt and trying to get it out of your eyes and ears and stop it from raining down on your chest. Just before everything goes black, maybe there'll be a big illumination for you, and you can talk to all the other people he's killed. You think that's the way it's going to come, Dave? That the earth will crush the light out of your eyes and in your last seconds you'll realize there's no mystery about life, that you're just a sorry sack of worm food down there in the hole with all the other sacks of worm food?"

"Do what you're going to do and be done. Listening to you is a real drag," I said.

His eyes locked on mine, and for a second I saw his self-assurance slip, as though the ridiculing voice of his father, a gangster who had run all the vice along the Texas coast, was echoing in his memory. Then the glint of cruelty that defined the Sally Dio I had known on Flathead Lake years ago came back into his eyes. The tip of his tongue moved over his lips. "Watch closely."

He walked to the three men who had been waiting inside the cargo van when we arrived. He rested his right hand—the one that resembled a shriveled monkey's paw—on the shoulder of a blond man and looked at him. "The woman hit you in the face with a tire iron?" he said.

"I got careless, that's all," the blond man said.

"We can't have broads doing that to us, can we? You want to do the honors?"

"Sir?"

"Want to pop her? I'm going to let Moo-Moo pop my wife if he wants to."

"No sir, we were just doing a job, Mr. Wellstone."

"No, no, when somebody hits you with a tire iron, it's personal. Come over here, fellows. Jimmy Dale ruined another man's marriage and deserves a special fate. The woman, however, is just a meddlesome pain in the neck. I think she should receive rough mercy, don't you?"

The three men from the van followed Sally Dio to the edge of the pit and stared down inside it, looking at one another, looking again into the pit, unsure what they should say next. It was obvious none of them wanted to be there. It was also obvious they feared the man who called himself Leslie Wellstone and did not want to displease him.

Then Sally Dio turned around and said, "What?" He said it as though someone behind him had spoken to him. "Wait here a minute, fellows," he said, and began walking toward his brother. As he did, he nodded to the man holding the Mac-10.

I had seen a Mac-10 at a weapons exhibition and had even held one in my hands. But I had never seen one fired. I had been told that a Mac-10 could discharge from one thousand to sixteen hundred rounds of forty-five-caliber ammunition per minute. It was difficult to imagine firepower of that magnitude in a weapon so compact it could be held and aimed like a handgun.

Billy opened up, the suppressor eating most of the sound of the discharge, the spent shell casings clinking and bouncing on the ground. In a brief instant, the three victims seemed to stare in disbelief at the reversal of their fortunes, their mouths dropping open, their palms rising defensively. Then their clothes erupted with red flowers, their faces and skulls bursting into a bloody mist. They jackknifed backward into the pit, and I heard them strike the earth heavily, and then it was over except for the sound of the last ejected shells tinkling on the dirt.

Jamie Sue Wellstone was weeping in the background, her arms

clenched across her chest, her back shaking, as though she were standing inside a cold wind without a coat.

"Do you want to get down in the pit by yourself, Clete, or do you want our friend Harold to put you in there?" Sally Dio said. "No matter what you do, no matter what you say, the end result will be the same. You can put yourself in the ground, or Billy can shoot you in the legs, and he and Harold can do it for you. But you're going into the ground, Clete, and you're going into it alive. Then Jamie Sue and Dave are going to join you. Maybe you and Jamie Sue can have a chat, a last bit of pillow talk."

"I guess that means we'll never be pals. So how about we leave it at this?" Clete said. He gathered all the saliva and bile in his mouth and spit it full in Sally Dio's face.

Dio recoiled. He lifted his shirt and wiped Clete's spittle off his mutilated face. But before he could speak, his hired man Billy, who had dropped the empty magazine from the Mac-10 and replaced it with a fresh one, clutched his arm. "There's somebody down the slope, Mr. Wellstone. I just saw him."

"Nobody came up the road. Nobody could be there. You probably saw a bear," Dio said.

"No sir, I saw a guy in a hat."

"Get down there, Moo-Moo, and check it out," Ridley Wellstone said to the other gunman.

"What do you want me to do with him, sir?"

"Bring him back or kill him."

"Are you gonna be all right, sir?" the gunman asked.

"Yes, I'm fine. Do what I say."

But Ridley Wellstone was not fine. The strain of standing up on his braces was taking its toll. His face was gray and deeply lined, his forearms starting to tremble slightly. "This is all on you, you incompetent idiot," he said to Dio.

"If you and Sonny Click had let that college girl alone, none of this would have happened," Dio replied. "You couldn't wait to put your dick in a coed who worked as a janitor. Then you let her boyfriend shove you down the stairs. You destroyed everything we put together, Ridley."

"You're right, my friend. I let you and your degenerate family bring your graft and misery into our lives, and I was a colossal fool for thinking I could turn a piece of shit into a gentleman. In his way, my brother was an honorable man. He didn't deserve to have his name soiled by a man such as yourself. My father wouldn't have let you clean our toilet."

Out in the darkness, I heard the man with the cut-down shotgun shout, "Down here. He's down here."

"Who's down there?" Dio called out.

But there was no reply.

TROYCE NIX KNELT behind a huge boulder shaped like the top half of a toadstool extending from the soft carpet of grassy earth that surrounded it; he was careful not to clink the aluminum bat against the stone. Down below, he could hear small waves sliding up on the rocks along the lakefront. Up the slope, the fir and pine trees pointed into the mist and glistened with moisture against the glow from the clearing. He could hear someone working his way down the incline a step at a time, trying to find safe purchase, his feet sliding on small rocks.

Whoever the man was, he had not been a combat soldier. Rather than zigzag through deep cover with the hillside solidly at his back, he had found a deer trail below the clearing and was following it in parallel fashion, so that his silhouette was backlit by the headlights of the Wellstone pickup truck.

But Troyce soon realized he had misjudged his adversary. The figure stooped over, temporarily disappearing from sight. Then Troyce heard a hard object knock against a tree behind him. He jerked his head around for an instant. When he looked back up the slope, the figure had not reappeared. The man had probably thrown a rock through the canopy, and Troyce had taken the bait.

The man up the slope was not using a flashlight, either, or trying to bang his way through the undergrowth or stay on the deer trail. He was somewhere immediately above Troyce, his eyes sufficiently adjusted to the darkness, occupying the high ground. Troyce hunkered down, one knee sinking into the velvetlike, damp earth, the coldness seeping through his trousers. He pulled his nine-millimeter from the back of his belt and clicked off the safety. But he also knew the minute he gave away his position, or gave away his identity, the Wellstones would immediately use Candace's life to force his surrender, provided she was in the clearing.

That was the problem. He didn't know what he was dealing with. Was Candace somewhere else? What if he got smoked on the hillside in an effort to rescue a couple of rogue Louisiana flatfeet? Candace would probably be killed, never knowing that he had tried to save her. But that was the way his entire life had been: never knowing who his adversaries actually were, never understanding the rules, never trusting anyone or anything except his own primal instincts. Early on, he had learned that the world respected brute force and brute force alone, no matter what people claimed. They made a show of venerating saints and men and women of peace, but when they were against the wall, they wanted their enemies hosed down with a flamethrower.

A sour odor rose from his clothes, like the sick smell the glands give off after a long fever. His stomach still felt nauseated and his body weak, as though an intestinal infection had spread throughout his system. He shifted his position, but when he did, the tip of the metal bat scraped against the boulder. He froze, his heart racing. Up above him, he thought he heard a twig break.

"Who's down there?" the voice of Leslie Wellstone called from the clearing.

But there was no answer. Troyce could hear his own breath wheezing in and out of his chest, and he hated every cigarette he had ever smoked.

Candace, Candace, Candace, he thought. *I'm out here. I won't let you down. Even if they put a bullet through my brain, I'll be at your side.*

He swallowed, closed his eyes, and opened them again. Time to give the guy a taste of his own medicine, he told himself. Troyce pried up a large rock from the sod, hefting it in his palm like a shot put. On one knee, he threw it in an arc down the slope. The trajectory was perfect. It smacked the ground at least forty-five feet below him, then rolled end over end down the hill, creating a sound like a man running.

The man who had gone into hiding stood up from behind some scrub brush and began descending the slope, holding a cut-down shotgun in front of him, digging his shoes into the dirt to keep his balance, using his elbows to knock tree branches away from his eyes.

"Wrong choice, pilgrim," Troyce said under his breath. He stepped out from behind the boulder and swung the aluminum bat with both hands, twisting his hips, whipping his arms and wrists and shoulders into it. The bat landed squarely across his pursuer's face, flattening his nose, shattering bone, splattering his dark blue Hawaiian shirt with a spray of what looked like brain matter.

Troyce stared down at the figure at his feet. The man's eyes looked back at him, glasslike and disjointed in their sockets.

Troyce scooped up the dead man's shotgun and moved away into the brush in a simian crouch. Above him, Leslie Wellstone called out into the darkness, "Moo-Moo, is that you?"

No, Moo-Moo is taking a long nap, Troyce thought. *And now it's your turn, you freak.*

THE MAN WITH the Mac-10 had put Clete and me on our knees. I wanted to believe that Troyce Nix could turn the situation around for us, or that Alicia Rosecrans would show up in a helicopter loaded with her FBI colleagues. I did not want to believe that this was how Clete and I would meet our end. But I knew of many instances when it had happened to better men than I: the two FBI agents who may have been executed on the Oglala reservation in South Dakota; the L.A. cops abducted out of the city and taken to an onion field outside Bakersfield; and closer to home, the three Lafayette cops who were killed by a shotgun at point-blank range when they tried to arrest a man getting off a Greyhound bus.

It can happen as quickly as a drunk driver swinging his car across the center stripe of the two-lane, crashing head-on into your grille.

It usually comes when you least suspect it, often in the most innocuous of situations. I guess I had accepted all the aforementioned; I just didn't want to buy it on my knees.

"Listen to me," I said to Ridley Wellstone. "When Sal is done with us, you'll be next."

"Not true, Mr. Robicheaux. He needs me," Wellstone replied. I started to speak, but he cut me off. "Don't say any more. Don't degrade yourself. I tried to reason with you. Fact is, I begged you to stay out of our affairs. You invited this fate into your life, sir. Accept it like a man."

You arrogant bastard, I thought.

"What do you think you're doing?" he said.

"Getting to my feet," I said. That's exactly what I was doing, rising from the ground, pushing myself erect, my knees popping, my hands no longer clasped behind my neck.

"Get down on the ground," the man with the Mac-10 said.

"Sorry, partner. You're going to have to haul a hundred and ninety pounds of dead meat to that hole if you want me in it," I said.

Out of the corner of my eye, I saw Clete rising up beside me. "That makes two of us, asshole," he said.

"Get up here, Moo-Moo," Sally Dio shouted down the slope.

Again there was no answer, and Sal knew he had a problem on his hands. The man in the mask began walking toward us from the pit. "Give me the Mac. I'll have all this cleaned up in two minutes," he said, his words reverberating inside the plastic hollows of the mask.

"Harold?" said Jamie Sue. "Harold, is that you? My God, what are you doing?"

The man in the mask didn't reply; instead, he seemed to hang his head slightly.

"Harold, look at me," she said. "What are you doing? You were my friend. I trusted you. Leslie hired you because of me. I told him what a gentleman you are. You came to our revival. You can't allow yourself to be part of this."

"Shut up, Jamie Sue," Dio said. "This guy has been snuffing Ridley's enemies for years. How do you think those two Hollywood characters ended up dead? The porn producer had been indicted and was going to give up Ridley to a grand jury. So our friend Harold tuned him up and tuned him out at the rest stop."

"You got a big mouth," Harold said, turning his gaze on Dio.

"We'll work this out later. Right now you get down that hillside and see where Moo-Moo is," Dio said.

"I don't take orders from you," Harold said.

A breeze blew through the clearing, showering more pine needles into the electric glow, the air blooming again with a smell that was like lake water and schooled-up fish. Then I saw something I couldn't believe, an image that was both incongruous and nonsensical: the top half of Jimmy Dale Greenwood rising from the pit, both of his hands gripped on a snub-nose thirty-eight revolver, strips of duct tape still hanging from his wrists. It took a moment for me to realize what had happened: The three men who had been machine-pistoled into the pit had been armed. Somehow Jimmy Dale had gotten loose and had taken a weapon off one of their bodies. He aimed the revolver straight out in front of him. I saw him close one eye and pull the trigger.

The report sounded like that of a starter gun at a track meet. The shot went wide and disappeared with a pinging sound down in the trees. Jimmy Dale pulled the trigger twice more, and Sally Dio's left leg buckled under him, just like someone had kicked him behind the knee. Billy tried to swing his Mac-10 clear of Dio for a shot, but Clete Purcel was all over him, pinning his arms at his sides, picking him up and slamming him to the ground, kicking the gun from his hand, stomping the side of his head, picking him up again and driving his fist into his face.

I got Sally Dio's nine-millimeter from his hand and aimed it at the man in the mask. Dio tried to fight with me, but his best blows were like those of a dried-out crustacean—weightless and empty, like Sal himself, a shell of a man whose strength existed only to the degree that he could inculcate fear in others. Oddly, the man in the mask showed no reaction that I could see, as though he was merely a witness to all the events taking place around him.

Clete was still hitting Billy, holding him down with one knee in his chest, hitting him so hard he had started to beg.

"Cletus, ease up," I said.

"You're right," he said, getting to his feet, the Mac-10 in his right hand, his attention focused on the man in the mask, his finger curling inside the trigger guard.

"Don't do it," I said.

"He's going to skate. The sicker they are, the easier they get off on an insanity plea," he replied.

"That's just the way it is. We're not executioners, podna. Lower the piece."

"No, I'm going to walk him into the woods. Call it Q-and-A time. Who knows how it might work out?" His green eyes were charged with adrenaline, his face slick with sweat, his cheeks as red as apples.

"We don't give them power. We don't become like them. Waxman will rot in a cage, and he'll take Ridley Wellstone down with him. We'll take two guys off the board instead of one. You want to do their time?"

"Good try," Clete said.

"You always said it, the Bobbsey Twins are forever. Who am I going to drink Dr Pepper with?"

I saw hesitation in his movements, like an elephant in must suddenly becoming pacified, his size actually deflating, a suppressed grin on his mouth. "You can really rain on a parade, Dave."

He made Harold Waxman take off his mask and lie down on the ground, then pulled Candace Sweeney and Jimmy Dale Greenwood out of the pit, brushing off their clothes for them as he did, maybe reassuring them in his clumsy fashion that the world was a better place than they had thought.

But in truth, I cannot tell you with any exactitude what happened inside that clearing during a midsummer electric storm west of Swan Lake, Montana. I know that the rain falls and the sun rises on evil men as well as on the good and just. I know that on that particular night we were spared a terrible fate. At the same time, men a theologian would probably term wicked were put out of business. Perhaps we even made a dent in the venal enterprises they represent.

But if there is a greater lesson in what occurred inside that clearing, it's probably the simple fact that the real gladiators of the world are so humble in their origins and unremarkable in appearance that when we stand next to them in a grocery-store line, we never guess how brightly their souls can burn in the dark.

Or at least that's the way it seems to me.

EPILOGUE

Troyce Nix had never thought of himself as a liar, or at least not a very good liar. However, he discovered he was far more adept at it than he had thought, particularly after being interviewed by both the Missoula County and Lake County sheriffs and then a team of FBI agents.

The latter group questioned him on the shore of Swan Lake, directly below the clearing where the mass shooting had gone down, asking him to describe again, in detail, how Jimmy Dale Greenwood had drowned.

"It's like I said. I chased him through the trees, but he just kept on hauling ass. He hit the water running and swum out about forty yards and then started fighting in the water and went down like a brick shithouse."

"It was pitch dark. How could you see anything?" one agent asked.

"There was lightning flashing up in the clouds. I think he probably had a cramp or them goons busted him up inside. I seen his arms flailing around for just a minute, then he sunk under a bunch of bubbles. Throw some grappling hooks out there. He probably ain't floated very far."

"That lake has mountain peaks under it. The drop-offs go straight down a hundred and thirty feet," the same agent said.

"Really? I guess that's how come all them big pike are in there," Troyce said.

"Did you try to go after him?" a female agent asked. She was the same Amerasian woman he had seen the night Quince Whitley tried to throw acid in Candace's face.

"The last time I got close to Jimmy Dale, he cut me up and left me to bleed to death. If you ask me, he was a mean little piss-pot and worthless half-breed and deserved worse than what he got. I wish he hadn't drowned. I wish I could have had the opportunity to stick him in that wood chipper by the log house."

The Amerasian woman looked at Troyce for a long time. "Do you know it's a felony to lie to a federal agent who is conducting a criminal investigation?"

"If I got a reason to cover up for that nasty little turd, it's lost on me. Y'all keep up the good work," Troyce said. "Say, y'all think I might have a chance of becoming a FBI agent?"

Two weeks later, I placed flowers on the graves of both Seymour Bell and Cindy Kershaw. I didn't try to contact or console their families, because I believe absolutely without reservation that the worst thing that can happen to human beings is to lose one's child, and the words we offer by way of solace become salt inside the wound. Instead, I said a prayer over their graves and told them that I hoped they were all right, and I also asked them to watch over me and my family and to keep all of us safe from those who Jesus said should fasten millstones around their necks and cast themselves into the sea.

But sometimes neither prayer nor visiting the graves of homicide victims expunges the images associated with the manner in which they died, and I knew I had to go to the source of their suffering and look him in the face, in the same way a child has to open a closet door and confront the darkness inside in order to be free of it.

Harold Waxman was being held in the Lake County jail, the first of a series of lockups in which he would reside until both state and federal authorities agreed to let him be prosecuted in the jurisdiction where the greatest amount of damage could be done to him by the legal system. The chances that he would be gassed, electrocuted, or injected were minimal. Unlike Ted Bundy, who deliberately committed heinous crimes in Florida—including the rape and murder of a twelve-year-old girl—knowing he would fry if he were caught and were caught and prosecuted there, Harold Waxman seemed to have no death wish and killed people for only one reason: He enjoyed it. Consequently, he was more clever than Bundy, less compulsive, and not given to the thespian temptations of televised trials.

I have known police officers and soldiers who I believed to be sociopaths. I have also interviewed sociopaths in death houses in the Huntsville pen, Raiford, Angola, and Parchman. They have one commonality that never varies from individual to individual, replicated in such exact detail that you feel they all know one another and have rehearsed their statements and are taking you over the hurdles. They not only lack remorse for the deeds they have committed; they are bemused when you indicate they should.

I was surprised Waxman consented to the interview, since I had no legal jurisdiction in the state of Montana. For the interview, he was moved from a lockdown unit to a holding cell, one with a barred rather than a solid door. He was wearing an orange jumpsuit and waist and ankle chains, his wrists cuffed close to his hips, his whole body tinkling with steel as he shuffled into the cell. He had been interrupted during his lunch and had brought a sandwich wrapped in foil with him, clenching it with his fingers, although there was no way he could raise it to his mouth. The turnkey locked him in the holding cell and brought me a chair so I could sit outside the bars and not inside the cell.

Waxman's expression was as flat as a skillet. He'd had a jailhouse haircut, one that had mowed off his sideburns and left a pale rim of skin around his ears and the back of his neck. He was sitting on a steel bunk suspended from wall chains and seemed to have no interest in my presence; if he recognized me, he gave no indication.

"I went out to the graves of Cindy Kershaw and Seymour Bell," I said.

"Who?" he said.

"The kids you murdered."

"Oh, you're talking about those college students. I didn't kill them. It was Quince Whitley."

I believed Whitley had been his partner, but to what degree and in the commission of which crimes were open questions that would probably never be resolved. What I did not question was that Waxman was a pathological liar and enjoyed the power his lies gave him and the injury and confusion they caused.

"Tell me, sir, do you think at all about the suffering those kids' parents have to go through for the rest of their lives?"

"I don't know their parents. I didn't know the kids. I won't say it again." He kept leaning forward on the bunk, trying to see past me down the corridor.

"Expecting someone?" I said.

"Why are you here?" he replied, ignoring my question. "I mean your real reason, and don't tell me it's those kids."

"When Jamie Sue Wellstone recognized you in the clearing, I saw you hang your head for a minute. Why did you do that, Mr. Waxman? Were you ashamed you sold her down the drain?"

"Yeah, I remember that. I bought a guitar. I paid three grand for it through Musician's Friend, out in Portland. She was going to show me some chords and runs she used in her songs. So I knew that was out. I wouldn't have put up three grand for a Martin guitar if I'd known how things were going to work out."

"Purcel wanted to smoke you. I stopped him," I said.

"Yeah?" he said, still focused on something behind me.

"Nothing," I said. "Enjoy your life in the gray-bar hotel chain. I'd ask for lockup and eat out of cans, though. The inmates in the kitchen don't like psychopaths in main pop."

"What?"

"Most cons aren't that much different from the rest of us. They don't like guys like you," I said, wondering why I was explaining myself to him.

I walked back down the corridor and wasn't sure whether he had heard me or not, or even if he cared about the implications of my statement regarding his future. The turnkey was walking toward me, grinning good-naturedly.

"He's all yours, Cap," I said.

"He give you what you want?" the turnkey asked.

"More or less," I lied.

"Good," the turnkey said. "He didn't want to talk to you, but I told him I'd find some seasoning for him."

"Pardon?"

"They aren't allowed condiments in lockdown. So I told him to bring his sandwich down to the holding cell and I'd find something for him in the coffee room. We got our own little items tucked away. See?" The turnkey held up a bottle of Evangeline hot sauce to illustrate his point.

Down in the pit that had almost become their grave, Candace Sweeney had gotten Jimmy Dale Greenwood loose from the duct tape that had bound his wrists. But Jimmy Dale had effected an escape of another kind without any help from anyone. He had broken out of the prison of fear in which he had lived most of his life. Jimmy Dale had not tried to run and was ready to take his fall and go back to prison. Except it was Troyce Nix who proved to be the surprise in the Cracker Jack box, when his aborted desire for revenge went through a strange transformation. Nix and Candace Sweeney and Jimmy Dale had walked into the trees together, then Nix and Candace had come back without him, and I never saw Jimmy Dale again.

Nix stuck by his story and continued to maintain that Jimmy Dale had drowned in Swan Lake. One month after the shooting, Jamie Sue and her son disappeared from Montana, and I heard nothing about or from her until four months later, when I received a letter postmarked in Upper Hat Creek, British Columbia. It read as follows:

Dear Mr. Roboshow,

We got us an Airstream and seventy acres of alfalfa in a place that doesn't need mentioning. We raise buffalo and red angus and provide rough stock for rodeos that probably come to your town. The point is I wanted to thank you and Mr. Purcel for all you done. Jamie Sue and me sing duets sometimes in saloons, but mostly we write songs and one or two has been recorded, although our names are not necessarily on them.

Tell Mr. Hollister I appreciate the trust he put in me and I'm sorry for causing him any trouble. I hope things have worked out for Miss Candace, too. If you don't mind, burn this letter. Jamie Sue says hi and says she apologizes for being rude to you, but sometimes you were a pain in the neck.

She didn't really say that.

You ever seen the Royal Canadian Rockies? I'm writing a song about them. Everything Woody Guthrie wrote about is still up here. Every morning when I wake up, all them big blue mountains fall right through my window. Don't let nobody tell you Woody's music isn't still on the wind.

> Your bud in E-major

The letter was unsigned.

Ridley Wellstone and Sally Dio? Their families had been in business together for decades, in the same kind of symbiotic alliance that had existed in the nineteenth century between the street gangs of New York and Boston and the blue-blood families whose names have been polished clean by success and the passage of time. Sally was under indictment when his plane crashed into the mountainside on the res, and he needed a new identity, one that would allow him access to all the resources he had amassed through his partnership with the Wellstones. Ridley, on the other hand, needed Sal's connections to the hotel and casino industry in Nevada after Ridley had lost a fortune during the collapse of the oil market in the early 1980s.

The last I heard, both of them were going down for at least twenty-five years. But who cares? As players in the building and the deconstruction of empires, they're merely ciphers. Jefferson in his letters to John Adams foretold their advent long ago. Perhaps the greater problem is their constituency. A confidence man chooses only one kind of person as his victim—someone who, of his own volition, invites deception into his life. Eventually we catch on to charlatans and manipulators and ostracize or lock them away. But unlike the fifth act of an Elizabethan tragedy, order is seldom reimposed on the world. The faces of the actors may change, but the story is ongoing, and neither religion nor government has ever rid the world of sin or snake oil.

Clete joined Alicia Rosecrans in San Diego, then she left the FBI and went back to the Big Sleazy with him. Molly and I went back home, too, but I couldn't rest and I still don't and I can't explain why. Maybe it's the times. Maybe I cannot rid myself of images of towers burning against a blue sky, the smoke an ugly scorch at forty-five degrees, the tree-shrouded neighborhoods of New Jersey just across the Hudson River. Maybe, just as in Clete's dreams, I see us all inside a maelstrom, past and present and future, the living and the dead and the unborn, all part of one era that is so intense and fierce in its inception and denouement that it can only be seen correctly inside the mind of a deity.

In the late fall I went west again, this time by myself, and visited the café in the Cascades run by Troyce Nix and Candace Sweeney. There was already snow up in the mountains, and the larches had turned gold among the fir and pine trees, and log trucks boomed down with giant ponderosas were gearing up for the long pull over a pass to a sawmill town on the Washington coast. I wanted to tell Candace and Troyce that I was just traveling through and coincidentally had found their café. In actuality, I didn't know why I was there. Maybe it was because of the clean smell of the air, the boulders encrusted with the skeletons of hellgrammites in the creek beds, the bluish-white outline of the Cascades themselves, the autumnal suggestion of death on the wind, followed by winter and, with good luck, another spring.

When I place my hand in a cold pool and fingerling salmon nibble the ends of my fingers, I know the pool will freeze over and the fingerlings will live under the ice until May, when the ice will thaw and the adult salmon will swim into the river's main channel and eventually work their way out to sea. All of these things will happen of their own accord, without my doing anything about them, and for some strange reason, I take great comfort in that fact.